M000223241

Announcing her palms against the bedroom door. Shrieking stopped as the banshee tried to stab into her intuitive power, not even making a dent.

Julie, I'm here to help. Don't be afraid. After sending her telepathic message, she felt a definite shift. The young girl now had hope.

Sensing another female entity in the bedroom, Vivien tuned in sharper. A spirit connected to the house stood in front of Julie, also protecting her.

"That horrible noise stopped." Neal eyed the door urgently. "Is that good or bad? I mean, is Julie safe?"

"Yes, she's safe. I put a protective light around her."

Heaving a sigh of exhaustion, he rubbed his temple. "Oh, right—the light thing. This is all so weird." Neal's head popped up. "No offense."

"None taken." She grinned like a debutant about to dance with the coolest boy in school.

"What now?"

Bay of Darkness

by

S. K. Andrews

The Kelly Society

This is a work of fiction. Names, characters, places, and incidents are either the product of the author's imagination or are used fictitiously, and any resemblance to actual persons living or dead, business establishments, events, or locales, is entirely coincidental.

Bay of Darkness

COPYRIGHT © 2019 by S. K. Andrews

All rights reserved. No part of this book may be used or reproduced in any manner whatsoever without written permission of the author or The Wild Rose Press, Inc. except in the case of brief quotations embodied in critical articles or reviews.
Contact Information: info@thewildrosepress.com

Cover Art by *Debbie Taylor*

The Wild Rose Press, Inc.
PO Box 708
Adams Basin, NY 14410-0708
Visit us at www.thewildrosepress.com

Publishing History
First Mainstream Paranormal Edition, 2019
Print ISBN 978-1-5092-2779-2
Digital ISBN 978-1-5092-2780-8

The Kelly Society
Published in the United States of America

Dedication

This book is dedicated to creatives everywhere—
Writers, actors, singers, dancers, artists, and the like.
Never give up on your creative journey,
for it is your sacred space.

Acknowledgments

To my editor, Dianne Rich, for help and support and believing in my story and me. Also, thanks to Rhonda Penders, Lisa Dawn, Debbie Taylor for my brilliant book cover, and all my fellow authors at The Wild Rose Press for a warm welcome and invaluable advice. I feel like I've come home.

Many thanks to family: Aunt Pat, Kenny, Robby, Krista, Karen, Roxana, the M&M's—Marri & Maher, Anthony & Maura, and Suzy. Though they have passed on, support and inspiration came from Kaye, Hazel, Vivien, Merle, Timmy, Ernest, and Marina.

Thanks to my friends: Heather & Spencer, Corinne & David, Dawn & Mark, Alisa, Nancy, Courtney, Dean, Aliza, Ayako, and the Pearl Girls from Alpha Chi Omega—Stacey, Lisa, Jill, Marilee, and Di, Karen & Bill, Danielle & Nicole, Vicki, Louise, the Pai family, Colette, Didi, Amber, Maura & Lowell, who also gave me my furry tabby cats Audrey Hepburn and Vivien Leigh, who sit on my printer while I type out stories.

Thanks to writing spaces & places: The Posh Moon in Half Moon Bay—Monica & Carol, to all the women behind the counter at Society Café in HMB for those mocha lattes and zucchini chocolate chip muffins, and Paragraph in NYC. Thanks to Jim Harold and Maddy Hilker from the Paranormal Podcast, and to the talented creatives who run Thrillerfest writers conference each year in NYC, especially Kim and Sandra. Thanks also to Randy & KC, my beautiful cozy town of Beacon, NY and the ARE group there. I'm grateful for my Irish clan and for those at my NY day job who have listened to me talk about my book and supported my goal.

Chapter One

Vivien leaned back, enjoying the trees adorned in little white lights along Park Avenue while Philip relayed his latest story of intrigue. En route to attend a dinner in Philip's honor as Journalist of the Year, a sigh of pride escaped her lips. No one deserved it more than he, and even in the midst of his glory, he remained humble.

As she pulled away from the glow of the MetLife building, while adjusting a beaded shawl over her black velvet evening gown, something caught her eye. A strange cloud of thick black smoke hovered in front of Philip's face. When she grabbed his arm, the smoke dissolved instantly.

His brows furrowed. "What?"

When she didn't answer, his lips curved into a grin, and mischief danced in his glistening sapphire eyes. Black hair fell over his brow. "Kiss me."

"Hang on." Frantically, she searched the limousine.

"What's the matter?"

Vivien turned back in utter confusion. "I swear I saw a cloud of black smoke covering your face just a minute ago."

He gazed around, and back at her. "I don't see anything."

"But I saw it."

"If it makes you feel better, I'll check with the

driver." Philip slid the glass partition open. After a few moments, he slid the glass back. "All his gauges are fine, so there's nothing on fire."

With a huff, she reclined back. "So, I'm insane now?"

"Yes, and that's why I love you." He suddenly tickled her midsection.

Vivien cackled while flicking his hands away. "Stop!"

As Philip kissed her deeply, she let herself go, and then nudged him.

"What's wrong?" he uttered huskily, giving her an innocent stare.

"Well, I suppose it makes no difference to you that I'm all made up for this award dinner of yours, and you just ruined my lipstick."

His arm wrapped around her shoulders. "It's okay. I asked the driver to go back to my apartment. You can freshen up there."

"Why are we going back to your apartment?"

Philip smiled boyishly. "I forgot my speech."

Howling with laughter, Vivien threw her head back with abandon.

"Shut up!" he snapped, through his own laughter.

"I promise not to tell anyone."

"Good."

"On one condition."

He studied her suspiciously. "Yes?"

"You have to make love to me all night."

"You've got a deal."

Just as she zoomed in to kiss him, the car stopped at the curb.

"Here we are, sir," the driver announced.

"Thanks."

Vivien's emerald eyes and deep chestnut hair glimmered when silver moonlight suddenly beamed into the car. She watched as Philip grasped a wisp of her hair that had come undone in the back and clumsily tried to reattach it. She'd been at the salon all afternoon, giving birth to an elegant swept-up hairstyle, accented with tiny crystal hairpins. Knowing Philip would never succeed, she put him out of his misery.

Vivien laughed and clutched his hand. "Let me do it."

Her skin tingled as his fingers gently stroked her cheek. He gazed upon her sweetly while she magically replaced the wayward locks in an instant.

A shiver abruptly passed over her body. Without even knowing it, Vivien wrapped her arms around Philip's neck and held tight. "I love you."

"I love you, too."

Outside the window the building took on a menacing shadow, and suddenly the thought of going back to the apartment filled her with dread.

"Viv, what's wrong?"

Reluctantly, she let him go, allowing her arms to slide down. "Something's not right."

"You wait here. I'll be right back." Kissing her hand, he got one leg out of the limo.

"No!" Her voice shot out of her throat like a cannonball, surprising not only Philip, but herself.

Philip gazed back, concern clouding his eyes.

Shaking her head, Vivien wondered how she'd become so paranoid. They'd only left his apartment ten minutes earlier, and everything was fine. What was wrong with her? She forced herself to brush off the feeling of foreboding and smiled. "I'm okay."

She knew Philip wasn't buying it. He knew her too well.

"What's really wrong? C'mon, Viv."

"I'm nervous about tonight because it's your big night. That's all."

He studied her face for a long moment. "All right, but we're going to talk later. Let's make this quick or we'll be late."

Relief flooded Vivien as she emerged from the limousine. He believed her fib—at least for now. She hated to lie, but until she could figure out why she was so irrational, she had to behave normally.

As they entered the foyer, Philip greeted the concierge. "Hi, Bruce."

"Hey, I thought you were off to your dinner?"

"Yep. Just forgot something." He pushed the elevator call button.

"All I want to do is check my lipstick."

"Well, you won't have much time." They entered the elevator. "I know just where I left my notes."

"Really?"

"Yes. They are on my bedroom bureau."

"Interesting, because I'll bet they're sitting on your mantel."

He chuckled, leading her through the elevator door and down the hall. "I'll take that bet."

"Okay, let's see." Vivien's head cocked to one side. "I need a new pair of gloves."

Opening his front door, Philip beamed with delight. "Done! If they're on the mantel, I'll buy you the most expensive pair of gloves in Manhattan!"

"I'm holding you to that." Her laughter ended

when unadulterated fear erupted in goose bumps all over her arms.

Philip stopped in the doorway. "Are you coming in?"

"I'll be right there." She opened her purse.

"Okay." He walked inside, leaving the door open.

The clasp snapped as Vivien closed her evening bag, the sound resonating in her ears. As if she had no will of her own, her head slowly turned to gaze past her shoulder. Her eyes settled on something unbelievable. A dark crawling mist in the shape of a man hovered in the hallway. It seemed to be staring at her. After a chilling moment, the thing propelled itself through the wall.

All breathing stopped. Had she lost her mind? She would blame fatigue for the hallucination, but she felt fit and well.

Oh my God! It's in the apartment with Philip!

The sudden realization snapped her out of the trance. Vivien catapulted herself inside with a pounding heart and found Philip in front of the fireplace.

"You were right. Here are my notes." Shaking his head, he caught her gaze with a smirk.

She latched onto his arm and pulled him out of the room. They had to get out now. There wasn't a second to lose. "C'mon, we'll be late."

Puzzled, Philip pulled back. "Wait a minute. Didn't you want to fix your lipstick?"

"No!" Not wanting to alarm him, she tried to sound blasé. "So, how does it feel being Journalist of the Year?"

His lips wrinkled into a smug smile, as Vivien pulled him. "I'll have to ponder that for a moment."

A loud crash startled them. Shattered remnants of a glass vase lay on the living room floor.

"What the hell?" Philip yanked his arm back and ran inside to investigate.

"Philip, no!" Vivien tried to snatch his hand, but he moved out of reach.

A skinny, dark-haired man emerged from behind the sofa, dressed in tattered jeans and a black fleece. His eyes appeared dilated. A second passed, which felt like a century. Then he turned on Philip, wielding a gun. Two shots fired. Philip fell to the floor and barely choked out, "Run, Viv!"

Leaving Philip was not an option. Instead, Vivien ran in his direction but slipped on her heel. Another shot rang out. Burning flashed through her chest as her body slammed to the floor.

Labored breathing echoed in Vivien's ears as her hand slipped off her thigh and landed in something sticky. Blood seeped through her elegant velvet dress, creating a large red puddle on the hardwood floor.

A tear slowly drifted down Vivien's cheek as beautiful parties danced on the ceiling like ghosts in the night. Knowing they took place in the very room where she now lay dying brought an agonizing, yet sweet nostalgia to her heart.

That jolted her. Giving up was never her style. Even with the room spinning and death creeping into her body, she had to do something. Vivien reached for her purse to get her cell phone. The dark stranger leapt out of the shadows and threw it well out of her grasp. His viciously curling lips suggested he wanted her to bleed out. He knew she couldn't run and pleasured himself by watching her moment of salvation lost.

The black clutch seemed suspended in time as it gracefully landed on the exact spot where she'd become engaged. Vivien sat on that brown couch just six months earlier, when Philip kneeled down and slipped a diamond ring on her finger. He'd invited all their friends and surprised everyone by proposing on the spot.

New determination emerged from the depth of her being. Blinking away tears, Vivien grabbed the wooden leg of the side table, and pulled herself toward it. Shooting hot pain filled her body, but she didn't care. She had to get to Philip. His legs were just visible beyond the overstuffed chair in front of the fireplace. He was so close, but every movement stung, and her head felt like it was about to explode. There was no telling how much longer she'd be conscious.

The predator lurked in the corner like a cobra—watching and waiting. Vivien didn't know what he waited for, but she was not afraid. Fear had no place to fill when all she could feel was sorrow and guilt. She'd known something bad was going to happen. She'd had at least three signs before they entered the apartment. So why hadn't she heeded the warnings and get them out of the building five minutes sooner? That's the question that would now haunt her forever.

With a sharp inhale, Vivien grabbed the other leg of the table and dragged herself forward. Suspicious of her movements, the perpetrator emerged from his dark corner and stood over her. Defiantly she glared back at him. He seemed to be frowning, but that didn't make sense. Was he remorseful for his actions? Her gaze fell upon a scar below his lower lip. He's eight years old, crying, a fishhook caught in his mouth. The images came so sharp, so clear, flashing in her head at lightning speed.

Then Vivien saw the decision in his cold black eyes. He cocked the gun, aimed, and leered. He intended to give her a final shot between the eyes and then leave them for dead. The white area rug soaked up her crimson life force like a thirsty sponge as a small breath escaped her lips. "Forgive me, Philip."

There would be no final embrace with the man she loved. In Vivien's mind she ran her fingers through his hair and laid her head upon his neck, taking in his favorite cologne. Her fingers traced the line of his face and prickled at the touch of his slightly rough skin. A five o'clock shadow had begun, and he'd been too nervous to shave that morning. Embracing him tightly, she buried her face in his hair and inhaled. His sweet essence smelled so good. She could stay there forever.

But all she could do now was meet him on the other side. Vivien made that her ending wish.

After closing her eyes and welcoming death, the thought haunted her again—*I could have stopped it.* The words pounded in her brain as warm tears ran down her face.

Vivien blinked hard, and when her eyes opened, the man holding the gun was now a black stone chasm of darkness. It seemed to go on for miles. The more she stared, the more she got pulled in. Hopelessness descended like a damp, clammy fungus settling in her bones. Buried within the malevolence existed an odd feeling of comfort. This wasn't just any evil. This was an evil she knew.

A loud bang echoed from down the hall, and in an instant the man and the chasm vanished.

Gasping into reality, she hastily crept to Philip, no longer aware of her aching body. Vivien's breath caught in her throat, and fresh tears stung her eyes at the sight of him. He lay in a pool of blood, absolutely still, eyes glazed over. The white index cards now smeared in red remained in his hands. Catching sight of one card, she read the lines: "There are no words to express the gratitude I feel for my fiancée, Vivien. I cherish her love, beauty, and spirit every day, and thankfully, for the rest of my life."

The moment her eyes left the page, heart-wrenching sobs filled the room. She didn't realize the sound came from her. Not caring if she lived or died, Vivien laid her head on his chest.

"I love you, Philip. I always will."

****

Warm sunshine bathed Vivien's face. Each golden ray wrapped her up in its glow, eager to share. Upon opening her eyes, breezes comforted, while soothing sand slid between her toes. She angled her head to one side to take in her new environment. The beach she rested upon vibrated with each element of nature, as a shimmering indigo sea rolled waves effortlessly to shore.

Vivien sat up and discovered she was on her favorite bit of Cape Cod.

Then a movement took her attention away from the tranquil beach.

Philip.

She immediately ran to him, and he spread his arms out to receive her. Embracing each other tightly, they rocked back and forth in pure bliss.

Her breath exhaled with relief against Philip's

chest. "I had the most terrible nightmare."

"I know."

"We haven't been here in years. It's still gorgeous." She lovingly gazed out at the water.

"Yes, it is."

Just then, she looked down to see herself in a white muslin dress and Philip in a white cotton shirt and tan pants.

"Where did we get these clothes?"

He stroked her hair and smiled tenderly.

"What's happening?"

"Come with me."

Vivien took his hand as he led her to a spot on the beach. They sat, and he pulled her in front of him. Taking his arms, she wrapped them around her.

"Isn't this peaceful?" Philip breathed in her ear.

"Yes. The sky is so clear, and the sand feels so good." She looked up and down the beach. "Hey, how come we're the only ones here?"

"I wanted us to be alone, even if just for a moment."

Vivien swiveled hard to face him. "What do you mean just for a moment?"

Calm, understanding eyes gazed back. "It wasn't a nightmare, Viv."

"No! It didn't happen!" She struggled against him. "What are you saying?"

He held her tightly, yet she only felt tenderness. She stopped fighting, leaned into him, and wept.

"Don't cry. It's the way things are meant to be. You still have a lot of work to do, and you're going to help people."

"But I don't want to help people!"

Philip roared with laughter. "I know you don't mean that. Viv, I love you, but you have to go back." He placed fingers under her chin and lifted her face. "You fought for your life whether you know it or not. Our time together has come to an end, I'm told."

"Told by whom?"

He released her chin and dropped his arm. "Your spirit guide. She would be speaking with you now, but I asked if I could deliver the message."

"What message?"

"The message is this—you have extraordinary psychic and physical power, and it's going to be even stronger when you return. There is a man of dark energy who will have the same strength as you. He must be defeated."

"What will happen if he's not defeated?"

"The world will change in a horrifying way. That's all I'm allowed to tell you."

Normally, the words Philip just shared would be plucked from his vast catalog of dark humor jokes, but Vivien realized he spoke in earnest. "What is this energy you're talking about?"

"It's an evil force. It will entice those who are confused, and many will follow him."

"But what can I do?"

"I can't say what the outcome will be because that depends on many people." He grinned with those dimples she loved. "But you have the power to stop him."

Vivien laid a hand on his cheek, cherishing the moment as long as she could. "Maybe I could help from here?"

Philip chuckled.

She heard his thought as if he spoke aloud. *That's my Vivien, always negotiating.*

"Are you sure I have to go back?"

"Yes."

Out of ideas, she clung to him desperately. "I don't want to leave you."

Philip pulled her up, and they stood. "I'm out of time. I will always be with you, Viv." She felt his hand upon her heart. "Here."

"I won't say goodbye. I can't," she choked out through tears.

"Then don't."

His lips brushed against hers one last time. Then, he turned her around.

"No!"

"Viv, you have to go, but remember—I love you."

Viciously pulled into darkness, she landed hard. Her earthly body ached, and Vivien resented being back in it. The beach was gone, the warm sand was gone, but most of all—Philip was gone.

****

Someone screamed.

Vivien looked up to see a white ceiling and tried to claw her way through it.

"Aaron, hurry!"

As the orderly held her down, a cold needle pierced her skin. Everything felt heavy—her body, the mattress, and especially, her head against the pillow.

Vivien quickly glimpsed a nurse all in white, with arms akimbo. Then she heard the words she dreaded.

"In all my days I've never seen a patient wake up so violently from a month-long coma."

Just before the drug took over, cold truth hit Vivien

between the eyes. Her life was now in uncharted territory, and on top of that, she'd inherited a devastating responsibility.

Chapter Two

Through bay windows, Vivien eyed a mother bird feeding her babies on an evergreen branch. Their innocent chirps felt like a cry of faith against the pale gray sky. Once sated, they nestled under their mama's feathers, keeping warm from the late winter chill.

She closed her eyes. How sweet and simple life seemed for the birds in the tree.

That very morning, she entered her thirty-fifth year. If someone told her she'd celebrate her thirty-fifth birthday in an upstate New York counseling facility, she would have called them crazy. She could almost laugh at the irony, if she could laugh.

Dreams of Philip still haunted her nightly. Red blood sprayed across the white mantel and after turning to help him, her own body descended to the floor utterly helpless. The end was always the same no matter how much she tried to change it. Happier dreams replayed Christmas shopping in New York City and sleeping in his arms. When those memories rose, she awoke with bittersweet longing. But the nightmares kept her in a constant sleep-deprived state, until she could no longer function in a healthy capacity. Taking a leave of absence from her creative-writing teaching position at Columbia, Vivien did not know when, or if she'd return.

Heaving a sigh, she slid deeper into an antique

rocking chair and massaged her neck, attempting to soothe tense muscles. At least her surroundings provided comfort. The stunning Victorian house looked like it leapt out of a Thomas Kinkade canvas. It sat on a meadow at the end of a long gravel drive surrounded by evergreen trees.

After her morning ritual of journaling, Vivien stared out the library windows. Black ink spread across white pages searching for answers. But each day she felt better. That helped. Her counseling sessions helped as well, but the most amazing development became her psychic abilities. She simply knew things. Several times she helped office workers find lost articles. They swore her to secrecy and never mentioned it to the counselors. Vivien smiled at that thought and closed her eyes, deciding to take a nap before her daily walk.

Just as her muscles relaxed, she felt a shadow pass by. Vivien looked up. The figure of an elderly woman stood before her. Shifting her head to see clearer—she vanished. The woman was nowhere to be seen. Shrugging it off, Vivien sank back into her chair.

A few moments later a beautiful low voice in an Irish accent uttered the words, "Hello, Vivien."

Her eyes flicked open to see the same elderly woman standing in front of her. She looked to be about sixty. With short, curly gray hair, she wore a sensible navy-blue pant suit, and yet maintained a graceful style. Silver Celtic knot earrings added a touch of elegance to her ensemble. Her face likened to a pixie with a petite, chiseled nose delicately placed upon creamy white skin. Even though she stood no higher than five foot two, a powerful vibrancy emanated from timeless amber eyes. It was as if staring into them long enough would bring forth another era.

Vivien looked behind her chair and then back at the woman. "Excuse me, but were you here just a moment ago?"

The woman nodded with a smile. "Ah! You must have seen my Fetch."

"What?"

"In Irish folklore it's called a Fetch. That is when you see a vision of a person arriving, just before that person has truly arrived."

"So, you're sure you weren't here just a minute ago?"

The woman casually waved a hand in the air. "No, that was my Fetch."

Vivien stared blankly at her Irish visitor.

"Don't be surprised you saw it. You do possess second sight, you know." She lifted her chin. "In fact, I'm glad you saw it in the morning hours. Belief has it, if the Fetch is seen in the morning, its original is expected to enjoy a long life. If seen at night, a speedy death awaits that person."

Blinking a few times, Vivien nodded slowly. "Aha...I'm sorry, but who are you, and how do you know my name?"

"Oh, do forgive me!" The woman laughed, her eyes twinkling as she pulled up a wooden chair and sat across from Vivien. "I was going on about the Fetch! I'm Katherine O'Hara. I was a friend of your parents when you lived in County Cork, Ireland. Oh, but you were a wee lass. I only knew you until the age of three. Sure'n you don't remember me."

"How did you know I was here?"

"How did you know Carmen's confidential memo

fell through the crack in between the desk and the filing cabinet last week?" Katherine declared, with a playful grin.

Flabbergasted, Vivien's mouth fell open. Not knowing how to respond, she scrutinized the woman.

"Don't be afraid of me. You have the same talent I do."

"What talent?" Vivien's voice came out as a squeak. Clearing her throat, she turned to check the hallway and found the coast clear. "What are you talking about?"

Katherine leaned closer with intense focus. "I have a proposition for you. Come to Ireland with me, and together we will hone your skill."

Who was this woman? The last thing she needed was a crazy lady hijacking her out of the country, even if she did know her parents. But was that even true? Vivien stood. "I don't mean to be rude, but I still don't know who you are, and I have to go to my room now."

Katherine shook her head while digging into a large cream-colored purse. "Oh, for the love of all that's holy! I had a feeling you might be needing some physical proof, so there ye are." A stack of letters tied with a forest green ribbon bounced onto the rocking chair.

All her doubts about Katherine vanished in a flash. Vivien recognized her mother's writing instantly. Touching the printed words, a vision of her mother addressing an envelope at the kitchen table touched her mind. Untying the ribbon tenderly, a feeling of sacredness enfolded her.

On the morning of Vivien's graduation from NYU, she saw her mother holding a letter as they were leaving and remembered the last line of the address going to Ireland.

After the commencement, Vivien turned to her dad, who stared back with hopeful eyes. "I want to teach at Columbia."

Her father drew her close. "I'm so proud of you, and I'm very happy you chose my alma mater."

They laughed, and the memory slipped into slow motion. Her mother's blonde hair danced in the wind. She kept it long and always looked younger than her age. Vivien remained grateful to possess her mother's green eyes and her father's dark hair, the perfect blend of both of them.

When Vivien glanced up, Katherine held a sympathetic smile. She must have known memories flooded Vivien's mind at the sight of her mother's letters. Emotions threatened to run away with her, so Vivien abruptly sat. After taking a few deep breaths, she looked up. "How long have you had these?"

Katherine's Irish brogue came out in a wistful tone. "Your mother and I wrote to each other for over twenty-five years, and I kept all her letters. That's just some of them. Those of us who were friends with her and your da in Clonakilty were heartbroken when we heard about the plane crash over the water."

"Wait a minute! I do remember my mother saying she was going to see her friend, Kate."

"That's what she always called me. I suppose you know your mother had the Gift as well?"

"Yes. She gave readings to people in our neighborhood." With a tilt of her head, her brows knitted. "But how come she never told me about you?"

"You mean she never told you about the mysteries

we solved together?"

"What mysteries?" Vivien fired back, nearly coming out of her chair.

"It started with small requests from the locals—a lost necklace, or a young girl wanting to know if her fella was faithful. Then, your mother and I traveled to Cork. We helped find a missing child and assisted on a robbery investigation."

Fascination filled her senses. "I never knew this. Mom never talked about it."

"I don't suppose she did. Your da was open to her Gift. But after she met him and soon had you, she retired, so to speak."

Amazed, Vivien moved closer. "How long did you two do this?"

"Oh, I'd say about five years. I was eighteen and your mother was only sixteen when people started coming to us for help. We knew we had the Gift and soon found we could talk to each other without words."

Making sure the staff was out of earshot, she stared Katherine down. "Are you talking about telepathy?"

"Aye—telepathy. It didn't happen all the time, but now and again we could do it."

"That's incredible." Suddenly, another thought struck Vivien. "Did you two ever work on a murder case?"

Katherine's face became grave. "Only once. It's not a pretty sight revisiting the act of a murderer. It attacks you emotionally and sometimes physically. Your mother and I got sick. That was before we learned to protect ourselves." Sighing wearily, she sat back. "It still doesn't make the sad cases any easier. It takes strength and courage, but I know you have those qualities."

Crossing her legs, Vivien looked down at her mother's letters. "I don't know how courageous I am."

"You're very courageous," the older woman threw back, her face beaming.

After an uncomfortable pause, Vivien placed the batch of letters on a side table. "Anyway, the idea of traveling to Ireland is intriguing. My mother always wanted to take me to visit…" The moment she uttered the words, they both fell silent.

"She and your da wanted to come sooner, but there never seemed to be enough time. Then, when they finally got the chance…"

"Ironic, isn't it? It happened eight years ago, and it feels like yesterday." Reaching over, Vivien brushed her fingers along the top letter. "At least they died together. That was the only thing that comforted me. They loved each other so much." Suddenly, her head popped up. "Wait a minute. Didn't you or my mother feel anything bad about that flight to Ireland?"

Crossing her arms, Katherine eased back in the chair. "I've often thought about that meself. Neither of us felt the danger. I believe it's because not everything is revealed, even to people like us. If something is meant to be, it will be. We cannot stop it. I did have an extremely vibrant dream the night before they were to arrive. Your mother said goodbye. She wasn't afraid. In fact, she appeared joyful. I usually wake up after dreams, but this time I didn't. The next morning, I phoned your parents, but it was too late."

Vivien's tormented eyes met Katherine's. "I should have had a premonition, even if my intuitive powers weren't as sharp at the time. I should have felt something and stopped them."

Katherine placed a hand over Vivien's. "Don't blame yourself. Their time had come. Otherwise, one of us would have gotten a sign. At least they are happy. They want you to be happy too."

Holding back tears, her eyes dropped to the journal in her hand. "I've seen them in my dreams. They're around me, encouraging me. But the confident woman I was is dead." Vivien didn't mind opening up to Katherine now that she knew her history. In fact, as Vivien was an only child, Katherine was the closest thing to family she had. "I think deep down I want to be happy. I've just forgotten how."

"Then come with me to Ireland!" Katherine snatched the stack of letters from the table and stuffed them into her bag.

"I can't just take off to Ireland. I need to…"

"To what? You don't have classes to teach, you don't have anything holding you here, and you just said you wanted to go to Ireland."

"How did you know I taught?" Vivien's head shook. "Oh, never mind. I said the idea of going to Ireland sounds intriguing, but I'm just…so tired."

"Are you sure you're not after staying because you're scared?"

Vivien pretended sudden importance with twisting the top of her ball point pen.

"You have to get on with your life, love. It's been two years since Philip's murder. He wasn't making it up when he said you had to come back and that you'd have powerful intuition, you know."

Vivien's head darted up. How could she possibly know about the message Philip gave her on the other side? Words formed a reply in her head, but she was afraid to speak, in case Katherine knew what she was going to say. Hell, she was probably listening to her thoughts right now.

"You're a strong, creative woman. You know this, and you're going to get awfully bored if you stay here much longer."

Her mind worked quickly.

"I also know your mother left you with enough money to sustain yourself. So, you're not tied to a job."

Finally, Vivien met her stare head on. "Well, since you know so much, my father left me with money too. So, you're right. There's nothing keeping me here, but I do have a goal. I'm going to write a book about exploring one's intuition." Holding her journal close, she gazed at Katherine with a tiny smile. "Also, it'll be nice for you to have someone in the house again after being a widow for four years."

With only a flicker of astonishment on her face, Katherine took in her words. "I'll make a deal with you. Come with me to Clonakilty, and you can write your book. All I ask is a few hours each day to hone your skill."

Actually, the idea sounded much sweeter now. While Vivien wouldn't admit it, she was getting very tired of her lovely surroundings.

"How long would this take?"

Delicate shoulders rose and fell. "As long as it takes. As long as you want it to take."

Vivien shut her eyes. Surprised to have a feeling of hope wash over her, she believed she may have a future, and this was the right thing to do. Her palm shot out. "It's a deal."

"The saints be praised!" shouted Katherine, vigorously shaking her hand.

Vivien laughed.

It was the first time in two years.

Chapter Three

Vivien buttoned up her tan trench coat. At a cool fifty-five degrees, the weather in Ireland was about the same as in her home state of New York. Stifling a yawn, she covered her mouth and blinked hard, trying to wake up after sleeping most of the flight.

"That's strange." Katherine stepped forward, craning her neck to scan the roadway. "Hanna is always on time."

"Well, it's only been five minutes."

"No, you don't understand. She's always early." All of a sudden, Katherine gazed into the distance, with eyes shining. "Your mother taught you about Celtic mythology, didn't she?"

Not sure what brought up the subject, Vivien shrugged. "Yes, from the age of ten. I was mesmerized by the creatures, gods, and goddesses of the folklore."

She nodded, with a delighted smile. "Good."

Suspicion rushed through Vivien's mind. "Why is that good?"

A small blue car skidded, bounced, and finally slammed the curb with its front tires. It reminded her of the clown car stunt in the Big Apple Circus. A tall, mid-fifties woman with vivid blue eyes and a long blonde braid, dressed in jeans, tan boots, and a white cable knit sweater rushed out of the car.

Dynamic strength struck Vivien the moment she

saw her.

"I'm sorry to be late! Shannon decided to try my hair dye." Her words came out between panting breaths, as she threw her arms around Katherine.

"Oh dear! What did you do?"

"I have Gregory giving her a bath right now. She's not happy about it, but that's her punishment."

"Sure'n it's Gregory's too!"

Both women howled with laughter and had to calm themselves before turning around.

"Hanna McTavish, meet Vivien Kelly."

"Hello." Vivien extended her palm.

Staring in wonder, Hanna took her hand. "Holy mother of God! It's like I'm looking into Rebecca's eyes. You are the spitting image, and she was so beautiful."

Blushing, she lowered her arm. "Thank you."

"I can't wait for my husband to meet you! His name is McGregor, and he's to teach you the ancient art of Celtic warrior combat!"

Vivien's face showed a look of panic. "Huh?"

"Hanna dear, I hadn't told her that part."

"Oh." Hanna let out a sheepish laugh and grinned. "Well…we best be off."

Vivien snatched Katherine's arm. "Celtic warrior combat?"

"We'll talk later."

"No! Hanna, please!" Vivien called out when she grabbed her bulging suitcase.

Hanna winked back. "I'm not as old as I look, love."

Climbing into the back seat, Vivien suppressed a chuckle. These two Irish ladies were quite a pair.

Katherine took the front passenger seat. "Now, I want to know what's been going on here while I've been away." She gazed back at Vivien while fastening her seatbelt. "Sure'n you don't mind if we catch up?"

"No, go ahead. I'd like to look around."

"Oh, there's no greater landscape than Ireland, especially in our beloved West Cork."

As they got onto the highway, Vivien gasped. The hills extended in green waves, as if someone tossed out an emerald ribbon. Sunlight through puffy clouds cast shadows, spotting the meadows. Patches of green were broken up by slim roads and charming white houses. Looking past a rocky summit, she saw what looked like little cotton balls. As they got closer, she discovered they were a flock of sheep trotting beside a clear blue lake. Magical—that's the only word she could use to describe the images enchanting her vision. Her parents constantly showed her photos, but to see Ireland's beauty in the flesh astounded her. Leaning against the car window, she let out a peaceful sigh. Everything felt like home. She knew it had to be her mother's lineage rising to the surface. How could she not feel at home in Ireland? This was where her mother and father met. It was why she existed. She shared their happiness in the land itself and delighted in her decision to come.

After they exited the highway, she caught sight of a charming white cottage poised effortlessly on the side of a green knoll, complete with a classic brown thatched roof. To her left lay the edge of Clonakilty Bay and what looked like a private cove. She noticed ripples in the twinkling water and followed the wake to see two striking swans gliding past. She didn't know what Katherine's view looked like in the winter

"You know, the internet. I need to book a flight back to New York."

Katherine grabbed her shoulders. "Vivien!"

Stunned, she stopped dead.

"First of all, I do have internet, but you will never be able to hide from this phantom, whatever it is. It simply isn't possible. Stay with me, and you'll learn how to banish it for good. You'll be able to help others do the same."

Wiping away tears, Vivien tucked the laptop back into its case.

"Propelling that dark being into another dimension without any training was incredible. You're more powerful than you realize, but you have to solve this mystery, or you'll never be rid of it."

"I thought I could do this, but I can't. I won't put everyone around me in danger." She gave Katherine a hard look. "Please take me back to the airport. I need to leave."

With hands on hips, Katherine sighed. "You'll never get a flight out tonight. So, I'll make a deal with you."

Vivien's eyes tightened. "Another one of your deals?"

"Aye. Stay the night, and if you don't feel differently in the morning, I'll take you to the airport."

Her head bobbed up and down. "Okay, but in the morning I'm leaving."

Katherine laid a hand on her cheek. "Now, wash your face, come downstairs, and instead of tea, we'll have a whiskey."

"Amen to that."

****

Katherine circled the house with salt to secure the outside and burned sage to protect the inside. Then, linking hands, both women covered the entire property with white light. Vivien had to admit the protection ritual made her feel much better.

Over caramel-colored liquid floating in her glass, she stared Katherine down. A delicious dinner of traditional Irish stew and garlic soda bread had been hungrily consumed, but before taking another sip of her whiskey, there was something Vivien needed to know. With a deep breath, she asked her burning question. "I know there's more to the story of you finding me in upstate New York. There's something you're not telling me."

Katherine rested her chin on her hands. "As it happens, the visitation of a very fine-looking forty-year-old man woke me in the dead of night."

Vivien's eyes widened as she absorbed her words, but deep inside she was not surprised. That was just like Philip—still looking out for her. "What did he say?"

"You have to help Vivien." Twisting the cap on the whiskey bottle, Katherine returned it to the shelf and then sat. Reaching for her glass, she continued. "That's what he said. Then, he revealed the scene on the beach at Cape Cod after that horrible night and where you were staying." She gazed into her drink. "I'd already planned on fetching you, but when Philip showed me your situation, I booked the flight immediately."

"Why didn't he come to me?"

Katherine shook her head with a compassionate smile. "He knew you'd be too emotional. He also made me promise to give you a message."

After shifting back in her seat and breathing in,

Vivien's voice still came out in a cracked whisper. "What's the message?"

"He forgives you for that night, even though no forgiveness is necessary. He also wants to remind you that he's the one who bolted back into the living room when the glass broke."

"But I could have stopped us from entering the apartment, I—"

Katherine's hands flew up. "His point exactly. It was no one's fault. You need to forgive yourself."

The moment those last two words left Katherine's lips, Vivien's neck unwound. She'd suffered with sporadic neck pain for the past two years. Suddenly, the aching released. After the tragedy, friends, counselors, and even strangers told her not to feel responsible, but their words fell on deaf ears. Her heart still yearned for her lost love, but at the same time—a new sense of freedom crept into Vivien's psyche. As she massaged her neck, years of emotional stress abruptly flooded down her cheeks.

Katherine gently wrapped her arms around her.

****

Vivien felt a man beside her—the essence of a man. As her body turned, there he was in the flesh. When her fingers ran along his bare chest they tingled at the smooth, yet strong feel of his skin. She couldn't see his face clearly—only an impression—but she felt his smile. He embraced her tightly, tenderly, and in his arms Vivien exhaled, surrendering to the peaceful warmth of his love. She didn't know who he was, but there's one thing she did know—she held someone new. He was not Philip.

Vivien filled her senses with his aroma—an earthy,

spicy musk. It calmed her. Curiosity would not wait, so she pulled herself out of his embrace with a direct glance. *Who are you?*

He gave her a charming grin, but then his image began pulling away.

Wait!

I am Neal.

Her eyes shot open. "Neal?"

Guilt suddenly soared through her mind, laced with excitement. Had she really just dreamt about another man? Focused on the white ceiling above her bed, she chanted in a lone whisper.

"It was only a dream. It was only a dream."

Chapter Four

"Where is she?" a voice thundered from somewhere beyond.

Vivien's eyes fluttered open. She turned onto her stomach and stretched. Low voices arose from the kitchen, but she relaxed deeper into her pillow hoping to recall a blissful dream.

When her bed actually shook, she bolted up.

"Vivien!"

Whoever this huge person was, his pounding footsteps were now climbing the stairs to her room. Like lightning, she threw on a robe and ran into the closet.

Her bedroom door blasted open and smacked against the wall.

"Where are you?"

Vivien held her breath and didn't move.

Heavy footfalls trudged to the bathroom and then came right in front of her closet door. Her clumsy fingers tried to hold the doors closed from the inside, but to no avail. They burst open.

There stood a husky man of fifty-five, well over six feet, with a full head of gray hair, dark brown eyes, and a scar on his left temple, all decked out in black workout gear.

His mouth formed a crooked smirk. "You hiding, woman?"

Fear turned swiftly to indignation. Vivien stepped out to face him. "No!"

The smirk turned into a wide smile. "That's grand. You're not a fearful one. I'm McGregor."

"Oh, no!"

"Aye! And you're late for your first combat training session."

"And if I refuse?"

"Then I'll be back every morning to personally escort you to class," McGregor proclaimed with arms akimbo.

Mimicking his arms, Vivien glared back. "Well, it doesn't matter because I'm flying back to New York today."

"You would, yeah?"

Katherine entered the room. "I tried to stop him, but as you can see there's no stopping McGregor."

In the blink of an eye, Vivien stared at floorboards.

"You're coming with me, lass!"

"No!" Katherine cried, waving her arms.

There she was hanging over McGregor's shoulder like a sack of meal, about to be hauled down the stairs. She threw up her hands as best she could upside down. "Oh, my God! All right! I'll go to your class on one condition!"

"Aye?"

"First, put me down!"

McGregor gently placed her feet on the floor.

Vivien jerked away from him as fast as she could. "You're insane!"

He grinned back. "Here we say daft."

"You're daft then!" Straightening her hair, she threw a dazed look at Katherine.

Katherine simply shook her head from side to side.

"Don't ever do that again!" Retying her robe sash, Vivien composed herself. "Here's my condition—after I take this class, Katherine picks me up with my suitcase in the car and drives me to the airport."

She observed carefully as McGregor turned to Katherine, who placed her hand on his arm and answered for both of them. "That will be fine."

"Great. Now could everyone get out of my bedroom!"

Exiting without another word, they left her to change into what Vivien could only guess would be combat gear.

****

After slamming Katherine's passenger door and watching her drive off, Vivien took a hard look at the old, abandoned barn which would function as her training site. It sat in the middle of a field and resembled ruins. Two pigeons flew out between broken boards, their wing flaps reverberating against ashen clouds. This gloomy, decomposing building was where she was supposed to learn fighting techniques? Wiping an already sweaty palm down her top, she reviewed her version of combat gear—a denim jacket over an old pair of sweatpants, a Columbia University T-shirt, and a pair of five-year-old sneakers with a hole in the left sole.

Vivien still didn't understand what she was to fight, besides her own fear and anger.

Crossing the road, she came around the far side of the structure. The front door must be somewhere. She kept walking until she found herself back where she started.

"How can there be no door?"

Retracing her steps, she observed withered vines which covered wooden planks and a metal handle. When her fingers pulled the vines away, a small door revealed itself. She seriously wondered if this was all a joke. She expected to see McGregor and Katherine pop out from behind a rock laughing their heads off and holding a video camera.

"This is so stupid."

For a second, she thought of walking back to Kate's Cottage, even if it meant getting lost. But after being given a taste of McGregor's determination, she realized that would only delay the inevitable.

With a hard sigh, she lifted the metal handle, pulled the door open, and bent down to enter. Immediately a combination of flies and dust attacked her face. Frantically waving her hands and nearly coughing up a lung, she surveyed her surroundings. A wooden ladder led up to rafters where hay lay dormant, but that was all. She stood in a deserted barn.

Her eyes closed as she tuned in, exercising her gift. No one used the space except to pass by—several men walked through, only to disappear. But where was McGregor? Her patience wore thin.

"McGregor!"

"No need to scream, lass."

Vivien whirled around. There was that Irish smirk.

"Where did you come from?"

"I'll show you." He walked away.

"Wait."

McGregor stopped.

"What is all this? I know you don't practice here, and it feels like this is all a front for something else."

Vivien watched him continue to the far corner. He pulled back a large section of boards, exposing another door, which he opened. Following him down a short hallway illuminated by two ceiling bulbs, they halted at a staircase leading down.

She threw him a sardonic smile and nodded. "I get it—secret entrance."

"Aye. Katherine protected this location for us, and we also had it blessed by the local priest."

"Did it work?"

"No spooks yet!" McGregor laughed.

Vivien suddenly lost humor. "Can we get started? I have a plane to catch."

Her glib comment felt like an old shoe thrust in his mouth. That's the energy she picked up, but he nodded respectfully.

While descending into the training center, she immediately regretted her tone of voice toward McGregor. This was his livelihood, and she should not dismiss him. Then she stopped short.

When her gaze met the floor, Vivien recognized special black rubber found only in the most exclusive of gyms. It ran the entire length of the barn and beyond. The middle of the room held a boxing ring, and in various areas, state-of-the-art fitness machines beckoned. As her body turned, she took in a gigantic floor mat facing a row of mirrors, complete with a flat screen TV and stereo system. Reluctant to admit its glory, her hand abruptly whisked the air. "Not bad."

"You will mostly work over there." He pointed to the floor mat.

Unexpectedly, a picture of McGregor standing beneath the Hollywood sign flashed in her head. "Why did I just see you beneath the Hollywood sign?"

The surprise on his face amused her.

"Katherine wasn't kidding about the level of your psychic ability. Now and then, I do combat training for the movies."

"Ah, now that vision makes sense."

Eight men emerged from a hallway. All the men possessed height—some athletically lean, some extremely muscular. The oldest of the bunch had to be thirty-five tops. They stared in awe. Vivien almost looked behind her to see who they were gawking at. Then, she entered a surreal moment when McGregor made a sweeping gesture with his arm.

"These are your warriors! They have been specially selected for you. Lads, this is Vivien Kelly."

They nodded in respect.

Cackling loudly, Vivien enjoyed the joke. "Wow! I never had my own warriors before."

McGregor's face told her he wasn't joking, but her mind couldn't accept reality. "Don't tell me—they all have matching tattoos?"

McGregor crossed his arms, gazing upon her with stern eyes. "This entire facility was built for your training."

Vivien's heart sputtered. "What are you talking about?"

"We've been waiting for you these past five years."

A hot flash of fear made its way from the top of her head to the tips of her toes. She only agreed to one combat lesson. The secret lair and buff warriors went over the top. All these people, including Katherine, were crazy. What were they thinking? She was not a warrior. She was an out-of-work creative-writing teacher. Her next mission became getting up the stairs, getting on a plane, and getting back to New York City as fast as possible.

Backing away slowly, Vivien turned and ran.

Two steel arms enfolded her waist. All at once, vibrant energy surged, bringing her cells to life. Unlocking the arms pinning her, she spun around in defense before she even knew what happened.

In a split second, Vivien curled into a ball and felt her other hand grab a thick wrist. Next, she saw a body flying through space and figured she was about to come down on her head. Maybe that would be better. Then she wouldn't have to be everyone's heroine. Closing her eyes, she prepared for impact.

"Feck!"

Silence.

Curious, she peeked. With legs three feet apart, Vivien faced the men, her body still vibrating. It felt weird, but at the same time, it felt great.

They gawked at her.

She looked down to see McGregor lying on the floor. He didn't look hurt, just shaken. "What just happened?"

Grinning widely, McGregor stood. "You threw me, lass."

"What? And what does feck mean?"

"Fuck." One of the warriors resembling Colin Farrell answered.

She witnessed McGregor dart a scolding glance at the warrior who spoke up and then, a bit embarrassed, turned back to her. "Uh…you took me by surprise. I didn't realize how linked you already are to your destiny."

"Are you telling me I knocked you down?"

"No, you threw me. There's a difference."

"Good throw!" One of the men shouted.

In confusion, she watched as McGregor chuckled, obviously pleased with the first showing of her skill. The warriors joined in his laughter, nodding their heads in agreement.

As they praised her move, Vivien caught sight of something misty in the mirrors. After a moment, the mist transformed into the shape of a woman. Raising her head slowly, deliberately, the woman gazed back at Vivien. Glowing with timeless, fierce beauty, she stood naked. Then, she donned a long black robe against flowing cranberry red hair, creamy skin, and brilliant green eyes. An image of tall slabs of stone circled behind her faded in and out.

Who are you?

The woman did not answer, only observed. Her emerald eyes bore through Vivien. Then, a string of words pounded into her mind.

It is your heritage, Vivien. You can do what I could not.

She vanished.

Concentrated power swiftly ran through Vivien's bloodstream as goose bumps emerged all over her body. For once, they were the good kind.

McGregor snapped his fingers in front of her face. "Vivien!"

"Huh?"

"Are ya well?"

That was a good question. Was she well? She flicked her eyes shut and connected to her emotions. Amazed to feel pride and honor in her newfound talent,

Vivien glowed. She wasn't sure who the spectral woman was, but now it didn't matter. Being able to protect herself gave her new vitality. She still wasn't convinced she was to lead all these fighters, but now a desire to learn burned.

An undeniable urge to turn around stung Vivien's mind. When she did, a long row of shining silver swords gleamed back. With lifted brows, she faced McGregor.

"Those you'll learn later on."

She gulped. "Oh."

"Are ya ready to begin?"

Vivien chucked her jacket, smiling from ear to ear. "Okay, tell me their names. I've decided to take the first lesson." Seeing McGregor's lips twitch, trying to hide a grin, sent a rush of joy to her heart.

He quickly moved to the first man in line. "This is—"

Vivien's hand rose up. "On second thought, don't tell me anything."

She tuned in.

Astonished at how swiftly pictures of their lives rushed through her mind's eye, she stifled a giggle of delight. "I'd like to hear your band Sons of Blarney sometime, Donal. You play guitar, right?" At twenty-eight, with roasted brown hair and hypnotic brown eyes, Donal played beside Aidan in the band.

"Aye!" Donal shook his head, shocked and happy at once.

The next man put out his hand. "I am Aidan."

Taking his palm in hers, she discovered this thirty-five-year-old held the position of lead singer. Olive green eyes lit up, alongside auburn hair. Aidan's looks reminded her of another man, but she wasn't sure who.

"You started Sons of Blarney. I'll come to hear you play very soon."

"Anytime, lass!" Aidan chortled, turning to his mates in awe.

Another man approached her with hands slapped on his waist and a smug smile. "My name is Brendan. What are the lottery numbers?"

Hilarity echoed around the gym, but McGregor stood with crossed arms and furrowed brows, glaring at Brendan.

Merriment died down as she examined Brendan's face. Amused, she clasped hands behind her back. "I'm afraid it doesn't work that way."

At thirty-two, Brendan was the only one married. With black hair and hazel eyes, he cut a very handsome figure. Besides helping people lose weight through his uniquely designed training program, his poetry writing had been published.

"Tell Maggie my favorite teacher was in sixth grade. I know her students feel the same way."

Pure emotion swept over Brendan's face. He covered it well, but she'd obviously struck a chord in his heart. Denying a connection to these men would be to deny her very soul. No wonder their stories unfolded easily in her mind.

McGregor pointed to the next man in line but kept quiet.

Finn possessed the classic Irishman's looks—thick black hair, alongside striking blue eyes. His age settled right in the middle of the group at twenty-nine. His life goal was to one day climb Mount Everest. "I believe you will climb Mount Everest one day, Finn."

Smacking his fist into his hand in excitement, Finn beamed. "Aye!"

"I'm Carroll, and now I want to ask you a question. Do you know everything?"

"Hell, no!"

Guffaws abounded from the men.

So, Carroll was the blunt one. Images of him fiddling next to Aidan and sometimes picking up the banjo flashed by. Always outspoken, he advised the younger lads at his rugby club and kept them on the run, even at thirty years old.

"Carroll, I look forward to hearing your fiddle."

With arms stretched out, he nodded vigorously. "My fiddle is class!"

Groans echoed. It was obvious they repeatedly heard Carroll boast.

Chuckles emerged from Vivien until someone tapped her shoulder.

"I'm Ronan, the youngest of the clan." He put his arms around two fellow warriors, one on each side. "Can you read all three of us at once, then?"

Vivien took on his challenge.

Ronan spoke correctly; at twenty-five, he was the youngest. Very buff, he flicked back dirty-blond hair and smiled with light brown eyes. He taught Tae Kwan Do at the Martial Arts Club.

Liam stood next to him, only two years older. Tall and muscular with rosy hair, he boasted of being the toughest soccer coach in town. Also an avid reader, he had a book with him at all times, especially books on history.

Sean flanked the other side of Ronan. He worked behind the front desk of his parents' establishment, aptly named the Clonakilty Hotel. At thirty-three, he grew up with the family business and offered their guests personal training sessions. Bearing a resemblance to Colin Farrell, he never lacked for a date.

"Ronan, I'd love a Tae Kwan Do lesson sometime. Liam, when I yearn for the written word, I'll ask you to recommend a book. Sean, whenever someone tells me they'd like to visit Clonakilty, I'll recommend your family's hotel." Slowly, Vivien's chin came up. "In fact, I'd love to have some of your mother's chocolate potato cake at the Copper Pot."

Ronan's arms flew up. "Feck!"

"Mind the language!" McGregor boomed, putting a stop to their stunned faces.

She repressed a snicker. He was like a father to them all. "Believe it or not, it will still take time for me to get all your names. So, bear with me."

Vivien stepped back to stand next to McGregor and suddenly knew any one of them would lay down his life to protect her. Their faith honored and humbled. But what was so threatening they would be willing to die?

****

Sliding into Katherine's car, Vivien uttered one sentence after closing the door. "I'll need to unpack."

Katherine smiled widely and accelerated down the road. "Now, I'd like to show you my town and introduce you to some people. What do you say to lunch at Mick Finns?"

"That sounds good to me. I'm starving." Katherine didn't seem surprised by her decision to stay. After the pause became unbearable, Vivien studied her face. "Aren't you going to ask about my lesson?"

"I assume you'll tell me when you're ready."

"Let's see. Well, I threw McGregor to the ground without even realizing it, and then—"

With a smack of her palm on the dashboard, Katherine laughed heartily. "I knew you had it in you!"

"Did you also know I was going to see a woman in the mirror?"

"Go on." Gazing at her for a moment, Katherine's hands shifted on the steering wheel.

"She stood tall, with long wavy red hair, and had on a black cloak. Her thoughts entered my mind. Her exact words were—'It is your heritage, Vivien. You can do what I could not.' "

Katherine's face revealed nothing.

"Do you know who she is?"

"She is part of your journey. I cannot interfere."

Vivien's eyebrows shot up. "Really? Because, up till now, it seems you've known everything about me."

While still focused on the road, Katherine hinted at a smile, and then her brows knitted. "Who do you think this woman is?"

"I have no idea."

"All will be revealed in time."

They rounded a corner, and there stood a statue erected in honor of Michael Collins.

Vivien couldn't take her eyes off the figure. "Can we stop for a moment?"

Katherine followed her gaze. "Of course. Oh, I see Rose." A woman standing in front of a church waved to them as she parked the car. "I need to talk to her about our next quilting club meeting. I'll join you here in five minutes."

"Okay." Stepping out, Vivien walked up to the statue. The gray stone base alone came to the top of her head. Engraved words read—Michael Collins, 1890-1922.

The figure of a very tall man speaking to a crowd filled the sky as she leaned back. It portrayed him stepping forward, very well dressed, stressing a point with his hands. Upon touching the stone, a streaming flow of powerful energy entered Vivien's hand. Here was a man who helped lead the Easter Rising. A true Irish patriot, who fought alongside other members of the Rising leadership. The Rising only lasted six days, but they achieved a goal of holding their positions for the minimum time required, justifying a claim to independence from Britain. Vivien had seen the film depicting his life starring Liam Neeson, but to feel the residual energy of Michael Collins' soul invigorated her.

"Here we are," Katherine announced as she approached, linked arm in arm with another elderly woman in a moss green sweater and an onyx coat.

"Vivien, this is my friend Rose Flanagan."

Rose shook Vivien's extended hand, her hazel eyes shiny with enthusiasm. "Hello, dear! It is a treat to meet Rebecca's daughter. We all knew her, you know."

"It's wonderful to meet you and to be here."

"Rose wants to personally invite you to our next quilting gathering this Thursday."

Vivien pushed away the impulse to decline the invitation once she stared back at the eager faces of Katherine and Rose. "Oh, well…I've never done it before, but I can learn."

Rose laughed, pulling keys out of a small black pocketbook. "Sure'n you'll have plenty of teachers to help you. I must go, but I look forward to seeing you,

Vivien."

"I'll be there." First combat fighting, now quilting. What would be next?

Katherine said goodbye and popped back into the car.

"You know I don't quilt."

"I thought it would help you relax."

Vivien rethought the idea. "It actually might."

Looking out the window, she finally absorbed the beautiful town she now inhabited. Tight roads turned and twisted between colored buildings, with brass lanterns emerging like figureheads. Although the structures connected in long rows, each had their own unique character—some blue, some yellow—all appearing clean and fresh. Each storefront displayed handcrafted shingles proclaiming their offerings amongst a burst of potted plants in rainbow colors.

Just five minutes later, Katherine pulled up to a charming tavern with a red door, blue shutters, and a row of leafy green plants within a yellow window box. Over the door upon a red wooden banner, gold letters spelled out Mick Finns.

Vivien stepped onto the sidewalk and turned in a circle. "Clonakilty is so beautiful and quaint. I love this city."

"I thought you might."

As they walked inside Mick Finns, Vivien's eyes wandered over burnt orange walls and a winning jersey framed under glass. An inhale brought shepherd's pie, pear cider, and Irish stout into her senses—thick and sweet. Part of the walls, covered in slate rock, contrasted with stained glass windows, giving a warm and earthy feeling to all who crossed its threshold.

Katherine walked ahead. "Follow me."

The owner, a beautiful, tall woman of about forty-five, with thick red-brick hair stood behind the bar. For Vivien, she emulated Maureen O'Hara from the film, *The Quiet Man*. Her fiery, yet kind command pulsated within its walls.

"Bridget!" When Katherine extended her arms, the women embraced.

"Katherine, it's so good to see you! How was your trip to America?"

"Lovely!" Katherine turned. "In fact, I brought a friend back with me."

"Hi, I'm Vivien."

"Welcome, Vivien."

They shook hands.

"Thank you. How long have you owned this restaurant?"

Bridget let out a small sigh. "Going on six years now. My husband and I owned the pub together, until last year when he passed."

A knife plunged into Vivien's heart—at least that's what her sorrow felt like. On the outside Bridget showed no signs of distress and held a light smile. "I'm so sorry."

"Thank you. Are you ladies hungry?"

"Aye," Katherine answered swiftly, marching toward a booth.

"Molly will bring you some menus. It will be more for Vivien's benefit."

Katherine laughed. "I have their menu memorized."

A teenage girl in a black T-shirt with gold Mick Finns letters approached.

"Hello, Molly. How are you?"

She handed them menus. "Grand. We missed you around here."

"That's nice to hear. This is Vivien."

"Hello." Molly gave a bright smile and pulled a pen and pad from her black apron pocket.

"What do you recommend?"

"Well, we're known for our fish and chips."

Vivien closed her menu. "Done."

"We'll have two."

"You'll be wanting an iced tea with that?" Molly broached. "That's Katherine's favorite."

"I'll have that too."

As they enjoyed lunch over a pleasant conversation about Clonakilty history, the meal came to a close. But as it did, the feeling of profound sorrow returned to creep along Vivien's skin. Katherine didn't seem to notice and rambled on about tea cakes she wanted to buy.

All of a sudden, Vivien's iced tea glass flew off the table, just grazing her ear, and smashed to bits against the wall behind the bar.

Every single patron turned to gawk at her.

Vivien's eyes widened in embarrassment. "I didn't do it!"

She knew Bridget saw the whole thing and wasn't surprised when her red hair whipped around, and she peered at her in astonishment. "What's all this, then?"

"I...I..." Vivien stammered.

Next, the sound of clanging metal took her attention. Vivien smacked her hand down, barely able to stop her fork from following her glass on its fateful journey to the bar. She looked up at Bridget.

51

This time a man stood next to her—six feet tall, with dark hair and matching beard. The name Ian flashed in her mind. He looked frantic, and she now knew where the second attack of emotion came from.

Did you throw that glass?

Yes.

Why?

Tell Bridget to stop Michael! He's going to kill himself this night!

"Well?" Bridget demanded.

Katherine placed her hand upon hers. "I'm going across the street to get my tea cakes. I'll come back to fetch you."

"Wait—you're leaving?" Vivien projected louder than intended.

Smiling thoughtfully, Katherine walked away.

Knowing she needed to speak with Bridget, Vivien swallowed hard and approached the bar. A busboy was already sweeping up broken glass.

"I'm sorry. I can explain."

Bridget crossed her arms, with eyes of steel.

"I need to talk to you in private."

"You come in here with my friend Katherine, you seem very nice, and then start smashing glassware? No! You give me your explanation right here."

Bridget never suffered fools, so she had to be direct. Looking behind her, Vivien found everyone gaping. Some people actually had forks in mid-air, about to put a morsel of food into their mouths but frozen to hear the juicy explanation.

"Fine." Vivien released a sharp breath and whispered close to Bridget's ear. "Ian wants you to stop Michael from killing himself tonight."

Bridget melted. That's what it looked like. Her eyes softened into puddles, while her entire body slid to the floor. Vivien barely had time to grab the lapels of her shirt from the other side of the bar. "Help!"

Two men flew out of their seats. They lifted Bridget up, and she revived immediately. Blinking a few times, she put on a strong demeanor, not wanting to appear weak.

Vivien tried to avoid their gaze, but one of the men shot her a venomous look.

"What did you say to her?"

Bridget put her hand on his shoulder. "It's all right, Simon." She spoke low, making eye contact with Vivien. "Let's talk in my office."

"Are you sure?" Simon pressed.

"Yes."

"Let me help you."

Bridget leaned on him as he led her down the hall, while Vivien followed. They entered a small room on the left just past the restrooms. Bridget sat on a beat-up red vinyl couch opposite a roll top desk and computer monitor.

"Take some water." Simon filled a small cup from a cooler in the corner. Handing the water over, he eyed Vivien.

Bridget touched his arm. "I'm fine—really."

After she took a few sips, he finally walked to the doorway. "I'll be just down the hall."

"Thank you."

Simon closed the door behind him.

"Let me speak first." Bridget put her paper cup down on a small table beside the couch. "Ian was my husband. He died last year in a car accident, and

Michael was driving. It wasn't his fault. It was a rainy night, and Michael hit a hole in the road. The car jolted, and Ian broke his neck. Michael only got a bruise, but Ian's body hit at just the right angle to be fatal. Even the coroner said so, and he's been punishing himself ever since because he had a pint in him when he drove. I saw him leave that night, and I know Michael wasn't pissed."

"You thought he was angry about something?"

"No. You know…pissed."

"Oh, you mean drunk?"

"Aye. I knew he was all right to drive Ian home."

"They were close friends?"

"Like brothers. They grew up together."

"I see."

"Anyway, I dreamt of Ian last night. He said Michael was in trouble, and I needed to talk to him. But this morning I convinced myself it was just my imagination. I was scared to face the truth about Michael. He hasn't even walked in here since the accident. He apologized to me over and over, and I told him so many times that I don't blame him. It was a freak occurrence. The car didn't even roll over; it just swerved."

When Bridget stopped to take a long sip of water, Vivien moved closer. "Now I understand your reaction when I gave you his message."

"Aye, and I already know about your abilities because Katherine is my friend. She told me about you before she went to America. So, you don't have to convince me that you saw Ian and what he told you is true."

Both women sat in stillness, absorbing the fate of

the day.

"So, what will you do now?"

"I'm going to pay Michael a visit."

"Good."

Bridget grasped Vivien's hand. "Thank you."

Heartwarming energy immediately filled her. "I'm glad I could help. I'm sure you above anyone else can convince Michael to keep living."

"If he doesn't listen to me and change his attitude, I'll give him a one-way ticket to the afterlife meself!"

Their combined laughter bounced around the small office. In that instant, Vivien knew they would become friends.

"I'm off!"

As Bridget gathered her keys to drive to Michael's house, Vivien watched her face change from stressed to relieved. At that moment, she grasped the rewards of her new life and glowed with gratitude for her decision to stay and learn more.

Chapter Five

Even though her second day in Clonakilty proved turbulent, Vivien fell into an easy routine as the months progressed. In the mornings, she practiced meditation and then took up occupancy at her writing desk. The late afternoons remained devoted to psychic training, and four days a week she reported to McGregor.

On top of everything else, she couldn't deny a compulsion to learn Gaelic. When Katherine offered lessons, she soaked up the language like a dry sponge dropped in a bucket of rainwater. The rhythm of speech became part of her. But on one particular day, while reviewing language notes at her desk, she caught sight of her watch.

"Feck!"

She'd adopted the Irish form of the swear word and used it accordingly. In fact, she discovered feck to be a lighter version of the word *fuck*. Her warriors used it in her presence out of respect.

McGregor would give her hell when she walked in late, so she bolted up. Didn't he know dashing about Clonakilty's tiny lanes in Katherine's little car proved a huge challenge? Especially on the wrong side of the road. But each day she got better and better. At least residents no longer ran for their lives when they caught sight of her behind the wheel.

Rushing into the gym, she scanned for McGregor,

but Ronan caught up with her first.

"I'm to keep a keen eye on you today, lass."

While stretching her quadriceps, she couldn't help but laugh at Ronan's eager energy. "You are, huh?"

"Aye." He winked, faking a left hook to her face.

"Well, we'll see about that. Especially since McGregor didn't want you to tell me before my lesson."

His youthful grin dropped. "You won't tell him, yeah?"

"Yeah—I won't tell him." She smiled sympathetically, letting him off the hook.

Ronan nodded quickly and trotted off to join the rest of the clan.

After getting a funny feeling, Vivien turned. A man with a very rigid countenance stood in the corner. At six foot two, with red hair and freckles, he looked to be in his early fifties. She took two steps toward him. "Hello, Michael."

He inclined his chin. "Vivien."

"Are you working out?"

"I've come to join up."

She whipped her head around to McGregor.

"It's true. He's part of the clan now."

"I hope I didn't do anything to—"

"No. This is something I want to do. It's given me a new purpose, and from what McGregor says, you'll need all the help you can get."

A slow grin spread across her face. "Gee, thanks."

"You know my meaning."

"Aye, I know your meaning."

He nodded again, and she realized he didn't know what else to say.

Bridget definitely inspired him when she talked him out of suicide that day. Michael joining the clan not only filled Vivien with gratitude, but also brought a warm glow to her heart.

McGregor broke the silence. "Come, lads! And turn off that telly!"

Sean creased his face with a groan. "But the match is on."

"You know this is an important day." McGregor sent them a look that could obliterate.

"Aye." Sean clicked the remote, and the game went dark.

McGregor then stared Vivien down with arms crossed above his chest like a genie.

"I know. I'm late. I'm sorry. It won't happen again, but if you guys drove on the correct side of the road, I wouldn't have been late!" Vivien worked herself up to match his glare.

As he turned away, she caught amusement in his eyes.

"As I said, today is an important day because..." Striding over to the far wall, McGregor pulled down one of the swords.

"I thought you were kidding!" Vivien's shrill voice rebounded off the dumbbells.

McGregor ignored her outburst. "The Celts were brave warriors, dating as early as 500 B.C. The close combat sword was the chosen weapon in battle. Its flared blade possessed a deadly sharp edge that could be wielded quickly and with great power." The blade turned around in his hand, then he took her palm and laid the handle upon it. "See this?"

Her head moved up and down, almost

unconsciously.

"A solid brass crescent moon guard and pommel reflects the Celts' worship to the heavens. It looks like a handle, but it's referred to as the hilt. Each blade is nineteen inches in length and hand forged from high carbon steel, replicating the materials as close as possible to the period. This sword possesses all the attributes needed for a true Celtic warrior to achieve victory in battle." McGregor's intense brown eyes met hers. "Take it."

The honor of what he presented pulsed through her veins, and she could do nothing else but receive his offering. Vivien wrapped her fingers around hard, cool metal. He let go, and she expected the sword to drop to her feet. Instead, she held it in a tight grasp, astonishing herself.

A tender smile touched McGregor's lips. "You knew I wasn't kidding didn't you, lass?"

"Yes, I knew." She didn't look up.

"Ronan!"

Ronan grabbed a sword from the wall. He raised his steel and stood before Vivien.

Eyes wide with alarm, her head spun about. "Wait just a minute! You are not going to throw me into this! I could get killed or kill one of you!"

"Relax." McGregor's hands went up. "We just want you to dance."

"What?" Vivien watched him walk to an MP3 player sitting in a sound dock.

"I'm putting on what Katherine told me is your favorite song. So, just feel the music. Ronan won't attack unless you do." He pushed a button and "Let's Get It Started" from the Black Eyed Peas came on.

That Katherine was a crafty one. It was one of her favorite songs, but she'd never shared that piece of information. Knowing McGregor wouldn't give up, she decided to try.

Ronan joined her on the mat as Fergi's sultry voice filled the room with the apropos words—let's get it started in here. At first, Vivien's sword awkwardly moved around. Then, she closed her eyes to the music. When she opened them, her blade swung toward Ronan. He blocked her, and Vivien dipped her body into another angle.

Soft leather boots soothed her toes as she moved like silk over moist green grass. A long wool dress twirled while her opponent made her heart race. Tall and powerful, he didn't hold back. His sword thrust as if in battle, knowing she would protest if it didn't. Sweat, heat, and pounding blood added to their passionate combat. Their swords linked. Laser blue eyes bore into her. Breathing ramped up. He wanted more than swordplay, and so did she.

Slicing hot pain shot through Vivien's shoulder. She'd stopped in midswipe, and Ronan's blade carved a three-inch cut.

"Feck!" Throwing his own sword down, Ronan clutched her arm. "I'm sorry! I couldn't stop it!"

Still in a fog, Vivien turned to Ronan. "It wasn't your fault. I…I lost focus."

McGregor strode to her in a flash, examining the wound. "Someone get the first aid kit." His command was given in a calm, controlled tone as he ripped her sleeve open.

Immediately three of them ran to the cupboard. Ronan turned a fearful glance to McGregor. He told him to clean the blades and put them away. "We're done for today's training."

When Ronan took the swords but didn't budge, McGregor made eye contact. "You're all right, lad. You did nothing wrong."

An audible sigh of relief escaped Ronan before he stepped away to fulfill his task.

When Vivien sat on a bench and McGregor began first aid treatment, she fessed up. "A strange vision overtook me."

"Well, it must have been powerful, because you kept the poor lad on his toes for a full five minutes."

A sharp inhale filled her lungs. "Really?"

"I know there is some force you're tapping into here. But eventually you'll have to control the images invading your mind. It will put you and the clan in danger."

"Yes, I know. Katherine and I are working on that."

Finn approached, slapping hands on knees and bending down. "How's herself?"

Sighing, Vivien gave him a slanted smile. "I'm fine."

"That's grand." Finn turned to McGregor with a hopeful grin. "Can we put the match on then?"

The rest of them hovered nearby with excited faces until McGregor caved in. "Go on."

A flurry of cheers pounced upon the air as her warriors ran to the television.

Vivien snickered, leaning her head against the wall. "You'd think you gave them a pot of gold."

An announcer's booming voice overran the large room.

McGregor shook his head, with a chuckle. "Aye." He finished dressing her wound and swiftly packed up the first aid box. "I won't be putting you in that position again. You took to this so quickly...I should have listened to you."

"Hey, it wasn't your fault."

Moans from the other side of the gym got Vivien's attention.

"This is a BBC news special report."

Trembling heat seized her body.

Liam grabbed the remote, while the clan yelled for him to get the game back on.

Vivien's heart raced as she sprinted to the television. "Leave it!"

They gazed at her in utter confusion, but Liam set the remote aside.

"An alarming development in climate change has just occurred. Early this morning a solid blanket of black clouds descended upon the Sahara Desert. Not just part of the desert, but the entire region. That's three million five hundred thousand square miles. Meteorologists and scientists alike are baffled but are meeting the challenge of solving this mysterious event."

The remaining words coming from the female, blonde-haired, British reporter fizzled away. Photos of darkness filled the screen—a gigantic black mass floating above, just waiting to expand.

"Holy mother of God!" Carroll shouted.

Ranting strange words, Vivien couldn't take her eyes off the TV.

McGregor listened to her speech and tried to translate. Being fluent in Gaelic, he was the only one who could attempt it. When Sean asked what Vivien ranted about, McGregor shook his head. He'd never heard the language before and could only assume it was so ancient, none of them could ascertain its meaning. When her intensity spiraled and she began screaming, McGregor slapped her hard across the face.

When her head swung back, Vivien spoke English again, not even feeling the slap. "Don't you understand? It's not climate change. This thing wants me to know it has begun. Now the world knows, even if they call it by another name. This is just the beginning. If we don't stop it, I see the entire planet covered in darkness, and we're ruled by…"

"By what?" a few of the men barked at once.

"I don't know!"

Crumpling into a ball on the floor, Vivien wept, especially since, while the clouds filled her with dread, they also filled her with exhilaration.

McGregor picked her up. "You're for bed."

****

After her episode at practice, she slipped into an aromatherapy bath to calm herself. The suspended black clouds made her blood run wild. Part of her wanted them to spread over the planet, but one thing she did know—eagerness for evil was not Vivien Kelly.

Heated voices rose from the kitchen below. Even without hearing Katherine and McGregor's dialogue, she sensed fear. They'd believed nothing malevolent would arise on the planet until her training had completed. The strange phenomenon over the Sahara changed everything. Her training would now be accelerated.

"All is well…and I am safe." She pronounced her daily affirmation out loud before dunking her head, lingering in peaceful silence under rose-scented water. Then, she took her mother's advice and prayed for an answer.

After donning a cream terrycloth robe and stepping into her bedroom, she had to shield her eyes as a powerful light hit her full on. When the illumination subsided, a woman emerged.

Flowing black hair framed luminous blue eyes, set in brilliant white skin. A gown of silver cascaded down her body, but the lustrous fabric equaled nothing Vivien had ever seen on earth. Wisps of narcissus dangled from her long tresses, and she held a moonstone in her right hand.

After inhaling a rush of lavender, a shocked whisper issued from Vivien's lips. "The goddess Rhiannon."

Then all went dark.

****

Fluttering eyelids opened.

Vivien found herself propped up in bed by three pillows. Rhiannon stood four feet away, with a sympathetic countenance.

Blinking a few times, Vivien's voice came out as a whisper. "You're real. You're really real."

"Aye."

The voice of a goddess sounded just as she'd imagined—like the echo of a moonbeam upon dark lake water—sultry, deep, and unearthly.

"I'm sorry I fainted."

A caring smile complemented Rhiannon's rich, soothing voice. "I am your spirit guide, Vivien. I have been with you from the day you were born, but I did not wish to reveal myself until now. Your mission in this life is very important, and I am here to aid you on your journey."

"Seriously?" With elated nervousness, Vivien raised her body off the pillows and leaned forward.

"Aye—seriously." On waves of laughter, the goddess sent assurance. "You need not fear me. Just know that I am here, and you can call upon me at any time."

"Thank you."

"Now that an example of dark power can be seen on earth, there is something I must show you. It will answer your question of how evil was unleashed unto this world."

Vivien's eyes grew wide as she moved to the end of the bed, sat cross-legged, and grasped the hands of a goddess.

Four teenagers—two girls and two boys, about fifteen years old—slowly came into focus. Both girls wore forest green and blue Pendleton skirts over navy blue tights, and an even deeper blue sweater. A gold school emblem sat at the top right corner of each sweater. The boys matched, but instead of skirts and tights, they wore dark blue slacks.

Vivien wondered why they huddled together, and then her vision widened. They sat inside a black rock cave near the sea. Moist with years of existence, mustard gray and silver mineral deposits created a frightening display of rock icicles, seeming to glow. A mixture of fresh ocean air and stifling hot pressure invaded their nostrils.

When the tide went out, kids snuck into the cave on a dare. Local Clonakilty legend proclaimed dark spirits lived within. Such a tale fascinated young minds, and they took the bait. That particular night proved even more daring, thanks to the creepiest part of the legend. It was said on the eve of the summer solstice an evil witch awakened and roamed the seashore.

Brows knotted as Vivien's eyes lifted to Rhiannon. *They're in a cave?*

Yes. That is where they exist.

They? Her heart dropped.

The other students laughed as one of the girls screamed. "See, I'm still alive!"

One boy scrunched his nose. "It smells like wet cats in here."

"But tonight, is the summer solstice! Sacrifice her to the witch!" The other boy snatched the girl, making her scream and laugh at the same time.

Trying to stand erect, the first boy laid a hand on the cave wall. "Fuck!"

Their heads snapped around.

"What's all this?" The other boy laughed with a snort, wanting to get in on the joke.

"The cave is vibrating." Grabbing his friend's hand, he smacked it onto smooth black rock. "Feel."

Eyes enlarged with fear. Then, yanking his hand away he shook his head. "I didn't feel anything."

One of the girls ran over, very excited. "Let's have a séance!"

The first boy began to walk out, leaning down so as to not hit his head. "This is stupid!"

"Scared?" She challenged him, head cocked and leaning on one hip.

Stopping in his tracks, he turned back to the group. "I've never been scared of anything in me life."

"What about that math test last week? You were

scared of that."

"Shut up, Thomas!"

"C'mon!" The girl beckoned with a wave of her arm.

He hesitated, but then ran back. "All right, but you better be fairly lively. I'm for home."

"Sit in a circle," she commanded.

They did as she asked, except the other girl.

"Brenna, do you really think we should?"

"Oh, shut up, Darcy!"

She slammed down to the ground, having forgotten no one countered Brenna.

"Close your eyes." Holding out her hands, she smiled playfully, enjoying the dramatic moment she'd created. With her head raised, Brenna shouted to the cave ceiling. "Whatever is here, let yourself be known to us!"

An eerie stillness fell upon them—no sound—no dripping moisture—not even their own breathing.

After the quiet became too much, one of the boys rose in aggravation. On his first step, he flew backward into the center of the circle. Before he even had time to recover, the cave rock cracked open, revealing a deep black chasm.

"Oh, God, no!" Vivien breathed out in a raspy choke. "It's the same dark chasm I saw that night in Philip's apartment."

A massive, growling black storm cloud ran them out of the cave as the teenagers screamed in unison.

The images abruptly cleared from Vivien's head. It felt like she'd been punched in the stomach. She stared blankly at Rhiannon. "What happened to the teenagers?"

The goddess instantly placed answers into Vivien's mind.

Each child's death was made to look like an accident, and they died in pairs. First the girls, and then the boys. It didn't happen until a year after their séance in the cave, but they were dead all the same. Rhiannon flashed a date in her head. The darkness broke free just three months before that horrifying night in Philip's apartment. It chilled her to the bone. Tears streamed down her face. Not only did she weep for herself and Philip, but for the innocent children who only wanted to play a game with the supernatural.

Rhiannon waved her arm, and Vivien's cheeks went dry. As her spirit guide gently disappeared, Vivien rejoiced in a feeling of trust and the knowledge she was not alone. The vision she just experienced motivated her to train harder than ever, and that's what she would do.

Whatever creature lurked in that dark chasm—one day she would challenge it face to face.

****

Breathing in organic musk, Vivien pulled his body against hers. Before she could see his features, he kissed her, and her heart lost itself in pure bliss. When he finally pulled those sweet, moist lips away from hers, she grabbed him by the shoulders and stepped back. She had to get a good look at him. Reddish, brown hair framed his handsome face, and then she gazed, transfixed, into his strong, green eyes.

Hello, Neal.

She found it funny they didn't need to communicate with words. They heard each other's thoughts.

Hello, Vivien.

His strong, sweet smile made her melt, and how the hell was he aware of her name?

Do you know me?

Neal's head cocked in puzzlement. *No, but I know of you.*

Vivien laughed. *You know of me?*

What I mean is...I feel you. Then, Neal reached for her.

That's when she woke up, vowing to find him one day.

Chapter Six

Murky brown liquid churned, seemingly enjoying the glass it filled. Its dance complete, white billowy foam collected on top, as the carefully drawn masterpiece was placed before Vivien.

"But I told you guys, I can't drink Irish ale. It's too strong for me."

"Actually, it is an Irish stout. So, you've had one before?" McGregor asked, with a mischievous angle to his lips.

Vivien examined the glass. "No...but it looks strong."

"It's the only way to truly be one of the warrior clan. It's like an initiation, if you will. We should have done it months ago, but no matter." McGregor moved the pint closer to her fingers resting on the bar.

Over McGregor's shoulder, six of her clan stared in anticipation, the other three glaring from Mick Finns stage while performing as Sons of Blarney. The men she'd been training with for the past eleven months and who'd shown patience and care in her progress, anxiously waited for her to drink a beer.

"But...it's just a beer."

Serious faces moved closer.

Brendan stepped forward. "No. It's Irish stout."

Feeling the pressure now, Vivien reached for the stout and sniffed it first. "It smells like wet wood."

They glared back.

She let out a long sigh, brought the glass to her lips, and then paused. "How many calories are in it?"

Thunderous laughter sliced through surrounding conversations. The clan practically fell over themselves. "For the love of God, stop stalling and drink!" Sean shouted.

"Just do it, love. They'll never let you be," Katherine crooned, leaning against the bar next to Hanna and Bridget.

Vivien turned to see the ladies smiling broadly, knowing she delayed the inevitable.

"Okay, okay! But I'm not chugging it in one gulp."

"You don't have to!" McGregor threw up his arm, as the chortles grew louder.

This time Vivien brought the glass to her lips and drank. Surprisingly, the fluid went down smoothly. Her tongue tingled with the dense, rich flavor of the brew. A slight bite of chocolatey bitterness followed, but nothing like she thought. Licking her lips, Vivien held the glass high. "I did it!"

Bridget enthusiastically slapped her on the back. "I'm honored your first pint was in my establishment!"

"Thanks!" Vivien choked, trying to hold her drink steady.

Their cheers deafened as all pints in the pub lifted to match hers. Aidan halted Sons of Blarney's playing to call out she'd just drunk her first pint, embarrassing her with the crowd—in a good way.

Just as the cheering died down, Michael walked in. Even though he'd got the message from Ian months ago, he still hadn't entered Mick Finns. People stopped talking. People stopped moving. Not sure which way it would go, Michael spun to leave.

Bridget snatched Michael's arm and pulled him into a tight hug. He shed tears as she held him.

Immediately, people turned and began talking again.

Vivien took a second gulp of her stout and walked over to McGregor. "Do you think he'll be all right?"

"Aye, but it will take time."

"Let's get this man a pint!" Bridget announced, bringing Michael to the bar.

Sons of Blarney spontaneously began "Galway Girl" at full blast. Carroll's fiddle buzzed as people darted onto the dance floor. McGregor pulled Hanna out, and Liam gently took Katherine by the arm. To her amazement both women erupted into an energetic dance.

Shocked, Vivien laughed with abandon. Then Michael's face flashed in her mind. He needed to dance. Snatching the pint out of his hand, Vivien yanked Michael to the floor.

"Hey!"

"Oh, hush!" She knew he might hesitate at first, but as roars of encouragement from his fellow warriors and friends surged, Michael let himself go.

Vivien released inhibitions as well. Her body remembered. She and Philip had danced beautifully. Whenever they attended a wedding, people commented on their effortless moves on the floor. Since it was her first dance in almost three years, delight rippled through her very being—delight that her heart had begun to open.

McGregor formed them into a circle, and Vivien hooted, pounded her feet, and drew in all the joy of the moment. Michael danced with full gusto right next to her. But after a third song, she tapped him on the shoulder and shouted over the music. "Thank you for the dance! I'm going back to my pint now!"

Michael bowed ceremoniously. "Let me escort you to the bar, my lady." As he playfully held out his arm, Vivien looped hers around.

After reclaiming her stout, Vivien spied Hanna and Katherine seated in a booth.

"You looked wonderful out there!" Hanna grinned.

Sliding opposite them, Vivien leaned back against hard wood. "It's been a while, but I always loved to dance. You know, this stuff really isn't bad at all." She took a hearty swig.

Katherine slapped her hand on the wooden table. "You truly have become part of the clan!"

After chuckling, Vivien gazed wistfully at the dance floor. "Philip always loved to dance. When other women sat begging their partners to get up, we were already twirling."

The women sitting opposite her looked at each other.

"What is it?" Vivien leaned in, sensing a shift in their energy.

"There's something I haven't told you." Katherine glanced intensely over her pilsner glass of pale stout. "You're not the only one who's lost someone. When I was married at twenty-one, I had a bad feeling about my husband who was driving to Cork. I thought I was overreacting, so I didn't say anything. He died on that trip in an auto accident."

Vivien wrapped fingers around her sweating pint glass. "Oh, my God. I'm so sorry. Wait. I'm confused. I thought you were married for thirty-five years?"

"That was my second marriage. I was still a newlywed when my first husband died."

Suddenly, Vivien knew whose black and white photograph Katherine pulled out of the drawer when she had her tea. The pain and guilt must have been unbearable, but somehow, she found love again. "Do you want to tell me about it?"

"There's nothing else to tell. I got a message, and I ignored it, but I never did that again. My point is—you aren't ignoring your intuition. You're acting on it."

Vivien had no idea Katherine suffered such a loss. Part of her didn't want to bring up painful memories, but at the same time, she needed to know something.

Her mentor looked Vivien square in the eyes. "You can ask."

"All right." Vivien sucked in a long breath. "When does the pain go away?"

"Never."

"What?"

Katherine reached for her hand. "The difference time creates is how you react to the pain."

"Aye." Hanna nodded.

Tumbling those words around, Vivien realized she sat with two very wise women. The pause that followed halted when Hanna asked Katherine about her new quilt in progress.

Moving her pilsner glass aside, Vivien's head rested against the end of the booth as she stretched her legs lengthwise. Sons of Blarney were on a break and the huge plasma TV above the bar cut to yet another report about strange clouds covering the largest desert in the world. Fear grew daily, but most people thought it was a global warming side effect. Some fanatical religious leaders spread dogma about the end of the world, but most of the world laughed at them. If they only knew this time, they could be right. Vivien reached for her glass and took another swallow.

McGregor looked up at the report, tossed a glance at her, and asked Danny the barkeep to change the channel. If she looked at the darkness too long, it pulled her into a trance like the first time she saw the BBC airing. It happened at Kate's Cottage one night, and she had to be drawn out of it. Thank goodness for Katherine's high energy and intuitive skill, otherwise, she didn't know what would have happened.

When the channel switched, stony sand beaches stretched below rocky cliffs, on which dwelled the most beautiful homes she'd ever seen. They appeared organic—that was the only word to describe them. Dark wood and elegant gardens adorned the bluffs, making Vivien's heart skip a beat.

A newsman stood next to the local sheriff's station in a town called Half Moon Bay, California. He held up a photo of a twelve-year-old girl with brown hair and sweet eyes. Astonishingly, the local sheriff's daughter had been kidnapped five days earlier. He showed a police sketch of the alleged kidnapper, but they only had one witness. The woman still wasn't sure of the face and the simple drawing was the best likeness they had. The event shook the small seaside town because kidnappings were not a common occurrence.

"What the hell?" Vivien looked down at her feet, to see the same brown-haired girl from the television tickling her ankles.

Giggling, she smiled up at Vivien. "My daddy

loves it when I tickle his ankles."

Hanna and Katherine continued their conversation, completely unaware of her young visitor.

"I'm Elaine. My daddy is trying to find me, but he can't. He's very sad. I can feel his sadness in my heart." Her small hand covered her chest. "I'm sleeping because the man won't feed me anymore. All I get is water now, and tomorrow he says the water will stop too." Her face turned ashen. "I'm scared."

Vivien looked up at the TV, but the sound had been turned off and the band began to play. Muted pictures moving on the screen portrayed highlights of Irish soccer. No one else saw the news report from Northern California—only her.

"What does the man look like? Do you know where you are?" Vivien asked Elaine's spirit, with calm urgency.

Immediately Elaine leapt up and put small white palms over Vivien's eyes. "I'll show you."

****

"Sheriff's station," a brisk, male voice grunted.

"It's vital I speak with Sheriff Harris. It's about his daughter."

The man on the end of the line cleared his throat. "Okay, we've been getting a lot of anonymous tips about Elaine's whereabouts. So, if you'll just give me the information, I'll pass it along."

"My name is Vivien Kelly. I'm a psychic, and Elaine is with me now." Not wanting to waste time, she'd placed the call from Bridget's office phone in the back of Mick Finns.

"Right!" the man sarcastically spat, about to hang up.

"Wait! Ask the sheriff why he put on that pink shirt today. He wouldn't be caught dead in a pink shirt, but no one is teasing him because Elaine liked it and made him buy it last year."

"You probably saw him wearing it on the street today."

"First of all, I'm in Ireland, and how did I know his daughter made him get the shirt?"

The phone line turned into dead air.

"Herman, please transfer me to Sheriff Harris!"

"How do you know my name? Never mind, I've had enough."

"No, you haven't! Especially since you're worried about how you're going to tell your own daughter that her friend disappeared. Of course, that's if you don't find her."

He spoke low into the phone. "How did you know my daughter is friends with Elaine?"

"Herman, please, just put the sheriff on the phone. We don't have much time!"

Herman finally gave in. "All right, hang on."

Precisely ten seconds later a very angry man answered. "This is Sheriff Harris. Who the hell is this?"

"Vivien Kelly. I'm a—"

"Yeah, yeah, I know. Herman told me about your psychic talents. Five other people called claiming the same bullshit. What makes you so different?"

Pausing with enough time for him to come down a notch, Vivien's voice came out in a gentle tone. "She likes to tickle your ankles when you watch television."

"What?"

The sheriff's desperately hopeful answer let her know he would now listen.

"Elaine showed me a black gutted-out old Victorian house in Monterey County. It's where two dirt roads cross, about twenty miles east of Cannery Row. He stopped giving her food today, and starting tomorrow, he stops giving her water. He also has a gun, but it's only one man, and the police sketch is accurate. He told her you did something very bad to him a long time ago. So, I assume he's punishing you."

A tearful gasp escaped Sheriff Harris before he checked himself. "I'm passing you back to Herman. Please give him all your contact information. I have to go, and Ms. Kelly…"

"Yes?"

"Thank you." The relief of hundreds could be heard in his voice. Not only was he anguished over his daughter's disappearance, so was the entire town.

Vivien was put on hold, and at that moment she knew he'd find her. This time when Herman got on the line, he sounded like a different person—friendly, grateful, and in awe.

Upon hanging up, Vivien's head dropped onto her arms. Images of Half Moon Bay processed through her brain like a cleanly timed slide show. Places she'd never seen appeared in crystal clarity, with a mixture of emotions—some blissful, some frightening. No matter what the pictures foretold, one thing Vivien knew—she had to be there. Tomorrow she'd ask Herman for a Realtor's name.

She'd found a new home.

Chapter Seven

Voices mumbled in the distance.

Vivien arched.

A child giggled.

Booming laughter jolted Vivien's eyes open. She tried to focus. People stared down at her. Some repressed laughter, while others expressed concern.

"Mummy...mummy! Look, she's awake!" A skinny boy pointed right at her.

Getting up on one elbow, she raised her hand to block cruel light from assaulting her pupils. To Vivien's horror, she found herself lying on hard ground in the middle of the Drombeg Stone Circle, a popular historic Druid landmark. A tourist van had just arrived, emptying several travelers into her sleeping area.

Hot panic swarmed her chest. *How the hell did I get here?*

The last thing she remembered was curling up in bed the night before.

A middle-aged man with a concerned face and a British accent took her by the elbow. "Are you quite well?"

Normal. Appear normal.

"Yes, thank you." Vivien gave him a weak smile.

Now standing, her body wavered.

The man's wife observed under troubled brows. "Do you need a doctor, love?"

Looking down, Vivien found she'd donned sneakers, sweats, a Mick Finns sweatshirt, and a down coat yanked out of Katherine's hall closet. Thank God she hadn't wandered out in her nightgown; with March temperatures being in the low forties, she'd be hypothermic by now. Aware of her disheveled appearance, the woman probably assumed she'd been on a pub crawl the previous evening. "No, but thank you." Pulling a few pebbles out of her hair, Vivien moved through the crowd with as much dignity as possible.

Frantically searching, her gaze settled on Katherine's white Fiat parked along the road not ten feet away. Keys jingled in her left jacket pocket, and with glorious relief, Vivien got in the car and sped off.

Halfway to Kate's Cottage, she pulled over.

Planting her head upon the steering wheel, she racked her brain to reveal why she'd awakened smack dab in the middle of the Drombeg Circle. Nothing came. Finally, she reached out to Rhiannon for help, and visions from the previous night flooded Vivien's mind.

****

The Drombeg Circle had been a Druid site for sacrifices as far back as 945 B.C. Such thoughts entered Vivien's psyche as she stood under shafts of moonlight glistening against seventeen stones standing thirty feet high. But she was not alone. The same woman from the mirror on her first day of combat training peered back. She was clothed in a tan animal-skin tunic, leather arm bands, and deerskin boots, and a long pewter sword extended from her right hand. It was the same sword Vivien had wielded in her practice session months ago.

The woman's face and arms displayed circular patterns of Celtic battle paint in red and blue, as emerald eyes mesmerized her.

The words *honor and courage* blazed into Vivien's thoughts as the woman approached her, pushing back striking red, tangled hair.

"This is where we took our life."

Vivien's heart tightened. "We?"

"I would not be made an example by the Romans. They would have exhibited my head on a pike. My people deserved better."

"Who are you?"

Taking Vivien's arm in a tight grip, her proclamation echoed upon the night sky. "We are Boudicca!"

Knowing of Boudicca's legend, Vivien scoffed at the entity who somehow was able to hold her by the flesh. "Are you talking about Boudicca, the Celtic warrior queen who led all her clans to near victory over the Romans centuries ago? The same legend whose gold statue stands in London, erected in her honor? No! I don't believe you. Whoever you are, what do you really want?"

"For you to accept that I am part of you." The Celtic warrior queen placed her palm on Vivien's head.

Images of brave battles emerged in Vivien's mind—so real, she felt the horse beneath her thighs. Tears gushed as Boudicca witnessed her daughters raped by the Romans, her own flogging, and the adrenaline rush from her blade slicing through bodies.

The specter standing before her told the truth. Vivien had walked the earth as Boudicca.

Jerking her body away from Boudicca's, she

dissected the spirit with eyes of rage. "I know the Romans dishonored your people, but no part of me would kill!"

"Ah, but the energy is there. It simply lies dormant."

"Well, it's going to stay dormant!"

Boudicca cocked her head, studying Vivien intensely. "What about passion?"

Taken aback by her question, Vivien shifted her feet. "I'm...passionate."

Boudicca laughed heartily. "Fearing a black chasm is neither passionate nor honorable."

"What?" Vivien hissed, like a cat about to attack. "How dare you judge me!"

"Find your passion, Vivien. I am you, and you are me. We are us." Gliding away, the Celtic warrior queen dissipated with each step. Hopeful eyes glistened as she sent her a smile of compassion just before vanishing.

"You were a murderer!" Running after her, Vivien tripped and smacked the dirt hard. A thin trickle of blood ran down the corner of her lip. "You stupid bitch!"

Flipping over, she gazed up at the tall, formidable stones. All of a sudden, they held peace. Midnight dew stung cold against Vivien's fingers. The rocks of earth empathized with her pain. No—the Romans would not defile her body, nor would they find it once her loyal tribe members collected her remains and gave her a secret burial. Her fate was to simply blend back into the earth. Pulling a leather cord out from against her neck, a silver vial arose. After a Celtic prayer to her people, her husband, and daughters in the spirit world, she touched the vial to her lips. Cool fluid drifted down her throat.

One final thrust of her head brought the last drop into her body.

Stars above transformed into a beautiful design as all those slain welcomed Boudicca upward into peace and glory.

****

Bolting her head up from the steering wheel, Vivien viciously gripped the rearview mirror. A line of dried blood under her lip reflected back.

"It really happened...it really happened." Her lips muttered repeatedly, before finally snapping out of her own trance-like chant.

Heaving a weary sigh, and suddenly needing a hot bath, she turned the key, and started the engine.

A man walked out from behind a nearby cottage and stood in front of the car. When Vivien looked closer, she realized it was Aidan. He appeared very stern. She lowered the window and popped her head out. "Aidan, what are you doing?"

His face remained stoic. "Turn off the car and get out."

What the hell was wrong with him? She knew from training with the warrior clan that they were all normal, decent men.

"Why do you want me to get out of the car?"

"Just do as I ask."

"What?" Vivien barked sharply.

Just then Brendan stepped out and stood next to Aidan. They stared her down in silence.

"Would one of you tell me what the hell is going on?"

They did not respond.

Angrily turning off the ignition, Vivien jumped

out, slamming the door behind her. "Okay, I don't know what weird joke you're both trying to pull, but this is not a good time. I have to get to Kate's Cottage, so would you two please get out of my way?"

They glanced at each other, crossed their arms, glared back at her, and replied in unison, "No!"

"What the fuck! I mean feck! Whatever!"

Spinning away from them, Vivien took a deep breath, trying to control her anger. When she felt more centered, she turned back. "Look, I had a really tough revelation last night. I slept on the ground, I'm cold, I'm exhausted, my face is cut, and I just want to take a bath and have a cup of peppermint tea. So, get out of my fucking way!"

They stood their ground.

Just as she was about to treat them to a new onslaught of vulgarities, McGregor emerged from behind the cottage wall.

"Good morning, Vivien. If you don't come with us, we will be glad to gently escort you to the next location."

"Gently escort me? You don't gently do anything."

McGregor actually smiled. "You'd be surprised."

With a gyrating index finger, Vivien tried to stall whatever they had planned for her. "So, in my country, when someone says they're taking a woman to a secondary location, it usually ends with a homicide!"

None of the men reacted.

Vivien's voice rattled the air. "Tell me where you're taking me!"

"No!" McGregor blasted with calm force, before she even finished her last syllable.

"Fine! Take me, but it better be quick because I

had a hard night!" Shedding tears on those last words, she wiped her face with her sleeve and opened the car door. "Just let me get the keys."

Falling into the driver's seat, Vivien pulled the keys from the ignition. Rage and devastating sorrow hit her anew. They didn't understand how she felt inside. How could she perform in a combat session? She knew it had to be something like that. Her concentration was shot, and her body worn out.

In the blink of an eye, Vivien reinserted the keys, and turned the engine over. Unfortunately, she had to look down to get the gear out of park, and in that instant, all three men pounced on her.

She screamed when Aidan wrenched the door open. Then, he wrapped his arms around Vivien's waist and yanked her out.

"Let go of me!" Her legs and arms thrashed about like a tired toddler.

McGregor opened the passenger door, turned the engine off, pulled out the keys, and locked the car.

Vivien's strength became too much for Aidan, so Brendan joined him in restraining her. As they did, McGregor came around, dangling the car keys.

"Now listen to me, lass. You will come with us if you want these back."

Shocking even herself, she thrust her body forward, trying to get out of their death grip. They could barely hold her.

McGregor shoved the keys into his pocket. "Have it your way."

"All right! But you promise after I do this I can leave?"

"Aye."

"Okay, I agree. Now let go of me!"

"Let her go, lads."

They released her.

"Follow us." McGregor walked across the grass, away from the road.

"Fine!"

"And stop acting like a wee babe!"

"Shut up!"

Why couldn't she control her emotions? One minute she raged with anger, and the next she fell into a pool of melancholy tears. Holding her head high, Vivien tried to focus. Soon she would be free to cry on her pillow and cuddle under a down bedspread. She couldn't wait for that moment.

They walked up a small hill and came down the other side. Upon descending, Vivien's eyes fell upon Donal and Finn.

Then, McGregor pointed. "Stand there."

"Why?" As Vivien walked to the spot, McGregor threw her a grave look. She glared back with arms crossed.

Immediately, Carroll, Ronan, Liam, Sean, and Michael came down the hill.

Vivien threw up her hands. "What is this?"

No one answered. They formed a wide circle around her.

"I said, what the hell is this?"

"This is your final test," McGregor finally confirmed, and gestured to the clan surrounding her.

Her mouth dropped. "Wait...I thought I did that in practice last week with Sean, Ronan, and Michael."

"I never said that was your final test, lass. I only said it was a test, and it was without swords. But this time…" McGregor added, with a devilish smile.

As he spoke, Donal and Finn pulled blades out of four wooden cases she hadn't even noticed. Each warrior grabbed one.

Her heart fell into her stomach. "You don't mean…"

"Aye. You will fight us all at once." He placed Vivien's Celtic sword into her hand, closing her fingers around the hilt when she refused to hold on.

True panic rose up into her throat. "You're daft! You're all daft!" She gazed at McGregor with beseeching eyes and stabbed the tip of her steel into the ground. Vivien hoped he would sympathize with her plight or postpone her final combat test. Instead, he addressed the clan with blades raised.

"Brace yourself, lads."

They moved closer, ready to battle.

"Wait! You don't understand. Something happened last night, and I'm in no condition to fight."

They continued moving in—slowly, but deliberately.

"Stop it!" Vivien crumpled into tears. A small part of her brain was embarrassed for herself. What was wrong with her? Lowering her head, she hoped to gain pity. But when her head popped back up, Liam pulled his blade back to strike. Vivien yanked up her sword and clumsily blocked his attack.

Ronan whipped her around—striking Vivien to the ground. Lying on her back, she opened her eyes. A circle of long silver metal loomed above. Perhaps they would leave her alone if she didn't move. After all, she was the one they counted on to fight the evil thing, right? A decision must be made.

Something happened in that next second. The valor of Boudicca and the passion of her psychic gift created a powerful tonic within her. But unlike the previous night, Vivien allowed pure strength to channel through her mind, body, and spirit.

White light filled her torso, propelling her up from the ground. Her sword flowed as if choreographed. Vivien existed in the eye of the storm—no panic, only stillness.

Behind her, Vivien blocked oncoming attacks with just a thought. She wanted them pushed back, and that's what happened. Surprise at her ability didn't even enter her mind. She knew all along, deep inside. It all happened with quick precision—a blur of legs, steel, and arms, flying through the air. Understanding all Vivien had come there to learn, she'd evolved into the perfect blend of herself—enlightened and potent.

McGregor's voice suddenly boomed. "Let's go, lads!"

Vivien looked around to see each man get up or lean over. Some had small cuts, while others rubbed their arms and legs. They walked back up the hill, except for McGregor, who came to her.

"What happened?"

McGregor's smile spread from ear to ear. "You passed. You knocked us on our asses! You're ready."

Vivien smacked her forehead in shock. It seemed like only a few moments had passed. She'd successfully fought off ten men at once, and with swords. "I did it! I really did it! Oh my God! Is everyone okay?"

"The lads survived. You're coming with me."

"Wait, where are you taking me now?" She almost fought him off again as he took her by the arm and handed her sword to Donal.

"Mick Finns. It's your graduation party, so to speak."

"But I have to go back to Katherine's. I have her car, and I'm a total wreck. I mean, have you looked at me?"

McGregor guffawed. "Aidan, come here." Aidan walked down the hill. He threw him the keys from his pocket. "Bring the car."

"Aye."

"Why won't anyone listen to me?" Vivien's protests fell upon deaf ears as he dragged her to the top of the grassy knoll.

"You're coming to your party and that's final. One more thing…"

"Yes?"

"I'm proud of you."

When Vivien glanced up, he didn't meet her eyes, but she felt his words. Getting into the passenger seat, she promptly fell into an exhausted slumber.

****

Walking into Mick Finns felt like walking into a dream. Katherine, Hanna, Bridget, and the quilting club immediately came forward to congratulate her.

After waves of accolades, the quilting ladies turned her around. "You have blood under your lip, dear. Hold still," Rose observed.

"Um…that's okay," Vivien protested.

Rose yanked out a handkerchief and licked the white starchy square. Enthusiastically she dabbed at the wound as the other ladies looked on, directing her hand.

"All done." Rose tucked the handkerchief back into her purse. "Now put some ointment on that, and it will heal in no time."

Vivien held back a grimace. "Thanks." She scanned the room but didn't know how everyone in the tavern became aware of her final combat test. Katherine must have had a hand in it.

"Breakfast for all!" Bridget announced. Snatching Vivien's arm, she led her to the bar and grabbed a pint. "You've earned it!"

"I can't drink stout at nine o'clock in the morning!"

"Sure'n you can! Besides, it goes perfect with a traditional Irish breakfast." Thrusting the pint in her hand, Bridget disappeared into the kitchen.

Katherine approached holding a cup of tea. "Let's sit."

"That sounds good to me." Releasing a calming breath, Vivien slid into a booth. With elbows on the table, she rested her chin on her hands and, with slits for eyes, sized up Katherine.

Hiding a guilty grin, Katherine raised her palm. "All right, then." She dropped her hand. "It was me who called McGregor before sunrise and told him it was time for your final test."

"I'm sure you know this, but it was the worst timing ever. I mean, I'm glad I did well, but I just found out…"

Katherine put her cup down after taking a sip of chamomile tea. "Aye?"

Lowering her arms, Vivien spoke softly. "I was Boudicca in a past life. I killed men like it was business as usual."

"I thought as much."

"Excuse me?"

Katherine smiled sympathetically. "You know

what I mean. But you can now make peace and understand that she was protecting her people in every battle."

"That's what I felt when I was fighting off the clan. But I was so emotional beforehand. I was afraid I couldn't even fight."

"You got past that. You focused and connected."

"You knew they had to attack me when I was at my lowest, most vulnerable point. When I felt so insecure, I wanted to disappear."

Katherine silently sipped her tea.

"I know there's more to this. Are you going to tell me the rest?"

"All I know is when the time comes, you are going to be under extreme stress and emotion. It had to be done."

When she leaned back, Vivien took in the room, suddenly feeling nostalgic about her experiences. "So…I'm finished."

"Aye." Katherine placed a hand over hers. "I'll be fine. I understand you worry about me, but I'll be fine."

"I know you will. You have an entire community of people looking after you. I just can't help it. I'll get us set up on instant video messaging."

"What?"

"You'll find out."

Laughter from the bar turned Vivien's head. The clan teased each other about the wounds they acquired from her thrashing.

Bridget appeared with two gigantic plates of food on her arms. "Two Irish breakfasts. Eat up, ladies!"

"Thank you, Bridget. I'm ravenous." Picking up a fork, Vivien wanted to pounce on her food.

"Now mark my words—if I hear of you coming back to visit and you don't come in here, I'll hunt you down!"

Katherine and Vivien laughed wholeheartedly.

"Do we understand each other?"

Vivien nodded several times. "Aye, we do."

"Good luck in America!" Bridget charged off to deliver more meals.

"I'll be right back." Vivien dropped her fork and slid out of the booth. With pint in hand, she moved toward the clan. A hush fell as she raised her glass. "To all the wounded men—"

Groans rattled her ears. Then, Vivien became solemn. "Let me rephrase that. To my fellow warriors. Thank you for nurturing my power and confidence in combat. I know we will be together again under very different circumstances…" She didn't mean to pause at those words, but overwhelming compassion emanating from them choked her up. After getting herself together, she continued. "I honor all of you."

They raised pints, clinked loudly, and drank. Vivien felt their admiration and respect and witnessed a few hiding their eyes. Wishing her safe journey back to America and asking about her new home filled the gap when they didn't know exactly how to say goodbye.

After she and Katherine finished eating and walked out to the car, Vivien pulled McGregor aside. "I just told Katherine I'm getting us video conferencing, but you already have it, don't you?"

"Aye, and I'm available anytime you need me." With concerned eyes, he whispered, "You'll be careful, yeah?"

McGregor was thinking about the dark mass

hovering over the planet that wouldn't budge. "Definitely." About to burst into tears at the thought of saying farewell to her coach and mentor, Vivien held her breath. McGregor had consistently challenged with full confidence in her skills, even when she didn't feel it herself. Before blubbering like an idiot, her hand came out. "Thank you for everything."

Vivien promptly got pulled into a bear hug. "Come here, lass! We'll kick this thing's ass, come back, and have an even bigger party!"

She laughed and cried as McGregor released her.

Hanna wrapped her up in a gentle embrace. "It seems you just arrived, and here we are saying our goodbyes. Safe journey."

"Thank you." Vivien's head lowered while she wiped away tears with her fingertips.

She turned to Katherine one more time. Their final parting would be at the airport, but it felt like her true sendoff in front of Mick Finns.

Katherine took her hands, and tears welled up for both of them.

Vivien tried to speak, but nothing came.

"I know." Katherine smiled. "You're so grateful for me finding you and helping to strengthen your intuitive skills."

She nodded.

"I'm proud of you."

"But I haven't done anything yet." Vivien's voice eked out.

"Yes, you have. You've aligned with your authentic power."

Absorbing her words, Vivien stared back in utter silence.

"You stay here. I'll get the car." Trotting off to her parked Fiat, Katherine left her curbside.

Golden streams of sunshine flowed through morning clouds, making dew on the streets glisten like diamonds. The next time she'd arrive in Clonakilty, her life would be completely different.

How? She didn't know.

Chapter Eight

Vivien's eyes fluttered shut as she melted into an enormous powder blue crocheted pillow in a cozy front window seat. Dripping sounds from the big silver espresso machine, combined with aromas of rich mocha coffee and organic chocolate-chip zucchini muffins soothed her soul. With a turn of her head, she watched the magic of Half Moon Bay's Main Street. A barefoot painter collected red curls into a loose hairband, packing up her easel on the sidewalk, while a couple in stiletto heels and three-piece suits crossed the street for an early dinner at Pasta Moon. Half Moon Bay truly expressed a delicious combination of elegance and bohemian style. While Vivien was only an hour south of San Francisco, she had the city available but could still enjoy a quaint beach life. No other place on earth did she long to call home.

Java Hut had become her favorite hangout ever since arriving in the charming seaside town two years ago. After retiring from professional surfing, Matt Johnson had opened his coffee establishment. The moment she met him, with his scraggly gray hair, scruffy beard, twinkling blue eyes, and constant sense of humor, Vivien knew they would become friends. At fifty-six, he acted as if he were still in his twenties. It wasn't an immature attitude, but one of absolute delight for all things relating to the ocean.

Known surfers from their local, internationally renowned Mavericks competition covered the walls— Peter Mel, Ken "Skindog" Collins, and Grant "Twiggy" Baker. A few photos portrayed Matt in his heyday, but the rest displayed surfing stars from all over the world. Their smiles were infectious. She believed that was why so many people loved Matt's place, and of course the outstanding coffee. Dried reeds placed on the front awning gave it the finishing touch, making it worthy of the word "hut."

"Hey, Vivien! How's the ghost-hunting business?" Matt stood before her with arms akimbo and a huge grin.

With a smiling sigh, Vivien set her paper coffee cup down. "It's just great." Her eyes twinkled and she cocked her head. "When are you going to join me for a banishing?"

Matt laughed with gusto. "Nope! Sorry, but I don't do spooks. Now, surfing—that's something I could show you."

A jazzy piano tune emitted from Vivien's cell phone. She fished it out of her purse. "Ah! Saved by the bell." Beaming up at him, she gripped the square piece of metal. "One day, Matt…one day."

He sauntered away with a chuckle and a shake of his head. "Yeah, that's what I always hear."

Eyeing the caller, Vivien picked up quickly. "Hi, Donna. Is everything okay?" Something had panicked her best friend, the owner of a local metaphysical store called Luna Books. She wondered if something happened at the bookshop.

"Oh, thank God you picked up!"

"Why wouldn't I pick up?"

Donna's voice came out in breathy gasps. "No, that's not what I meant...I mean...I'm just so glad you're available."

"What's happening?"

"I'm sorry! I never got a call like this before. Some little girls were trying to do a séance, and now a man's ten-year-old niece is trapped in her bedroom by a banshee!"

"A what?"

"A banshee! That's exactly what he described, and he can't get the door open. He's desperate."

Waves of dread engulfed Vivien's heart. Something had changed in her sweet little town, and she intended to find out why.

"Give me the address."

"Gladly!"

****

Upon pulling up to the dark wood house, warm shivers hastened her heart and tingled her body.

For Vivien, it felt like she'd come home.

Blinking hard, she wiped cheeks dry of spontaneous tears. What the hell was happening? She had the right address, but why this emotional reaction to a house? Gazing at her reflection in the rearview mirror of her midnight blue hybrid SUV, Vivien's mind spun. She'd trained in combating evil and had come a long way in the past two years utilizing everything she'd learned in Ireland. Why didn't she see this coming? Not getting a psychic hit on a banshee felt like a red flag. Ever since her intuitive awareness book, *The Truth Within* hit the New York Times best seller list, she cleared homes of unwanted ghosts and worked with authorities on missing persons cases. In fact, the satisfaction Vivien felt when helping people in need was like nothing she'd ever experienced. People were scared, confused, and most of the time angry, because dealing with the supernatural was never covered in school. It was something people believed only inhabited their nightmares. She never realized how rewarding it would feel to give people peace in their lives. Between leaving Ireland and settling in California, she relaxed into her true calling—banishing evil and enhancing love. Vivien truly found happiness in her work. And now, there was a banshee…

With swirling thoughts rushing inside, her head dropped against the steering wheel. She took a long, deep breath. Vivien had been on many cases before but never experienced such strong emotions while parking her car.

Relying on her paranormal cleansing skills, she'd already projected shielding white light, which now protected the little girl trapped inside the beautiful house in front of her. In fact, when Donna told her it was a banshee, she almost didn't believe it. Creatures such as those only appear in homes where a death is imminent, and she intuitively knew the owner had a long life ahead of him.

Concentrate, Vivien. You need to concentrate.

But temptation won out, and her eyes turned back to the dwelling before her, looking like it was carved by a giant from some far away land. A simple one-level structure, there were no harsh angles—only a flow of curves. Beveled windows greeted, while miniature lanterns lining the walkway enhanced a rich green lawn and two cypress trees reaching for the sky. A real garden gnome darting across the grass would not have been a surprise.

Finally emerging from her car, Vivien took in a salty, crisp summer breeze. In the distance, yellow lights popped up along the marina, mixed with amber golden hues—one of her favorite sights of dusk falling upon Half Moon Bay. Taking in another calming breath, she smoothed out her navy-blue designer jacket, worn over jeans and a white cotton top. Clicking the lock button on her key fob, a sharp chirping sound echoed down the quiet street.

What was a banshee doing here anyway? She'd heard of sightings in County Clare, Ireland, and the Northwest Highlands of Scotland centuries ago, but California in modern day? Could it be related to the mass of dark clouds over the Sahara? The whole situation mystified her.

While puzzling over this odd reality, something caught Vivien's eye. A strange black mist slinked out from behind one of the cypress trees. It started crawling toward her like a predator. As it crept closer, her heart raced. She didn't realize she held her breath until the front door flew open.

When a man came out in a dark blue T-shirt and jeans, the strange vapor vanished. Walking briskly, he held a look of grim hope. Everything depended on her.

"Vivien Kelly?"

"Yes." Swallowing quickly, she tried to forget the eerie fog that just came out of nowhere. For once, she hoped her eyes played tricks on her.

"I'm Neal Harrington."

Meeting him halfway, her legs abruptly halted. It was him. The man who'd occupied her psychic dreams for the past three years. He stood before her in the flesh.

Power vibrated through him, and yet, he wielded such strength from a place of kindness. A wonderful combination. At six foot one, with tanned skin, auburn hair, and thoughtful green eyes—her adrenaline shot up.

His thoughts swiftly entered her mind. Besides taking in her beauty, she suddenly made him feel safe and happy. A shy smile grew on her lips at the thought. Never had a person been so open, so fast. Confusion shown on his face, but one thing he did know—he wasn't the same man he was ten seconds ago.

As Vivien exhaled on a moan, her purse flipped upside down. She kneeled, thrusting lip balms, a nail file, and tissues back into her stylish black and white satchel as fast as possible.

Neal gently, yet firmly, pulled her up by the elbow. "We've got to get in there now. That thing has my niece prisoner."

Vivien met his eyes. They held fear, restrained only by his own strength to remain calm, something he'd learned long ago. "I know. I've already sent light to Julie, so she is protected."

With eyes swimming in apprehension, he cocked his head. "Light?"

"Yes."

Realizing she was serious, Neal led her into the house. "I'll take you to her."

The touch of his skin sent warm waves through Vivien's body when his grip switched from grasping her elbow to holding her hand.

As they crossed the threshold and the inhuman screams devastated the air, his anxiety rose anew. He released her hand.

"All will be well shortly. Julie's friends are in your bedroom, correct?"

Nodding, he strode to the hallway. "Yes. Julie's room is—"

Vivien looped her purse straps onto a coat rack nearby. "I know where it is."

Now in the living room, she couldn't help but take in gorgeous wood molding at the top of each wall. The design not only looked like a forest but felt like nature—vibrating serenity. Rich red-brown Santos mahogany floors extended to a stone arched fireplace, enhanced by organic brown couches and Adirondack style lamps. A redwood tree embellished the square lamp shades, complementing a round frosted-glass ceiling fixture covered in an outline of maple leaves.

Vivien jerked herself away. She'd never been so sidetracked on a case before, but then again, this was no ordinary case. She had literally come face to face with the man of her dreams.

Announcing her presence, Vivien slapped open palms against the bedroom door. Shrieking stopped as the banshee tried to stab into her intuitive power, not even making a dent.

Julie, I'm here to help. Don't be afraid. After sending her telepathic message, she felt a definite shift. The young girl now had hope.

Sensing another female entity in the bedroom, Vivien tuned in sharper. A spirit connected to the house stood in front of Julie, also protecting her.

"That horrible noise stopped." Neal eyed the door urgently. "Is that good or bad? I mean, is Julie safe?"

"Yes, she's safe. I put a protective light around her."

Heaving a sigh of exhaustion, he rubbed his temple. "Oh, right—the light thing. This is all so weird." Neal's head popped up. "No offense."

"None taken." She grinned like a debutant about to dance with the coolest boy in school.

"What now?"

Vivien desperately prayed for someone to slap her in the face. Where was Donna when she needed her? Clasping her hands tightly, she pressed on. "I go in and—" Her mouth stopped moving. A dustbowl of black energy swirled through the house coming from Neal, as well as Julie's friends.

"Please bring the other girls to me. Tell them we need to help Julie."

"What?" His horrified face reflected his confusion.

"Do you trust me?" Relaxed eyes connected with his.

Neal's voice came out in a whisper. "I do trust you. I don't even know why."

The universe ceased movement while they gazed at each other again. Finally, Vivien cleared her throat and Neal turned on his heel.

"I'll get the girls."

After he rounded the corner, Vivien's head dropped into her hands. He distracted her to the point of possible error, and that she couldn't afford. Why did she have to meet him on a case? A damn weird one at that.

Bringing her head up, Vivien found three nervous girls peeking out from behind Neal's legs.

Neal looked down upon them with an encouraging smile. "It's okay. Vivien is here to help."

They gawked at her like fawns caught in the

headlights of a tanker truck.

A red-haired, freckled girl held Neal's hand, a brown-eyed girl grasped his thigh like a rope tow on a ski slope, and a sandy-haired, blue-eyed girl sporting a pink kitty shirt clung to his second hand. All three held guilty faces. Then it hit Vivien like a shot to the chest—they believed they'd abandoned Julie to a horrible fate. Neal got them out, but before Julie could escape, the creature sealed the door with an oozing black substance.

"I want to tell you all something—and you too."

Neal looked at her with surprise. "Yes?"

"I feel and can see the terror you're all in right now. Everything in this world has energy, and you're sending out powerful fear. That's what the creature wants. So, when you're scared, you're actually feeding the banshee and making her more powerful."

Her helpful speech made the girls burst into tears.

Stretching out her arms, she kneeled in front of them. "Wait! I know how we can fix this."

"We didn't mean to! We really didn't!" The girls proclaimed between sobs.

"Now, listen to me."

Beautiful young eyes gazed back at her expectantly.

"Go back to Neal's bedroom and sit in a circle. Hold hands and think of the best, most fun memory you have with Julie. I see you all at the beach making sand-castles. Use that one, or another, but focus on the joy of that day. It's like a daydream. Keep that vision going until I'm done."

Neal came forward. "I'll do it with them. Let's go."

Amazed at his instant acceptance of her task, she

stood.

Suddenly the girls sprang to life, all smiles and nods. They pulled Neal down the hallway, chattering about which memory they would choose.

Neal walked with them, but gave her a last, concerned glance before turning the corner. He wanted to protect her but didn't know how. Glowing from the inside out, Vivien realized it had been a long time since a man worried about her well-being.

Abruptly banging her hands on the ectoplasm wrapped about the door, she watched as it dissolved with a hiss into black smoke. After stepping back, a wave of love embraced her from behind. Pink, sparkling light filled the hallway. *It didn't take Neal and the girls long to send their support. Good for them.*

Crashing the door open with a bang, Vivien's combat kick splintered wood.

Damn it!

Sometimes she forgot her own strength. Neal would need to fix the doorframe, but she had the distinct feeling he would forgive her.

Frenzied laughter ricocheted off the walls as Vivien stepped inside. The banshee floated underneath a filthy black robe. Radiant red eyes dissected her every move, while disgusting nails clicked in excitement, flicking back greasy strings of midnight hair upon dead white skin.

Vivien caught sight of a thin ten-year-old girl huddled against the far windowsill. With hands clutching the end of a long yellow braid, her beautiful blue eyes hazed with fear, Julie could not see the white glow of light vibrating around her. Vivien's protection would embrace her until their skin touched. Once that happened, she hoped the creature would be gone. She gave Julie a playful wink before turning to face her adversary.

All of a sudden, the banshee transformed. Now, the creature's face could rock the runway of fashion week and her model thin body donned a flowing white gown. Vivien upped her own protection of light, knowing the monster's supernatural grin had stopped a human's blood from flowing many times before.

A Baobhan Sith?

The creature nodded.

As she dashed in front of Julie, Vivien's maternal instinct kicked in, even though she had no children of her own.

The *Baobhan Sith* hailed from the highlands of Scotland as a particularly evil and dangerous form of banshee. As a hybrid, she also possessed a strain of siren—hungering for handsome young men. A common tale told the account of four male friends on a hunting trip. After entering an abandoned cabin, they drank and made merry. One of the men wished for female companionship and after a knock at the door, four beautiful maidens joined them. A few dances later, blood splattered across the cabin walls, but one man escaped. With the fourth *Sith* at his heels, he took shelter between the horses outside—creating a barrier she could not cross. When dawn approached, the *Sith* had vanished.

Vivien racked her brain to remember what held off the monster. Something connected to the horses kept the man safe. A horseshoe popped into her mind. *That's it!* The iron on the horse's hooves stopped the Sith. The hag feared metal. Not having dealt with this entity before, any information helped. Vivien wore a Celtic *Triskele* around her neck, but the quarter-sized silver medallion would not be enough. Looking for something metallic, she decided to play it cool. Crossing her arms, she cocked her head. "Shouldn't you be seducing some hot surfer dude right about now? I know you strike after sunset."

Hovering, the *Sith* sneered and hissed.

Taking Julie's arm, Vivien hauled her toward the door. After getting the girl out, she'd resume her search for metal, but she had to get her out now.

"The child stays!" Transforming back into its true gruesome form, the *Sith* blocked their exit.

Fear boiled up from the pit of Vivien's stomach for the first time in two years. Almost unfamiliar with the emotion, it took her back to early psychic training days. How could she let this thing get to her? Angry now, she connected to her inner strength. "Fine! But before I banish you into whatever dimension you hail from, why are you here picking on little ones?"

The hag glided closer, until they were almost face to face. Julie's quivering form huddled behind Vivien's back. The monster snarled, with a grotesque incline of her head.

"Boudicca."

Every fiber in Vivien's body hastened to alarm. It knew who she was.

Without warning, claws lunged for Julie's face, aiming to slash her young skin to shreds.

Vivien waved her left arm—sending the creature flying against the opposite wall with a loud whack. She hoped not to demonstrate her unique talent, which accompanied her psychic power, but otherwise the girl would be hurt.

Julie gasped, and then giggled when she watched the old hag squirm on the wall. "She looks like a wiggle worm!"

Repressing a laugh, Vivien addressed Julie in a serious tone. "Go to your uncle's bedroom and join your friends. When I'm finished, I'll let you know. Okay?"

"Okay!" Rushing down the hall, Julie's voice rang out. "Uncle Neal! Uncle Neal! The pretty lady stopped the monster!"

Hiding a smirk, Vivien knew when Julie told them of her unseen strength, they'd believe she exaggerated, caught up in the high emotion of the moment.

The *Sith* spoke in a voice akin to sizzling bacon. "I keened at many a household from your deeds."

The creature spoke the truth. As with most historic battles of justice, Boudicca slaughtered many people in the process. Combining extraordinary psychic power and her commanding Celtic past, Vivien now used her skills to help others.

"That was then. This is now."

The *Sith* drooled on her chin.

"Why are you really here?"

"He has released us! We shall live in a new world—this world, and it shall be turned to darkness!" The hag writhed, viciously trying to free herself.

"Who released you?"

"Dagda!"

Images of a giant portly man, pale of skin, unkempt long red hair, in a tartan cloak and primitive kilt, carrying a large club rushed through her memory.

"Dagda? You mean that rosy-cheeked, fat, father

figure, Celtic god we used to worship for good harvest?"

"Aye!"

Horror forgotten, she guffawed—reveling in absurdity. "Dagda?" She nearly choked on laughter. "That's so stupid!"

Crimson eyes flashed back. "He holds you in favor, but now you shall be punished!"

Throwing up the other arm, Vivien channeled all her power into the banshee's banishment, bored with her ridiculous threats. Usually an entity would be halfway to hell by now, but somehow the hag began to wriggle free. She needed metal. Luckily, just behind her sat a silver metal princess tiara perched on a white pillow. To reach it, she'd have to release the bonding power holding the *Sith* in place. If she grabbed it fast, the beast would recoil just as her nails touched Vivien's hair.

Leaping onto a cream white comforter on the four-poster bed, Vivien's fingers snatched the tiara. Triumphantly about to fling it at the despicable thing, her body suddenly slammed onto the hard wood floor. Then, slimy nails viciously yanked her hair backward.

Both claws reached out to seize her skull.

"My, my…what have we here?" With a raised eyebrow, Vivien whipped out the crown.

Palms smacked onto her ears to keep them from melting, as the *Sith*'s howl burst forth. When the banshee took a breath, Vivien sprang into action.

Coming out as rich smooth silk, Vivien's voice beckoned. "You are now helpless on the wings of night. Go from here with your hollow fright. For this home is for the living and the light!" With one last thrust of her arms, a final command emitted from her lips.

"*Dibir!*"

Blazing white light wrapped around the *Baobhan Sith*, throwing it into a frenzy. Blackness opened the opposite wall and spread like an oil slick. Twisting into its new dimension, the monster created a gale force wind, sending dolls flying everywhere. Not wanting to damage any more of Julie's toys, Vivien quickly caught them before they landed, turning around just in time to see the wall solidify into its original state.

Releasing a thankful breath, she placed the dolls on the bed, smoothed back her hair, and then froze.

Red combat blood covered her hands.

Boudicca's memories came crashing down— severed heads leaving a trail of blood, while jugs of wine passed amongst raucous laughter.

Vivien dropped to her knees.

"Stop...please stop."

The steaming stench of sweat, blood, and death sickened her. It became increasingly difficult to push gory scenes aside after a paranormal battle.

Two hands grasped her arms. "Vivien? Vivien?"

"Honor and courage!" Her head raised high.

"What?"

Vivien checked her hands. They appeared normal.

Reality slammed back when she looked directly into Neal's worried, yet gorgeous, sea green eyes. Not knowing why she spoke those words, Vivien's legs shot up, bringing her to a standing position. "Sorry about the door. The creature is gone. I banished her. She won't return."

Suddenly, her body wrapped up into his arms.

"Thank you!"

All thoughts of monsters, death, and blood fled as Vivien relaxed against him. He smelled like organic musk. Just like her dreams.

"You're bleeding."

"Huh?" She pulled back.

"Come with me. I have a first aid kit."

"That's funny." Vivien emitted a hasty chuckle for Neal's benefit, knowing full well her wound was no laughing matter. She'd never been injured during a banishing.

Once in the kitchen, Neal grabbed a paper towel and pressed it against her skin. As a red line expanded on thin white paper, his eyes caught hers.

After a time of suspended animation, Vivien spoke. "Where shall I sit?"

"Right here." He gestured over her shoulder.

Settling into a redwood chair, one of six surrounding a large round matching table, she gazed about. A huge French country-style kitchen stared back. Copper pots hung above a block island, countered by a rounded window seat with a view of the ocean to die for. But the most charming quality had to be the antique potbelly stove in the corner.

"This is a beautiful kitchen."

Rummaging through medical supplies, Neal sent her the most charming smile she'd ever seen. "Thank you."

Electricity ran through Vivien's body. She cleared her throat. "Are you in business for yourself now?"

"Yes. A year ago, I still worked for a large architectural firm in the city, but now I have my own clientele."

"You've wanted that for a long time." Vivien

didn't mean to say it, but she couldn't hold back her psychic hit.

Looking up at her with sparkling eyes, Neal didn't seem to mind her probing his thoughts. Just the same, she vowed to stay polite and managed an awkward smile. "How are the girls doing? They must be scared."

"Actually, they're pretty savvy. They read some book that warned about this."

"And they still did it."

"Yes, but from what I can tell, they won't be in analysis for years."

She snickered. "That's good."

"What does *dibir* mean?"

Neal threw out the question so quickly, he took her unaware. "I'm sorry?"

As he unwrapped a butterfly bandage, Neal didn't look up. "I know you told me to stay with the girls, but I was worried about you."

Vivien's entire body went rigid. "What else did you hear?"

"Only some kind of poem, or chant. Nothing else." Gently reaching for her hand, he removed the paper towel, replacing it with the bandage.

Confident he'd only heard the last part of her exorcism, Vivien decided to answer his question. "Well, I've never told anyone this before because my clients are always out of the house when I'm working, but *dibir* means exile—to cast out. It's the Gaelic word for banishment. My mother hailed from Ireland, and I draw from my Celtic heritage." She purposely left out her extra power as a warrior queen from a previous life. "The poem part—that's an Irish Triad. Three sentences manifest energy in a threefold nature, and I command entities in a magical way by using my mind, body, and spirit." Having revealed much more than intended, she gulped. "What I mean is—it helps me concentrate when I cast something out, and each time I improvise in the moment."

Studying her face, Neal appeared deep in thought, as if he were trying to solve a puzzle. Gently, he uttered, "That's very interesting."

Vivien knew he pondered her process. Wanting to change the subject quickly, her mouth opened, but shut again when he spoke first.

"Actually, I need to ask you a favor." Neal's eyebrows creased as he wrapped gauze around her hand.

"Yes?"

"Will you talk to the girls? I'm afraid they won't come back to play with Julie. I don't want them to be scared of my house."

"Are you scared?" Vivien asked calmly.

With a half laugh, his head shook up and down. "I was, yes. I'm not ashamed to admit it." Grasping the table with both hands, Neal looked her straight in the eyes. "As an architect what I create I see, touch, and comprehend—but not this. I know there are strange things out there, but that doesn't mean I'm ready to see them face to face."

"I completely understand. Sometimes I wonder how I'm still doing this work. Then, I remember I'm giving people their homes back—their lives back."

"Yes, and I for one am very grateful."

The air shifted. Vivien raised her chin toward the archway kitchen entrance where a beautiful blonde in a yellow dress smiled at her. Holding a small bunch of spring flowers, she urged Vivien to speak.

"There's something else. A protective spirit stood in front of Julie the entire time."

His shoulders leveled.

"A female connected to you."

Shock did not register on his face.

She waited.

Releasing a long breath, Neal locked eyes with hers. "That was my wife. Darlene. She died two years ago while I was building this house for us."

Surprised she hadn't picked that up, Vivien held her newly bandaged hand. "I'm very sorry."

"The first night I moved in, about three months ago, I entered the bedroom and smelled her favorite flower. Roses seemed to be everywhere. But I didn't think it could be real."

"It was."

Neal's lips curled into a reflective smile. "Well, at least I know I'm not crazy. Her appearance doesn't surprise me. She loved Julie."

After a moment, he stood.

Darlene walked through the opposite window, nodding to Vivien before vanishing, a look of pure peace on her face.

Neal leaned into the hallway. "You can come out now, girls!"

The running of small bare feet echoed down hardwood floors.

"We're so sorry! Really, we're so sorry!" Julie exclaimed, throwing her arms around Vivien's neck.

"Hold on there. I've put a special Band-Aid on her."

The girls gasped in unison.

Julie's hands cradled her own face. "Did she scratch you?"

"No. My hand hit something. It happens sometimes in my job." Vivien knew it wasn't quite the truth, but close enough.

"How did you get rid of the monster?" the girl with red hair asked.

"By the way, this is Sam." Neal laid a hand on the freckled girl's shoulder.

"Well, Sam, that was a banshee. She came because you girls were playing around with the supernatural." Vivien's stomach tightened knowing there was much more to the story, but they had to know the dangers of dabbling with forces they didn't understand. "You must be very careful when you play in the spiritual realm. But the good news is she won't be coming back. I banished her."

"How do you banish something?" Two girls behind Julie excitedly screamed in stereo, jumping up and down.

"Stop right there!" Neal held up his hand. "I don't want you girls trying to do anything Vivien does."

They went quiet. Before they could speak again, Neal pointed out Pamela, the sandy-haired dreamy girl and Becky, whose long black curls eagerly nodded at everything Vivien told them.

Pulling in their attention, Vivien spoke crisply. "Before you do a séance, you must imagine a white light all around your body that protects you."

"Actually, I forbid any of you to do a séance anytime, anywhere—especially in this house." Neal made eye contact with each girl, driving his point home.

Julie lowered her head. "I'm sorry, Uncle Neal."

"Yeah, we won't do it again," Pamela droned.

Taking pity on their wretched faces, Vivien reached her arms out. They circled around her instantly. "You have to obey Neal's house rules. But if you're ever in a place where the energy doesn't feel good, imagine the light."

Neal stood with arms akimbo. "You'll all remember what Vivien said, right?"

"Right!" the young chorus echoed.

Before the doorbell rang, Vivien pushed her chair back. "That's my team."

"Okay, I want you girls to wash up. We're going to eat in fifteen minutes."

Bare feet sprinted again, but Julie held back. She beckoned Vivien to bend down and whispered in her ear. "I didn't tell them about your special power. I knew that was a secret."

When Vivien lifted her head to reply, Julie was already halfway down the hall. What a smart little girl. Instead of selling her out, she became an ally.

Chapter Nine

Neal opened the front door and welcomed the rest of Vivien's team. Little did he know this was their first official case working together as the Kelly Society. John and Jason had entered Vivien's life unexpectedly one night in a club. She rarely went out anymore, but it was a blind date debacle set up by Donna. After sensing a dangerous entity, John approached Vivien. He introduced himself as a retired Celtic mythology professor and paranormal investigator, and Jason as his former student and professional photographer. The combination couldn't have been better.

"Hi, I'm Jason," a fresh-faced, dark-haired, twenty-six-year-old with a huge grin stated, shaking Neal's hand.

Jumping in, Vivien made introductions. "Yes, this is Jason Lee, our photographer and videographer. When he's not taking shots for *National Geographic*, he helps us out. And this is John Patrick, who runs all that scientific equipment I don't understand."

The weathered, yet kind, face of a man about sixty, with salt and pepper hair and blue eyes, stood in the doorway. In tan khakis and equipment hanging all over his body, John nodded. "Hello."

"Thanks for coming." Shaking hands, Neal gestured for John to enter.

"Sure thing." Suddenly, John observed Neal and

Vivien in utter astonishment—darting his head back and forth.

"What's wrong, John?" Vivien questioned, suddenly mortified.

"Uh...nothing," John blubbered. Looking up at Neal, he shrugged. "I thought I recognized you for a second. Never mind."

Jason glanced at Vivien's hand. "What happened to you?"

"Oh, it's just a scratch."

John's eyebrows knitted. "Are you sure?"

"Yeah, I'm good." John already took on a father-figure role with her, so she knew he'd be concerned. She turned to Neal. "We want to make sure there's no residual energy. So, we'd like to conduct a sweep with the equipment. That way we've covered all the bases."

Neal shook his head. "All right. But you've got to understand—I've never had to do this kind of thing before."

"Oh, you're in good hands with Vivien!" Jason piped up eagerly.

Seeking to hide blushing cheeks, she looked down, faking an itch on her good hand. It was nice of Jason to talk her up, but Vivien didn't want promotion at this point.

"Hey, I'm heating up lasagna for the girls, and I made a salad. Do you want to join us?" Neal asked all of them but stared directly at Vivien.

Gazing into his joyful face softened her racing mind. Can the heart open up a second time? Part of her wanted to stay, but the rest wanted to run.

All eyes turned on Vivien. Adrenaline pounded. Even knowing Neal to be her soul partner, primal panic set in. "I don't think so, because we—"

"That's a great idea!" John interjected loudly. "Yes, we'll all stay and have some lasagna!"

John refused to look back when Vivien glared at him—all of a sudden, fumbling with his electromagnetic field meter.

Neal's eyebrows raised. "Maybe you have other plans?"

"Nope," Vivien retorted with a timid smile.

Smacking his hands together, Neal nodded. "Okay, then. I'll be in the kitchen if you need me."

John set his mechanisms on the floor just when Julie and her friends rounded the corner.

"Are these the other ghost hunters?"

"Yes, these are the other investigators." Trying not to laugh at Julie's reference, Vivien swung her arm toward her team.

Pure awe filled the girls' faces as they stared.

John coughed to suppress a chuckle.

"John, Jason—this is Julie, Neal's niece, and these are her friends Becky, Sam, and Pamela."

"What's all this stuff?" Julie cried, in pure glee.

"I still don't know, but he does." Vivien referred to John, who kneeled down in front of the girls.

"Tell you what—I'll show you the machines after dinner."

"Yay!" The girls resounded with delight.

Neal cleared his throat. "I could use some help."

They raced off in a flash to join Neal in the kitchen.

Jason snorted. "Cute kids."

"Yeah, too bad they conjured up a banshee."

"What?" John almost choked on his gum, while

Jason's eyes grew bigger, not with fear, but with eagerness.

Crossing her arms, Vivien stared their young rookie down. "And not just any banshee—a *Baobhan Sith*. A very special breed—part Siren, which means she feeds on handsome young men. She'd eat you for breakfast and spit you out before you could say flapjacks, Jason."

"I know. It's just so amazing." Pulling out his camera and scanning the walls, Jason anticipated another paranormal event instantly occurring.

Vivien shook her head. He'd barely heard a word.

In contrast, John sought out her insight. "What's really happening?"

Gathering them close, Vivien spoke low. "Something evil has entered our world, and for the life of me, I can't figure out what it is."

"Really? You? I thought you were uber-psychic," Jason said.

As she sighed, a hand belonging to John wacked Jason on the arm.

"Well, I'm just saying."

Stalling for time to think, Vivien massaged her neck where a knot began. Not wanting to frighten them with ramblings of a *Baobhan Sith* and her empty threats of a Celtic god releasing dark creatures, her head came up. "When I know more, I'll fill you both in. I promise."

"I'm keeping you to that promise," John declared with conviction and an index finger almost in her face.

A moment later Neal walked up to them. "I hope you're all hungry."

****

Each time the rocking chair came down, Vivien pushed off, creating a tiny squeak from her wedge sandals. Next to her, Neal sat in front of an unlit fire pit of gorgeous brown marble in the middle of a stunning redwood deck.

Having finished a delicious dinner of homemade lasagna, John and Jason now swept through Neal's home. It was easier to pick up electromagnetic energy created by the paranormal with all electronics switched off.

It also made it easier to stargaze.

"There it is. There's the Big Dipper." Neal pointed up to the night sky.

Playfully, Vivien let the chair swing her back. "Oh, yes. That makes us even. I found the Little Dipper and you found the Big Dipper."

The warmth of Neal's smile reflected in his eyes. Then, they turned somber. "I need to thank you again. If anything happened to Julie or the girls, I don't know what I'd do. I've never felt so irrelevant in my life."

"I'm glad I could help."

"You're very brave."

Vivien shrugged. "This may sound strange, but it's all in a day's work."

He leaned in. "I know what it's like to enter a dangerous situation. Believe me, I respect that."

Neal looked like he'd elaborate, then a wave of pain flickered through his face. If her sensitivities weren't so sharp, she would have missed it.

Rocking backward in a chair that matched hers, Neal released a deep breath. "I'm glad I finally moved in. Now I can enjoy this patio and stargazing. Maybe I'll even buy a telescope." His arms extended, with a gigantic grin. "You know, one of those big ones."

Laughing, Vivien crossed her legs toward him. "I think that would be the perfect addition to your new home."

With a firm gaze, Neal began to speak, then his eyes dropped in embarrassment.

A classic picture of an old woman sitting in front of a crystal ball snapped into Vivien's head. Trying to hold back a smile, she swayed back lazily. "I'm not what you expected, am I?"

"No, you're not." With a hand to his forehead and a look of dismay, he chuckled.

"You were expecting an old woman with pocked skin, crazy black hair, a tasseled gold scarf wrapped around her head, a flowing gypsy skirt, with a lazy eye and a scratchy voice."

Waving a hand in the air, Neal laughed harder, trying to dismiss her stereotype. "Not at all!"

"Just try to deny it." Vivien's voice sputtered, guffawing just as hard as he. She had become accustomed to his reaction. When she crossed the threshold of many a house, people stared in shock to see a woman looking like she just stepped off the cover of *In Style* magazine. Once, she had to expel a negative basement ghost just after attending a celebrity-studded fund-raiser and arrived in a little black cocktail dress.

"I'm sorry...I'm sorry. Actually, I didn't know what to expect." Neal's voice smoothed. "You're a very pleasant surprise. So, when you show up, do people ask where you got your sense of style?"

It happened a few times just like he said. "Yes— from my mother."

"Oh?" His brows raised in curiosity.

"She owned a little designer dress shop in Manhattan, and I helped out starting from five years old. I used to separate ribbons by color. Each winter, she ran a coat drive for lower income families, and each spring she did the same with donations for children's clothing. Her loyal customers brought in tons of stuff." Vivien resumed rocking her chair. "Anyway, you can guess where I got my prom dress."

"I bet you were beautiful."

Joyful tingling traveled through her. Locking eyes with him, words escaped Vivien's mind. She decided to study her left thumbnail. "So, does Julie stay here often? I noticed her bedroom is fully furnished and lived in."

"Yes. I'm sorry I couldn't introduce you to my sister earlier, but she had to get home." Moving forward, Neal slapped his hands onto his knees. "Pam went through an emotional divorce a year ago. Her ex-husband now lives in Madrid with his new wife and has no desire to see Julie."

"Oh, no." The little girl's sorrow sliced through Vivien's heart.

"I always hated the guy, but that's another story. Pam is establishing herself as a real estate agent in Santa Cruz, where she lives. Sometimes she shows homes on weekends, and that's when I help out." His shoulders lifted with a shake of his head. "I know I may be going overboard, but right now Uncle Neal is the only father she has."

"Julie loves you and looks forward to every time she comes here. Your sister is extremely grateful." Vivien couldn't help sharing her intuitive ping and touched his arm without realizing. As she pulled away, he placed his hand over hers.

Suddenly, it felt like one of those freeze frames in a movie—no words, no sound—just the two of them set against an unforgettable summer evening of glowing stars and the fresh smell of the sea.

Nervously, Vivien rose and grabbed the wooden railing at the far end of the deck. Feigning a desire for astrological education, her finger shot up. "Is that Cassiopeia?"

Neal had moved right behind her. With a sweet smile, he pointed. "That's the Milky Way."

"Oh." Quickly, her arm dropped.

Many miles out to sea an illuminated fishing boat drifted by. One of the men ordered to anchor down for the night.

"I haven't figured it out yet, but you look so familiar."

"What?" Blocking thoughts of the fishermen, Vivien focused on Neal. "Oh. Well, I have a book out, and my photo is on the last page. Maybe—"

"No, it's not that. It's something else."

Unanswered questions hung between them. Questions she couldn't even answer. For some reason she could only get so much from him. His mind opened to her, but he also held a mystery she couldn't seem to penetrate.

As he leaned against the railing, Neal moved closer. "I noticed you were very quiet at dinner. Is it because of the work you do? I imagine it's very draining emotionally."

His words sounded almost clinical, but the way his soft green eyes searched hers told her he authentically cared. Vivien's feet shifted awkwardly. "Well, every case is different—" In the next second, she plummeted into him.

"Look out!" Neal's arms snatched her around the waist.

Peacefully resting against him, she forgot where she was. His thoughts gently entered her mind. He hadn't held a woman in years. To hold her felt like a miracle. So strong and yet, so feminine. When Neal leaned in, lowering his lips to hers, she wanted to accept his kiss but stopped dead.

"Sorry about that—new sandals."

"Huh?"

She killed the moment. Now she wanted to kick herself.

"Oh." Neal looked down at her shoes.

Maybe he'd be brave enough to try again. He started to let her go, and that's when Vivien pulled him back. "You were saying?"

This time his lips parted, and so did hers.

"Well, we're done!" John announced in a booming voice and a loud clap of his hands.

Vivien jerked, knocking her forehead right into Neal's.

"Ouch!"

"Oh, my God! I'm sorry!" Grimacing in utter embarrassment, she stepped back.

Neal laughed with a pained grin. "That's okay."

"I didn't mean to startle you two," John mumbled, looking remorseful.

Panic gripped her. She'd made a fool of herself. Neal opened his mouth to say something, but she moved away. Switching gears, Vivien focused on John. "Did you find anything?"

"No. The readings were normal. I left the digital recorder going, and I'll let you know if we get any EVPs."

Neal turned to Vivien, completely lost. "EVPs?"

"Electronic Voice Phenomena."

"Which is?"

"Sometimes the voice, or sound of a spirit can be captured on a digital recorder." Vivien rambled, planning a quick escape.

"Oh…uh…okay. Let me get these lights back on." Neal entered the house.

John began packing up.

Vivien grabbed her satchel from the coat rack. "Okay then, we'll get out of your hair. Let us know if you experience anything else."

"Do you have a card?"

"Yes. Here it is."

Neal held the business card between them; his green eyes searched hers. "Will you have dinner with me Saturday?"

Silence fell over the room. The reptilian part of Vivien's brain engaged, putting her into fight or flight mode. She took the flight option.

"I'm sorry. We have an appointment that night."

John threw a bag over his shoulder. "No, we don't."

"Yes, we do. Remember, it's the follow up at Ruby Lounge. I have it marked on my calendar."

"Check your calendar."

"What?" Vivien's voice barked with flashing emerald eyes.

"Check your calendar," John repeated, calm as a cucumber.

Briskly, and with a sigh to end all sighs, Vivien pulled out a six by eight-inch black book. Regardless of modern technology, she still preferred to carry a hard copy calendar where she could pencil in time commitments.

"Fine. I'll show you." Turning to the date in question, blank pages mockingly stared back.

"See." John pulled up his cell phone calendar. "It's the following Saturday, and it's in the afternoon."

"Can I see that?" Neal reached out for her black book.

"Why?"

"Please?"

Neal took her calendar, then opened a kitchen drawer, pulled out a pencil, scribbled something, and handed it back.

Vivien read the words—Dinner with Neal Harrington at 7:00 pm. Upon looking up, she caught John and Jason reading over her shoulders. "Excuse me!"

They scattered like wounded animals.

"So, I have your number, and I'll call you midweek to get your address."

"Well, um…all right." Vivien shoved the book into her satchel awkwardly, wondering what just happened.

Jason walked up to Neal. "I took a bunch of shots, and I'll call you if anything turns up. Sometimes this phenomenon doesn't appear on digital. I have to wait till it's printed the old-fashioned way. They're sneaky like that."

"Okay, thanks. Here's my card." Neal handed one to each of them.

"Good night." Vivien snatched his card and

quickly retreated through the front door.

John waved, very pleased with himself. "Bye!"

Opening her driver's side door, Vivien angrily thrust her purse inside. "Thanks, John!"

Jason erupted in a snort-laugh, trying to hold it back.

"What? You told me it's been five years since you had a date. Isn't that long enough?"

"That's not the point. I'll know when I'm ready to date again."

"That's true, but maybe it's also true that you're scared?"

"Okay, when it comes to this, I want you two to leave me alone." Leaping into her SUV, Vivien locked the doors, refusing to look at them.

When John tapped on her window, and as Jason walked away, she eased it down.

"Do you want to know why I looked at you and Neal so strangely when I first arrived?"

Vivien buckled her seatbelt. "No, but I think you're going to tell me."

"I saw a pink aura around both of you. I don't know what it means, but I know you need to spend more time with him. Just get to know him."

John appeared sincere in his description, which excited and frightened her—just like the first time she saw Neal's house.

"You're not the only one who gets signs from the universe. Mine aren't as common and strong as yours, but it does happen." With that, John walked away, leaving her speechless.

Chapter Ten

Reveling in bright lights shimmering off dark water from the ferry building, Nicholas Williams leaned against the glass of his ultra-chic Embarcadero loft. He loved being in the center of San Francisco's financial district and savored his contacts there. With a grunt of satisfaction, he brought a flute of champagne to his lips. After knocking back the sparkling wine in one greedy swallow, he unbuttoned his white silk shirt. "Where are you?"

"Coming!" the sexy brunette from a cocktail party he met two hours earlier answered.

Nicholas chuckled, moving into the kitchen. "Pun intended?"

When she appeared from the hallway in red bra and panties, she wrapped her arms around his neck. "Definitely."

Moving his mouth over hers, he started slow. Nicholas knew women liked that, but just as he shifted to deepen the kiss, a vibration of energy shook him.

Someone called out. Someone just as powerful as he. The energy came from a female. That excited Nicholas. This unknown woman found herself in a dilemma and didn't know what to do. In fact, she wasn't even aware he'd picked up her psychic signal. He had to enter meditation and find out who she was without delay.

Nicholas pulled away from his hot conquest. "You have to go."

"What's wrong?" the dark-haired beauty begged in a whiny tone.

In a brief moment of compassion, he touched her cheek. "It's not you, honey. I just have something I need to do."

She clung to him, trying to rekindle the lust. "C'mon. I'm sure it can wait."

"No!"

Flying two inches above the black and white designer tile floor, her body slammed against the opposite wall. He hadn't touched her. Grasping the black granite kitchen counter, Nicholas tried to regain control.

With a scream of hysteria, she'd already run away. He didn't mean to scare her, but this was too important. After the front door slammed, Nicholas raced to his bedroom.

He lay down and centered himself. As his eyes closed, each end of his lips lifted into a sly smile. Keen intuition had brought Nicholas amazing success, which he now enjoyed to the fullest. Not only was he the most sought-after motivational speaker on the scene, but his book sales rocked off the charts. His self-help group, the Foundation, continued to grow, and he luxuriated in celebrity status.

But right now, Nicholas focused on finding this vibrant woman and decided to have some fun with her.

****

Anticipation rushed through Vivien while she drove down the familiar two-lane coast highway on her way home from Neal's house. If the banshee's proclamation was on the level, she would have a lot on her plate. She thought about Neal. What kind of life would she be involving him in? Maybe she should avoid a relationship altogether until her battle with evil ended. But when would it end?

Struggling with her decision, Vivien grasped the quarter-sized piece of silver dangling around her neck. Her mother gave her the Celtic Trestle on her sixteenth birthday, knowing she'd inherited her psychic gift. Swirling lines within a circle signified life eternal—never ending. Rubbing her fingers over the cool metal always reassured her, as well as her mother's motto—*Every problem has two sides, the negative and the positive. Search for the positive. There you'll find the answer.* The talisman had been on her person every day for the past twenty-two years.

All of a sudden, a strong male presence entered her car. He felt familiar. As Vivien eyed her rearview mirror, she saw the intruder leering from the back seat.

Tall and muscular, he wore a brown tunic under a fur-lined black cloak, with a thick wooden club atop his shoulder.

A stunned whisper hissed out of Vivien's mouth. "Oh, my God!"

It was Dagda. But instead of the rosy-cheeked, jolly man who brought them good harvest in Roman times, he now appeared as a green scaly-skinned vessel of horror, with a gnarled face and red eyes. Over the centuries he'd transformed into a demon. The banshee told the truth.

Angry at how she could have worshipped such a creature even in another life, Vivien's gaze raked him up and down. "You! You're disgusting! You used to be

Dagda! God of harvest and our protector! Now look at you! You're a demon! What happened?"

In a voice oozing like hot lava, Dagda answered in Gaelic. "I shall live anew. You will take the journey with me to the highest point of power." He made the statement matter-of-fact, as if the deal was done.

"Like hell I will!" Facing a demon should have tested Vivien's courage, but in this case, anger won out. "You're pathetic! You're in the modern world now, and the last thing we need is some ancient loser Celtic god turned demon to mess it up! We already have terrorism, and we don't need you added to the mix! My answer is no! In fact, I'm going to do everything I can to send you back to where you belong—in hell!"

"You always were a fiery lass!" Dagda roared, shaking her car. Pulling back his club, he took a mighty swing.

Suddenly, the steering wheel jolted out of Vivien's hands.

Dagda no longer occupied her back seat, but someone else was with her—someone just as horrible. She knew it was a man, but that's all she could get.

An invisible foot smacked down on the gas pedal, swerving her SUV off the highway and onto the dirt shoulder of the cliffs.

"Stop it! Stop it right now!"

Vivien's shouts only increased his energy. Terror flushed her system, but quickly she protected herself with light, imagining her foot lifting off the gas pedal. Seeing and believing it with every cell in her body, Vivien channeled all her energy to that image.

Her foot released, and Vivien immediately hit the brake.

After skidding on the dirt for what seemed like forever, the car stopped. Her finger hit the park button on her dash, then she slammed down the emergency brake, turned off the engine, and leaned back. Now that it was over, fury ensued.

Like a bolt of lightning, Vivien opened the door and bounded out. "You have exactly two seconds to show yourself, or else I'm coming after you, and you know I can do it!"

The crunch of loose gravel under his shoes invaded her ears. As footsteps got closer, Vivien stood her ground, ready for a fight.

A tall, dark-haired man, possessing piercing blue eyes and perfectly chiseled facial features, was the last thing Vivien expected to see. Women lost their souls in those eyes. As he stood there in black dress pants, an open white silk shirt, and a very expensive watch on one wrist, she instantly knew he enjoyed toying with women. After glaring with a lustful leer for three tension-filled seconds, he vanished on a breeze of sultry laughter.

Looking down, Vivien's body went numb. She'd stopped just ten inches from the edge of the cliff. Waves thundered in the darkness, echoing her fear.

Falling back into the driver's seat, Vivien suddenly realized the identity of the mystery man.

He is the one Philip warned me about.

As she shuddered in foreboding, Vivien's hands covered her face. She didn't have one enemy, now she had two—a demon and a malicious psychic man just as powerful as she.

Chapter Eleven

Streams of yellow morning sunshine broke through partially open plantation blinds, striking Vivien's eyelids and reminding her of a crucial task. Getting answers had become key, and she would do nothing else before summoning Rhiannon. Nearly tripping on her favorite lilac silk nightgown, Vivien rushed down the hall. Upon opening the third door to the room dubbed her meditation room, she slipped inside. As her body settled onto a black pillow, she ignited a stick of sage with a snap of her fingers. White swirling smoke cleared any hovering energy. Snapping her fingers again, a white pillar candle came to life upon a low round table encircled by twelve clear crystals. A soft glow shone through each crystal as the flame's orange brilliance illuminated the small space.

With eyes closed, Vivien inhaled deeply. "Rhiannon, goddess of the moon—I call upon you."

Rhiannon continued to give advice and comfort, especially when Vivien first returned to America and got pangs of homesickness for her Clonakilty family. Rhiannon also brought the healing power of forgiveness, perhaps because her own soul knew deep sorrow. In ancient times, Rhiannon fell under false accusation for killing and feeding on her own son. As penance, she stood before the castle gates of Dyfed telling her story to each traveler passing through. Proof of her son's existence vindicated her of the crime, and she reunited with her beloved family. As a true goddess, Rhiannon bore the horror with courage and grace, transcending injustice. But most importantly, she lived in dreams waiting to renew the passion of humankind.

"Hello, Vivien."

Such a greeting, with her velvet rich voice, always made Vivien feel she'd entered a sacred place. In formal recognition, she stood.

Rhiannon's scoop-necked dress vibrated in amethyst hues, appearing almost liquid. Her gown complemented cascading rich blue-black hair and hypnotic purple eyes. The goddess's silver moonlight embraced the small room, while a black songbird with a yellow belly sat on her forefinger. As she petted the bird's short gray beak, the goddess gave her a sideways glance. "You wished to speak with me?"

Vivien swallowed hard. "Yes, I did. I mean…I do." Drawing in a breath of courage, she pressed on. "The message you gave me years ago, through Philip, foretold of battling one man with psychic power to match mine. I find that's not the case."

"Meaning?"

"Meaning, I not only have a strong psychic man of dark energy, but also a powerful demon to destroy!" Vivien abruptly stopped her mouth, knowing it wasn't a good idea to get pissy with a goddess.

Gazing timelessly into Vivien's eyes, Rhiannon compelled attention. "The prophecy has altered, but you are strong. Believe that."

"Who altered the prophecy?"

All of a sudden, her front doorbell rang at a frantic

pace. Vivien tuned in. No life-threatening scenario came to mind.

Tiny sparkles of light fluttered about as Rhiannon dissipated before her.

"No! Wait!"

Her guide had departed.

"Damn it!"

Vivien blew hard on the candle wick. She'd honed her skill to spark candles with a snap of her fingers, but not to extinguish them. Grumbling, she trudged from the room, no longer resonating an air of meditation.

As she moved through the hall, it now sounded as if a man's voice called her name from her own bedroom. Half panicked, her feet raced forward, but paused at the doorway. No living being could be seen, but her name still floated on the air in desperation.

Then it hit her.

Jason.

Vivien moved through the bedroom and thrust open her balcony's French doors. She awkwardly tugged on her favorite cream terry cloth robe.

"Vivien! Thank God! You've got to help me!" Jason begged as loud as he could without screaming at eight o'clock in the morning. Planted on her back lawn, he looked as if his sanity hung by a thread.

Surrounding Jason stood four elderly ghosts. Astonished, Vivien took in a man straightening his red bow tie, two women in house coats wearing pink sponge curlers in their silver hair, and a bald man adjusting a pair of thick black glasses onto the bridge of his nose.

Vivien's hands smacked hard onto the wooden railing. "What did you do?"

"You said she could help us!" the man in the bow tie bellowed.

Throwing Jason a venomous look, her eyes narrowed. "Oh, you told them I would help, huh?"

"I had to tell them something. Meet me on your front porch, please!" Jason blubbered, with hands over his ears.

"Can you see them?"

"No, but I can definitely hear them!"

With crossed arms, Vivien glared. "All right, but they are not coming into my house."

"Thanks!"

After one step from her balcony, she turned back. "Wait a minute. How come the doorbell kept ringing while you were down there?"

The ghost in thick glasses slowly raised his hand with a guilty face.

Shaking her head, Vivien grabbed the bowl of sage which always sat on her bureau.

The minute she opened her front door, Jason dove into her house.

"You wouldn't believe it! They were in my car telling me how to drive!"

"Was it helpful?"

The ghosts guffawed on her front porch—the one with glasses slapping the back of the man with the bow tie.

"You realize why we scolded this young man, don't you? He was going so fast, we were afraid he would join us!" one of the women in curlers proclaimed with hands on hips.

"All right, you can all shut up now!" Jason shouted into the air and then faced Vivien. "If you help them, I promise I'll never do this again."

"You mean a half-assed exorcism attempt?"

His head dropped as he expelled a grunt. "I thought I could do it."

She put a hand on Jason's shoulder, finally letting him off the hook. "I feel they are ready to go. They're just confused."

"Okay. What should I do?"

"Make some coffee."

"Coming right up." Darting to the kitchen, Jason started brewing strong espresso drip coffee, turned, and sprang backward.

A striking young woman with deep blue eyes and wavy blonde hair stood before him.

Jason blinked a few times. "I'm sorry... I didn't know anyone else was here."

"I'm Shawn—Vivien's new assistant. I just moved into the guest house." Shawn's hands went into pockets of faded jeans, beneath a flowing white cotton beach tunic.

"I'm Jason. I do photography and video footage for our investigations." Shaking hands, their gazes linked. Jason couldn't seem to speak further.

Slowly Shawn pulled her hand away. "Nice to meet you, Jason. Is that a spider monkey?"

"What?"

She pointed to the arm tattoo above his left elbow.

"Oh!" Jason laughed. "Yep. I had a photo shoot in the Amazon rainforest. When they wouldn't let me take one home, I figured I'd take it this way. I loved those little guys."

The front door opened and closed.

"I heard voices in the backyard, so I came in to see

if you were all right," Shawn explained as Vivien entered.

"That's okay. I planned on introducing you to Jason anyway. Now it saves me the trouble."

"I didn't know you had an assistant."

Suppressing a chuckle, Vivien could almost see waves of attraction coming from Jason when he glanced at Shawn. "I'm also mentoring Shawn's psychic abilities."

"That's great! So, you do what Vivien does?"

Pulling a hairband out of her jeans pocket, Shawn tossed curly locks into a ponytail. "Well, I have a long way to go before I reach Vivien's level."

"You'll be there before you know it," Jason encouraged, with a grin almost too big for his face.

"Thanks." With a shy gaze, Shawn walked to the rear kitchen door. "I still have some stuff to do in the back. Just knock if you need anything."

Jason quickly pulled down a mug. "Do you want some coffee?"

Vivien sat on a stool with elbows on the counter and a smug smile on her face. "Yes, please join us, and I'll tell you how I transitioned four spirits pathetically clinging to Jason."

"Now, wait a minute. It was kind of a weird situation." Jason laughed gruffly. "Hey! Did you tell Shawn how the Kelly Society came together?"

Vivien knew Jason sought to take attention off his supernatural error. Crossing her arms, she stared back at him. "Not yet."

Almost attacking the coffee pot, Jason poured black brew into a cup for Shawn. "Have a seat."

"I am curious about the beginnings of your group."

Taking the caffeine offered, Shawn eagerly snatched a stool and sat.

Grasping her own mug of hazelnut-flavored coffee Jason so graciously prepared, Vivien relayed the odd birth of the Kelly Society.

Chapter Twelve

Thundering bass challenged Donna's brain when all she wanted to do was think. She usually enjoyed herself at Ruby Lounge, but tonight the DJ cranked the volume. After a while, people didn't notice the smell of sweat and alcohol from the dance floor, or smoke that hovered on jackets after a cigarette drag in the alley. They just danced.

A redhead cried into her dirty martini. Watery teardrops flowed down a speared green olive, disappearing into clear liquid. Donna felt bad for the woman in the dark corner booth but wanted to keep her own spirits up.

As soon as her handsome blind date left their table for the men's room, Donna quickly reapplied rose red lipstick. Who would have thought a blind date would go so well. Good looks, and a brain. Nothing like the men she used to date. Checking in the mirror to make sure she didn't resemble the Joker, Donna packed up her purse. The final step had to be executed, and she did it with the precision of an artist—flicking her hair back. Shoulder-length blonde tresses settled into place as hazel eyes glittered. She'd skillfully prepared for his arrival back to their table.

In perfect timing, Roger appeared. His six-foot-two frame glided across the club floor, with eyes focused on her. Underneath his humble, nonchalant manner crackled an undeniable sexiness. Donna picked it up the moment they met. When Roger settled in next to her, she smiled back. His ruffled coffee-colored hair and intelligent, yet sensitive brown eyes behind vintage black-rimmed glasses elevated her pulse instantly.

"I think we're perfectly matched."

"What?" Donna had to yell, turning away from the DJ.

"I think we're perfectly matched!"

Delightful shock played on her face. "Oh yeah? You surmised that after one hour?"

"Yes. The astrologer and the engineer. We're ideal."

Roger's notion struck a chord with Donna. They both looked for answers in scientific, yet creative ways. She in the stars, and he in design. Impulsively, Donna wrapped her arm around his neck and gave him a peck on the lips. "I always believed in love at first sight." When Roger didn't answer, she pulled back. "I'm sorry. Sometimes I'm too forward." Donna figured he had better know now because she'd always been a woman of high energy and blatant honesty.

Laughing, Roger took her hand. "Don't be sorry. You just surprised me. I've never met anyone like you." He hesitated, clicking his fingers on the table. Finally, he looked up. "Can I be utterly frank?"

"Absolutely."

"You're a combination of natural beauty and scientific intelligence. That's what I've been looking for in a woman all my life. I feel like I already know you."

"So, that's a good thing?"

With a sweet smile, Roger pounced on her last

syllable. "That's a good thing."

Cascading laughter enhanced Donna's beautiful lips.

"Okay, are we done now?" He leaned back.

Donna pulled her chair closer and laid her left hand on his arm. A diamond wedding ring glistened.

"Gee, who gave you that?"

Furrowed eyebrows marked her pretty face for only a second. "You did!"

Kissing her quickly, Roger grinned. "That was fun, I will admit. But can we go back to being newlyweds now? I don't think we need to relive our first date again."

"I'll drink to that!" When she reached for her cosmopolitan, the hair follicles on Donna's arms flared up. She noticed a black shadow on the far wall. Darkness spread above the redhead's straight thin bangs like an expanding beach umbrella, until the rim of a cloak became visible. Donna gasped in horror. A hooded figure covered the woman's body. "Hey! Get away from her!" The words just flew out of her mouth. She couldn't help it. Several patrons stared, sniggering into their drinks. After all, the redhead sat alone in the booth. Lost in her own sorrow, she didn't even notice Donna's shouts.

After she gave her husband a pleading glance, Roger slowly draped his arm around Donna's shoulders, staring down the onlookers. The group of early twenty-year-olds turned away, laughing at a new text on one of their phones.

Roger breathed sweetly in her ear. "Are you okay?"

Donna looked again to see the sad redhead peering

into her glass. The hooded figure no longer existed. Imploring hazel eyes turned on him. "I thought I saw something. I'm not crazy."

"I know you're not."

"You believe me, don't you?"

Roger nodded, bringing a pilsner glass to his lips.

"Well, of course you do. You're my husband. But whenever I'm at a party, there's always someone challenging me, just because I'm an astrologer—"

Upon making accelerated contact with solid wood, the pilsner glass cracked in half. Golden fluid burst in all directions, like a washing machine gone mad. Donna frantically wiped her little black dress with bare hands. Among the sarcastic cheers, groans, and swear words of customers in close proximity, Donna zeroed in on her husband's face. Stone-like, pale, and with bulging eyes, Roger gawked at the corner booth.

"Oh, my God! You saw it!"

Roger's mouth tried to create sounds on their way to words, but nothing came out. He finally closed his lips and bobbed his head up and down.

"Excuse me!" A very pissed-off waitress appeared, wiping their table with a dirty white towel. She threw three large pieces of glass into a gray plastic bin. With one hand on her hip, she thrust disapproval into Roger's face. "And, no—you don't get a free beer. You broke it—you bought it!" Off she went, in a huff.

Pushing through the dark hallway entrance of Ruby Lounge, Vivien wanted to kick herself. Why did she do it? Why did she let Donna talk her into a double date? Donna wanted to pretend it was a blind date for both of them, even though she'd been married to Roger for almost a year—one of her adventurous games. Vivien wasn't ready, but then again, she was never ready. Donna only met the attractive blond-haired restaurant owner for a few minutes in her bookstore. The next thing Vivien knew, a date had been set up. Her heart pounded hard. Staring down evil—no problem; a first date—terrifying.

On a long exhale, Vivien scanned the murky, dimly lit room. There they sat at a small round table dead center. Two empty chairs waited expectantly opposite them. Her heart rate shot up again.

Donna saw Vivien and waved her arms wildly, resembling an octopus.

Clenching her jaw, Vivien marched over and sat. "I need to tell you two something right now."

"Wait!" Donna yelled.

Vivien leaned in so she could hear. "I came to apologize, because I can't stay. I called you both, but I'm sure you couldn't hear your phones, and I didn't want to be a no show."

Roger huddled over the table and pushed up his glasses. "He canceled anyway, but there's something else we need to tell you."

"I knew it!" Vivien's hands whacked onto her thighs. A brand-new dress would now go to the back of the closet. She bought the frock on the off chance she'd actually have a date. Instead, she'd donned jeans and a black sweater. "He freaked out because I'm a psychic, right?" With elbows on the table, Vivien's head rested between her hands. She wavered between wanting a relationship with a man and living on her own, satisfied with a life of service to others.

"No, it's not about your deadbeat date!" Donna shrieked.

Vivien's head came up like a bloodhound catching the scent of a fox. "Something's in here." Her gaze became glued to the corner booth.

"C'mon!"

Vivien's body flew, as Donna yanked hard on her arm. Roger followed, until the redhead was now flanked by all three of them, as she remained tucked against cinnamon plastic cushions.

"What's your name?" Vivien attempted a smile.

The woman shook her head. "Get away from me!"

Donna touched her hand. "We want to help you!"

Without warning, a subzero gust pushed them backward. Vivien narrowed her eyes in concentration. Deep shadows bearing a hooded figure swirled around the weeping woman. This time the creature glared directly at them through hollow white eyes.

"Holy shit!" Donna shouted like a hot steam kettle.

Three bodies soared onto the floor, as if a giant air blaster went off.

Flat on her back, Vivien took in a grimy, slow moving ceiling fan. Sitting up, she winced, wiping gritty dirt off her hands. She started to stand.

An older man with a friendly face offered assistance. His blue eyes held the youthful excitement of a mystery unsolved.

"Thank you."

"I'm John Patrick."

"I'm Vivien Kelly."

"I know who you are." John acknowledged her with a happy smile.

Roger and Donna scrambled up to join them.

"Hey! Are you guys okay?" a fresh-faced, mid-twenties man asked, filling the space beside John.

145

Reticently, Vivien answered the eager stranger. "Yes, we're fine."

"It's gone again, isn't it?" Donna's body lurched as a vivacious couple leaped to the small hardwood space masquerading as a dance floor.

Vivien's eyes scanned the room. "Yes, but not for long."

"Okay, I'm the manager here, and I want all of you out now!" a short, scrappy-haired man demanded.

"What are you talking about? We're not drunk. We tripped!" Donna proclaimed, very convincingly.

The cynical man crossed his arms. "Oh yeah, right! You all tripped at the exact same time?"

"That's right!" John moved forward. Pointing to a thick black electrical cable snaking along the edge of the booths, he got the man's attention. "Do you realize that's a safety hazard? You'll be lucky if none of these patrons are injured or sues you."

Suddenly shamefaced, the manager extended his arm. "All right. You can have this large booth over here and a round of drinks on the house."

"And the cable?" John wasn't letting him go.

"It will be taken care of." The scrappy man darted away.

"Thanks." Roger shook John's hand. "That was brilliant thinking."

"I'm a retired professor, so I've dealt with some whiners in my day."

Donna waved everyone over to the booth. "Let's all sit down. We need to make a plan of attack. Right, Vivien?"

Vivien peered at the red-haired woman now covering her face in utter sadness. She did not answer

Donna but deliberately moved to their new booth.

John eased into the opposite side. "So, you all saw that black mist over her as well?"

"More than that," Donna spat, not surprised John saw the entity.

"By the way, I'm Jason Lee," the captivated young man announced, moving into the booth. "I was a student of John's at U.C. Berkeley. I took his Celtic mythology class, and that's when I found out he used to investigate hauntings. He's got all the equipment and everything. Next time he goes on one, I'm taking the photos. I'm a professional photographer, but my dream is to get a ghost on film." Jason rambled like a kid on Christmas morning, intrigued by the notion of other worldly realms. "Or, at least an orb."

The frenzied waitress arrived, gazing at Donna and Roger under lowered lids. "You guys again!" She plucked drinks off her tray, banging them down on the table. "You two had a cosmo and a pale ale." Her focus switched to John and Jason. "And another dark beer for each of you." She locked eyes with Vivien. "I didn't know what you wanted, so you get water." The waitress disappeared.

"Jason's excellent if you need a photographer on your cases. In fact, he just got back from New Zealand on assignment for *National Geographic*."

Vivien held John's glance as she wrapped her fingers around the chilly water glass. "You're a retired professor of Celtic Mythology?"

John nodded, raising the beer to his lips.

"Then you know what a *fear dorcha* is?"

Black ale splattered across the table when John choked. "You're not serious? It's a Dark Man?"

Vivien rose from her seat, leaning toward them with hands on the table. "I need to begin a Celtic Triad chant while all of you make sure she doesn't get near that front door."

"If she goes out the front door, something bad will happen, right?" Donna's concerned eyes met hers.

"Right."

"You'd better be careful." The Dark Man's confirmation resonated in John's worried voice.

"What is a Dark Man anyway?" Jason whispered excitedly before taking a drink.

John wiped his spilled ale with a cocktail napkin. "He's hungry—unfortunately, for a soul. The legend goes, that he comes to women in their sleep on the eve of Samhain. It's alarmingly weird that he's shown up here, and in waking hours."

Jason looked utterly lost. "Samhain?"

"Halloween." All four voices retorted in sharp unison.

Vivien's face hardened. "I'll be damned if I'll let him take an innocent woman's life on my watch, just because she got dumped this morning."

"Ah…that's why she's so sad." Roger nodded slowly.

"How can we help you?" John gazed at her with arms outstretched.

"Actually, I've always worked alone—"

Slapping her hand on the table, Donna stared her down. "Vivien, let us help you. For some reason, this time we're all seeing this creature."

Donna had a point. In the past, only Vivien and the victims witnessed a paranormal entity. The rules had changed and she didn't understand why, but she could use additional forces on her side. "Okay. But be ready for anything—and I mean anything. I'll tell you exactly what I need, when I need it. For now, stay right here." Just before Vivien turned to cross the floor, a voice stopped her.

"See, that wasn't so hard, was it?"

When she glanced back, Donna cracked a crafty smile.

Playfully rolling her eyes, Vivien walked away and seated herself opposite the redhead. As if entering a bubble, the temperature dropped. Vivien's body shuddered. The Dark Man stayed hidden, existing within frozen air.

"Hello, Melanie."

Looking up for the first time, an unfixed gaze tried to make out Vivien, and then the redhead gave up. Snatching the thin clear stem of her martini glass, she polished off her drink, smacking it down hard. "Get lost!"

Suddenly clasping Melanie's hands across the table, the elegance of Vivien's voice came out as a ray of hope. "Your life is now. This I vow. Renounce the sorrow which looms upon you, for you alone hold a heart that is true."

Pools of desperation shone in the eyes Vivien beheld. The true Melanie surfaced, and now she knew something was terribly wrong. Something had hold of her. "Help me," she uttered in a small, broken voice.

Ascending the wall, the shadow grew. In that moment, Melanie's eyes changed. The Dark Man tried to enter her body. Soaring from her seat, Vivien yanked Melanie from the booth to a standing position, and then turned her around to face the *fear dorcha*.

"Let me go!"

Laser focused, Vivien answered in a soothing tone, "This monster is going to kill you. He's taking advantage of your distress. You have to say it with me and remember, Chris isn't the only man on Earth."

Melanie's body twisted. "You bitch!"

"My life is now. This I vow. I renounce sorrow which looms upon me, for I alone hold a heart that is true."

While Vivien began her new version of the Triad chant, Melanie thrashed about, but when one voice became two, everything changed. The club patrons gathered in a semi-circle around Vivien and Melanie. They couldn't see their plight but knew something extraordinary to be taking place. Glowing light spread from their bodies as the poem rose to a crescendo. Being no match for their combined power, the Dark Man made his exit, taking the wall with him.

Having greeted the floor for the second time, Vivien leaned up on one elbow. People raced around like hummingbirds—hummingbirds that screamed. Three guys in the alley stood agog, staring into the club and waving dust out of their faces. Sights and sounds whirled, and yet, a quiet vortex encompassed Vivien. Her own quivering hand touched her cheek to find moisture. Tears hadn't graced her skin for two years, but renouncing sorrow for Melanie forced her to feel her own loss.

"Did you see that?" The men howled with laughter in the alley. Suddenly, an exploding wall became the most hysterical thing they ever saw; of course, their intoxicated state enhanced the hilarity. One of them had to hold his groin to avoid peeing his pants, which got the other two laughing even harder, falling to their knees.

Roger and John helped Vivien to a standing position. The group encircled her. Donna pushed loose hair out of Vivien's face, her mouth in constant motion. Sound seemed to have taken a well-deserved break. Donna's mouth continued to move, but she heard nothing.

Philip.

His presence embraced her. He's one spirit she would not see. Philip knew that would be too painful, but her freedom was all he wished. Loving warmth filled every particle of her body. As she breathed his essence in, her heart lightened.

"Vivien! Are you all right?" Donna demanded.

"What?" Shaking her head, Vivien came back to messy reality. "Yes, I just…never mind. Is everyone okay?"

Jason stepped closer. "Yeah, you screamed for everyone to get down right before the wall exploded."

Vivien faced him with a blank stare.

John's brows creased. "You don't remember that?"

"I must have been in the zone, as we call it. Where's Melanie?"

Roger, being the tallest, searched the room. "I don't know."

"We need to find her now! Quick, everyone outside."

Bouncing against hysterical people, they spilled out onto the sidewalk. Faces turned at the loud clanging of a cable car as it jostled by. Tourists waved at riders on board, apparently unconcerned why so many people ran out of the night club. Snapping photos with cell phones, they yelled back jubilantly, enjoying their quintessential San Francisco experience.

A sickening thud broke cheers of the crowd, as the cable car lurched to a stop. Blood covered the street. Melanie lay on her stomach for the very last time.

"No!" Vivien shrieked, actually stopping people in their tracks. It proved to be only a vision—a vision that would become reality if she didn't find Melanie. As Vivien tuned in, an alley ten yards away called out. The group of friends followed her when she ran down the street.

There stood Melanie, right in the middle of the dark alley. Her back faced the street. What was she waiting for? Whatever it was, it would be her doom. The *fear dorcha* would try again, but to stop that deadly end, Vivien approached casually.

"Hey, I've got a bottle of shiraz from a new Napa Valley winery. Let's go to my house, and I'll pour you a glass. Sound good?"

Melanie swiveled her body at a strange angle to face Vivien. "How did I get out here?"

"It doesn't matter. Let's go." Taking Melanie's hand, they started down the short thoroughfare.

A screech equipped to wake the dead impaled her poise. "Vivien, no!" Donna yelled, with an arm around Melanie's shoulder at the other end of the alley. Next to her, John, Jason, and Roger stared as if she stood on the edge of a skyscraper on a windy day.

Whose hand held hers?

In one quick movement, Vivien kicked hard against the chest of the body standing next to her—but it was only a shadow. Then, biting cold ripped through her soul.

An ancient voice entered her mind. *I prefer you lass, but I'm not allowed.*

Not allowed? What do you mean you're not allowed?

Instead of responding, the creature concentrated on Melanie. Throwing herself against his massive shadow, Vivien demanded an answer.

Then, the Dark Man took flight toward her friends.

Quickly. She had to think quickly.

Are you afraid to fight me in solid form? I know you can take solid form, but you must be afraid! Short of calling him chicken, that was the best she could do. Even the Dark Man had an ego.

Hovering above, the entity hesitated. Then, deliberately turning inch by inch, the *fear dorcha* came to face her. A sly motion intended to frighten only brought a smile to Vivien's lips.

"What did you just do?" John screamed out, anxious for her safety. He knew something went down, even though no words were spoken.

"I'm okay. Just get out of here!"

"We're not leaving you!" Donna roared back.

Sighing with joy at having such loyal friends and guilt for putting them in danger, Vivien moved farther back into the alley.

Black boots hit damp pavement, shattering the red neon sign reflection in a nearby puddle. As Vivien's gaze lifted, sleek black pants led up to an obsidian colored sweater—all worn by the most handsome man in the world. Of course, he sported black hair and radiant golden eyes, but the translucent skin gave him away. She expected as much. When he seized women's souls as they slept, it was done with seduction.

"Putting yourself on the line for a stranger? That be wise, lass?" His sexy Irish brogue began its spell on her.

Digging a nail into her palm, Vivien allowed the pain to ground her as his evil, enticing power expanded. The attractive monster actually made it feel good to entertain wicked thoughts.

"About that glass of wine, you offered…" His fingers temptingly ran through her hair. "We shall drink in front of a roaring fire and let the heat consume us."

When Vivien held fast, the *fear dorcha* gripped her roughly by the shoulders. His voice dropped into a sultry confirmation. "There be darkness in you. Aye—there be darkness."

"Shut up!" Vivien closed her eyes and saw herself with Philip. They walked through Central Park on a crisp autumn afternoon hand in hand after lunch at A Voce.

Shaking her, the monster demanded attention. "Your Philip be dead!"

Clutching him in an iron grip, Vivien flipped his rock-solid body over her head. By the time Vivien turned, his face came up against hers. It didn't matter. The vile creature had crossed a line no one crossed before. Vivien's words crackled out of clenched teeth. "Don't ever speak his name! He's in a place you will never be!" Before another heinous utterance left his lips, she focused on two dumpsters ten feet away. They jolted forward. Sliding next to each other, the metal boxes blocked her friends' view. Their anxious screams resounded down the short alley.

The darkest of men eyed the trash containers, glaring at her with a leer. "Impressive for such a wee lass."

"I didn't want my friends to see me destroy you." Vivien knew they'd think the *fear dorcha* moved the dumpsters, never guessing it was her.

Maniacal laughter boomed from the entity like an earthquake. "You cannot kill me!"

"No, but I can banish you, and I'm not a wee lass!" Emitting a battle cry, Vivien threw herself onto him, slashing his face with her nails. "*Dibir!*"

Immediately, dark concrete beneath opened up and swallowed the Dark Man. Within seconds, the pavement popped back into its normal, solid state.

Breathing hard, falling on her knees, Vivien realized she'd never banished a dark creature so violently. The Dark Man knew a yearning for evil lived deep within her. Lately that hunger had become more tantalizing. She had to resist. Doing her best to dial back the power rush, Vivien rose as her friends tore past the dumpsters.

John made it to her first, asking all kinds of questions, then the rest caught up.

"He's gone. He's banished." Vivien kept repeating the words as they pounced upon her. "Wow, okay, group hug!" Their relief lifted her spirits. "Thanks, guys, but I need to breathe!"

Melanie stood to the side in tears. "Thank you! I don't know what else to say but thank you."

They pulled her into the mass embrace, as Vivien gazed into her eyes. "It's all right. He's gone."

Jason suddenly jumped into the air. "Oh, my God!"

"What is it?" Roger yelled, watching the sky and expecting something else to swoop down.

Jason pointed at Vivien. "You, John, and I should

be a new paranormal team! Like those shows you see on TV. Wouldn't that be great?"

"I don't think—"

"That's a fabulous idea!" Donna said.

"No, I really don't—"

"Sure! I have the equipment. Jason has all the cameras we'd ever need, and Vivien has her incredible talent," John agreed.

Roger joined in, his eyes bright with excitement. "What will your group be called?"

Donna put a finger on her chin. "Well, since Vivien is the core, it should be named after her."

Jason threw his arms out with a big smile. "I've got it! Team Kelly!"

Horrified, Vivien flinched, while the others cracked up.

"Nice try, Jason, but it has to have a little more class." Thinking for a moment, Donna gasped. "I know! The Kelly Society!"

Cheers reverberated between the buildings as their new name took root.

Roger pulled out a small pad and pen. "I'll have your business cards made up. Come by the store in a few days, and they'll be ready."

"This is so cool! We are totally the Kelly Society!" Jason screamed to the heavens.

"Totally." Vivien echoed, releasing a long breath on a wispy smile.

Leaping up, Donna clapped wildly. "Roger and I will have your cards at both cash registers and posted on the bulletin board!"

"Thanks." Vivien nodded. Deep down, she knew her new team would be the best thing for her, and her community. Since now she'd be working in a group, she decided to be truthful about Celtic power running through her from Boudicca, but not about her ability to move matter. That could wait until another day.

Donna draped her arm around Vivien's shoulders. "So, were you serious about having shiraz from a new Napa Valley winery?"

"Yes."

"Okay, everyone, let's go! Dinner and wine at Vivien's house! Roger and I will pick up some North Beach pizzas on the way. That means you too, Melanie."

Melanie's head nodded up and down. "Sounds good."

"You can ride with me and Roger. No driving after what you've been through tonight."

"I came by cab anyway." Melanie sniffled.

As they started toward the sidewalk amongst eager jabbering about her new paranormal investigative group, Vivien looked up at the night sky.

Their battle had just begun.

Chapter Thirteen

Luminous, frightened eyes faced Vivien as Shawn released a long-held breath. "Wow. I'm so glad you got rid of that Dark Man thing. I don't know how you stayed so focused and confident."

Sensing Shawn's fear, Vivien laid a hand on her back. "You don't have to go up against creatures like that. Your energy will help us in other ways."

"That's good." Relieved, Shawn slid off the stool and added her mug to the dishwasher. "I better finish getting myself organized. I'll check back in about an hour. Is that okay?"

"Take your time. We'll continue the work we started yesterday." Vivien went for a second cup of coffee.

"All right. Bye for now, Jason."

"See you around." Jason stood, craning his neck to see her move down the hall and out the back door. "Why didn't you tell me? She's gorgeous!"

After stirring in chocolate hazelnut creamer, Vivien tapped her spoon, set it down, and faced him. "She's only twenty-two."

"So! I'm twenty-six. That's actually a good age range for us." Jason plopped onto a stool, smiling like a kid who just got an ice cream cone.

As Vivien's eyes bore into him, his cheer vanished.

"I met Shawn on the beach yesterday morning. She

just came out of a horrible relationship with a guy who cheated on her and took her money. She didn't have anywhere to go when I found her, but I sensed her strength. Shawn has just begun to heal, so if you think you're going to have some fun and move on—you'll have to answer to me."

Visibly pale, Jason straightened. "Jeez…you just gave me chills."

"So?"

"So…I'll be professional. I won't make any moves on her."

Finally, Vivien's lips formed a half smile.

Testing the waters, Jason continued. "But if it happens naturally, that's something else, right?"

"I'm not saying you two could never be together. I'm just saying Shawn needs time."

"Okay!" Silly happiness occupied his face once more.

Vivien laughed, shaking her head. Knowing Jason to be a good soul, she didn't truly worry, but also felt protective of Shawn. "All right, so tell me how you ended up with four ghosts in tow?"

"My friend lives in a house built after a retirement home burned down. It's on the exact spot. Four of the seniors died in the fire. The next thing you know, he has four house guests."

"And you went over to exorcise them."

"Yeah, that worked out great!"

Vivien chuckled with abandon. "Actually, I'm gonna come clean. I had a paranormal mishap at thirteen. My friends and I started to do a séance, when one of the girls shouted out for something to make a terrible noise. The door started breathing."

"What the hell?"

They guffawed over hot mugs of coffee as she explained how they finally opened the door and ran out into the street, while her friend's mother yelled after them for being idiotic girls. Vivien knew Jason would not try a stunt like that again, but she also wanted him to know he wasn't alone.

****

Nicholas's sexy, lean body sauntered toward City Lights. Usually an independent bookstore would not be on his list of places to frequent. Especially in the heart of North Beach, best known for the beat generation in the fifties—but Vivien Kelly was inside. After pissing her off on the cliff the other night, Nicholas hoped to remedy the situation.

Artistic types loitered around the front windows. Bad perfume, strange cigarettes, and people laughing too loud split before him as his power pushed them aside. Most assumed they'd been bumped, but one teenage girl with purple hair and black lipstick eyed him suspiciously before turning back to her group.

Once inside, Nicholas gripped the doorjamb to remain standing. Vivien's aura encompassed him, and it was like nothing he'd ever felt before—courage, beauty, grace, intelligence, and compassion for humankind. Truly in her element, the store pulsated with her pure energy.

A store clerk stopped with an armful of books. "You okay?"

"I'm fine." Abruptly moving down the aisle, he found a quiet corner among the philosophy paperbacks. Nicholas closed his eyes. Never before had he felt such a lack of control. Vivien opened parts of him he'd closed off and possessed a wisdom he needed to enhance in himself.

Ramming a fist into his hand repeatedly, he felt the overwhelming emotion finally cease. The good part about his slip in discipline was that it brought anger back. With anger, he could protect himself. Nicholas arched, throwing a psychic boundary around his body. Then, he made his way up the tight wooden stairway to the metaphysical enthusiasts. Bodies clung to each other in the small space in an effort to fit, making him want to vomit in disgust. Instead, he'd wait his turn.

****

"Thank you for coming!"

Applause rose from the audience. In a midnight blue blouse, black pencil skirt, and designer black boots, Vivien gave readings, answered questions, relayed psychic cleansing stories, and conducted an exercise to open intuition. The crowd roared in approval. Next, she prepped to sign books.

Vivien's book signing marked Shawn's first event as her assistant, so she expected her to watch and learn. But when the manager, Cleo, suggested writing each name on a slip of paper as they approached, Shawn jumped right in. Standing next to the signing table, Shawn greeted people in line. Jotting down their names, she enjoyed her task.

An elderly man revealed he'd just become a widower. Vivien met his eyes when she handed his signed copy back. "I'm so sorry. When did she pass?"

"It will be a month tomorrow, and there's something else."

"Yes?"

Leaning in, he whispered in Vivien's ear. "Twice

I've smelled chocolate chip cookies when I had almost no food in the house. I don't even know how to cook, but my wife loved to bake, and she would surprise me with chocolate chip cookies. Have I gone mad?"

Vivien laid her hand on his. "No, actually our loved ones communicate in all different ways. One way is through smell. She is letting you know she's around."

"Thank you." The elderly man turned away, moved to tears.

Coming around the table, Vivien embraced him before he started down the staircase.

The signings continued until they reached the last person in line. As Vivien wrote out her name for a shy college girl, her hand slipped. The air became thick and heavy. Her arms erupted in goose bumps. She held a poker face and smiled at the girl, who timidly walked off.

"It looks like that's it," Shawn stated with a happy sigh.

"No. There's one more." Boldly, Vivien snatched Shawn's arm. "Remember what I taught you yesterday about psychic protection?"

Nodding, Shawn's eyes widened.

"Do it now."

Wearing a sleek business suit, Nicholas appeared from behind a bookshelf. Smelling of the most expensive cologne on the market, he glided, holding her book out for signature. To Vivien, he looked like a black panther coming in for the kill.

Vivien's trepidation ended when she stood and pointed right at him. "You!" The ad for his seminars flashed in her brain. Nicholas Williams, an extremely popular motivational author, speaker, and leader of a group called the Foundation, stood before her. He claimed to come from a spiritual base, but before he discovered metaphysics, he made his money as a ruthless corporate attorney. She didn't judge people their vocations, but in his case, ego and lust for riches remained intact.

Delightfully amused, his lips curved into a smile, but actually looked like a sneer.

Realizing her outburst could call attention to them, Vivien turned around. The room had cleared out. Only Shawn and Cleo remained, talking in the corner. They watched closely but made no move to intervene. Angrily, Vivien grabbed his copy of her book and scrawled her name as if signing for a second mortgage. "You're that Foundation guy! So, what's your angle?"

Nicholas laughed, eyes twinkling, and with a pearly white smile, held out his hand. "It's nice to meet you too. I'm Nicholas Williams."

"Yes, I know your name." Vivien meant to shake his hand hastily, but the moment skin touched skin, the room disappeared.

****

Cries of conquest echoed off the moors, like rays of light thrown against darkness. Candlelight glowed against brown burlap walls. Boudicca's bare feet embraced the rich soil of her Celtic land she fought so hard to protect. The fight had just begun, but tonight they reveled in victory. Romans would never see their clans the same.

A single beam of moonlight shone between two folds of the perfectly structured camp tent. Dragging a bloody sword behind her, Boudicca followed the path of the moon.

Amergin.

His name echoed through Boudicca's mind. After months of grieving her husband's death, he'd been a delicious retreat from sorrow. With the audacity to luxuriate in a Roman officer's bed, Amergin beckoned her. They all fought bravely—her clan and his. As leaders of their tribes, they deserved a victory celebration, especially if that meant ravaging each other's bodies. Her erotic smile betrayed her thoughts. Amergin displayed his beautiful naked body, striking long black hair, and dazzling blue eyes for her perusal.

After taking in the sensual picture he portrayed for her, Boudicca cocked her head. "You tricked me. I thought you'd gone back with the clan to celebrate."

"Aye, I started to go. Then, I beheld you."

Boudicca's eyes narrowed. "Where were you?"

"Hiding in the shadows."

"You're always hiding in the shadows."

Laughing heartily, Amergin's fingers ran through her thick, cranberry hair. "You know me too well, my sweet."

Plunging her mouth onto his, Boudicca's arms roughly wrapped around his neck. Her body burned.

When Amergin hesitated and clutched her wrists, she grunted. "Must you stop?"

A leer of satisfaction spread across Amergin's face as his gaze raked over her hands. "A successful slaughter of our enemy. Our crops will remain with the clans. Dagda will be pleased."

She followed his gaze. Dried red blood covered Boudicca's palms and ran between her fingers.

Falling onto silk bed sheets in raucous laughter, they savored their well-deserved triumph among

Roman abundance.

****

Vivien yanked her hand out of Nicholas's grasp. Brushing her hair back with shaky fingers, she hit a chair. It fell with a harsh bang.

Shawn and Cleo ran over instantly, darting accusatory glances at Nicholas.

"Are you all right?" Shawn demanded.

"I'm fine."

"You don't look fine."

Vivien already knew Shawn to be brutally honest. There was no fooling her. Nicholas retrieved his book from the floor. He'd dropped it, but she didn't even hear it hit the ground. Obviously affected by the intensity of their vision, Nicholas had his game face on.

No wonder an array of violent, arousing emotions sprang to life when she touched him. He'd fought beside her against the Romans all those centuries ago, and the rest she couldn't even think about. His commanding presence carried over into this life, which gave Vivien an idea. If she could win Nicholas over to her side, he'd be an ally. They could fight Dagda together.

"Cleo, may we use your office for a moment? I need to speak to Mr. Williams privately."

"Ah...sure. Follow me." Sandy tan eyes tightened beneath her chestnut brown bob haircut.

Vivien placed a hand on Shawn's shoulder. "Wait for me?"

"No problem."

Giving Shawn a wink accompanied by a comforting smile, Vivien turned away.

Cleo started down a thin hallway between packed

bookshelves and then stopped at an open door. "Here it is."

"Thanks." Vivien entered the small office.

Nicholas closed the door behind them and immediately took charge. "I knew you looked familiar." Laughing at his own joke, he reached out for her hand. "I'll pick you up tomorrow night, and we can have dinner at—"

Vivien pushed hard on his chest. "What the hell is wrong with you? I almost drove off a cliff!"

Stunned, Nicholas barely recovered from bouncing off the opposite wall and almost falling on his ass. Once shock ceased, he hooted with pleasure, throwing her a look of respect. "Boy, are you strong! I was just testing you, that's all."

"Testing me, huh?" With a disturbing whisper, Vivien got in his face. "How about I test you?"

Nicholas's smile broadened with eagerness. "Ah…there's Boudicca."

A smack cracked the air as his head flipped to one side. Vivien had slapped him—and hard. Not even realizing she'd done it, she twisted away, fingers kneading her temples.

The walls seemed to close in. Cloe's office turned out to be much smaller than anticipated. Stacked hardback books traveled up the walls from retro green shag carpet. To avoid being too close to him, Vivien moved to a small black desk in the opposite corner. From her peripheral vision, she caught Cloe's top of the line ergonomic chair twirling in a circle. Was that her doing? Reining in rogue energy, Vivien turned to face him.

Nicholas didn't seem to mind her outburst of

violence, but she did. What happened to her? He made her temper flare like no other man. In fact, Vivien had never slapped anyone before. She had to pull herself together.

Nicholas moved in like a predator, but also with desire that would have weakened the knees of any other woman. "I had you pegged all wrong."

Throwing up her hands, Vivien channeled power into creating a wall between them. She'd never attempted it before and went purely on instinct.

In awe, Nicholas stopped short. "My God, Vivien. I can actually see the barrier you've put around yourself. You're more advanced than I thought." He scoffed. "You know, in the sixteen hundreds they would have called you a witch."

"I'm sorry for hitting you. But will you just answer my questions?"

Moaning, Nicholas nodded. "All right, but on one condition—after I answer your questions, you have to answer my question."

"Done." Vivien's wall dropped. "What are your intentions in this life?"

"I want to help people, just like you."

Vivien didn't believe him but would let that one go. Right now, with a demon on the loose, she had bigger problems. "Why is Dagda in the twenty-first century?"

Nicholas spun away. His anger and frustration hit her like a Mack truck. "That, I can't answer. I saw him in a meditation years ago when I was just starting my group, the Foundation. I thought it was just a previous life memory. Now he appears to me more and more."

She pressed on. "Why do you think he's drawn to

you?"

"Oh, I know it has something to do with my status. What I've achieved is very seductive to him. I thought at first he just wanted to be around power, but now he's aggravating me." His expression suddenly lightened. "But I think he will move on soon. He can't stay in this realm for long."

While Nicholas spoke, an image emerged before Vivien. Dagda struggled to get inside his body. Nicholas fought him off with all his strength.

"Vivien."

When Nicholas touched her cheek, Vivien grasped his hand, locking eyes with him. "He's much more dangerous than you know, Nicholas." A rush of sympathy engulfed her. Goodness existed within him. Her soul remembered.

When Nicholas pulled her close, Vivien didn't resist. Love flowed from him, and she felt warm and protected. But soon, sensations of control and obedience jaggedly entered her peaceful state. Nicholas tried to keep them out of her sensitivity.

"I would never have let you go over that cliff's edge. As long as I was there, you were safe."

Gentle affection quickly transformed into primitive craving. Flushed with heat and shocked by her own reaction, Vivien pushed away, trying to keep her voice level. "So, what are you going to do about him?"

"Who?" He followed her, still in a daze of desire.

"Dagda!"

Sparkling blue eyes tantalized. "Can't we go back to what we were just doing?"

"No!"

With a grunting sigh, Nicholas set his arms

akimbo. "I told you, he won't be in this realm for long. Now, are you going to answer my question?"

"Why do you keep saying that? When he appeared to me, Dagda said he wants to rule the world."

Leaning to one side and switching arms behind his back, Nicholas exuded complete confidence. "I just don't think he's that strong. He can't maintain himself here unless he gets help from someone. I'm not going to help him, and you're not going to help him, are you?"

"No." Vivien hissed with disgust.

"So, there it is. Dagda will fizzle out soon."

"But what if Dagda goes to someone else?"

"I don't see that happening."

Cautiously, she regarded him. "Even though what you say could be the outcome of all this, I don't believe it, and deep inside, you don't believe it either." Sitting back against the black desk, Vivien continued. "I have a proposition for you. If we work together, we could vanquish Dagda, and all the dark creatures he's releasing, for good."

Nicholas flashed a bright smile. "Will you have dinner with me?"

With a growl, Vivien marched past him, yanking the door almost off its hinges.

Chasing her, Nicholas stomped down the snug stairway as fast as he could.

Shawn waited at the front door holding Vivien's purse. "Everything okay?"

"One second."

Meeting him at the foot of the stairs, Vivien extended her card. "Call me in a few days and think about my proposition."

169

Taking Vivien's card, Nicholas looked very pleased with himself. "Excellent! I'll take you to a fabulous new restaurant—"

"A few nights ago, I banished a *Baobhan Sith* from a ten-year-old's séance attempt. There was no reason for that creature to be there. When I showed up, the banshee told me Dagda had come back specifically to turn our world into darkness, with himself as ruler. I don't see how that translates to 'He won't be in this realm for long.' I also know there's something you're not telling me, so if you think we're going to have a romantic dinner—think again!"

With that, Vivien stormed out.

"I don't know what you said, but you left him with his mouth hanging open," Shawn huffed, quickly catching up to her in the parking lot.

Sliding into the driver's seat, Vivien depressed the brake pedal, pushed the start button, and doubled over. Sudden pain in her stomach felt like she'd been stabbed.

Boudicca's hands dug into the earth in utter horror as she cried out.

Amergin fell to his knees—bloody hands covering his face.

"Stop!" Vivien pulled backward with all her strength, until the scene in her mind vanished.

"What's the matter?"

"I haven't felt that much sorrow since Philip's death," she rasped, in between gulps of air.

"Philip? You mean your fiancé who was murdered?" Shawn had started reading Vivien's book, which began with her own tragedy.

Vivien nodded, resting her head against the car seat

with eyes closed. "Something happened to Nicholas and me in a past life that devastated both of us."

"What was it?"

"I don't know. I could only feel the pain."

Opening her eyes, Vivien attempted to clutch the steering wheel, but her hands slid right off. "You're going to have to drive. I'm too exhausted."

Shawn's eyes opened saucer wide. "You trust me to drive your car?"

"Of course."

After switching places, Shawn nervously settled into the driver's seat.

Vivien seized a tissue from the glove compartment and dabbed stray tears away. "I'll give you directions as we go."

"Okay."

After a long shaky sigh, Vivien slapped her hands onto wobbly knees. "I really need to take my mind off what I just experienced, and there's something you haven't told me. What happened to your stepfather Adam?"

Pure angst took up residency on Shawn's face. "No, no, I can't." Yellow hair flickered within dim light as her head shook back and forth.

"I know you don't want to talk about it, but you have to. I can feel it eating you up inside."

A long uncomfortable silence expanded like waves of radiation.

"Turn right at this light, and you'll be at the on-ramp. I know you weren't responsible for his death. When did he marry your mother?"

Shawn still didn't answer, and that's when Vivien looked directly at her. "I'm just as stubborn as you are.

I'll just keep asking, and then—"

"When I was ten. My mother remarried when I was ten."

"What happened to your real father?"

"He died when I was eight. It was a car accident, and my mother never got over it—not even to this day."

"I'm sorry."

After a moment, Shawn tilted her head. "My mother never felt good unless she had a man around. I think she really loved my father, but when he died, she got scared. After running through a bunch of loser boyfriends, she finally settled on Adam."

"You're from Arizona, right?"

"Tucson."

After a dead pause, Vivien forged ahead. "My feeling is that your stepfather never touched you inappropriately."

"No, thank God. In fact, he just ignored me. Adam didn't know how to deal with a ten-year-old girl, so he didn't. I was fine with that because I didn't like him either. But my mom always put him first, and it made me feel like..." Shawn stopped, her eyes welling with tears.

"Made you feel like what?"

Shawn's voice quivered. "Like I was nothing."

"I know it's hard to understand, but that had nothing to do with you as a person. Your mother, overwhelmed by her own fear, clung to him."

"Yeah, I know."

Vivien pulled fresh tissues from the box and handed them to her. "But it still hurts."

Shawn wiped at her eyes. "What a pair we are tonight."

"Good thing we have plenty of tissues!"

They laughed for a few moments, watching the highway, until Vivien looked back at her. "I just have one more question."

"Yeah?"

"When did you discover your psychic abilities?"

"Speaking of—I have the feeling this 92 Freeway is ours?"

"Right. That would be great intuition, except the sign says Half Moon Bay in huge letters."

Chuckling, Shawn pulled over a few lanes and entered the freeway. "Anyway, to answer your question, I discovered it right after my father died."

"Many times, that happens after a personal crisis."

"I loved my real father. He held us together and took care of my mother. He co-owned an auto repair shop, but his partner took over the business when he died. So, my mom worked as a waitress. Without any schooling beyond high school, that's all she felt she could do. She's a wonderful seamstress, and I told her to open her own store, but she never believed she could do it."

Shawn's face turned grim. "Okay, since you asked about Adam, I'm going to tell you what happened. But...after I tell you, I never want to talk about it again, all right?"

"All right."

"It happened six months ago. I knew Adam took drugs, but I didn't know he was also a dealer. My mom kept it a secret, and for some reason I didn't pick it up intuitively. I got home early one night, and this guy came to the door. I'd only seen him once before, but I knew he was an associate of Adam's. He asked me where he was, but I didn't know. I really didn't. He knew where my mom worked and I was scared for her, so I focused on Adam. I saw an image of him at a local diner, so I told the guy. He left immediately and an hour later the cops found Adam shot in the chest in the alley behind the diner."

Vivien remained calm when Shawn glared to check her reaction.

"The moment I focused on Adam's location, I swear I didn't feel danger. If I had, I would have told him another place, or called the cops. But in the end, I was responsible for his death."

"Shawn, listen to me. My mentor Katherine told me this, and now I'm going to tell you. Everything is not revealed to us. You can't blame yourself. That man would have found Adam eventually, and I know in my gut the same thing would have happened."

Shawn's shoulders tightened. "Well, my mom didn't see it that way. She blamed me and then threw me out of the house."

Vivien smiled at her. "You are a very courageous woman."

Taken aback, Shawn's head snapped from Vivien to the road. "Seriously? I never expected to hear that!"

Delightfully surprised by Shawn's level of psychic talent, Vivien made a spontaneous decision. "I have a proposition for you."

"Oh yeah?"

"Besides being my personal assistant, how would you like to join the Kelly Society and investigate hauntings?"

Shawn's mouth gaped open. "Ye…yes, I would. Oh my God, that would be incredible!"

Tossing the box of tissues back in the glove compartment, Vivien laughed. "Okay, then."

For the remainder of the drive, questions about the Kelly Society investigations flew from Shawn's lips, as if she'd discovered treasure. When Shawn stopped to breathe, Vivien tried to answer her rapid-fire inquiries.

Descending the hills into her cherished waterfront town, Vivien realized a new life for Shawn had just begun.

Chapter Fourteen

Vivien exhaled in relief when Neal pulled into Vivien's driveway as she felt his heart race. She didn't want to be the only one nervous about their first date. In fact, Vivien had to admit to being more frightened of a first date than of fighting a *Baobhan Sith*. While wiping sweaty palms against a pleated purple cocktail dress, she checked the buckles of her new black ankle-strap sandals.

When the doorbell rang, Vivien took one last look in the mirror. "Okay, this is it."

Simba meowed, looking up with luminous eyes. She'd adopted the gray tabby from the local shelter right after moving into her new home. He always picked up on her emotions and in his own feline way, reassured her. After a pat on his adorable furry head, Vivien moved down the hall.

Beveled glass upon the top half of the front door revealed Neal's shape. Turning the knob, she inhaled, reminding herself to be cool and calm. "Hello."

"Hi," Neal greeted with an easy smile.

That's the last thing Vivien heard for a full ten seconds. Neal's eyes shimmered, full of life. In a black sports coat, white shirt, and navy-blue slacks, he epitomized handsome elegance. Taking in his cologne of musk and spices, her mind eased.

"You look beautiful," Neal whispered, not able to

find his full voice.

"Thanks, so do you."

Neither of them spoke.

Finally, Vivien broke the spell by slapping her hands together. "Shall we have a drink here first?"

"Well, I made a reservation for seven thirty, so I guess we should go."

"Okay. I'll grab my purse. Come in. Feel free to look around."

As Neal stepped inside, Vivien caught him marveling at her home.

Light maple-wood floors extended throughout. In the living room, a long white couch, housing different colored throw pillows beneath a wrought-iron chandelier, invited relaxation. Her black and white framed photographs also added depth. A shot of a New York City brownstone pulled Neal into the room. Vivien knew that particular photo would call out to him. Nostalgic warmth vibrated from the picture. Next to it hung the Eiffel Tower, Mick Finns tavern, and a gorgeous sunset shot of Half Moon Bay in color.

Wandering farther, Vivien followed him into her kitchen. Another wrought-iron chandelier hung in a square design. Vivien's pine cupboards framed glass doors, allowing for flower-painted white plates and mugs to be appreciated. She trailed him again when Neal walked away to examine the curved staircase leading to her second floor. The maple-wood banister topped a black iron design of roses and leaves, giving off a classic, romantic vitality.

Smiling, Vivien crossed her arms over her waist. "So, what do you think?"

"This is stunning!" Looking up at the high arched

ceilings, Neal's brows furrowed in concentration. "Wait a minute, I know this work. Did Elizabeth Weston build this house?"

"Yes! Wow, you're good. But then again, this is your field."

Neal grinned widely. "A former colleague said she lived in this area, so that helped."

"I bought it from her a few months after I moved here." Snatching her purse off the small foyer table, Vivien found him calmly gazing upon her.

"The beauty of this house suits you."

His words hung in the air like soft snowflakes on a magical winter day.

"Thank you."

Their gazes locked, and Vivien couldn't seem to move.

This time, Neal broke their trance and extended his arm toward her front door. "Well…shall we?"

"Yes." Putting one foot in front of the other, Vivien reminded herself not to act like a smitten schoolgirl. *Just breathe, Vivien.*

As they passed the archway to the living room, Neal stopped and pointed. "That black and white photo of what looks like a New York brownstone really struck me."

A wistful smile crossed Vivien's lips. "That was the home I grew up in on the Upper West Side."

"Really? Do you rent it out or something?"

Taking a black sweater off the antique coat rack that stood by the door, she looked down. "No. I sold it after my parents passed away."

"Oh, I'm sorry." Neal followed her out.

After getting into his black hybrid SUV, a similar

car to hers Vivien noted, they backed out of her driveway in silence.

The dreadful silence grew.

Vivien inhaled sharply. "Okay, here's what I believe—if there's a pink elephant in the room, introduce him. So, I need to tell you that I haven't dated in a while, and I'm very nervous."

Neal let out a long breath. "I'm glad you said that. I'm in exactly the same boat."

"That's good. I mean, not good—but…well, you know what I mean."

"Yes, I know what you mean."

Sharing in laughter, their conversation from that point on flowed with little effort.

****

Relishing the cozy table Neal secured for them at the end of the patio, Vivien lazily stirred the ice inhabiting her margarita glass. Camacho's was one of the most popular restaurants on the marina, and after crafting the addition of their banquet room, Neal formed a friendship with Alejandro, the owner. They never ran out of chips and salsa, and she could swear the water glasses were checked every five minutes. Their waiter stayed his distance but made sure they were hydrated and cared for.

Filled with happy patrons, the long red Spanish tile patio extended in a semicircle around a cream-colored stucco building. Long windows lined the edge so customers inside could also enjoy the ocean view. Rose, gold, and pink clouds reflected a spectacular setting sun. When the horizon grew dark, flickering candlelight from the table votive accented Neal's dreamy sea green eyes. Vivien relaxed against the tan padding of her carved wooden chair amidst a fresh ocean breeze and tangy spices from meals placed upon nearby tables.

"So, what got you into architecture?"

Neal angled his head. "Let's just say the inkling was always there. At nine years old, I used to make my parents stop in front of historic buildings to examine the shapes. It got on their nerves after a while."

Resting an elbow on the table, Vivien delighted in his childhood memory. "So, it really did start early on?"

"Yes, there was never a question. I was lucky, too, because my parents supported me. My sister is an artist, so she had to graduate from business school first."

"Of course."

"Pam hated business. But the Realtor job is working out, and she's started painting again. That makes me happy."

A smile graced her lips. "You're a very good brother."

Neal leaned closer. "So, do you have brothers and sisters?"

"No. I'm an only child."

He scooted the bowl of tortilla chips across the table.

"Thanks." Snatching a chip, Vivien chewed it up after a quick dip in Camacho's homemade salsa.

"Actually, I'm really curious to know how you got into the ghost-hunting business. I'm sorry, is that the right term?" Popping a chip in his mouth, Neal crunched it down.

With a short laugh, Vivien's shoulders rolled back. "It's as good a term as any, but we refer to ourselves as paranormal investigators. Then, if we find the haunting to be legitimate, we cleanse the space. So, we're ultimately paranormal cleansers."

"I'll remember that." Smiling, he nodded respectfully.

"Anyway, that came later. I used to teach creative writing at Columbia."

With brows raised, Neal reached for his beer. "Really? What inspired you to teach?"

Playing with tiny salt crystals on the rim of her glass, Vivien mused on the answer. "In my elementary school days, I wrote short stories and enjoyed being my English teacher's pet. But as I entered high school, students came to me for help. I began tutoring and found I loved that even more. Hence—the teaching." Taking a sip, she enjoyed the salty sweetness of her drink.

"And here you are writing again. You came full circle."

Vivien set her glass on a small white napkin. "It all started with my father. He was a literature professor at Columbia and read me fairy tales before I fell asleep. My dreams came alive with everything from blue pixies with snow-white wings to dark creatures with slimy hands. But he finally slowed down on the monsters because I'd end up in my parents' bed in sheer terror." She quivered with laughter.

Neal laughed with her. "I bet your mom had something to do with that."

"Yes, she did."

"So, why did you stop teaching?"

"Because…"

After a numb pause, Neal shifted, getting closer to her by placing his elbows on the table. "Because?"

He sensed a change in her—that she knew. Soft

waves against the sand below echoed inside. How did they get to this subject so quickly? If Neal had read her book he would know. But he hadn't even searched her out on the internet, wanting to learn about her on his own. Vivien had to be honest, but also wanted to pace herself.

"I probably shouldn't talk about this on a first date."

"A wise woman once told me if there's a pink elephant in the room—introduce him."

Breathing deeply, Vivien focused on the dancing candle flame on the table between them.

"Five years ago, I lived in New York City. My fiancé and I left his apartment to attend a dinner in his honor. But we returned to get his speech notes. An armed man jumped out from behind the couch and shot us both. Philip died, and I lay in a coma for four weeks. I didn't go back to teaching because I had a tough recovery, and then my psychic skills accelerated. My mentor, Katherine, found me and trained me for a year in Ireland. When I completed my training, I settled here in Half Moon Bay."

Glancing up, Vivien found his eyes wide with shock, but filled with compassion.

Her lips continued to move. "It feels like I'm living two lifetimes in one. My life felt like Camelot. I loved my students, my friends, my fiancé, and my parents. Now…they are all gone."

Snapping back to the present moment, Vivien stopped. She'd run off at the mouth. Sitting back, her hands fell into her lap. "I'm sorry. I don't know why I just told you all that. I've never shared those thoughts with anyone."

Softly, Neal touched her arm. "Maybe because I can relate to a second life within one as well."

"Here we are!" Two iron frames descended onto the table, quickly filled with steaming fajitas.

They separated as white smoke hovered, filling their lungs with succulent sizzling green peppers and onions.

"Enjoy!" Their waiter slapped down plates and tortillas.

Perusing her noisy dinner, Vivien inhaled deeply. "Smells good. Looks good too." Meeting Neal's eyes, she found him contemplating her.

"Vivien, I'm so sorry."

His tenderness sent waves of warmth through her entire being. "Thank you."

"I hope you don't mind me saying, but I completely understand why you haven't dated in a while."

"I don't think people get the healing process. Sometimes, it takes longer for some than others."

"Exactly. Over the past year, friends have been pushing me to date. But there were times I just wanted to be alone."

"Yes."

Neal finally looked down at his plate. "I guess we better eat before it gets cold."

"I agree." Vivien pulled her tan cloth napkin out of a rose-painted porcelain ring.

After a moment, Neal cast an amused glance. "Hey, I bet you don't watch shows about heroes fighting the supernatural. For you it would be like watching another day at the office."

Almost choking on her food, Vivien swallowed.

Recovering with a drink of water, her eyes caught his. "Actually, I love all those supernatural shows. It's wonderful to see someone else fight evil for a change."

With a chuckle, Neal picked up his beer and held it out. "Cheers to that!"

Snatching her glass, Vivien clinked it against his. "Cheers to that!"

****

As the brush flowed through her chocolate brown hair, Vivien examined her reflection. *What happens now?* She had no clue.

Upon exiting the restroom, she eyed Neal lurking near the hostess station. Suddenly a thick manila envelope flashed in Vivien's head. "Oh, no! I completely forgot. I have the photos and digital recorder from your investigation back at my house. I was supposed to review them with you."

Grabbing two peppermints wrapped in clear plastic from the podium, Neal shrugged. "How about we go to your house and have that drink you offered earlier. Then, you can show me the stuff and answer any questions I have."

"Great." Taking the mint he offered, she had her answer about what would happen next. Post dinner investigation follow-up was not what Vivien expected, but that was okay with her.

****

Arriving at her front door, laughing about their favorite movie, Vivien put her key in the lock. In contrast to Neal's house, wooden stairs led up to a wraparound porch framed by two columns. The two-story home presented a stunning sight in the classic Barn Style white, accented by forest green shutters upon each upstairs window.

All of a sudden, a distinct cologne filled Vivien's senses.

Nicholas.

She froze.

"Is something wrong?" Neal's gaze showed concern.

"Just a second." Vivien pulled the key out of the lock and closed her eyes. *Please leave.*

Nicholas's reply came fast and hard. *No!*

Impulsively, Vivien threw her arms around Neal's neck. "Hold me tight."

He did as she asked, and Vivien wrapped them up in protective light. She also covered the house, guest house, and focused on all the doors—just to be safe.

Dark energy hovered for a moment, and then jettisoned away.

Instantly relaxing, Vivien's body melted into Neal's.

"Are you okay?" he breathed in her ear.

How could she explain? Deciding to go with vague, Vivien's head popped up. "I'm sorry. I felt some bad energy. Everything's fine now." Smiling cheerfully, she opened the door. "Red or white?"

"I'm sorry—what?"

"Red or white wine?"

"Red."

"Okay."

Neal took off his jacket and hung it on the hallway coat rack. "So, what did you mean when you said you felt bad energy?"

Fumbling for a bottle of merlot, Vivien wasn't ready to explain about Nicholas and their past life together. "Sometimes I just tap into stuff."

Neal sat on a bar stool at her kitchen counter and peered back. "How do you deal with that?"

Vivien awkwardly battled with the cork. "Oh, it doesn't really happen that much." Little did he know, it happened often.

"Do you want some help?"

"This one is just being difficult." After another yank, the cork was out, and she hastily pulled down two wine glasses. "Would you like to go over your investigation results in the library?"

"Sure. You have a library?"

Pouring the wine, Vivien handed him a glass with a twinkle in her eye. "Follow me." Leading Neal down the main hall to the back of the house, she opened a door with a light touch of her fingers. Upon entering, she turned on two Tiffany lamps.

"This is incredible!" A high arched ceiling offset a floor of dark brown oak. A cranberry velvet couch and two overstuffed velvet chairs—one emerald green, and one deep purple—sat in front of an oak fireplace. Books filled built-in shelves, amidst a beautiful bay window with a tapestry window seat beneath. The last dramatic element lay in a pair of long red velvet curtains framing the window, displaying the Pacific Ocean beyond the cliffs.

"I can tell this is your creative haven. Am I right?"

Vivien bordered on a blush. "That is exactly right."

"I feel like this place is very important to you."

"Now who's the psychic?"

The corners of Neal's lips curled. "It must be rubbing off."

Snatching the manila envelope from her desk,

Vivien snickered. Since Jason was busy on a photo shoot, they would be the first to look at the evidence of the paranormal—if any. Jason didn't even have time to print the shots. A friend did it for him.

"Shall I sit here?" Neil pointed to the cranberry couch.

"Yes."

Seating herself next to him, Vivien opened the flap. "Why don't we start with the pictures?"

"Sure."

"We're looking for anything that looks like a wisp of smoke, or an orb."

"An orb is?"

"A spirit taking the form of a ball of light. They can be small or large, and when you zoom in, they resemble a vortex."

"Amazing."

"Yes, it is." Vivien continued to flip through the photos, finding no indications of light or orbs.

The next picture finally showed a glimpse of something spiritual. Jason must have taken it just as dinner began. Neal stood at the kitchen counter reaching for a glass, and just behind him a strip of white mist extended to the ceiling.

"Okay, here's what I'm talking about."

"Wait a minute." Neal examined the photo more carefully. "Do you mind?"

"Not at all."

Taking the picture from her, Neal leaned toward the stained-glass lamp. After a long moment, he put it down and placed a hand to his forehead.

Picking up the photo, Vivien held it to the light. At first, it did simply look like a smear of white mist, but within the haze the shape of a woman appeared. Gazing out the kitchen window, the woman wore a summer dress with her hair held up by a shiny silver clip. She even detected a smile upon her face.

"It's Darlene, isn't it?"

"Yes," Neal answered in a troubled voice. Reaching for his wine, he took a sip.

"I'm sorry. We should stop now."

"No."

"No?"

His face held a combination of sadness and peace. "Thank you."

"For what?"

Neal studied the picture. "For allowing me to see she's happy. Darlene always stood in that pose when she felt serene."

"Maybe that's why she appeared." Vivien studied his face. "So, you're sure you want to continue?"

"Yes, I'm sure."

"I feel strong emotions stirred in you. I know this isn't easy, even if it has been two years."

Neal took another sip of wine.

Sitting silently, she let him think.

Setting his glass aside, Neal leaned forward, hands clasped. "I just feel like I want to do this with you."

Neal's confidence in her talent sent a glowing shudder through Vivien's heart. "All right." Reaching in, she pulled a small metal box from the tan envelope. "Do you want to play the recorder for any EVPs?"

"Yes. When was this recorded again?"

"While we ate dinner on your patio."

"Got it."

"The recorder is sound activated, so you may hear

us going outside. But after that, we'll see." Vivien pressed the button. Little girls' voices came out first, as they moved from the kitchen to the patio. Then, a sudden noise emitted from the recorder. She played it back.

Laughter—like wind chimes in a Zen garden.

"That's her laugh." Neal said it flatly, then comprehended what he'd just heard. "Oh, God."

"We're stopping."

"I'm okay…I just…didn't expect to hear that. To be honest, I didn't really expect to hear anything."

Vivien sensed Neal's anxiety level raise several notches, but he tried to cover it up. Usually her focus would carry her through a situation like this, but Neal wasn't just any client.

"Many times, we don't get EVPs. To have this one come out so clearly is astounding."

"When Darlene set out to accomplish something, she always succeeded." Neal's hands clung to his kneecaps.

Vivien felt his shock, but also his contentment to be with her. Giving him an out, she got up and put the recorder on her desk. "I'm so sorry. I know this upset you. Maybe we should call it a night."

After pushing himself off the couch, Neal paced. "Frankly, I just don't know how to react to this. I mean, give me a two-by-four or a blueprint, and I know exactly what to do. But this…"

A wave of pain and embarrassment hit Vivien full on. Neal didn't want to show his distress and distance her. Going with instinct, she interrupted his pacing by enfolding him in a tight embrace. His love, his pain, and his hope flooded her. Vivien's eyes brimmed with tears. She actually needed to calm herself before speaking. "May I tell you what I'm picking up?"

"Please."

"Darlene is just saying hello. She doesn't want to interfere with your life, but she wanted you to know she's okay."

He exhaled, long and deep.

Vivien watched thoughtfully as Neal pulled away from her. He ran a hand through his hair, grappling with this new part of the world he didn't believe existed. Neal's reaction did not surprise her, but she desperately wanted to make it easier.

"Why don't I make us some tea?"

"That sounds good."

While they stared at her silver tea kettle, Vivien asked Neal about his current project. Trying to get his mind off Darlene would be a challenge, but she would try.

Neal spoke briefly of rebuilding an estate on the cliffs, but then stopped. As the conversation stagnated, she leaned against the kitchen counter. "How are you doing?"

"I think it will take some time." He shifted on the bar stool.

The teapot finally whistled. Vivien filled their cups and took a seat on the stool next to him.

Neal shook his head. "You know—no offense, but I'm very glad your investigation of my case is over."

"I don't blame you a bit." Vivien raised her cup and gave him an understanding smile.

Uncomfortable silence amplified as they sipped their tea.

"How is Julie?"

"She's fine. The incident at my house is their big secret now."

"Yes, I'm sure they'll never forget it."

Neal took another sip and set his cup down. He wanted to leave but didn't want to hurt her feelings.

Vivien stared into her chamomile tea. "I know you need to go."

"You must have read my thoughts." Neal smiled sheepishly.

"Seriously though, I apologize for putting you through all that, when we could have had a nice evening."

"I was the one who suggested it. You were just doing your job. I didn't believe how real this stuff obviously is, even after seeing a banshee." Neal moved off the stool, picked up their mugs, and made his way to the sink.

"Oh, please. I can do that."

After setting them down, he made a beeline for the front door. "Okay…well, I'll give you a call in a couple days. How's that?"

Vivien walked behind him. "That's fine." Something shifted. He felt hesitant to call but didn't want to tell her.

After grabbing his coat, Neal opened the door. Turning, he gave Vivien a quick hug. "Well, thanks again."

"Thank you for dinner."

"See you later."

"Bye."

After closing the door, Vivien returned to the kitchen, opened the dishwasher, and grabbed one of the cups.

Why did she show him the photo and play the EVP? Neal wasn't ready for that experience. She scared him away. The mug slipped from her fingers. Pieces of white ceramic shattered in slow motion. Tears flowed down her cheeks. Bracing her forehead on her palms, Vivien leaned against the counter. She had a chance to begin something new with Neal, and she blew it.

Someone turned her body around.

"I'm an idiot." Neal's hands gently held her shoulders. "Can you forgive me?"

Vivien gazed up. "Can you forgive me?"

When Neal pulled her close, her arms wrapped around him. Their lips finally met, and her entire body seemed to dissolve into his. At first, they kissed tenderly, but passion soared, and soon they found themselves in an ardent embrace.

Finally coming up for air, Vivien opened her eyes to find him holding her face between his hands. "I'm sorry I made you cry. I feel better thinking this other worldly stuff is fake, but that's not true. It's part of your work, and I just need to accept it."

"I thought I scared you away."

Neal lifted his head in contemplation. "For about two minutes."

Grabbing his lapels with relieved laughter, Vivien planted her lips onto his. After ten minutes of no further language and leaning farther and farther against the counter, they came up for a breather.

Vivien stepped back. "I hope you understand that I can't…"

"I know," Neal uttered in a husky voice.

"I'm just not…"

Swiftly, she felt herself enfolded in his arms.

"Hey, I didn't expect to spend the night. How about a picnic on the beach?"

"That sounds wonderful." After one more kiss, Vivien walked him to the door, but this time they held hands. "I'm glad you came back."

"If I didn't come back tonight, I would have come back first thing in the morning. I'd rather spend time with you than be afraid of the supernatural."

Vivien suppressed a smile. She'd never heard that line before.

"Good night." Neal touched her lips gently with his.

"Good night."

Vivien watched him get into his car and drive away with a wave.

Closing the door and turning around, Vivien's head pressed back against the beveled glass. She would sleep well tonight, and if she had dreams that included a romantic lover—she knew exactly who he was.

Chapter Fifteen

Dusty Rose Cottages in bold red paint across a white-washed wooden plank proclaimed their location.

Vivien pushed the dashboard button into park as if in slow motion.

Her first murder case.

"This feels worse than when Nicholas arrived at your book signing," Shawn's dread carried in a whisper as she unlocked her seatbelt.

"I know. Do your protection."

An aura of death struck Vivien the moment she stepped onto the brick path. Beyond the roses, a fountain trickled below a stone statue of the Archangel Gabriel. Knowing such a horrible act occurred in such a beautiful place made her ache inside.

"Good morning," John greeted as he and Jason entered the garden.

"Good morning. John, this is Shawn, our newest member."

"Welcome." Shaking Shawn's hand readily, he didn't appear surprised. Jason had obviously told him about her.

Releasing his camera from its case, Jason shook his head. "I have to admit, I'm surprised a sheriff is soliciting our help."

"My vision led Sheriff Harris to his daughter's kidnapper a couple years ago. Elaine was rescued and came home safe. Ever since then, he's believed in me and the supernatural."

John eyed Jason in bewilderment. "Didn't you hear that story? It was all over the news."

"I was in Iceland at the time." Jason's mouth dropped in astonishment. "That was you? You have to tell me more."

Vivien turned. "Another time."

Just then, a six-foot-two bald man in his mid-forties emerged from the main cottage. He wore a navy-blue sheriff's uniform and a gold badge on his chest. His intense brown eyes betrayed hints of previous investigations, and those to come. "I appreciate you coming."

"Of course." Vivien raised her arm. "Andy Harris—meet my team. This is Shawn, Jason, and John."

Nodding, Andy stood with hands on his hips. "Nice to meet you all." Then, he angled his head toward Vivien. "A family member is about to pick up the mother, but before she does, I wonder if you could talk to her."

"I'd be happy to."

"She told me some things her son said just before he went into the green cottage, and it makes no sense to me. But it may make sense to you."

"Perhaps. Where is she now?"

Andy pointed to the opposite side of the property. "In the white cottage."

"I take it the boy is already gone?"

"Yes, the coroner left an hour ago."

"What is her name?"

"Grace."

"The boy's name was Daniel, right?"

"That's right."

"While I talk to Grace, would it be all right if my team investigates the cottage?"

"Yes, under my supervision. I'll take them in."

"I'll join you all in a few minutes. Shawn, can I talk to you?"

"Yes." Shawn stepped closer.

"Just make a sweep of the room and see what you pick up. If it gets too much, step out and wait for me. I know you're nervous."

With a jittery smile, Shawn scratched her nose. "Just a little bit."

"Remember—focus and protect yourself."

"I will."

While Andy led the rest of the team to the only cottage with yellow police tape stretched across the walkway, Vivien knocked on the door of the white cottage.

"Who is it?" a worried female voice inquired from the other side of the door.

"My name is Vivien Kelly. Sheriff Harris said I could speak with Grace."

Swiftly the door opened, held by a woman with dark ash hair, viciously pulled back in a headband. Frantic amber eyes looked Vivien up and down. "Oh, yes, he told me about you. Please come in."

When her feet crossed the threshold, Grace's sorrow threatened to suck Vivien down into an abyss. Inhaling deeply, she centered herself in light.

"I'm Nancy. This is my bed and breakfast. My daughter is watching the front office. I didn't want to leave Grace alone."

"I can understand that. Grace is in the bedroom?"

"Yes. Shall I take you to her?"

"In a minute, but I just want to ask a few questions first."

"Certainly." Crossing her arms, Nancy attempted to keep her body from shaking.

Reaching out, Vivien placed a hand on her shoulder, sending calm energy. "Did you have any problems with the green cottage before this happened?"

Releasing a long breath, Nancy's anxiety came down a few notches. "Yes. People started complaining of something smoky moving in the mirror about three weeks ago. After we lost three sets of guests that way, I decided to remove the mirror. But when I tried to take it off the hook, it wouldn't budge. I asked my handyman to do it and he couldn't get it off. He even took an ax to it, and the blade broke in half. After that, he ran out and hasn't been seen since."

"What did you do?"

"I covered it with a board. But even after that, people said they heard knocking coming from the mirror. So, I finally locked the cottage up and made it a storage room. Now, the only people who go in there are me, my daughter, and the maids. So, how that little boy found his way inside, I'll never know. We never left that door unlocked."

"I see." Vivien got an image of a blond-haired boy playing in the rose garden with a ball. He saw the Green Cottage door slowly open, and curiosity took it from there.

"All the same, I feel horrible. You must believe me, if I had any idea it would come to this, I would have had that cottage torn down. Now I'm going to do just that." Blinking away tears while looking at her watch, Nancy began to ramble. "I better take you to Grace. Her sister is picking her up in twenty minutes. Follow me."

Nancy walked down the hall, throwing words over her shoulder. "This was their last stop before driving down to L.A." Her crooked finger lightly tapped the door. "Grace? It's Nancy. There's someone here to talk with you. It's the woman I told you about."

After a moment, Nancy turned the antique glass door handle. Grace sat in a white wicker chair with burnt orange padding. Her fingers tugged at blonde locks of hair—exhausted grief invading her striking blue eyes. Standing unsteadily, Grace extended her hand.

"Oh, no, please. Sit down." Vivien spoke softly and shook her hand.

"I'm Grace." Her voice cracked.

"I'm Vivien. I'm very sorry for your loss."

"Thank you."

Vivien noticed a small matching wicker table holding a teacup, saucer, and a box of tissues.

"Grace, I'm going to brew some chamomile tea, all right?" Nancy said.

"Thank you."

"Would you like some, Vivien?"

"No, thank you."

Nancy slipped out the door.

As soon as Nancy made her exit, a little boy appeared standing behind Grace's chair. He wore green shorts with a white shirt and possessed the same blue eyes as his mother.

Please—tell Mommy I'm sorry.

The words rang out inside Vivien's mind, startling her.

"Sheriff Harris explained what I do?"

"Yes."

"So, you're open to speaking with me?"

"I told the sheriff I would."

I just wanted to bring her a picture of the ocean. She likes pictures of the ocean, and there was a real pretty one in the other cottage.

Grace stared at her with concern. "Are you all right?"

"Yes," Vivien assured, coming back to the conversation. "Was your son wearing green shorts and a white shirt when he was found?"

"Yes."

"I'm going to tell you something, because he wants you to know. Daniel is standing behind you, and he says he's sorry."

Grace looked behind her chair, then sharply back to Vivien. "Why are you saying this? He said you were a profiler. I know the sheriff gave you information. You probably know his name is Daniel and what he was wearing!"

With compassion, Vivien spoke slowly. "Daniel just wanted to bring you a picture of the ocean. He says you love pictures of the ocean, and there was a pretty one in that cottage."

All anger left her eyes as Grace understood the truth of Vivien's words. Covering her face, she cried—the deep, tortured cry of a mother.

Kneeling down, Vivien embraced her as best she could. Instead of speaking, she sent Grace loving white light.

All of a sudden panic crept down Vivien's body. Looking out the window—there stood Daniel—and this time he looked very different. Where his left eye had been, was now a gaping hole. Raising his arm, he pointed to the green cottage.

"It can't be." Vivien gasped in horror.

Grace lifted her head. "What can't be?"

"Tell me what Daniel said before he went into that cottage."

"But it doesn't make any sense."

"Please tell me!" Vivien demanded, almost shaking her.

"Daniel told me every time he passed the green cottage, he heard a man riding a horse."

"Oh, God!" Almost knocking down a steaming teapot and Nancy, Vivien blasted out the front door.

****

Andy touched the shoulder of the deputy standing watch. "Logan, why don't you take a break?"

"All right. I'll get some coffee." Deputy Logan made his way to the front office with only a curious look at the group with Andy.

Pulling up the yellow tape, Andy allowed Vivien's team to enter.

Shawn stepped inside and wrapped her arms around herself when biting cold promptly swept through her body.

Jason came up behind her. "How are you doing?"

"Fine. Thanks."

"Let me know if you need help. I know it's your first investigation."

"And your second," John interjected, unpacking his gear.

Shawn tried not to laugh. "Sorry."

Hiding a smirk, Jason pulled his camera out of a brown messenger bag. "That's okay. I guess the only real veterans here are John and Vivien."

Andy joined them. "So, as you can see this is the living room. Follow me, and be careful not to touch anything."

The mood took on a grim tone when they entered the bedroom and saw the chalk outline of a seven-year-old boy on the hardwood floor. Even though it was a large room for a cottage, everyone stayed several feet away from the chalk.

"Do you mind if I take some shots?" Jason lifted up his digital camera.

"As long as they are only used for the investigation."

"Absolutely."

With brows lifted, John crossed the small space to Andy. "I'm curious why you thought this crime to be supernatural?"

Shifting his weight, Andy grimaced. "Nancy told me they've had unexplainable disturbances in this cottage for weeks. That's why it's been locked up and changed to a storage room. But this is the first time anyone got hurt. So, I had a feeling I should call Vivien."

"Good feeling," Jason said in between snapshots.

Andy pointed. "What is all that?"

Starting a digital recorder and taking out his EMF machine, John demonstrated them. "I'm taking a reading of the room. Temperature, electromagnetic field—stuff like that. How did the boy die?"

"His heart stopped. It could have been a heart

attack."

"At seven years old?"

Andy squinted, rubbing his forehead. "I know it doesn't make sense, but nothing does in this case. No sign of forced entry and no signs of a struggle. But the thing that really puzzles me is the loss of his eye."

"What?" John uttered in a tight whisper.

"I haven't even had a chance to tell Vivien. All she knows is that his heart stopped. The boy's left eye is missing, and we still haven't found it."

The recorder bounced off the floor. Grabbing it before damage could be done, John faced Andy, almost stammering. "And no one saw anyone go in or out of here?"

"No."

John had a strong idea of what it could be from his days teaching Celtic mythology, but it seemed too unreal. Even though Vivien had banished a *Baobhan Sith* and a *fear dorcha*, he wasn't ready to believe the creature in his mind could actually manifest. "The hairs on the back of my neck are standing up."

"That was my reaction as well. I've seen some grisly scenes in my line of work, but this one feels very creepy—for lack of a better word."

"Did you ever read Washington Irving's book, *The Legend of Sleepy Hollow*?"

Andy grunted, with brows wrinkled and a sardonic smile. "Uh…yeah."

"Well, if I didn't know better, I'd say this was the work of a *dullahan*. You see, the headless horseman was fashioned after the *dullahan*. In Irish legend, he appears at midnight on certain festivals and feast days. He rides a black horse and holds his head under one arm. Ordinarily, the *dullahan* arrives to take a person destined to die to the afterlife by calling out their name. Next, he plucks out their eye using a whip made from a human spinal cord. Once a person makes eye contact, he takes their eye and stops their heart from beating. But the weird thing is—the *dullahan* is afraid of gold."

Andy's face contorted. "Oh, that's the weird thing?"

"Yes. Even a pinpoint of gold will frighten him." John stopped talking. Sheriff Harris was not ready to hear this level of paranormal revelation, so he looked down at his EMF machine. "I'm going to walk around and get some readings."

"Go right ahead." Shaking his head, Andy walked down the short hallway to check on Shawn.

Shawn stood inside the bedroom examining the opposite wall.

"Do you have any questions?"

"Why is that mirror boarded up?"

"The owner said it bothered the guests."

"Why didn't she take it down?"

"They couldn't get it off the wall."

Shawn crossed her arms. "Couldn't get it off the wall? How can that be?"

"It's very strange, but when I pressed her for more information, she ran off to help Grace."

A vision of the board bursting off and landing on the floor filled Shawn's mind. "Whatever killed that boy came out of this mirror."

Andy shifted his weight. "Excuse me?"

Unaware she'd spoken her thought, Shawn gazed at Andy for a moment. "I just feel like the mirror could be a clue, that's all. Maybe I'll see how Vivien's doing."

John tapped the glass on his EMF machine, certain he'd misread it. The needle shot up to the highest level once again.

Shawn took one step toward the door.

Pop.

The board concealing the mirror twirled in a circle on the floor, until it stopped dead.

Crazy laughter echoed throughout the room.

Andy drew his gun. "Get behind me!"

An unseen force pushed Shawn back, pinning her against the opposite bedroom wall. "I can't move!"

When Andy grabbed Shawn's arm, the same force catapulted his body into the hallway.

"What's happening?" Jason shouted. He tried to jump into the bedroom but was pushed back.

Pinned to the wall, Shawn tried to keep the barrier of white light around her, but fright took hold. Movement caught her eye. A smoky haze gathered in the center of the mirror. Thudding hooves of a galloping horse reverberated around the room. Squinting hard, Shawn could just glimpse a black horse and rider—only the rider held his head under one arm. The flesh looked like moldy cheese and the mouth held a hideous grin, but the eyes remained closed.

Vivien raced through the living room, to find Andy on the floor.

Andy shot up. "It's got Shawn!"

"Don't look in his eyes! Can you hear me, Shawn? Shut your eyes now! Nod your head if you can hear me!" Vivien screamed, leaning into the bedroom as far as possible.

The *dullahan*'s eyes began to open.

Quickly, Shawn closed her eyes and nodded.

"Don't give in to fear. I'm going to get you out of there!" Turning back, Vivien grabbed John's arm. "Give me your gold ring."

"What?"

"Give me your gold ring!"

John shoved his ring into her palm. "Oh, my God! It is him?"

"Yes, it's the *dullahan*. If Shawn looks in his eyes, she's dead."

"Don't go in there. Wait until I get more men." Andy pulled out his cell phone.

"You can't! This is something I have to do."

Pushing the phone back in his pocket, Andy nodded. "Okay, how can I help?"

"By sending positive energy to Shawn."

"Huh?" Andy's face twisted as he thrust his gun back into its holster.

"Believe it or not, that's how you can help." Vivien made it easier for him. "Just imagine her safe and free from that monster."

"I'll try." Stepping back, he gave her more space.

Jason's hand shot out. "Give me the ring. I'll do it!"

"No, Jason. You're coming from sheer terror."

"But I have to help her!"

"Right now, you're putting her in more danger."

Jason's hand dropped. "Then tell me what to do."

"All of you go to the living room and imagine Shawn walking away from this."

A sharp snap turned their heads. The whip of the *dullahan* burst through the mirror—a gray, slimy collection of bones, designed to pluck out Shawn's eye in a second.

Peeking quickly, Shawn screamed as the whip thrashed about the room. "Vivien, help!"

"The *dullahan* can't hurt you as long as you don't look in his eyes. His whip can't touch you. Do you understand?"

Desperately Shawn nodded, tears running down her face.

"Oh, my God!" Jason moved fast behind Vivien, trying to get past the invisible barrier to the bedroom. Before she could react, John grabbed Jason by the shoulders and hurled him into the living room.

Finally able to concentrate, Vivien closed her eyes with no time to lose. The *dullahan* would find a way to force Shawn to look at him. Throwing her arm out, Vivien commanded the creature's whip back into the mirror. Nothing happened. Why didn't his spinal whip react to her power? She tried again, flinging her arm out and willing his collection of bones back into the glass. Again—no change.

Vivien's ability to move matter had never failed since discovering her gift. She remained outwardly calm but had to deal with her own anger. Why hadn't she felt the *dullahan*'s presence when she arrived? And why weren't her powers working? Now she had to try something else.

After a long inhale, Vivien lay flat on her stomach, gripping the ring tightly in her hand. Slithering, she got underneath the mirror. Suddenly her leg jerked backward. The whip encircled her ankle and sliced through flesh.

The *dullahan* sought to distract her—to break the power of her focus. The pain became excruciating, but

Vivien held her ground. *That's not fair. I didn't look into your eyes.*

I'm not allowed to kill you, but you shall look into my eyes.

Blood ran down Vivien's heel as the sting became unbearable. Maybe she couldn't move things at the moment, but she still had the power of imagination. All her energy poured into an exaggerated vision so real it would plunge the *dullahan* into horror.

The *dullahan* stood within the Drombeg circle of stones. Boudicca and her warriors unmercifully buried him under a mountain of gold bricks.

Earsplitting shrills pounded through the cottage.

"Shawn, get down!" Her ankle now released and with no time to conjure a Celtic Triad, Vivien smacked the gold ring onto the mirror.

"*Dibir!*"

Tinkling sounds of glass settling from the shattered mirror still sounded when the men ran down the hallway.

Lifting her head, Vivien jerked back, John's face an inch from hers. "Oh, God! You scared me!"

"I scared you!" John almost laughed in wide-eyed surprise. "Are you all right?"

Jason ran to Shawn like a flash of lightning, while Andy scanned Vivien's body for any signs of injury.

"I'm okay, but my ankle is bleeding."

"No, it's not." Andy looked at Vivien in confusion.

"What are you talking about? It's…"

Pulling up her jeans, Vivien found her skin untouched. "He made it feel so real." They helped her to a standing position. "Where's Shawn?"

Supported by Jason, Shawn's voice came out in

spurts. "I'm okay—just shook up a little."

Taking Shawn in a tight embrace, Vivien gasped. "I'm sorry! I never should have left you." Releasing her, she gazed at the rest. "That goes for everyone."

"Is he gone?" Shawn anxiously glanced around.

"What does it feel like?"

Shawn gave a quick nod. "He's gone."

"I need to clear this room." Andy took command, leading Jason and Shawn out.

"What about my ring?"

Vivien moved glass with her foot. "There it is."

John carefully picked it up. "I never realized my wedding band would save a life."

"I'm glad you still wear it." Vivien breathed wearily, with a thoughtful smile. After John slipped the band back on, she held his ring finger. "I think Peter was looking out for all of us today." Vivien knew even though he'd been a widower for three years, John couldn't imagine taking his ring off—such was the love he shared with his late husband.

"So, when are you going to get out there and date?" she tossed back, brushing dust from her pants.

"When I see him, I'll know, and that's the day I take this ring off for good."

"Vivien?"

"We're coming!" Her answer came quickly, then Andy popped his head back in.

Andy addressed the group as Logan wandered back with his coffee, unaware of what just took place. "Okay, everything that just happened in there is confidential. Got it?"

"Yes," Vivien assured, looking over at her team, who all murmured agreement.

"Good. I'll say the mirror cracked and shattered unexpectedly onto the floor. I need to talk to Logan, and then I'll talk to Vivien privately."

They moved toward the parking lot. When Shawn began to shake uncontrollably, Jason peeled out of his jacket and quickly threw it on her.

"Jason, please drive Shawn to Luna Books. Donna sent me a text before I left my house, but I didn't get a chance to tell any of you. She's got a keen sixth sense of her own, and she knows we had a tough morning. Donna and Roger have their meeting room prepared for us in the back of their store."

"Right." Jason swung a camera strap over his shoulder.

"Shawn, drink lots of water, all right?"

Holding the jacket tightly around her, Shawn tried to smile. "Yes, I will."

"No worries. We'll go right now." Jason led her to his car.

"I'm right behind you," John called after them.

"Here comes Andy. I'll be there in ten minutes. Oh, and please help Shawn. It was her first investigation, and I threw her under the bus."

"Don't beat yourself up. I'm the one who should feel guilty. Andy told me the boy's eye was missing, and I knew it had to be a *dullahan*, but I wouldn't let myself believe it. If I'd turned the EMF on sooner, I would have seen the insanely high reading. You, on the other hand, didn't know what it was. If you did, you would have been there from the beginning."

Meeting his gaze, Vivien spoke in a low tone. "Let's face it—neither of us wanted to believe that creature could materialize in our world. We'll have to

209

stay sharp from here on in. We don't know what could show up next, and now we're dealing with murder—not scared little girls after an innocent séance."

John whispered, as Andy got closer. "It's like a living nightmare. I'd better go."

"See you over there."

Andy stared through her—shell-shocked. "I know you can't explain what just happened in there." He shook his head in dismay. "In fact, I don't even want you to, but I need to know if our community is in danger?"

Quickly processing the best explanation, Vivien listened to the peaceful dripping of water from the stone angel fountain. "All I can say…is that I've encountered very powerful entities lately. Creatures that should never inhabit our world."

Andy's gaze intensified. "Okay, I'll be on the lookout for anything strange. Are you sure you're all right?"

"Yes. It's all in a day's work." Vivien feigned a cool attitude, but her head throbbed.

"Well, I don't envy you your work, but I definitely have a new respect for what you do." With caring eyes, Andy grasped her arm. "It's been a hell of a morning. Take care today."

"Thanks. You, too."

As she walked to her SUV, Vivien's mind tumbled. Every time she tuned in for answers, she met a black wall. Now her telekinetic powers seemed off. Dagda was part of the puzzle, but she knew there had to be more.

Unlocking her car and settling in, Vivien noticed a red dot on her cell phone. She pressed down and retrieved voice mail.

"Well, hello, mistress of the psychic realm! I'm picking you up tomorrow afternoon for lunch. I know I promised dinner, but my plans got switched around. I'm calling you from my private cell phone, so you won't have to go through my assistant. Give me a call to confirm. Talk to you soon."

Vivien's blood boiled at Nicholas's off-hand way of ordering her about. He didn't even know her availability tomorrow, but psychically he did. Immediately, she returned his call.

"Well, well, well…"

"I don't have time for this."

"Ah, c'mon—"

"Listen to me! We've got big problems here."

"Go on," Nicholas answered, respectfully.

"I'm at a bed and breakfast where an innocent little boy was just killed by a *dullahan*. You will not pick me up. You will meet me at one o'clock at the Moss Beach Distillery. This is serious, Nicholas!"

Abruptly, Vivien clicked off. Tuning in to his reaction, she found he wasn't angry. Understanding her fury at the thought of a sweet boy's grisly murder—Nicholas would be there tomorrow.

Chapter Sixteen

A picturesque Victorian house, three stories high, sat at the end of a long block just west of Main Street. Sky blue paint contrasted with snow white trim above a dangling shingle in black calligraphy, displaying the words Luna Books.

Hanging petunia baskets along the curved front porch in pink, lavender, and deep purple brought a tender grace to the home's beauty. Roger and Donna inhabited the top two floors, leaving the first floor solely for books, browsing customers, meditation classes, psychic readings, healings, and author signings.

As the front door closed behind Vivien, a small shop bell chimed its welcome. Cherry wood bookshelves stood in rows. Two girls sat at a square table under a Tiffany lamp reading the latest book, *The Little Book of Saturn*. Various pendulums, crystals, wind chimes, and creative mobiles hung on display from ceiling crossbeams—their best seller being a cascading collection of painted paper butterflies. Down the hall, three small rooms housed their psychic readers and Reiki healers.

Vivien always breathed easier upon crossing the threshold of Luna Books. The store's energy calmed, refreshed, and invigorated all who entered.

When she moved down the stairway entrance, Vivien caught eyes with a Green Man mask hanging on the wall. Rich forest leaves surrounded a long nose and penetrating sapphire eyes. The nature spirit respected Donna and Roger, so she nodded, but resisted tapping into his overpowering essence—having bigger issues to deal with.

"C'mon." John waved her forward, walking back to the meeting room.

They strode to the new space provided for creative brainstorming. Upon Vivien's entrance, Roger tugged down blinds on the window facing the shop's interior. Jason, Shawn, and Donna sat at a round mahogany table with a tray of water bottles, string cheese, green grapes, apple slices, and red cherries. A small glass refrigerator housing more water lurked in the corner opposite a long bookshelf filled with paperbacks. A rolling whiteboard with colored markers sat on the other side, ready for ideas to be born.

Donna ejected herself from a sitting position and grabbed Vivien's shoulders. "How are you doing?"

A tsunami of grief threatened to burst. Swallowing hard, Vivien smiled directly at her friend. "I'm fine."

"Bullshit!"

Studying the floor, Vivien blinked. Donna's compassionate eyes would throw her over the edge.

Luckily, John intervened. "Sit down."

Vivien did. Confusion overtook her expression when John began wiggling with excitement.

"Did I tell you I run a dream group and they sketch their visions for me once a week?"

"No." Vivien rubbed her temple as Donna shoved cheese, cherries, and a bottle of water before her. "Do you have some aspirin?"

"Coming right up," Roger answered, leaving the

room.

"I think we got a lead." Eagerly, John pointed to the center of the table. "Isn't that the Celtic God, Dagda?"

As Vivien opened her water bottle and took a swig, scrawled printed pages of a burly man with a beard, tunic, and cape lay before her. Some drawings included him holding a club. Her skin went cold. "You didn't tell any of them about our investigations?"

"No. I have ten people in the group, and each week I ask them to email a sketch of something that created a strong emotion in their dream. I hadn't checked email lately, but I logged on the minute I got here. Seven out of ten came up with this."

Cold turned to heat, erupting inside her with every word coming out of John's mouth.

"Look at this one." He tugged a page loose. A striking woman possessing beautiful cheekbones, thick cranberry hair, adorned with swirling red and blue battle paint upon her face, stood in the foreground.

"*Loc na mhuice!*" Vivien screamed, bolting up.

"She just called someone pig shit," John mumbled in response to the questioning faces around the table.

Now Vivien had to tell them about the visitation from Dagda. How could she have so underestimated his warning? The demon's energy had expanded since his proposition to her and the killings had begun. How did it get to this point? She used to clear houses of irritating poltergeists, and now she fought to keep innocent people alive.

With arms flailing, Vivien ranted in Gaelic. But they had a bigger concern when books flew off shelves in response to her movements.

"What the hell?" Jason wrapped his arms around Shawn.

"Wow! She's telekinetic!" John grinned in awe before dodging out of the path of a flying paperback.

"Look out!" Donna yelled as more books flung themselves at a frenzied pace.

Pushing Shawn under the table, Jason ducked just as a copy of *Haunted Gettysburg* hurled at his forehead. Missing him, it whacked against the window shades.

Roger opened the door.

"Take cover!" Donna screamed.

Mouth agog, Roger slammed the door shut, just before two water bottles leapt off the table.

A small part of Vivien stayed lucid but could not stop her own tirade. She vaguely noticed Donna stepping toward her. Just as the white board levitated, Donna grabbed Vivien from behind. As she whispered a calming meditation in her ear, Donna refused to let Vivien go.

Suddenly both women dropped to the floor.

Popping her head up moments later, Vivien eyed the room in utter confusion. "What the hell happened?"

Before anyone could answer, someone knocked hard on the door. Placing an index finger to his lips Roger opened it, closing the gap with his body. After speaking briefly with Pamela, their cashier, Roger shut the door. He turned to meet the curious eyes of all in the group. "I told her we were releasing anger. You know, trying out a new healing exercise."

"Good thinking, honey!" Donna proclaimed with a proud smile.

Vivien stood slowly. "Oh, God. This was me, wasn't it?"

John nodded hard and crossed his arms. "Yep—and all in Gaelic."

Mortified, Vivien glared back. "What did I say in Gaelic?"

John scratched his head. "Mostly swear words."

"Shit!" Slapping a hand to her forehead, Vivien moaned. "I'm so sorry."

"Well, at least we understood that." Jason pulled out a chair for Shawn.

Vivien fell into another chair and dropped her upper body onto the table.

Roger tossed out a pill. "Take your aspirin."

"Wouldn't you feel better with a Reiki healing?" Donna suggested, brows raised. With a quick shake of Roger's head, she stopped. "Never mind."

Vivien did as instructed, swallowing the medication and trying not to look at her team picking up books and water bottles strewn across the floor. Then, she noticed John staring down Donna and Roger.

"How long have you two known about this?"

"How did you figure out we knew?" Donna shot back with a puzzled look.

"Neither of you appeared surprised by her power to fling objects around."

With the room back in order, everyone else sat around the table.

"I'll answer your question." Vivien straightened tousled hair with her fingers. "During my final combat test in Ireland, I discovered my Gift. I thought it was just extra power manifesting because I was in battle mode with a Celtic sword in my hand. But as soon as I arrived here, I learned I still possessed that power. I met Donna my first day, and as I reached for a coffee swizzle stick in Java Hut, it flew into my hand. Thank God it was only Donna and I who saw it. She pulled me out to the street, sat me down on a bench, and explained what was happening. From then on, Donna, Roger, and I have been the only ones privy to this information, and I've learned to hone my skill only for paranormal cleansings. Actually, I also use it to light candles and sage, but everything's changed as of today. That little boy would be alive right now if Dagda didn't want me." Her index finger extended toward the drawings. "That's me. That's Boudicca." Vivien elaborated by relaying the encounter with Dagda, an annotated version of her past life, and what he proposed to do to their modern world.

Her words rumbled like a shockwave over their faces. They didn't want to believe it, but Vivien's disclosure propelled them into an entirely new reality.

Heaving his shoulders, John brought up a subject many never cared to discuss. "The black clouds hovering over the Sahara Desert—are they connected to this demon?"

Nodding, Vivien reached for a red cherry and yanked off the stem. Plopping the cherry in her mouth, she pulled out the pit.

Shawn leaned over the table. "I had a feeling there was more to this. But there's no way you could have anticipated what happened to that little boy. Dagda is very strong. That much, even I can pick up."

After throwing Shawn a grateful smile, Vivien focused on John. "What emotions did the members feel when they had these dreams?"

"Rage, hopelessness, control, submission, fear, and darkness." After a silent moment, John gathered the

217

pictures into a manila folder. "I think we should let Vivien and Shawn rest. It was an intense investigation this morning."

Shawn straightened. "I'm fine. I don't want you guys to think I'm a wimp, or anything."

Vivien choked on her sip of water. "Shawn, we don't think you're a wimp. Far from it! You were left alone under the attack of a *dullahan*, and you're sitting here. A weaker person would be locked in the bathroom on tranquilizers by now."

Jason nodded. "True…that's true."

"The *fear dorcha*, the *Baobhan Sith*, and now—the *dullahan*. How can we stop Dagda from awakening all these creatures?" Donna pounded a fist on her last word as the table jumped.

All eyes turned on Donna.

"I mean…a boy is dead."

Roger pulled her close.

Vivien exhaled long and slow. "That's what I don't know yet. I'm meeting Nicholas Williams tomorrow, and I'm going to grill him. He is connected to this. We both are."

"The guy who started the Foundation?" Roger asked, incredulous.

"Yes. Nicholas was at my book signing, and when we shook hands, an intense vision of a past life overtook us. It felt like we were there." Her finger jabbed the folder of sketches. "That life. Nicholas was a Celtic tribe leader as well, and we were lovers. Dagda existed as the father god of the Celts and the protector of our harvest. We gave him offerings from our crops, and I was Dagda's favorite. When Nicholas started the Foundation, a new version of Dagda began entering his meditations. He thinks Dagda's just hanging out, but I know that demon wants more from Nicholas."

"Perhaps Nicholas knows more than he's letting on," Jason ventured, grabbing a bunch of green grapes.

"I know he does, and I have to keep my cool with him tomorrow. He makes me crazy angry."

Popping a few grapes in his mouth, Jason smiled. "He's an ex. They always do that."

Vivien glared back at Jason, and he pretended to cough. Kneading her forehead, she tried to alleviate the pounding. "Those pictures are a confirmation that Dagda's energy is growing. He has to be destroyed. The alternative is unthinkable."

"But you're doing the best you can right now." Donna squeezed Vivien's arm in a quick movement.

"Yes, you are." Shawn nodded fervently.

Vivien's gaze caught John, Roger, and Jason. "If you guys can scan the internet for any news on Nicholas or Dagda, that will help." Then she turned to Shawn and Donna. "Ladies, keep your intuition open for any messages or signs." As she reached for her water bottle, the container flew down the table and slammed into the wall with a hard splat.

"I'll get it." Jason retrieved her drink from the floor.

Vivien threw up her hands. "Unbelievable! Now my energy goes nuts, but when I focused on shoving the *dullahan* back into another dimension—nothing!"

Donna pointed at Shawn. "You were scared for her safety. Fear blocked you."

As she gripped the armrest of her chair, Vivien sat back. "You're half right. That was part of it, but I could also feel a powerful force holding me back. It was

Dagda." Sinking lower, she gazed up at the ceiling. "What I haven't told you is that every time I try to tune into Dagda, I'm blocked. I hit a wall. That's never happened before, and it pisses me off!" Vivien suddenly lurched from her seat. "I have to go home."

Roger stood. "Wait a minute. Do you want some lunch before you go?"

Shawn and Jason whispered in the corner.

"I'll get something on the way home, but thanks. Ready, Shawn?"

John rested his hands on her shoulders. "We will get this thing, you know. We will. Everything's going to be fine."

Vivien's expression softened a bit. "I hope so."

Jason looked at Vivien. "Shawn and I want to go to an early lunch, and then I can drop her off at your place."

"Okay, then."

A sweet jazzy tune erupted from Vivien's phone. Retrieving the thin piece of metal from her jacket pocket, she saw Neal's name.

"Hi." She attempted to sound blasé.

"How are you?"

"Can you hang on?"

"Sure."

Lowering the phone, Vivien scanned the room. "Everyone be careful and remember to protect yourself with light twenty-four, seven."

Donna wiped a hand across her forehead. "That's for sure. I'll walk you out." When they got to her SUV, Donna took her by the elbows. "Promise me you will eat, drink lots of water, and take a very long nap, okay?"

Vivien beamed. "Okay."

With a quick kiss on her cheek, Donna walked away.

Vivien lifted her phone. "I'm back."

"I heard everything. Are you all right?"

She launched into her car and relaxed against the buttery soft seat. "Honestly—no."

"Do you want to tell me what happened?"

"I do, but I can't talk about it now."

Neal paused for only a second. "Well, I actually called to ask a favor. You see, I got this delicious tiramisu and now I can't eat it all. If I come by later, would you help me get rid of it?"

Warm sparkles filled Vivien's heart. What a sweet approach to finagle his way into her house again.

"But maybe after what happened you're not up for it?" Neal said softly.

"That would be perfect. How about six o'clock?"

"Sounds great. I'll see you then, and please follow Donna's instructions."

"I will."

After hanging up, Vivien tuned in.

Neal worried he may be coming over at a bad time, but in fact, it was just what she needed.

Chapter Seventeen

Vivien waited, pretending to sift through a mound of sand in her right hand. Unexpectedly, a small spiral seashell popped out. So small, yet so intricate. Nature constantly amazed her. Drawing in a deep breath of fresh salty air, Vivien's thoughts came back to Neal. She'd just finished telling him of her ordeal at Dusty Rose Cottages. The *dullahan* didn't seem to jar him, maybe because Neal had already witnessed the wrath of a *Baobhan Sith*. Vivien went all the way back to seeing Dagda in her car the night she drove from his house. The only parts she left out were her past life with Nicholas and her telekinetic power. It was too early to share those facts with him. But if Neal was truly in for the long haul, he had to know everything else.

As they walked, Neal's arm encircled her waist to the brisk sound of waves rolling onto shore. When Vivien cast him a glance, confused dismay reflected in his eyes. In his gut, he knew she spoke the truth. Not only did Vivien just tell him demons exist and one wanted her as his queen, but also that a headless horseman killed a child.

"I can still see that little boy. I only saw him in spirit, but he looked so real—his face so innocent. He only wanted to get his mother a picture of the ocean." Tears she held back now flowed freely.

Vivien felt his arm shift, gently pulling her down

with him to a sitting position. Returning her palm of sand to the beach, she pulled a tissue out of her sweater pocket.

"I'm sorry. I had no idea, and there I was talking about a stupid dessert."

Vivien embraced Neal's cheek with her open hand. "You didn't know, and I just didn't want to crumble in front of my team. I held it together until now." *Except for almost destroying the new meeting room in Luna Books.* Gratefully, Vivien snuggled into his side when Neal wrapped his arm around her and held tight.

"I'm amazed you could face that thing in Julie's bedroom, let alone fight off that other creature and save the life of your assistant."

She felt his hesitation as he paused.

"I have to be honest—the part about a demon taking over the world—I can't even process that. I know you're not lying to me, that I know, but the survival part of me won't believe it."

Vivien examined his face. "I understand. But the survival part of me has to believe it. I just feel horrible for putting Shawn in danger."

Echoes of sea lion barks drifted down the beach—one of Vivien's most beloved sounds. Swimmers in slick black wetsuits on surfboards dotted the sea, waiting for that last perfect wave of the day.

"Maybe Shawn had to face her own fear in that situation."

Taking in his insight, Vivien's head tilted to one side. "I never thought of it that way. Not that I'd ever want to see her in that situation again, but my mentor, Katherine, always says we have our own journey. Shawn proved to be very strong."

"When will you get rid of this Dagda ghost?"

"He's a demon."

"Oh, right. When will he be banished?"

"That I can't answer. I'm meeting with someone tomorrow who can help our investigation. I have to find a way to eradicate him. Once Dagda is gone, all the other creatures will be cast out as well." Vivien prayed he wouldn't ask who she would be meeting with.

As she wiped a stray tear from her cheek, Neal's penetrating green eyes focused on her. "I can't wait until you just clean haunted houses again." After a long moment, he picked up a small piece of driftwood and threw it forcefully into an incoming wave's foaming water. "My instinct is to protect you and keep you from harm, but I know you'd hate that. You have to accomplish your goal, but I also can't help the way I feel."

Anger blended with love. Yes, he felt love, even if he couldn't say it yet. Neal wanted her safe and it proved very difficult to accept what she did, especially when it got dangerous. With nothing else to do for him at this point, Vivien stood. "So, what did you do growing up in Santa Cruz?"

Vivien heard his small grunt, acknowledging she no longer wanted to talk about her challenges. Then, Neal rose.

Smiling, Vivien took his hand as they began walking.

"I was a total surfer dude."

Hearty laughter echoed down the beach as she intertwined her fingers with his.

"Oh, and every Christmas my mother let me construct the gingerbread house."

"That's sweet."

"Yes, it was. My folks moved to Palm Springs to retire and now they live and breathe golf."

They continued to walk in silence, looking out at pink hues over the ocean.

"Julie says hello."

Vivien smiled and leaned against him. "Please tell her hello back."

"Will do. Sometimes Julie feels like my own daughter."

An intense stillness enveloped them the moment he uttered the word—daughter. Neal burned to ask if Vivien wanted children one day but didn't want to come on too strong. As soon as she picked up his thought, he pushed it away.

"Well, I better let you rest after the day you had," Neal breathed gently, halting their walk.

"I guess you're right." They turned around, making their way back toward Vivien's house.

Suddenly, Vivien passed Neal and turned to face him. Running backward with a big grin, she shouted back at him. "Oh, and by the way—I do want children someday!"

He grinned. Catching up with her, Neal grabbed her by the waist.

Laughing harder than she had in years, they fell onto soft sand and wrestled, tickling each other silly. Soon the wrestling turned to passionate kissing, and when they finally sat up, a sky-blue and pink horizon awaited them.

"It's beautiful," Vivien wheezed out on a long breath.

Neal wrapped her up in his arms. "Yes. Yes, it is."

****

Hard snorts from his horse fell in sync with his own sharp breaths. He'd commanded his men to ride in a different direction to pursue Boudicca himself. Underneath a brilliant night sky, he watched her dismount and pull into an abandoned stable.

He closed the thick wooden door behind him and stepped into darkness, strands of hay giving way under his sandals.

"Boudicca?"

Emerging from shadows, Boudicca flicked back her hood with a shrewd smile. "Gaius Marcus Antonius."

"I may have just saved your life."

Her eyes instantly filled with gratitude.

Gaius's fingers raked through his slick hair. "These attacks must cease. Nero has ordered more men against you, and you will be far outnumbered. I tried to convince him to vacate these regions, but he won't listen. He's a demented little bastard! Nero won't rest until my army has destroyed you and all your clans."

"Gaius, you do not understand our commitment. If we die, we die fighting—with honor and courage."

"Honor and courage." Unconsciously, Gaius placed a hand on her cheek. As a Roman general, he more than understood. "I cannot meet with you again."

He kissed Boudicca with such intensity, she gasped. Wrapping her arms around him, she met his passion. Gaius felt her heart. She loved him—it had become undeniable. He'd helped her many times before, and their connection blossomed.

Pulling back from his tender lips, Boudicca twisted away. "I'll not put you in danger. Nero and the other generals would kill you if they witnessed what just took place."

Gaius drew her back into his arms, caressing Boudicca's cranberry red hair with the back of his hand. "Come away with me."

"You already know I cannot. They would find us."

Silently, they stood. A moonbeam poured through a crevice in the wood, creating a glowing pool of light.

"I must go." Boudicca yanked at her horse's reins.

"Boudicca, wait! There must be a way."

"No." She pushed open the heavy door, gazing at the silvery meadow before her. "There was a time I wondered how my life would be had fate chosen a different path. If I wasn't in a position of leadership for my people, a life with a man like you may have been possible." Pulling the hood over her head, Boudicca mounted. Her voice caught when she peered into his cobalt blue eyes. "I thank you for your help, Gaius." Faintly, a smile crossed her features. "I shall meet you on the battlefield." In a flash, she galloped away.

Longing filled his soul. Yanking a sword from its sheath, Gaius leaned his forehead against it. The one woman he loved on earth was his sworn enemy and must be killed. Looking down, Gaius stared into his reflection on the glistening silver blade. A strong chiseled face stared back, framed by black hair. Casting his gaze down farther revealed a gold chest plate over red material ending just before his knees and dangling from his waist—a matching gold helmet.

Gaius left the sanctuary of the stable, mounted his horse, and charged off like the wind.

Amergin emerged from behind the stable, glaring after the man who was not only his enemy, but now his rival in love. How could Boudicca betray her clan? Part of him could not believe his eyes. If Boudicca truly allowed herself to be seduced by this scum of a Roman, then Amergin knew what he must do.

****

Neal jerked awake as trembling fingers groped for the lamp switch. Breathing like a marathon runner, he stood and found his way to the bathroom mirror. The face staring back at him remained the same he'd always seen, albeit now a mask of shock.

He stood in that stable. He would take an oath on it. The realism of the dream stunned him—the smell of the horses, the feel of the wooden door, her lips.

Neal splayed his fingers upon the mirror.

"Gaius?" he mumbled with a wrinkled brow.

The red-haired woman from his dream had become Vivien in this life. He knew it as well as Neal knew his own name—past and present. Instead of fear, relief washed over him. Vivien felt so much a part of him, he wasn't surprised he'd known her before. This time they had a fresh start and could finally live their lives together.

For now, Neal decided to keep the dream to himself. Vivien had enough on her plate. She had to focus on her confrontation with what they called a demon. For some reason, their previous life wasn't revealed to her, and he wasn't going to give her another blow. When the time felt right, he would share his vision if Vivien still hadn't figured it out.

With sleep impossible, Neal walked down the hall to the kitchen and filled a tall glass with purified water from the refrigerator spout. Taking a long cool swallow, he settled into the window seat. Shards of dawn splintered through the sky, sending whispers of orange light along his redwood patio. It was then grief hit him. Gaius had loved Boudicca so much her death devastated his spirit. Even knowing their love to be doomed from the start, Gaius still held faith they could escape together once the battle ended.

Boudicca died with honor. That gave him peace. They never found her body, and it was said she swallowed poison rather than become Nero's example to her people by torture and finally, displaying her head upon a spike. The Roman standard of punishment was well known, and Boudicca would not subject her clan to that horror.

Neal set down the water glass and massaged his face as emotions of loss spilled over into present life. The only reason he now sat in his own beautiful home was because of a promise. Before Darlene died, she made him promise to complete their house. Neal's first impulse was to sell and cut his losses, but it became important that he stand by his promise to her.

The world he knew crumbled the day Darlene passed. She opted for hospice and wanted to take her last breath in her own bed. Darlene sat up proudly in her favorite white silk gown, with her blonde hair in an up do. Her best friend and hairstylist, Charlotte, spent hours making it just perfect. Charlotte stopped a few times to cry in the bathroom, telling Darlene she needed more hair clips. Darlene knew it to be her emotions and not hair clips Charlotte needed to gather together.

Darlene's essence of peace amazed Neal that night. She remained the calmest one in the room, and she knew it.

With Darlene's coiffure complete, all their friends

and family came around to say goodbye. Some laughed over memories with her, while others cried openly. Darlene held each person and gave them her love. She'd already accepted she would die that night and told Neal it was her final day on earth that morning.

Neal lay beside Darlene as she took her final breath. She had turned to gaze at him once more, with a sweet whisper. "I love you."

Neal repeated those words with a soft kiss upon her lips.

Arching back, he sighed slowly and stretched his arms. Neal finished his water, rose, and set the glass down in the sink. Gazing at the ever-growing sunlight outside, he suddenly understood why she needed him to keep the house. Darlene wanted him to live in happiness with Vivien.

Neal made a vow to do just that. But for the present, he would support Vivien in this strange new battle. At least this time, he was not her enemy.

Chapter Eighteen

The Moss Beach Distillery stood dramatically overlooking the cliffs, harboring a lost soul. While Vivien took in white sands and an endless ocean, she pondered the ghost known as the Blue Lady. Always seen in a gossamer aqua gown, she would not cross over, refusing to leave. After several attempts, the entity retreated farther into shadows.

Built in 1927 and originally called Frank's Place during prohibition, the eatery doubled as a speakeasy. San Francisco politicians, gangsters, and movie stars walked through its attractive doors. A blazing image of Louis Armstrong singing "West End Blues" popped into Vivien's brain. How sweet—he wanted to say hello. His music had always cheered her up, especially his rendition of "Hello Dolly" from the film with Barbra Streisand.

After Louis faded into the ether, Vivien placed a hand on the window, feeling the buzz of the Blue Lady's energy. As the story goes, in the late 1940s, she fell in love with the piano player of the establishment and began an illicit affair. After her husband discovered her betrayal, a passerby found her lifeless on the beach just below the restaurant. The exact cause of death and her true identity remained up for debate by several paranormal investigators. Vivien never pressed the spirit for details because the Blue Lady didn't care to revisit her demise.

"Hi, Vivien. Are you here for another exorcism?" The waiter winked, weaving through two small oak tables filled with lunch goers.

Vivien tossed her head back. "No, Brad. Not today."

"That's good. The boss wants the Blue Lady to stay. She's good for business." Scanning the dining room, Brad whispered. "In fact, he almost had you banned from here—afraid you'd send her away."

"No!"

"It's true. He knows your track record." He chuckled. "Are you waiting for someone?"

"Yes."

"Would you like a glass of chardonnay while you wait?"

"No, just a sparkling water. Thanks."

"All right."

When she gazed out at the sea, she sighed as sunshine glittered like stars across a blue canvas. But Vivien's moment of peace got quickly stabbed.

He had arrived.

"Hey! You're Nicholas Williams!"

"That's me."

"Honey, this is the guy I told you about. He runs the seminar I'm taking. I'm signed up for the next one."

"Wonderful, then I'll see you there. What is your name?"

"Aaron Klein."

"Well, see me after the closing, and I'll sign my book for you."

"Thanks! I'll do that."

"I'm looking forward to it." Nicholas

enthusiastically shook Aaron's hand and made his exit.

Vivien witnessed the entire exchange from a silver framed mirror on the wall. Impeccably dressed in a gray designer suit, Nicholas insinuated himself into the chair across from her with the grace of a dancer.

"You're quite the celebrity."

Nicholas smiled broadly. "You should know. You're on the New York Times best seller list alongside me."

"You know, it's not about the fame." Vivien's head cocked to one side. "Oh, that's right—you don't know." Chiding herself for getting defensive every time he came near, she bit her lip.

"Must we start off our lunch fighting?"

Vivien cast him a glare that could decapitate when his hand reached for hers, stopping him cold. Easing up, she smiled. "I have a message from your sister. She visited me last night."

Never before had Vivien seen him utterly lost. Suddenly, Nicholas looked like a little boy.

"Holly still loves you. Her overdose was an accident, plain and simple. She wants you to know that, and she's sorry she left you alone. You'll always be the little brother who saved her life." The beautiful nineteen-year-old sitting on her bed at the stroke of midnight told Vivien how Nicholas snatched her arm just before a near fall to the bottom of the Grand Canyon. He was only five years old.

His face transformed to stony inertia. Nicholas wheezed out words in clipped sentences. "She made her own choices. Now she has to live in whatever dimension will have her. End of story."

"She wanted you to know the truth."

Brad returned with a tray in hand. "Here is your water, and what would you like sir? Oh, Mr. Williams! I just read your book. I loved it."

"Thank you." Nicholas responded with a satisfied grin, back to his assured self.

"So, what will you have to drink?"

"I'll have what the lady is having." He unbuttoned his suit jacket and settled deeper into the simple wooden chair.

"Coming right up. Here you are." Brad presented them with menus before whisking away.

Vivien's amazement grew at how fast he turned off human emotion. "I give you a heartfelt message from beyond…and that's it?"

Nicholas faced her with vibrant, yet stifled anger. "Vivien, I got her message and yes, that's it. It's done."

"Her name is Holly."

"Was. Her name was Holly."

His eyes shut down, all torment stuffed inside. Vivien didn't know how he managed it. Nicholas simply erased his sister's spirit and her love for him. He would bolt if she mentioned Holly again, so Vivien remained silent.

Nicholas eyed the menu. "I see one of the specials is shrimp scampi. I believe that's your favorite."

Vivien stared right through him. "I know what you want."

"Actually, you don't know what I want."

Slowly and deliberately, Vivien crossed her arms. "You want me to join your group and pull in more followers because I have strong psychic power and positive energy. You also want me to be your lover, and later, your wife."

Vivien had broken his casual composure, but Nicholas regained poise swiftly. "They are not followers. They are members."

With a sharp laugh, Vivien loosened her arms and leaned upon the table. "I'll stick with my former reference, thank you." She poured her sparkling water into a glass of ice and took a long sip.

"I see you don't want to waste time, so I'll be blunt as well." His gaze observed her affectionately after Vivien set down her glass. "I cannot deny everything you said is true. However, I asked you to lunch to find out what you want."

"What I want?"

"Yes, I want to know what your desires are. I want to know more about Vivien Kelly, not because I wish to manipulate you, but because...I have feelings for you." Crystal blue eyes gleamed on his final sentence.

"I thought this was a brainstorming lunch."

"No, I consider this a date."

Suspicious of his motives, Vivien's eyes closed. To her surprise, Nicholas opened to her. His love felt gentle—like sunshine inside a summer ocean tide. She basked in its peaceful glow.

Then, everything changed. Sensing something dark in the distance Vivien's head turned. Panic rushed inside her veins at warp speed as her hands flew out. Gripping the table in an attempt to hang on to reality, silverware hit the floor.

In a flash, the vision shut down.

Nicholas had covered up something from his past, and it took all the energy he possessed to keep it from Vivien's psychic sight. Usually an image would present itself, but for some reason this particular image remained a mystery.

"Let me get that for you." Brad quickly picked up Vivien's place setting and brought back a new one. He also set down a sparkling water bottle and a glass of ice for Nicholas. "There you go. So, have you decided?

Addressing Brad, Nicholas pulled his gaze from Vivien's glare. "Yes, I'll have the filet mignon cooked medium and the lady will have the shrimp scampi."

Brad snatched the menus. "Oh yes, that's one of Vivien's favorites."

"That's right." Vivien observed Nicholas closely. "Everyone knows that."

Brad turned on his heel, and they were alone.

Whispering forcefully, Vivien got in his face. "What have you done, Nicholas? Tell me. If you really want me to be your mate, you won't keep secrets."

Not able to hold eye contact with her any further, Nicholas slid his white linen napkin out from under a silver fork and carefully placed it in his lap.

Leaning back, Vivien searched his face. The angst inside finally dissipated. Letting out a long breath and feeling clear of negativity, she asked again. "What was that thing in the corner of my vision you didn't want me to see?"

Pouring sparkling water over ice, Nicholas did not answer.

"Would you like me to repeat the question?"

"I think you know already." He put the small bottle down. "It's my ego and lust for power. I'm doing my best to keep them at bay. Most women can't even sense that, but I knew you would."

"You're sure that's all it was?"

Again—no answer. Instead, Nicholas brought

fizzing water to his lips and drank.

Vivien shook her head from side to side. "You have a great capacity for good, Nicholas. It's up to you how you use it. Don't let Dagda sway you."

As Nicholas gazed into her eyes, she could see vulnerability. Then, he sat back. "Okay, we're getting off the subject here. I want to know more about you. What are your dreams?"

Exhaling, Vivien sat up straight. "All right, if you'd rather talk about me—fine. But only if you'll answer my questions later. Deal?"

"Deal."

"So, you want to know my dreams, huh?"

He nodded enthusiastically.

"Well, actually I'm living my dreams now. I help people with my psychic ability, work with the sheriff to find lost children, and wrote a book on intuitive guidance. I am very fulfilled."

"What about a partner?"

"A partner?"

Nicholas smiled. "Would you like me to repeat the question?"

"No." Vivien looked him straight in the eyes. "I'm going to be perfectly honest."

"I'd expect nothing less."

"I'm not discussing this subject with you."

Nicholas took her hand. "Vivien…"

"Don't do that."

Quickly, he let go. "I should know better."

"Yes, you should. Your charming smile and player moves don't work with me."

Adjusting the salt and pepper shakers, Nicholas murmured, "Then I don't know what to do."

"Seriously?"

"Yes."

He spoke in earnest. Nicholas trusted her enough to reveal himself. "Just talk to me, like you are right now."

"Complete honesty. I can do this."

Vivien laughed.

"I made you laugh. That's an improvement." Nicholas gave her an eager smile. "You want to ask me something, don't you?"

Vivien spoke lively. "Just for a moment, forget the power. Forget the journey you're on right now. Who are you? Who is Nicholas Williams?"

Pensively, he looked out to sea. "For one thing, I think I'm near the ocean, because I always wanted to be a professional surfer."

"You're kidding?"

"Ever since I was fourteen. You didn't pick that up?"

"No. But as you know, not everything is revealed to us."

"That's true."

"Here we are," Brad announced, as he laid down their plates. "Do you need anything else?"

"No, thank you," Nicholas answered briskly. "Oh, I'm sorry. I shouldn't speak for both of us. Vivien?"

Staring Nicholas down, Vivien slowly turned her head toward Brad and smiled. "Thanks, I'm fine."

Their waiter turned away.

Nicholas's face turned apologetic. "I meant it when I said I was sorry. I know you hate that."

"Then why did you do it?"

"Because I'm not used to being with someone at my psychic level, and who has…"

"Has?"

"A higher energy than mine."

"I don't believe that."

"What I mean to say is—your energy is pure."

Vivien cocked her head. "Yours is too. You just won't admit it."

At that, Nicholas looked down and she felt him closing off.

Lifting his fork, he spoke into his plate. "Our food is getting cold."

"So it is."

They finished lunch with lighter conversation. Nicholas wouldn't answer her tough questions about Dagda until they left the restaurant, so Vivien devised a plan.

As they made their way out, a pair of desperate eyes met Vivien's. It was Mrs. Klein. Vivien tapped into her thoughts. She worried about her husband sinking thousands of dollars into the upcoming seminar for the Foundation. Believing her to be Nicholas's girlfriend, she appealed discreetly.

"I'll wait for you," Vivien announced, stopping herself short.

Lips twitching at the corners, Nicholas gave her a wide smile. "Gee, how did you know I was going to the men's room?"

Vivien switched her straw tote straps from one shoulder to the other. A simple distraction.

"Be right back." Nicholas headed into the hallway.

As soon as he left, Vivien projected light around herself and the table she swiftly slapped her hands upon. Nicholas couldn't interfere, but she had to work fast. Vivien clasped Aaron Klein's hand almost violently.

"What are you doing?" Aaron stuttered in alarm.

Upon gazing into Vivien's compassionate, powerful eyes, Aaron opened to her vision of the future.

Losing his house, his job, and finally his wife after being seduced by the Foundation, Aaron had nothing left. Feeling like an utter fool, he sat on a toilet in a dusty, flea-ridden truck stop bathroom about to end his life. Pulling out a .45 caliber pistol, beads of sweat fell gently onto the black, cold metal.

"Oh, God!"

Aaron yanked his hand from Vivien's, snatching his wife's hand instead. Aaron felt his true destiny in that vision as if it had happened.

"Honey, I think I've changed my mind."

Lowering her forehead onto their entwined fingers, Mrs. Klein wept. Vivien reveled in the knowledge they were tears of joy.

The moment Nicholas emerged, Vivien took his arm and rushed them out the door. Remarkably, he had no inkling she'd just lost him one more follower. Taking her influence even further, Vivien decided to suggest a walk on the beach. Nicholas could discover his inner light with her guidance, and if that happened, they would definitely fight Dagda together. She knew there had to be a reason for her impulse to dress in yoga pants, a light sweater, and sandals.

"Do you have somewhere to be right now?"

With a sparkle in his eyes, Nicholas moved closer. "Not at all."

"Then come with me."

They walked up the parking lot and down a residential street adjacent to the restaurant, among million-dollar homes and eucalyptus trees. Nicholas didn't mind that, but when Vivien stopped at a posted sign which read Seal Cove Stairway, he annoyingly gaped at the rustic wooden stairs leading down to the beach.

"I'm not dressed for this."

"I'm sure you can easily replace those Italian shoes if they get damaged." One brow lifted as Vivien regarded him.

Laughing, Nicholas threw out his arm in a Shakespearian gesture. "Lead on, my lady!"

Once they reached sand, Nicholas took his jacket, shoes, and socks off. "So, what's this all about?"

"You."

He came to a standstill. "Me?"

Taking the wardrobe items out of his hands, Vivien set them down.

"Please be careful. Those are very expensive." Nicholas grimaced.

Ignoring his complaints, Vivien took his hands in hers. "Will you allow me to show you another aspect of yourself?"

"What the hell is this?" Nicholas jerked his palms down.

Knowing this would be her only chance, Vivien needed to show what his impact could do in a good way. He already knew she was up to something, so she resorted to drastic measures. Dropping her tote, Vivien wrapped her arms behind his neck, and pressed her lips against his.

Straightaway, a simple kiss turned to lust as Nicholas opened her mouth. No tenderness—only fervent hunger. Vivien couldn't deny her own reaction, albeit a carnal reaction. Heat spread, as she rode a wave of powerful energy. Almost forgetting what she'd come there to do, Vivien pried her face from his. Holding Nicholas back felt like pushing against a tiger.

Leering, he licked his lips. "I knew you'd taste like that."

Ignoring his crudeness and trying to catch her breath, Vivien kept him at arm's length. "Nicholas, if you'll indulge me this once, I promise never to do it again." She enticed, practically batting her eyelashes.

"Do we have to?"

With a sweet tone and a honeyed smile, Vivien traced his chin with her finger. "Please?"

After a moment, Nicholas nodded in resignation. "Okay. I do trust you more than anyone else, so go ahead."

They closed their eyes, but she could feel his playfulness.

"No peeking."

He shut his eyes again, accompanied by a charming smirk.

Immediately visions entered their minds in quick synchronized motion.

Within a brilliant crystal temple, a line of people waited to see Nicholas, who appeared clad in a long white robe. A lovely five-year-old girl with angelic brown eyes approached first. Shriveled skin covered her deformed left leg. Going down on his knees, Nicholas took her into his arms. The child gazed upon him in total surrender. When Nicholas smiled back at the girl, Vivien knew the innocence of her soul affected him. A bright light shone upon all in the temple, and then pulled back.

Moments later, actually sprinting to her mother on two healthy legs, the girl's laughter drifted through the stratosphere like little bells.

Vivien's heart swelled as authentic unconditional love encompassed them.

Tears of gratitude rimmed Nicholas's eyelids. But with a turn of his head, those same eyes froze Vivien out.

Charcoal slices of energy soared past her body and grew larger, until Vivien fell brutally from the scene.

Nicholas!

I will not do this!

Flicking her eyes open, Vivien found Nicholas striding away with his luxurious shoes and jacket in hand. Having fallen flat on her back, she scrambled up as fast. "Nicholas, wait!"

"You tricked me!" He broke into a run down the beach, blocking her with a wall of rage.

Nicholas's true healing power penetrated on a deep level. Vivien thought there was a chance he would embrace his enlightenment, but now she had her answer—Nicholas never would. Her brilliant plan also thwarted the opportunity to ask him about Dagda. Now she would have to pursue Nicholas in a very different way.

Grabbing her bag and sandals, Vivien began the journey back to the car, and stopped dead in her tracks. At the edge of the bluff stood Neal, staring down at her. His face revealed pain, even from a distance. Neal had witnessed the entire scene with Nicholas. Holding a blueprint in his left hand, he must have been on a client call.

"Neal!" She screamed at the top of her lungs.

Walking away, he presented his back to her.

"Neal, wait!" Vivien shrieked louder, running up the wood stairway as swiftly as her feet would allow. She couldn't believe her luck. After putting herself in danger time and time again to help others, her own life was now a shambles.

Reaching the top just in time to watch him drive away, Vivien got in her car, snatching her cell with quivering hands. One ring, two rings, and then voice mail. "Neal, I can explain what you just saw on the beach." Pausing only to catch her breath, Vivien continued. "It actually has to do with our investigation. I know that sounds crazy, but it's true! I'm coming over to talk. I don't know where you're going, but I'm coming over, and I'll wait as long as it takes. I'm sorry. I truly am."

Tapping into Neal's energy, she picked up hurt and anger, but mostly confusion. Vivien pulled up to his house and knew he waited inside. She walked to the front door and centered herself, but before she could knock the door opened.

Neal's face shattered her.

"I just wish you'd told me you were dating someone."

"But I'm not."

"You're not? What I saw was not a friendly kiss." He quickly reminded her with stunned anger.

"Can I come in?"

After Neal stepped back, she entered. Vivien wanted so much to hold him tight and tell him everything would be okay. But she couldn't do that— not the way he felt right now.

Neal led her into the living room.

Vivien sat on the couch while he descended into a chair across from the coffee table. Stretching back, Neal waited for her explanation.

Wringing her hands, Vivien wondered how to describe her past life, their primitive passion, and the attempt to bring forth higher energy from Nicholas. "Okay, I'm warning you, this is all going to sound nuts."

He shrugged. "I already know that."

Neal's relaxed exterior covered turmoil inside. The sooner she got it out, the better. "All right then." Exhaling sharply, Vivien began. "Nicholas Williams attended my book signing last week. He's the head of the Foundation group, but I'm not a member—far from it. Anyway, the minute we shook hands, we went into a past life vision. We're connected to Dagda, because we worshipped him together. Nicholas led a neighboring clan and we fought the Romans. In fact, I was known as Boudicca, the Celtic warrior queen." She looked down. "But Nicholas and I in that life were lovers." Bringing her head back up, Vivien checked Neal for any reaction. His face remained cool. "Back to the book signing. When we were talking, I got an image of Dagda trying to get into his body and Nicholas desperately fighting him off. So, don't you see? Dagda's trying to possess him, because he's growing in fame and followers and Dagda wants to rule the earth."

With hands on his knees, Neal tilted his head. "How does all that explain the wild kissing?"

"That was my idea."

Like a man shot from a cannon, Neal bounded from the chair. "Excuse me?"

Leaping up as well, Vivien paced the room,

rambling out her story as quickly as possible. "I needed to grill Nicholas about Dagda, but I had to get him out of the restaurant. So, we went down to the beach and I thought why not show him his healing power with a guided meditation? But Nicholas knew I was up to something, so I had to throw him off his game. Hence, the mad kissing scene!" Vivien's voice accelerated in pitch and speed as the urgency for his understanding became crucial. "It was the only way to loosen him up and show him his higher energy. But then it backfired because now Nicholas doesn't trust me." Halting her nervous feet, their eyes locked. "But the real kicker was when I looked up and saw your face."

Stepping away from her, Neal peered out the side window. "So, you don't have stronger feelings for him?"

"No. I feel compassion for Nicholas only because we have a connection, but that's all."

They remained in silence for what felt like eternity. Finally, Vivien spoke.

"I think I was supposed to tell you all this. Otherwise, why were you at that exact spot at that moment? I mean, think about it. What are the odds? It had to be fate. I was doing my job, and I made a judgment call. Granted, an extreme judgment call. But I can't let Dagda come to power. I just can't, and neither can you. It will never happen again. I promise."

Approaching Neal, Vivien laid a hand on his shoulder.

He jerked at the touch, sending her heart plummeting. Taking her hand away, Vivien fetched her bag. Neal believed her. She picked that up, but he remained affected by what he'd seen. "Please just think about what I said and call me when you feel ready to talk."

Barely holding back tears, Vivien turned to Neal one last time. "I would never choose to cause you pain. Seeing your face today felt like a dagger through my heart. I only want happiness for you, because you're not only a wonderful man, but a pure soul. I feel that." Taking a deep breath, she gathered her strength. "I'll leave now." Making her way to the door, Vivien heard something metal hit the hardwood floor. Curious, she ducked back into the living room.

Neal had something in his hand.

"What is that?" Vivien moved closer.

Neal remained silent, and then cleared his throat. "It's an antique tin Darlene insisted we get when we were in Carmel years ago. There's a turn-of-the-century woman hand painted on the lid." He handed the tin box to her. "Take a look."

Gazing at the tin gave Vivien instant goose bumps. The woman on the cover could have been her twin. It was as if she posed for the painter herself.

"Now I know why you looked so familiar to me the first time I saw you."

"I…I—" Sharply glancing at Neal and then back at the tin, Vivien shook her head. "Where did this come from?"

"Inside that bookshelf." Neal pointed to a cherry wood unit with sloping glass doors. Opening one of the doors, he gestured to a spot in the back corner. "You see that little empty space there?"

"Yes."

"That's where it's been for the past two months."

Still amazed at the likeness, Vivien pointed to the

tin lid. "But…this is me."

"I know it's you."

"Well, when did you take it out of the bookshelf?"

Neal shut the glass door and faced her. "I didn't."

"Then how did it fall on the floor?"

He laughed roughly. "You tell me! It never left that spot, where it was tucked behind a securely closed glass door."

Suddenly, Vivien realized Darlene executed the fall of the small metal box sitting in her hand. Darlene's intuition had been strong when she lived, but she never told Neal. When her cancer spread rapidly, she knew her time to be short. But being a strong woman, instead of wallowing, Darlene lived a full life. Having an intense feeling about the woman on the tin lid, Darlene knew Neal had to have it. She wanted him to see Vivien would not hurt him, and it all led to this moment.

Although grateful for Darlene's guidance, Vivien decided to quit while she was ahead. Starting for the door, she set the tin box on a side table. "Well, now you can put it back."

Neal took her by the arm. "I'm not dense, you know. I realize this is a sign from her, and I'm not going to just let you walk away." As he wrapped himself around her, the heat of Neal's kiss acted like sexual nirvana.

Vivien wept with relief, knowing he trusted her again.

Neal gazed down at her. "Damn. This is the second time I've made you cry."

He pressed his lips to hers, this time with a craving Vivien didn't know he possessed. When his hands reached under her sweater, that took her over the edge.

"Do you have any other appointments today?" Neal managed to get out.

"No. You?" Vivien rasped.

"No."

Instantly, her body lifted off the ground. After striding down the hall with superhuman speed and almost kicking down the door, Neal tossed her onto his bed. As she bounced off a forest green comforter, Vivien's husky laughter halted when his warm mouth smacked down upon hers. Neal rose only long enough to roll his shirt off in one swift movement and covered her torso again. Vivien moaned while her outstretched fingers slid down his back. She didn't know why, but it felt like centuries of aching to touch his bare flesh.

Neal removed her navy-blue striped sweater before she even knew what happened. Gently raising her back, he undid her bra with a quick snap. It too became airborne and joined Vivien's sweater on a chestnut recliner in the corner of the room.

"Oh, God!" Was that her voice? Having entered sensual bliss, she wasn't sure. Neal's strong, moist lips covered her breast. Slowly, he cherished her body, creating sounds of uncontrollable longing and joy from both of them.

His breathing accelerated when Vivien's hand slid down to stroke him.

Neal grasped her wrist with a smile and sparkling eyes. He kissed her palm. After he moved off the bed, his fingers rapidly loosened brass buttons, and soon blue jeans and white men's underwear fell to the floor.

A sharp inhale emitted from Vivien upon gazing at his beautiful body. In a daze of passion, she tugged at her navy-blue yoga pants.

"No," he whispered softly.

On a luxurious sigh, she let go.

Neal pulled the tight material below her hips while his fingers caressed her inner thighs.

A deafening cry echoed around the walls as Vivien's pants swiftly joined his jeans on the hardwood floor, and her back arched.

His gorgeous hard body covered her. She embraced every bit of his skin and then spread her arms back upon the pillow in utter happiness.

Neal's fingers interweaved with hers as his legs opened her.

Vivien closed her eyes.

"Honey?"

"Yes?" Eyelids flicked open.

"Look at me. I want to see you."

"And I want to see you."

Only seconds passed before they became one.

She didn't know such ecstasy existed, as true passion ignited. Vivien wrapped her legs around him instinctively and welcomed pleasure long overdue.

The words hadn't been spoken yet, but they swirled inside a wave of energy that could only be called...love.

Chapter Nineteen

Dean Marshall pulled out a mini flashlight and leaned in to check Joe's notes. They needed to get everything down, having forgotten some important details last time.

"Okay, now that we know what she's capable of, we have to keep our eyes on her. Remember, we're doing this for him." He flicked back sunlit hair as his smoldering brown eyes perused the group.

"Can't we just say his name?"

"No, Carl, I told you. We are never to say his name."

Hutch mumbled with a dumb face, holding back a laugh. "He who shall not be named."

"You better watch your wisecracks, Hutch." Dean sneered, pointing at him. Turning his sneer into a scowl, he examined the five men crouched shoulder to shoulder on the dark floor. "Why do you keep challenging me? It's non-negotiable. When all this is over, we'll be able to do whatever we want, live wherever we want, and have lots of money while doing it, all right?"

Carl, Hutch, Joe, Angelo, and Dan nodded their heads in agreement. Their muscular frames could rival Hercules, but the rules of pure evil confused them.

Dean glared them down. "We have our new assignments. When you're at the Foundation headquarters, act like everything is normal, especially around Nicholas. He's really psychic, and even though he's protecting us from his probing mind, I still need you all to be alert. If Nicholas discovers we're starting our own group with his benefactor, we'll be hurled off the Golden Gate Bridge. Got it?"

Very serious faces nodded back, except for Joe, who gawked with an open mouth and frightened eyes.

"Keep it together, Joe!"

Slamming his mouth shut, Joe nodded like a bobble head on a dashboard.

"You all have your instructions. I'll see you here next week at the same time."

Standing one by one, the men descended a tight wrought-iron staircase.

Dean caught sight of Angelo and Hutch standing near the window and strained to hear their conversation.

"I've never told Dean this, but I have a fear of heights. I can't wait till we find a different meeting place. Can you talk to him?" Hutch pleaded, trying to get out of their leader's line of sight.

"I don't know what power you think I have. I'm just the IT guy, and quite frankly, I can't wait to cash my big paycheck and go. This gig is getting worse and worse. Unfortunately, this is the only place the Foundation guys would never think to look for us."

"Yeah."

"Oh, and Hutch—I wouldn't mention a fear of anything. You know how Dean hates weakness."

"What are you two talking about?" Dean came between them.

Hutch spouted incoherent language while Angelo remained silent.

"Let's go!" Their leader growled, waving an impatient hand in the air.

Dean followed behind the line of men, shaking his head at the motley crew he had for such an important undertaking. He didn't care that his new boss happened to be a demon. He no longer wanted to be second to Nicholas Williams. When the dark entity came to him offering quick financial abundance, Dean's fearful shock dissipated instantly. Even though he maintained a presence at the Foundation headquarters, it was now for infiltration purposes only. Dean's focus for the future consisted of getting first dibs on which Hawaiian island he would call his own after Nicholas was out of the picture and the entire world transformed.

****

Vivien's eyes snapped open.

Nicholas had willingly connected with the demon. She knew he'd kept details hidden from her the first night they met.

Ruminating on the scene of her most vivid dream ever—six men referred to a benefactor. Vivien knew of whom they discussed—Dagda. Nicholas was not aware of Dean and his men crouched in a tight dark space conducting a clandestine meeting. They'd broken off, and Dagda now led them on his own. The demon must have gotten stronger to elude Nicholas's psychic detection. Either way, she now had leverage for the next time Nicholas got into her head. In fact, since Dagda blocked her, Dean and his unsuspecting guys would supply much-needed information. Vivien also knew they referred to her as the woman to keep an eye on, but anxiety didn't even enter her body. They had brawn on their side, but intuitively she knew them to be amateurs. Vivien's lips curved in triumph. She would now acquire vital data to hunt down and vanquish Dagda forever.

Turning on her side, Vivien gazed at Neal's peaceful slumbering face against a white pillow. Strands of reddish-brown rested upon his brow, and she imagined him as a young boy while gently raking his hair back with her fingers.

Stirring, Neal kissed her hand and pulled her close.

****

Vivien and Neal walked through the door of Java Hut, their favorite coffee house. They discovered they were both friends with Matt Johnson, the owner, but never knew.

"I would have stopped and stared if I'd seen you in here," Vivien told Neal with a glint in her eye.

"And I would have stared right back."

Abby, a local high school student and part-time Java Hut cashier, gave them a smile. "Hi, Vivien. Hi, Neal." She waved her index finger back and forth. "Do you two know each other?"

"Uh…yes, we do now," Vivien confirmed with rosy cheeks.

Like a shot, Matt ran out of the back room. "I knew it! I kept trying to get you two together, but you both refused me every time!"

"You mean, Neal was…"

Beaming, Matt nodded.

"So, Vivien was the beautiful brunette you kept telling me about?"

"Yes, you idiots!"

A round of laughter exploded from everyone as Matt put his arms around them. "I'm so glad you finally found each other. I guess you didn't need me, because fate stepped in." He leaned back with hands on hips. "But that was pretty psychic of me, huh, Vivien? I must have known something."

Rich chocolate hair tossed as Vivien guffawed. "Yes, you certainly did."

Slapping his hand on Matt's shoulder, Neal winked at her. "Say, Matt, you want to go ghost hunting with Vivien next time?"

Matt rolled with deep laughter. "No, I'm not ready for that, but now that I have you in my corner, can you help me convince this lovely lady to try surfing?"

Vivien's palm smacked upon her forehead with a moan. Matt asked the same question at least once a week. One day she would surprise him by arriving in full wet suit, with a brand-new surfboard hoisted under her arm.

"No worries. I'll take care of that." Neal grinned.

Matt snorted and went behind the counter. "Oh, this is a happy day! A happy day!"

Vivien laughed even harder. "I love him!"

"Me, too. I'll order for us."

"Okay." She sat at a free table.

Checking on Neal's progress with their order, Vivien's gaze landed on Josh, another local high school student and part-time barista. Sun-bleached hair flopped down as he prepared their drinks while listening intently to surf conditions from his cell phone on the counter.

Then, she caught sight of a magazine cover held by a man in line. Above what used to be white sands of the Sahara, hovered a black mass of clouds.

Blood stirred within, yet her body became utterly

still, as if entering a new energy field. Quickly, Vivien snapped her gaze from the image. Remembering what Katherine taught her, she executed slow, meditative breaths to calm down. Every time Vivien saw the Dark Matter Phenomenon, a title created by the media, her reaction got worse. The darkness pulled and repelled at the same time.

Neal took her hands in his as he sat. She jerked away sharply.

"Everything okay?" he asked, eyes wide with concern.

Stretching her muscles, Vivien pushed out the sinister waves of energy as fast as she could. "Yeah, sorry."

Abby smacked their coffees down on the small round table with a wink.

"One hazelnut and one mocha."

"Thanks, Abby." Vivien reached for her warm cup of hazelnut while the young cashier walked away.

"I think Abby is happy we're together." Neal smiled, lifting his coffee to his lips. "All right. Tomorrow is the Fourth of July. How do you want to celebrate?"

"I was going to swing by a friend's party in the early afternoon. Will you come with me?"

"How about this—I come with you to your friend's party. Then, we continue on to John's party, where he has a fabulous view of fireworks."

Neal gave her a peck on the lips. "Done."

"But that's only after we watch the parade in the morning. Have you seen it?"

He shook his head side to side before taking a sip of mocha. "No."

Vivien pointed out the window. "It comes right down Main Street. They throw out candy to the kids, drive antique cars, and the librarians push decorated book carts in a synchronized dance. It's so fun!"

"I can't wait." Neal smiled widely, reaching for her hand.

Weaving her fingers through his, Vivien lingered in the passion of his eyes. Something about Neal ran deep within her. She figured it must be new love, even though he felt like old love. Vivien brushed his lips softly with her own, not able to hold back.

"Careful," Neal crooned. "You don't want to start anything here we can't finish."

"True," she concurred, on a deep husky laugh.

Did you have fun last night?

A hair-raising pant escaped Vivien's lips as she pulled her hand back, nearly spilling her coffee. *Leave me alone!* Closing her eyes, she held her head in her palms. Neal repeatedly asked what happened, but she had to concentrate.

Please, Nicholas. I'm sorry for what I did.

No, you're not.

We need to talk again, but not now.

I won't be available.

Before you come into my house, make sure your own house is clean.

At that, Nicholas's energy cut off. Vivien didn't want to reveal Dean's betrayal yet, but at least that would get Nicholas thinking.

Tormented, Neal tugged at her arms.

"Bad energy gone," Vivien abruptly proclaimed, tenderly touching his cheek.

"Huh?" Neal eyed her, half crazed.

"Let's go to the Posh Moon. I need some crystal necklaces." Getting up, Vivien grabbed her coffee, but Neal quickly stopped her.

"Wait a minute. What the hell just happened?"

Perusing the coffee house, she murmured in his ear. "It's hard to explain."

Placing his hand on her lower back, Neal snatched up his cup. "Let's go."

They walked across the street to Vivien's favorite store, but before going in, he pulled her aside. "Tell me what you mean by bad energy. This happened on our first date too, didn't it?"

Vivien lowered her head and twirled a finger around the brown coffee lid, collecting her thoughts. Nicholas would not stop until their battle ended, so honesty became vital—especially since Neal already knew so much.

"It's Nicholas," she confessed, looking him straight in the eyes. "He can enter my mind, and I can enter his. He's jealous that I'm with you because he wants me to be with him."

Instinctively, Neal's arm wrapped around her waist, pulling her close. "Why doesn't he just leave you alone?"

Wanting to change the subject quickly, Vivien switched to the task at hand. "I'm going to make sure what happened to Shawn doesn't happen again. That's why I'm getting white crystals. They possess the absolute power of pure light. I can give one to you, my team, and my friends. I'm going to cleanse and charge them with even more energy, and that will guard us."

Neal embraced her tightly. "I just don't want anything to happen to you."

Breathing in his essence, she relaxed.

"And I want to kick his ass."

Vivien leaned back, surprised at his statement.

"Heaven help him if he comes near you, especially when I'm around."

Neal's face held strength Vivien had never seen before, as if he were fighting for her honor. He looked like someone else for a moment, but when her eyes narrowed, his face changed back.

With an affectionate nod, Neal took her hand and led them into the store. "Let's get your crystals."

****

Gold satin shimmered against candlelight as Vivien stepped onto an enormous Gothic stone patio. Rows of diamonds sewn into her elegant robe glistened brilliantly. Placing her hands between pillar candles lining the edge of a high stone wall, she rolled her eyes at the large gargoyle to her right.

The sun had gone. In its place weaved stunning black clouds. Like an eternal night, they never wavered from their decadent darkness. They called it the New World.

The wealthy elite had been spared subordinate living quarters and the New World Purge, which eliminated all inferior humans from the planet. Those remaining dwelled beneath the castle Vivien and Nicholas inhabited. The citizens addressed them as King Nicholas and Queen Vivien. They lived in what the Old World called the French Riviera. She loved her power, loved her endless money, loved her glamor, and loved being able to do whatever she wanted—assuming it didn't anger Nicholas. Vivien had to maintain some submission, but in reality, Nicholas indulged her desires and she reveled in it.

Voices whispered from the back of her mind. They felt familiar, but so far away. People she used to know? Vivien's head shook from side to side, clearing her brain. She didn't have time for past ghosts. Her massive power had silenced whatever pleas fell upon her ears long ago.

Two strong arms wrapped around Vivien's waist from behind.

Nicholas breathed sensually into her ear. "Good morning, my beautiful queen."

Purring, Vivien inclined her head toward the gargoyle. "Can't we get rid of that thing?" Her voice sounded spoiled and sultry.

He ignored her request as the toxic energy of his kiss came down hard on her lips.

Peering into his eyes, she saw Nicholas, but also recognized someone else. A red haze covered his pupils. Dagda inhabited his body.

Vivien turned in his arms and hoisted herself onto him playfully.

As they flew down the corridor to their bedchamber, her thoughts lingered on her upcoming spa treatment and a dress fitting for tomorrow night's dinner party.

****

Shawn ran at top speed while jabbing her arms into the sleeves of a terrycloth robe over sweats and a T-shirt. When she swung the front door open, Donna burst through in black leggings, flip flops, a long-sleeved blue chiffon dress—all covered with a black velvet jacket. "Vivien upstairs?"

Shawn chased after her down the hall, watching as

Donna pulled out a strange looking plant. "Yeah, she's still in her bedroom."

"Ginger root," Donna explained in answer to Shawn's look of disgust. "It's very healing when boiled. It comes out like tea." Fetching a pot, Donna filled it with water.

A long meow rose behind them. Shawn scooped up the hungry tabby. "Okay, you make your ugly tea and I'll feed Simba." Once chewing sounds commenced from the silver dish in the corner, Shawn gazed upon the long staircase.

"What are you getting?" Donna whispered loudly, stirring with a wooden spoon.

"I'm not completely sure, but whatever nightmare she had—it's bad."

"Yeah, that's what I got too. She'll be down soon."

"I'll make a strong pot of coffee."

****

Vivien yawned, stretched, and snuggled one more time before getting up. But after rising onto one elbow, she found herself caressing a pillow. Where was she? Where was Nicholas?

Her eyes blinked sluggishly as Vivien caught sight of the room reflected in her dresser mirror. French windows leading out to her balcony triggered the memory of Jason standing below asking for help.

As reality set in, her stomach heaved. Pitching the comforter off, she sprang for the toilet. Though she vomited three times, the vulgarity of Vivien's visions still clung to her body.

The shower came next. Ejecting half the concentrated gel bottle into her loofa, she scrubbed at what could not be cleansed. Soap suds flew everywhere. Simmering tears, blended with pulsating streams of water, ran down Vivien's face. Finally, she emerged, wrapping herself in her cream white comfort robe.

When she stopped at the wood framed mirror on her wall, Vivien glared at her reflection. "How could you do that?"

Nicholas and Dagda's plan had been laid out for her if they truly merged together. It was still a possibility, even with Dean's betrayal. But if they believed Vivien would submit to their abomination, they didn't know her at all. She'd die first.

An Irish ballad ringtone awakened Vivien's cell phone, and she knew Katherine also felt her virtual reality dream. After a reassuring conversation confirming her well-being, Vivien promised to check in more often.

Seeing Simba's face in her mind, she hurried down the stairs to feed him.

"We know something's wrong. Please tell us. We promise not to tell the team, and we know you're scared," Donna declared with luminous eyes. She stood next to Shawn at the foot of the staircase.

Vivien inhaled the steaming cup Donna placed into her hands with a grateful sigh. "Ginger. Good for the stomach. Thank you."

****

A morning fog bank rolled in, just enough to add a slight chill to the air. When it burned away in a few hours, Vivien hoped for a beautiful Fourth of July holiday. Having donned soft and comfy boots, she sat across from Donna and Shawn in a cobalt-blue cushioned Adirondack chair on her back porch.

Following two minutes of silence, Donna tossed a quick look to Shawn, then snapped her head back. "Vivien, you need to talk to us. We promise everything will stay in the vault, but you can't go through this alone."

Tears ran down Vivien's cheeks unchecked. "I just don't want Neal to ever find out what I dreamt and how I behaved."

"It wasn't real." Shawn spoke softly, leaning her body closer.

Vivien's back straightened with a cock of her head. "For me, it was. I felt it. I felt everything." She took another sip, swallowing hard. "Okay, I'm warning you two—it's very disturbing."

After imparting her visions and the state of the planet, they sat in quiet shock.

Shawn's gaze absently followed curls of misty fog moving over a patch of grass between the porch and the guest house, which she now called home.

Donna stared into her tea.

"You both know this will not happen, right?"

They nodded.

Setting down the ginger tea in anticipation of Donna approaching her, Vivien grasped her hands.

"Vivien, I see how strong you are, and you will stop at nothing to keep this revulsion from taking over. If I didn't believe that, I'd be finding survival places for us to live in abroad and hoarding supplies."

Laughter, the sound Vivien least expected to hear this particular morning, suddenly filled her backyard.

"You two and Katherine are the only ones who know. Got it?"

Donna held up her hand as if taking a pledge. "Got

it."

Vivien crossed her arms with the slightest touch of a smile. "You realize you just gave me the Vulcan hand signal for live long and prosper?"

"Well, whatever—that's good too."

With a deep inhale, Vivien raised pained eyes upon them. "There's a part I haven't told you. None of you were there. Not even Neal. You'd all been killed in what they called the New World Purge. I forgot about all of you, and I didn't even care." Slinking lower, she put a hand to her forehead. "How could I let my friends die? My soul mate? I just can't believe it! Nicholas, with a demon inside him, spoiled me lavishly and I loved it, while people suffered!" Her hands covered her face in tearful shame.

Donna pulled at Vivien's fingers. "Now, listen to me! You are not that woman! Do you understand? You are not that woman! If you were, I could never call you my best friend!"

Eyes distant, Vivien became very still. "I'm not even afraid of Dagda or Nicholas. I'm afraid of myself. If I had that strong a vision, it's possible."

"Okay, so you were a killing machine back in ancient times."

She winced.

"Sorry. But now you are an enlightened, modern woman. Just let all that other stuff go. I, for one, have complete faith in you."

"Me too." Shawn joined Donna, kneeling in front of Vivien.

With her hands clenched in theirs, she released a long breath. "Thank you."

After sitting back in their respective chairs, Shawn

eagerly propped herself to the edge. "You must have some clue on finding Dagda?"

Nodding, Vivien came clean. "Actually, I did get a big clue just yesterday. Some of Nicholas's guys have taken off on their own with Dagda leading them. They were conducting a meeting, but I can't figure out where—someplace dark and tight. Anyway, they also mentioned keeping an eye on me, but don't worry, Shawn. I've already put protection around the house. I even spread salt around the property."

"Oh, so that's the white stuff I keep seeing. I figured that's what you did."

"Keeping an eye on you. Ha! What a bunch of idiots!" Donna laughed.

"We'll just keep plugging away. Something has to break through soon." Vivien sipped the last of her tonic tea with hope in her heart.

Chapter Twenty

Luckily, Vivien's drive up the 101 freeway into downtown San Francisco flowed smoothly. She had to catch Nicholas in his office before two o'clock. He intended to leave town, and confronting him face to face would be the only way to gain information. After seeing what would have happened to Aaron Klein, one of many, she needed to stop the Foundation as well. Since Nicholas refused to answer her calls, she decided to simply show up.

As Vivien entered the lobby elevator of a posh office building, her skin tingled. He anticipated her arrival. At least Nicholas wasn't escaping down the stairway or faking a meeting. Walking through sleek glass doors, she approached the receptionist. A beautiful sandy-haired twenty-four-year old in a tight magenta dress and heels greeted Vivien. With too much black eyeliner, the young woman strived to look older, all for Nicholas. Because she couldn't manage her energy, Vivien instantly picked up that the receptionist and Nicholas had sex about three times a week. She made herself available for him whenever he liked and fancied herself in love. The poor deluded girl. Nicholas used her.

"Can I help you?" She bristled at Vivien's beauty, even in a casual vintage navy polka dot shirt, jeans, and boots.

"I'm here to see Nicholas Williams. My name is Vivien Kelly."

Checking the computer screen, she slanted her head with attitude. "You don't have an appointment."

"It's all right, Olivia."

They turned to see Nicholas filling the corridor entrance with his charming smile, impeccably dressed as usual.

Olivia immediately brightened. "Oh, certainly, Nicholas."

He gestured for Vivien to walk in front of him. "My office is at the end of the hall."

The décor reflected a hip style. Tan carpeting extended the length of the corridor beneath glass doors with shiny chrome handles. They passed ten offices before arriving at Nicholas's door, his being the only one etched in smoked glass.

The room occupied a huge space, and Vivien quickly noted books by billionaire authors on the shelves, framed photos of Nicholas shaking hands with celebrities, and only the highest quality black leather and chrome furniture. She sat in the first chair opposite his desk. "So, people can see inside your employees' offices, but not your own. That way you can see what they're doing, but they can't spy on you, right?"

Instead of sitting behind his desk, Nicholas sat across from her, the leather making a whooshing sound as he settled. "Well, I am the boss." He eased back with watchful eyes. "Have you come to convert me again?"

"I apologized for that."

Observing her, Nicholas sat in silence.

"Do you forgive me?"

His mouth revealed a hint of play. "I'll consider it."

Relief flooded her. Obviously, he'd cooled down since their beach vision and was inviting her back in. Vivien returned his blatant glare. "What?"

"I have a question for you."

"Yes?"

"What are we going to do about this other guy you're hanging out with?" Nicholas waved a hand, as if Neal were an annoying mosquito.

"Yes, I got that you're jealous. You only invaded my mind twice now. You need to stop."

"*Moi*?" With a hand upon his chest, he was going with funny and cute.

Vivien gave him a smile just as cute. "I know you're having consistent sex with Olivia and you don't see me getting jealous."

His cheek tightened, angry that she tapped into Olivia's mind so easily.

"Aren't you being a bit of a hypocrite?"

"Touché." His eyes relaxed. Then, Nicholas checked his watch. "I have to leave within the hour, so what else did you want to talk about?"

"Where are you going?"

"If you must know, I'm conducting a three-day training seminar in New York."

"New York City?"

Nicholas laughed. "No, Poughkeepsie! Of course, New York City! My group is growing faster than we can get instructors, and—"

"And you're prepping the planet for what you call the New World." The words drifted from Vivien's mouth as if in a trance.

Sweeping in, Nicholas took her hands. "You see, only you and one other person knows that, and I didn't even have to tell you. We're connected. We belong together in this life."

He kissed her tenderly, yet seductively. All reason left when Vivien's body recalled long hours of ecstasy in a Roman tent. But before she crossed a line she'd regret, her head jerked backward.

"Why did you stop?" Nicholas asked in a surprisingly sweet tone, leaning his head against hers.

Vivien became aware of his plan. He held back, trying to show his good side because that's what attracted her to men in this life. She couldn't deny Nicholas knew things about her only one other person did—Neal. But there was one big difference—Neal had authenticity on his side and allowed their relationship to evolve naturally. Soul mates weren't always romantic; Katherine told her that. They exist in many forms. Vivien would have been his best, most confidential friend if he would only drop the desire to be intimate.

Sliding further back into her chair, Vivien met his penetrating eyes. "Can you tell me more about your group? I know it's based on your book, but what is its purpose?"

Lengthening his posture with a condescending smile, Nicholas explained as if she were a child. "We have chapters in New York City, Chicago, San Francisco, Los Angeles, and Dublin. Soon we'll be expanding to Paris, Rome, and Tokyo. And that's just the beginning."

Tugging her sleeves down, Vivien hid goose bumps bursting forth along her skin. His group possessed an intensely dark energy, even without Dagda involved. It came from Nicholas and the people he handpicked to run his chapters.

Crossing her arms in an effort to deter creeping chills, Vivien kept at him. "But what is it? What do you teach all those people?"

Rising, Nicholas pulled one of his hardback books from the shelf titled *Foundation for Life*. Grabbing a pen, he signed his name on the first blank page. "Read this."

Grasping the book, Vivien repressed rage at his treating her like an intern. "Thank you, but I'm not leaving this office until you give me your mission statement." The words came from her mouth so crisp and sharp, she stunned him.

Sitting on the edge of his leather chair, Nicholas nodded. "You're right. If you're going to be involved with the group and me, you deserve to know. I help people reach their highest potential. That's it."

"That's it?"

"Vivien, after people take my seminars, they suddenly find the love of their life, get that dream job, and make more money—it's their potential come to life."

Connecting to the vision Nicholas described—a magical energy engrossed her—but not good magic. Each member existed in a spellbound state. They thought they had the things he described, but in reality, they didn't. Believing they lived in success, they actually dwelled in darkness, fear, and servitude to the Foundation. The group's essence made Vivien nauseous, and before she knew it, she doubled over.

Nicholas reached out to her with genuine concern. "Are you okay?"

She had to get it together—now.

"I tapped into the group's energy and got

overwhelmed. That's all." Tossing her head up, Vivien hoped her lie worked.

Drawing closer, Nicholas held her face in his hands. "No worries, baby. You'll get used to it, because you'll be leading the group with me."

In a flash, Vivien pulled his hands off. "Baby? Nobody calls me baby!"

"Okay, no 'Baby.' Note to self." Nicholas shook his head in amusement. "You never cease to surprise me."

Chopping off his head and feeding it to ravenous wolves seemed like a very good idea. Standing, Vivien took his dreadful book in one hand.

Rising with her, Nicholas stood with hands on hips and a smug smile on his lips.

She'd had enough. Barely controlling fury within, Vivien turned on him. "I know you've aligned with Dagda. I've seen your visions for me, and I'd die before filling that role. Oh, and here's another surprise—your right-hand man, Dean, has joined Dagda behind your back with five other key members. They want to overthrow your leadership, take all your established followers, and start their own group with Dagda at the helm!"

His ridiculous glass door flew open and burst into a million pieces with a wave of Vivien's hand as she stormed out. Her stylish boots stepped over shattered glass as employees rushed into the hallway in alarm. When they saw her face, each one backed away without asking what happened.

For the second time, Vivien left him with his mouth hanging open.

She hadn't planned on revealing Dean's betrayal,

but she figured maybe they'd destroy each other. That way Vivien could fight Dagda on her own—but she wouldn't count on it.

****

Slamming her body into the driver's seat, Vivien churned. Nicholas's stubborn nature drove her to near madness, but he thought the same of her. Nicholas couldn't see her side, and Vivien would never see his. Hoping Nicholas's new goal of exposing Dean and his treachery would buy her time, her next task clicked in—keep everyone safe.

All of a sudden, a grin of satisfaction spread across Vivien's face. Calling out to Rhiannon, she shared her plan, one that would banish all dark creatures and stop the torment of innocents, at least until she could defeat Dagda.

Vivien's smile grew as one hand opened the driver's side window and the other thrust Nicholas's book out into the street. She couldn't drive with that wicked energy in her car.

Loud ringing from her speakers interrupted Vivien's favorite song on the radio—a very apropos tune about bad blood. Tapping the answer button on her dash, she exhaled.

"Hello?"

"Hi, it's me," Shawn began. "Oh, my God. What happened? I feel like I'm going to be sick."

The exercise of cleansing her aura had not been a success. "Sorry about the negative debris. I'm just leaving Nicholas's office. I'll fill you in later. What's up?"

"Okay. I'm better now. Anyway, you got a call from a family in Santa Cruz. They had to move out. It

272

sounds really weird, but the mom said there's an entity that looks like a big ugly clown in a black coat, and he's taken over their house."

"You've got to be kidding me!"

"What is it?"

"It's the *bodach*! In Celtic folklore, he's their version of the boogeyman. Great!"

"You mean there's a real boogeyman?" Shawn wheezed in horror.

"Don't worry about it. You're not coming with me."

"No, I want to."

"I'm not putting you in danger again, Shawn. You're not coming."

"Yes, I am!"

"No, you're not!"

"I'm the one with the address in my hand, and if I have to hitchhike to get there, I will!"

Vivien wanted to protect Shawn, but also had to let her make her own decisions. "Are you sure?"

"Yes. If I'm going to be part of the team, I have to face my fears. I just didn't think things like this existed in real life."

"Well, that's our goal—to make them not exist in real life. Call John and Jason and give them the address. They can meet us there. I'll pick you up."

"Will do."

****

Vivien nestled her water bottle back into the cup holder. Shawn's face followed her action and jerked back to stare out the passenger window. After driving another mile in uncomfortable quiet, Vivien's voice rang out. "What is it, Shawn?"

273

Shawn jumped.

"Sorry. I didn't mean to scare you."

Twisting her body beneath black seat belt straps, Shawn faced her. "I need to ask you a question."

"Yes?"

"These creatures…where do they come from?"

"They come from the darkest caves in the middle of the earth. Those regions are the closest to their dimension. They come through the caves into our realm."

Wanting to ease Shawn's mind before confronting another monster, Vivien blurted out a thought. "How's Jason?"

Suddenly all smiles, Shawn looked out the window. "He's great. He's the first man to…"

"I think I know what you're going to say."

"He doesn't want to be intimate until I feel comfortable."

"You're not used to that, are you?"

"No."

"That makes all the difference, doesn't it?"

"Yes."

"I'm glad."

A shift in energy abruptly slowed everything down. No longer did they hear tires meeting the road, the swish of other cars passing by, or airstream blowing past the windows. In matched motion, their heads rotated.

The Pigeon Point lighthouse stood just a mile off the highway atop the cliffs. A dome of black smoke concealed the entire property—the same smoke covering Philip's face in the limousine that fateful night. The blackness warded off everyone. During the day the lighthouse functioned normally with visitors and tours, but at night it became shrouded, as if an invisible cloak fell upon it.

"Do you see that?" Shawn uttered breathlessly, jabbing a finger onto the window.

"Yes. Something is happening there, and it must be connected to Dagda. That might be his dwelling. I'm going to have to investigate and see—"

"Oh, my God. It's gone. Just like that. It's gone."

Like the click of a remote, dark smoke disappeared. The lighthouse once again appeared normal.

As the landmark fell behind them, Vivien spoke up. "I'm going to examine the grounds, particularly the tower itself."

"Don't go there alone." Shawn grasped her arm with desperate eyes. "Let all of us go with you."

"Well, they have daily tours."

"That sounds good. I just don't want anything to happen to you."

Meeting Shawn's anxious gaze, Vivien snatched up her water bottle. "What are you saying, Shawn? Do you see something happening to me in the future?"

"I feel like the possibility is there. It can go one way or the other, but you may be in danger soon."

Relaxing tight shoulders, Vivien stretched backward. "Well, no big surprise there. I mean, that goes with the territory, right?" After she took a long slug of water, her bottle found its home again.

"Yes, but this is serious." Shawn stared and wouldn't look away until Vivien said something to eliminate her fear.

"All right. Thank you for the warning. I'll be

careful."

Shawn heaved a long sigh of relief. "Good."

"Now, let's talk about something really important. You mentioned getting highlights. What shade are you leaning toward?"

They cracked up laughing, and the lighthouse seemed forgotten—but not for Vivien. Dean and his men crouched in a tight dark area magnified inside her mind. The tower had to be their meeting place. Vivien had waited five years to discover how the black mist connected to Philip's death, and her body now hummed at the chance of getting an answer.

****

The house sat beautifully nestled in the redwoods of the Santa Cruz Mountains and had been built in the sixties by a protégé of Frank Lloyd Wright.

Shawn let out a slow breath and undid her seatbelt. "The key is under the mat."

"No one will judge if you choose to stay in the car."

Shawn's gaze fixed on the front door. "No. I want to go in."

"All right, then."

They stepped out and Vivien locked the SUV.

"John and Jason are twenty minutes behind us."

"That's perfect. I have an idea. The *bodach* is horrific, but very dumb. We're going to play this one differently. Remember, I won't let anything happen to you. Just follow my lead."

"What do you mean we're going to play this one differently?"

"You'll see." A sly smile transformed Vivien's face.

Arching her brows to a new height, Shawn followed. "Okay."

After retrieving the key and turning the lock, Vivien marched directly into the living room. "Oh my God!"

"What?" Shawn squealed, lurking in the doorway.

"What a stunning fireplace! I wish Neal could see this. See how the wall curves like a wave and the natural rock brings an earthy quality to the room."

"What are you doing?"

Roaming the space, Vivien's voice projected. "I don't think this *bodach* is even here, Shawn! This must have been a hoax. A lot of families just want attention and they'll call someone like me, and I find out it was all faked. They think they'll get on television."

Shawn followed, her face perplexed. "Shouldn't we at least be burning sage or something?"

Finally, Vivien's arms shot up. "Yep! This was a fake! I bet those *bodach* things don't even exist! Let's go!"

At seven feet tall, the creature did indeed resemble a clown with white make-up smeared across his face, surrounding bulbous dark eyes. The black coat hung low, too big for his huge body, covering wrinkly, gray skin beneath greasepaint.

"Ah…there you are," Vivien murmured softly, facing him head on.

Shawn screamed at the top of her lungs the moment she turned the corner.

With a belly laugh, Vivien winked, gesturing for Shawn to join her in mock frivolity.

In wide-eyed shock, Shawn forced a giggle, sounding like a rodent about to be eaten.

"Ye dare laugh!" the *bodach's* voice, akin to tires over wet gravel, bellowed.

The wind of the monster's outrage blew Vivien's hair in all directions. Annoyed, she put her tresses back into place and crossed her arms. "That wasn't very nice. I just had my hair done at the spa." Vivien glanced back at Shawn. "You'll have to go with me next time. It's called the Journey of Beauty and they do a facial, mani-pedi, and end with make-up and hairstyling. You'll love it!"

Instantly, the *bodach's* horrid face existed an inch from Vivien's.

She didn't flinch.

"Yer beauty shall wither—"

"Blah, blah, blah." Calmly, Vivien smashed the *bodach's* body against a wall with a flick of her arm. It felt so good to have her power back. A titter came out at the sight of the creature twisting under her restraint. But having no time to dwell on restored energy, Vivien got straight to work. With eyes blazing through the *bodach*, she focused on one intention—to banish this creature and all his cohorts.

Shuddering, the monster reacted to Vivien's control but tried to hide it with a snort.

Closing her eyes, Vivien tapped into her Celtic spirit, combining it with her modern soul.

"I am Vivien, and I am Boudicca, and we are now banishing all dark realm creatures released by Dagda! Ye shall go back from whence you came! I call upon Rhiannon, goddess of the Moon, and war goddesses Morrigan, Badb, and Macha!"

Arms outstretched, Vivien circled the living room.

Swirling violet light shimmered overhead,

liquefying the ceiling. Rhiannon descended first, giving Vivien a nod. She glistened in a flowing gown matching the color directly above their heads.

Then a rumbling akin to thunder struck, and three war goddesses materialized beside Vivien, each one bringing her unique power to the circle.

The *bodach* paled beneath his white makeup.

Morrigan, with hair as black as night, flowing sleek underneath a silver battle headpiece and matching silver chest plate, glided forward. Olive skin gleamed with the dust of battles past. Gray eyes locked with hers.

Vivien nodded in recognition, feeling if she stared too long, she would cease to exist. Breathing deep, Vivien mustered courage. Even though the war goddesses were on her side, they still intimidated.

With her hand wrapped around a silver dagger tucked into a leather waist belt, Morrigan nodded in return. Morrigan frequently appeared by a river just before battle, washing bloody laundry of those warriors destined to die, for she knew who would perish and who would live. Her chosen shape-shift was that of a black crow to aid the army of her choosing.

Legend further told of a brief consorting with Dagda, which made Vivien peer deeper into Morrigan's radiant eyes. Smiling ever so slightly, her telepathic reply came instantly—only in his former state were they mated. Now, Morrigan renounced him and would do everything in her power to aid Vivien in her quest. The women shared an understanding as it became clear that Dagda might have killed Philip. Whether or not that theory proved to be true, Vivien too would utilize every drop of power inside her soul to slaughter him.

Macha approached next. Crimson hair mingled

with the blood of conquests fell in thick waist-length curls. A long cloak of rich amber surrounded a golden tunic. The pounded bronze shield Macha brandished bore the marks of combat as meadow green eyes glowed against translucent skin. With a wooden bow in her other hand and a bag of arrows slung over her shoulder, Macha's chin lifted. Instantly two fawns and two bucks marched onto the patio, gazing through the living room window. She had influence over forest creatures and protected them from man as much as possible. Being a nature warrior, Macha honored them. Pledging her faith in Vivien, she cocked her head in admiration. A magnificent falcon came into Vivien's mind, which is the form Macha would take on their day of combat.

Badb struck the floor with a long golden sword—the largest Vivien had ever seen. Her forest green robe fell to the floor with gold brocade outlined throughout. A gray wolf ran before Vivien, giving her a start. Badb smiled, for she revealed what she shall be on the battlefield against Dagda. Badb's shape-shift had assisted many soldiers in the past when time was of the essence. With long, acorn-brown hair, she folded her hands upon the handle of the mighty blade and stared Vivien down. *I honor you,* echoed into Vivien's brain as she gazed into Badb's mesmerizing cobalt eyes. She rode with Vivien while she walked the earth as Boudicca, and pure pride radiated from Badb at the memory.

Vivien suddenly realized they all rode with her in Boudicca's time. History shall be repeated, only this time the fate of the planet hung in the balance.

As for Rhiannon, she already knew which animal

she favored in battle—a stunning white horse. Vivien had dreamt of Rhiannon in that shape many times, knowing the animal to be her brilliant power manifested in nature's form.

Turning around, Vivien found Shawn cowering in the corner. With a soothing smile, Vivien extended her arm. "Come, Shawn."

With eyes as big as saucers, Shawn's head darted between Vivien's new entourage and the *bodach* squirming halfway up the wall, as if not sure which frightened her more.

"You're safer over here than over there, Shawn— now!"

Breathless, Shawn popped up and snatched Vivien's hand. The goddesses circled them as Shawn gawked in amazement. When she began to fear, Morrigan held her wrist, filling her body with vitality.

Fright danced upon the *bodach*'s face like an avant-garde ballet. He tried to dissipate, but the goddesses held him with a Celtic chant. Vivien and Shawn sang with them, the verses flowing out of their mouths effortlessly. The rhythm of the sound came in waves. Each surge charged the energy to a higher level until the whole house pulsated with brilliant deep purple light.

Bursting through the wall emerged the *Baobhan Sith*, the *fear dorcha*, and the *dullahan*. Thrashing in rage, they beheld Vivien, Shawn, and the goddesses, then stopped moving. Their wickedness could not conquer the power before them.

Spinning dots of gold gathered to form a rope, collecting the monsters in a tight bond. After their shrieking ceased—when the ivory shag rug swallowed them whole—peacefulness settled upon them.

Goddesses gathered close and encouraged Shawn to embrace her talent. One by one, they touched her hand, allowing Shawn to see her true self just before each dissolved.

Vivien gazed at the stunning mountains from the living room window. Thanking the goddesses on her own, she felt out of body watching pine needles fall in slow motion from the mighty branch of a three-hundred-foot coastal redwood.

"Oh, my God! That was so amazing!"

"Shawn?"

"Yes?"

"I can't breathe."

"I'm sorry!" Shawn released her from a skintight embrace. "I just got so excited!"

"I know." Vivien smiled gratefully.

"They're gone, aren't they? Those horrible things?"

"Yes—at least for now."

"I thought you banished the first three already?"

Shoving fingers into her back jeans' pockets, Vivien shifted weight. "I did, but I felt their presence resurface yesterday. Now, they're really gone until I kill Dagda."

"Why didn't you tell me?"

"I'm sorry. I couldn't risk Dagda picking up our thoughts."

The front door opened, and John's voice floated down the hall. "Hello?"

"We're in the living room!" Vivien shouted back.

"Sorry we're a little late." John jerked heat sensors off his shoulder in an attempt to choose which one to use.

Close behind, Jason wrapped his arm around Shawn.

"It's okay. I just need you two to check for residual energy. Shawn and I exiled the *Baobhan Sith*, *fear dorcha*, *dullahan*, and *bodach* with the help of four Celtic goddesses."

Jason blinked a few times, shaking his head. "Now there's a sentence you don't hear every day." He glanced at Shawn. "How are you holding up?"

"It was great! Wait till I tell you about it!" Shawn grabbed Jason's face and gave him an energetic smack on the lips.

"Which ones were they?" John's voice blasted, his excitement getting the better of him.

"Rhiannon and the Morrigan."

"The war goddesses! Damn! I wish I'd been here!"

Placing a hand on John's shoulder, Vivien's lips smirked. "I'm sorry, John. Today was all about the divine feminine. It's very strong, you know."

"Oh, I know that." He nodded vigorously.

Pulling car keys from her pocket, Vivien moved toward the door. "I'm supposed to give Neal a call, and I'm off to fetch my purse."

"Can you get mine?" Shawn called out. "Jason and I are driving back together."

"Sure."

John pulled out his EMF reader. "We'll do a quick sweep."

Slipping into the driver's seat, Vivien found a voice mail from Nicholas on her phone. Bracing herself, she retrieved his message.

"I want to thank you for the information you gave

me. You saw something I couldn't. I've ostracized Dean and his group from the Foundation, and they will never be allowed back. I also summoned Dagda, and he vowed loyalty to me—and only me."

"What?" Gasping out a breath, she steeled herself.

"We belong together, Vivien. What is not revealed to me is revealed to you. Can you imagine what our combined energies would create? We could have a whole new world. Think about it."

The line went dead. Vivien sat paralyzed while the pleasant female voice asked if she wanted to save the message or delete. Swiftly, she deleted. Had she made the situation worse? But then, Vivien reminded herself, Nicholas came from ego and greed, and she could not change him.

Attempting to shake it off, she called Neal.

"Hi." His soothing, deep voice greeted her.

Vivien's tension unraveled at the sound. "Do you still want me to come over later?"

"Yes, of course. I didn't tell you this, but I have a weekly poker game at my house, and that's what's happening earlier tonight."

She stretched. "Oh, really?"

"Yeah. I waited to tell you because I know how women feel about testosterone-crazed poker games, complete with cheese whiz, cigar smoke, and beer."

"I assure you, I won't disturb your man cave." Shoulders shook with her chuckles. It felt so good to laugh. Neal's smile flashed in her mind.

"We'll be done by eight o'clock, so if you want to come over at eight thirty, I'll have the place cleaned up."

"That sounds great. We just took care of some

business here in Santa Cruz."

"Anything you want to share?"

"I'll tell you later, but as usual, it's weird and other worldly."

"As usual."

Neal's understanding and humor lifted Vivien's spirit. On a peaceful smile, she said goodbye. After handing Shawn her purse, she returned the house key to its resting place under the mat.

"There's nothing here now," John confirmed.

"I took some shots. Not one orb or mist to be found." Jason closed the front door, making sure the lock took hold.

Shawn tossed her arm up. "I'm hungry! Who's with me?"

They echoed her sentiment as Jason took her by the hand. "We'll meet you two at Scott's Diner just down the hill."

"Sounds good." John turned to Vivien. "Do you know the place?"

"Yeah, I do. I'll call the Bradfords and tell them they can move back in. See you all there." After she notified the family, Vivien glided her car downhill. With one phone call, her Celtic warriors would join her. They waited for her communication even now, over five thousand miles away. But when would Dagda make his move? That's what she needed to know before the battle could take place.

Finally, being clear of lethal Celtic creatures, Vivien sighed. The fact that no more people would be hurt freed her heart, albeit, she thought it would feel better. Instead, a horrible dread tightened inside. Next would be her face-to-face battle with Dagda and

Nicholas. All her training had to come into play, and she could not waver for an instant. One second of lost focus could cause her own death, and in turn, the deaths of everyone she loved. Anger and frustration rose at not knowing when, where, or how Dagda would perpetrate his atrocity. Opening her intuition more than ever before, Vivien prayed for a sign that would give her something tangible to work with.

Chapter Twenty-One

As she pressed the button for her Celtic Woman playlist, Vivien longed to relax. At the end of their brainstorming lunch at Scott's Diner, John, Jason, and Shawn's faces changed when she revealed the malevolent purpose of the Foundation. To her surprise they held up well, ready more than ever to fight. Vivien had revealed the news to Shawn already, of course, that Fourth of July morning, but Shawn didn't reveal her prior knowledge to the rest of the team.

He's creating a new plan.

Inspecting her back seat for rogue spirits, Vivien saw no one.

Listen to me, you jerks!

Looking out her driver's window, there stood the lighthouse.

"It's them! It's Dean and his guys!" Vivien yelled out to no one in particular. Sitting up, she expected to receive more conversation, but only got static—like a radio station tuning out. She needed to discover their plan, especially after making a connection. A terrifically terrible idea struck. They would never guess she'd eavesdrop in person. Protecting herself would be paramount, but their strategy had to be found out. Vivien could wait no longer.

She turned her car into the long gravel driveway, strategically parking behind the youth hostel buildings.

The hostel had occupied the property for years, and Vivien could walk up the trail unnoticed.

The last yellow line of sun burned out under the horizon. Dean's meeting had begun early. Vivien surmised it must be urgent. The warning Shawn gave about danger flashed in her mind, and for a split second, she considered driving away. Still, Vivien had to take advantage of this golden opportunity to discover Dagda's design. She promised herself to be in and out. Pushing ahead with an extra strong protection ritual of white light, she slid her car keys firmly into her pants pocket.

The lighthouse door opened easily, with a musty smell hitting her nostrils. The dimly lit journey up the winding wrought-iron staircase commenced in her new high-heeled mahogany boots. From now on, Vivien vowed to keep a spare pair of running shoes in her car at all times.

Finally, she could see them, but made sure they couldn't see her. Holding tight to the black railing with both hands, Vivien sat on a step and peeked through the bars.

A husky, attractive blond-haired man about twenty-eight led the group. It had to be Dean. A variety of buff men surrounded him—all in their twenties, with most looking ready to audition for the role of Hercules.

"Don't communicate with anyone from the Foundation. That's an order."

"Did he tell you when he'll initiate?" Angelo asked, pulling up his knees.

"Yes, but if you betray his trust, he'll kill you."

Carl tried to cross his legs. "Yeah, we got that."

"His initiation will happen in December, on the

morning of the winter solstice, on these grounds."

Of course! Dagda entered this realm on the summer solstice, so he will initiate himself on the winter solstice. It all made sense.

Vivien knew what the word "initiate" meant as well. Most likely, Dagda would possess Dean's body. He had become more than willing.

Joe shifted, trying to get comfortable. "What about her?"

Everything inside Vivien's body froze.

Dean grunted in agitation. "He wants her alive. He says she's stronger than Nicholas, but I think that's a crock."

"What if she is?" Hutch threw up his hands with raised eyebrows.

Dean threw him a hard look. "That's none of your business, Hutch."

"Okay. I'm just saying."

Suddenly, getting out of the tower felt like a great idea. After all, Vivien got the information she came for. Their battle would take place on the winter solstice at the lighthouse. Now, Vivien could summon her warriors and prepare her team.

Upon rising to descend the stairway, a massive face of green scales blocked her exit, causing her designer heel to bang down hard.

Ye have knowledge of my command. Now—shall we see how strong ye truly are?

Clinging to metal as the sound from her boot echoed through the structure, Vivien's eyes tightly shut, then opened. Dagda had vanished, but he'd challenged her. He wanted her to fight the men huddled in the darkness above.

"What the hell?" Dean's big hands smacked onto the railing as he peered down at her, dumbstruck.

Vivien created the most innocent smile possible. "Am I too late for the tour?"

They all gawked back like dumb creatures.

Not waiting for an answer, Vivien clambered down the stairway.

"Get her, you idiots!" Dean hollered, waving his arms.

A thundering of boots reverberated through the tower as they flew down the stairs.

Hands and arms encompassed Vivien all at once. She bit one hand and kicked someone's leg.

"Ouch!" Joe screamed.

"Shit!" Hutch snarled.

With laser-beam focus, Vivien tried flinging them out of her path, but something pushed back on her power. She wasn't surprised. It was Dagda.

Dean's thugs got her to the top of the stairs, smashing her against the magnificent lens stored there. One man on each side held her arms back. Usually Vivien would have flattened them, but with the demon's power on their side they had an advantage.

Dean approached with a swagger. "Well...It's the famous Vivien Kelly!"

Staring calmly with eyes of seething ice, she gathered all her energy for the coming attack. Even though Dagda gridlocked her invisible forces, she still had physical strength.

"Dagda calls you a modern-day sorceress." Dean shook his head with a sneer. "I don't see it." When Vivien didn't take the bait, he leisurely clasped his hands behind his back. "Okay, so we can't kill you, but we can threaten you. We know who your friends are."

"Oh, that's intelligent, Dean." Her voice purred, coolly.

His face showed shock that Vivien knew his name, and he faltered and unclasped his hands.

"If you dare touch any of my friends, you can tell Dagda I'll never be his." The quiet potency of Vivien's demeanor sent a tremor down Dean's spine.

"We can't kill you, but we can beat you!" Dean bellowed, like an exploding car radiator, overheated and furious. He pulled a fist back to pummel her face.

Before his hand made contact, Vivien's legs shot up and pounded him in the chest. The men holding her arms actually helped that maneuver happen. Dean flew back against the windows as if hit by a tornado, sliding down to the floor with a pathetic thud.

"Holy shit!" Angelo stammered with a huge grin.

The men gaped in awe, letting her go. Then they turned against her.

"Bitch!" Dean clambered up.

Vivien attacked again. The only problem remained with the tightness of the space. She never imagined herself fighting off six men at the top of a lighthouse and without her telekinesis. They were getting their shots in, but she kept going, kicking all their asses.

Tired of playing under Dagda's rules, Vivien finally called out to Boudicca, allowing her to rise up inside. Suddenly, Dagda's hold on her released.

"Ha!" Vivien laughed as she pushed away the demon's followers with a flick of her wrist.

As they clung to railings lest they fall, their fearful gazes took her in anew.

"That will show you idiots!" Revolving around to

taunt them again, her foot stumbled over a loose bearing on the floor. Before Vivien could recover, Hutch seized her arm.

"That's it!" Hutch opened the door to a small balcony. Being the strongest of the bunch, he pushed the other men out of the way, ignoring their protests.

The fierce rebound broke them apart as Vivien blasted Hutch backward with a wave of her right arm. While Hutch landed inside, Vivien's body flew out over the balcony railing.

"You dumb fucking bastard!" Dean yelled as Vivien soared through the air.

As she fell through empty space, time halted. Swirling white foam pounded against the jagged rocks below.

Rhiannon swiftly entered her essence. *Grab the bars, Vivien. Grab them now.*

Very clearly, Vivien saw two steel bars even as her body hovered. Steadily grasping them below the railing, her boot heels smacked against the tower wall. Vivien swung in the mighty wind like a rag doll on the end of a fishing line. The location of the lighthouse already had a reputation for being a windy spot, but being at the top of the tower made the wind factor even more dangerous.

Voices sounded in the distance, but the only noise pounding in Vivien's ears came from the ocean. Horrified, she imagined herself falling, then pushed that thought away. She climbed up, but a massive wind pushed her back. She froze in panic. What could keep her from surrendering to sheer terror? Neal. She thought about Neal. Vivien thought about how sorry she was. Her ego got the best of her and instead of taking a tour with her team, she showed up by herself. Now her life hung in the balance—literally—just when she'd begun a second chance at love.

Neal! I'm sorry. Please help me!

Vivien didn't know why she called out to Neal, but she wasn't thinking clearly. It wasn't like he could actually help her.

After the men slammed Hutch to the ground, Dean ran to the balcony. Grabbing Vivien's arms, he tried to pull her up.

"Let go of me!" Albeit the survival part of Vivien wanted assistance, she didn't trust him.

"I'm trying to help you, bitch!"

"No one calls me bitch!"

"Fine!" Dean tromped back into the tower.

With renewed strength, Vivien put all her concentration into swinging her leg onto the railing. Her heel made it above the rail on the first try. Heaving herself over the top, Vivien fell onto the safety of the balcony. The drop knocked the wind out of her, but at least she no longer hung from the opposite side. Flat on her back, Vivien tried to fill her lungs with much needed oxygen. A hoarse whisper rose from her throat. "Thanks, Rhiannon."

Still reeling, Vivien's body rose up as if by itself.

"Just a little something to remember us by." All of a sudden, a hand covered the back of her neck. After smashing Vivien's head into the windowpane, Dean marched back into the tower.

"What did you do? I thought she wasn't supposed to be killed! You could have just done that!" Angelo cried, pushing Dean against the wall.

"Let go of me!" Moving his shirt back into place,

Dean got in Angelo's face. "Did you see how strong she is? She'll survive. Let's go!"

The stunned men followed Dean down the stairs in eerie silence.

Vivien's mind shut off as she heard them stomp down the staircase.

****

Neal threw a chip on the poker table. "I'll raise you."

Cigar smoke hung in the air as each man searched the expressions of the other players.

George laughed. "He's bluffing."

"I don't know. He looks like he means business," Don observed, blowing out a puff.

"Vivien?" Neal suddenly blurted, looking around the den.

His friends burst out laughing.

"He can't stop thinking about her for five minutes!" Ben rasped, choking on his cigar.

Guffaws filled the room.

Barely aware of their mocking, Neal's hairs flared up on the back of his neck. He could have sworn he heard Vivien call his name.

Something had to be wrong.

Pitching his cards on the table, Neal stood. "I fold."

His buddies protested, accusing him of being at Vivien's beck and call way too soon.

Once in the kitchen, Neal tried Vivien's cell. No answer—then voice mail. Next, he called Jason, grateful he got his number to photograph a house, Neal had just completed.

"Hello?"

"Jason, it's Neal. Is Vivien with you?"

"Oh, hi…uh, no. Hang on." Muffled noises emitted from his phone.

"Neal, I thought she was with you?" Shawn squawked urgently.

"No. She's not coming over till later, but I have a feeling something's wrong."

"Just a second. Don't talk."

After a pause, Shawn's voice boomed out of the phone. "Oh, God!"

"What?"

"She's at the lighthouse."

"You mean, Pigeon Point lighthouse?"

"Yes. We were supposed to go as a group, but she must have sensed something. I just saw a guy push her into a window, and she hit her head. I think Vivien's knocked out."

Neal's world went still, as if someone clicked the pause button. But the thought of Vivien in trouble swiftly got him back to reality. "I'm leaving right now."

"We'll meet you there."

Neal grabbed his keys and leaned in the doorway for exactly two seconds. "Lock up when you leave."

Flying out of the house, he left his friends shaking their heads.

"Boy, he's got it bad." Don sighed, as George dealt a new hand.

Dialing his buddy Frank on speaker phone, Neal peeled out of the driveway and flew down Highway 1. Frank, a volunteer fireman in Pescadero, would be much closer to the lighthouse. He could bring emergency equipment.

****

"Vivien…Vivien."

Vivien's eyes flicked open to see glimmering stars. As she moved her head, Neal's agonized face came into view. "Neal? What's wrong?" The lighthouse tower loomed behind his shoulder, reminding her of where she was. "Oh, no."

Once she awoke, Neal's expression changed to that of a seasoned professional in the medical field, which Vivien found very curious.

"I'm putting this around your neck in case you have any further injuries. Next, we're putting you into a stretcher." Neal secured a thick white neck brace onto her.

Vivien moaned with regret for what she'd done.

"What day of the week is it?" Neal's hands snapped the brace snugly.

Eyebrows drew together for only a moment. "Friday?"

"Right." He smiled.

Looking beyond Neal, Vivien's gaze fell upon a dark-haired man in his forties.

"Hi. I'm Frank." Frank moved inside to grab the stretcher.

"Frank is a buddy of mine. I've got to get you to a hospital. You have a concussion, and you're bleeding." Neal moved a stray hair out of her wound.

Vivien blissfully stared into his caring eyes with a happy smile. "I love you."

Neal stopped short. "I love you, too."

"I called out to you, and you heard me."

Raising her hand, which sought to find Neal's face, they locked eyes.

Taking Vivien's searching hand in his, he kissed her knuckles. "Yes, I did hear you."

Everything went black again as Vivien's lids shut.

Shawn and Jason soared up the stairs and onto the balcony.

"Oh, my God! Is she all right?" Shawn gasped.

"She will be," Neal assured them.

They stepped back when Frank came out with stretcher in hand.

"Hi."

"Jason, Shawn—meet Frank."

Murmuring greetings with confused nods, they kept out of Frank and Neal's way. Neal placed Vivien's body on the stretcher and strapped her in while Frank belted her legs down.

"You look like you've done this before," Jason said with a raised brow.

Neal looked up from his task. "I used to be a volunteer fireman."

"That's right," Frank confirmed.

Smiling broadly, Jason nodded. "A man of hidden talents."

Chapter Twenty-Two

Nicholas pulled Olivia's arm off his chest and rose from the bed. Processing Vivien's knowledge about Dean enraged him. He'd taken Dean under his wing from the moment he joined the Foundation years ago. Everything that traitor had now came from him.

Donning a black silk bathrobe, Nicholas's thoughts turned to the empire he'd built and now cherished. He'd be damned if anyone would take it away from him.

Sitting in a dark room at the end of a long hallway, Nicholas lit a special candle made of human fat. Ancient legend stated that a treasure seeker who took the candle into a cave would find his booty. If the candle sparkled brightly and hissed noisily, treasure awaited. Dagda, Vivien, and the New World had become his treasures. Whether the legend still held or not, Nicholas had sought out the candle for the power it held. Closing his eyes, he summoned the demon.

Dagda materialized instantly. Nicholas would have preferred to possess enough power to change the planet on his own, but alas, he needed the creature. Noticing scales and green skin flaking off, he suddenly became grateful they would inhabit his human body in the end. Dagda would only last in his current physical capacity until the morning of the winter solstice—hence, the urgency to sway Vivien his way.

Dagda's ancient voice shook the room.

"You failed me."

"How did I fail you?"

"She is stronger." Lowering his mighty club, it hit the hardwood floor with a bang. "You did not know your protégé summoned me."

A tic began in Nicholas's cheek as he took in the truth of the demon's accusation. The fact that Dean had sought Dagda out without his knowledge proved to be a grave error. He needed to turn it all around. Lifting his head sharply, Nicholas spoke with confidence. "That's why Vivien and I will be even more powerful together. What is not revealed to me, is revealed to her. I believe it occurred so you could see the compelling influence of our union. We are the only ones who can rule the New World."

Dagda considered his statement.

"Very well." The demon leered. "Sure'n it will require a sacrifice. Your loyalty must be renewed."

"My loyalty? How can you even doubt…" Nicholas shouted in argument, then stopped. Rationalizing with a demon was not possible. "Fine."

Dagda's gaze shifted toward the hallway and Nicholas knew what he had to do.

Walking slowly into the kitchen, he pulled a drawer open and grasped a carving knife. Holding the knife behind his back, he proceeded to the bedroom.

Olivia raised her arms with a yawn, blinking a few times. "What happened? I heard yelling."

Smiling, Nicholas reached out. "I need to show you something."

"Okay," she answered without hesitation, rising naked from his bed.

Making her walk ahead of him, he led Olivia to the

back room. Dagda had disappeared. Golden shadows from a single candle fluttered upon looming black walls.

Olivia's lips curled seductively. "What did you want to show me?"

Nicholas smiled again, exposing more teeth this time. His hand yanked down a chunk of blonde hair, and her neck jutted out. He sliced in one rapid movement. Gurgled choking sounded distant to him as Olivia's body fell to the floor.

Dagda flashed into sight once more, the timbre of his voice echoing in all directions. "Your sacrifice is accepted."

The candle hissed and sparkled brilliantly while Olivia's blood pooled around it.

Back in favor with the demon who would help him create the life of his dreams, Nicholas raised his head high.

****

Neal sat in an uncomfortable beige plastic armchair holding a hardback book.

"Doing a little light reading?"

Startled, he almost dropped his copy of *The Truth Within*. Leaping from his seat, Neal took Vivien's palm in his. "How do you feel, honey?"

"I'm tired." Nuzzling his hand, Vivien glanced up, eyes at half-mast. "So…do you like it?"

"What?" Neal followed her gaze to the book sitting half open on the chair. His eyes lit up. "You're a very talented writer."

"How does it make you feel?"

The top of his fingers lightly stroked her cheek. "It's been making me think about a lot of things."

Vivien stretched, then pitched forward. A hospital. She hated hospitals. "What am I doing here?"

Before she could make a run for it, Neal grabbed her by the shoulders. "Do you remember being at the lighthouse last night?"

It all came back in a blaze. "Yes! I remember everything. In fact, I need to talk to my team."

When Vivien started to yank the sheets off, Neal pressed her back against the pillows. "Slow down. You just woke up."

"But—"

"But nothing! You need rest." Shaking his head, he sat beside her on the bed. "My God, you're stubborn."

Shyly, she smiled up at him. "You're just noticing this about me?"

A sharp laugh emitted from Neal as he pulled out his cell. "I'm texting Jason that you're awake. He's with Shawn and John having breakfast."

"I have a foggy memory of you putting a neck brace on me."

Neal stared back with new solace. "Nothing foggy about it."

It was then Vivien realized the severity of her concussion had been plaguing him. "You must be furious with me."

"I was. Believe me, I was, and still am. But you can thank your entire team for talking me down last night." He paused, with a thoughtful look. "You know, you have a good group there. They care about you and are still pissed about what you did."

"I know. Let's see if I can gain their trust back." Gazing at Neal, her eyes welled up. "Thank you for coming after me, and I'm sorry for my stupid judgment call."

Pulling her close, Neal held on tight. "Apology accepted. But you have to promise never to do anything like that again."

All the fear and pain she'd caused him came upon her in waves. "I promise. I'm so sorry." As soon as she received his emotions, Neal pulled himself back. The happiness of her awakening began to overcome his previous agony. Vivien carefully felt a gauze bandage on the middle of her forehead and winced.

"Don't touch that." Neal took her hand away. "Only one stitch. I had better tell your doctor you're awake." Kissing her softly on the lips, he stood.

A dozen white roses sat in a vase on her nightstand. "Where did these come from?"

"Those are from Donna and Roger. I sent them a text, too. They have a family wedding out of town, but Donna wouldn't leave until the doctor assured her you'd wake up. Roger told me in confidence that he'd never seen Donna so upset." Neal walked out.

Fatigue set in, emotional and physical. Could she feel any worse for what she'd put her friends through? Closing her eyes, Vivien vaguely remembered Katherine coming to her in a dream—half scolding and half wishing her a speedy recovery.

After a few moments, a doctor entered with Neal close behind.

"Well, good morning! I'm Doctor Johnson." A stocky, kind-faced man in black rimmed glasses, about mid-fifties greeted her.

Vivien meekly replied, "Hello."

"I'm happy to see you're awake." Dr. Johnson grabbed her chart at the end of the bed and reviewed it quickly. "I'll probably keep you one more night for observation, but I need to look you over first."

"Sure." Smiling, she tried to exude confidence.

After going through a myriad of checkups, the doctor made notes on Vivien's chart. "It's just like I said, one more night for observation." Dropping the clipboard back, he thrust his hands into his coat pockets. "I've got to say, you must have a hard head to withstand a frozen ham hock thrown at it." Dr. Johnson chuckled as he exited, shaking his head and casting them an amused glance.

Vivien forced out a small laugh and turned to Neal in utterly confused embarrassment.

Sheepishly, Neal glanced back. "Jason blurted it out before Shawn and I could say anything."

With a big sigh, she pressed back against two white pillows. "Oh, my God."

Sitting on the bed again, Neal spoke softly. "Jason said we were all at his house and his nephews started a tossing contest with a frozen ham hock. You just got in the way."

"My…he must have strong nephews."

"Well, they are on the high school wrestling team."

"Ah." Vivien nodded hard and then touched her head. "Ouch. That hurt."

Neal moved closer, his arms on each side of her. "I am ordering you to rest, or I won't make my special batch of chocolate chip oatmeal cookies." His voice got soft and sultry. "I planned on following them up with an even sweeter dessert, but not until you're better."

Vivien's face flushed, and she knew it had nothing to do with her concussion. "I can't think of any better incentive to get well."

Neal smiled—that gorgeous smile that made her melt—and leaned in to kiss her. "I love you."

Her eyes popped open. Adrenaline rushed through Vivien's system as Neal's face pulled back from hers.

"Oh, God. You don't remember, do you? You said you remembered everything."

"I'm sorry. I think it's actually in bits and pieces." After an awkward silence, Vivien looked up from wringing her hands. "Please, tell me what happened."

Neal cleared his throat, obviously collecting his thoughts. "I was about to strap you into the rescue stretcher, when you turned to me and said…"

"I love you?"

"Now you say it like a question."

Vivien touched his arm. "It's not a question."

"Good to know."

Gently, she pulled her hand back. "So, then what happened?"

"I said I love you too. You also said you called out to me and I heard you." His head shook from side to side for a second. "Actually, while playing poker I heard you call my name. That's when I called Jason, and Shawn got on the line telling me you were at the lighthouse in danger."

Vivien's mind raced. She would praise Shawn for tapping into her energy so quickly, but the fact that Neal heard her telepathically sent a rush of joy through her system. She had not expected that, but then again, he did occupy her dreams for years before they met.

He leaned closer. "Aren't you glad I said it back?"

Looking down at her hands, Vivien nodded. "Yes."

Neal lifted her chin. "So…do you love me?"

"Yes."

"I see, but you can only say it when you're semi-conscious?"

"No, I didn't mean that."

"Hey, you started this."

Vivien blushed. "You're right. I did." Why couldn't she just say the words? Her subconscious could say them, so why couldn't she?

Vivien placed a hand to his cheek. "Thank you for hearing me when I called out to you."

Jason's booming voice exploded from the doorway. "She's alive!"

Her hand dropped. "A ham hock? Seriously?"

"You should be thanking me." Jason's head whipped around, making sure no one could hear them. "I thought it was a great idea. Unless you wanted me to tell them you were trespassing?"

A light smile lifted her cheeks.

Shawn immediately embraced her. "I was so worried about you."

"The doctor said just one more night for observation. I didn't heed your warning very well, did I? But thank you for picking up my location." When Shawn leaned back, tears rimmed her eyes. Vivien held her hands. "Listen, it will take a lot more than a bonk on the head to get rid of me."

Releasing a weak laugh, Shawn nodded. "Just so you know, I drove your car back last night and it's parked outside Jason's house. Simba and I are staying there for now. We just wanted to play it safe. Also, I packed a change of clothes, some toiletries, and brought your purse." She pointed to two bags in the corner.

Jason stepped closer. "Yeah, Neal and I agreed we didn't want Shawn at the house, and also...I'm glad you're okay." He squeezed her arm gently.

Taking them all in, Vivien exhaled wearily. "Thank you, and I need to apologize. I never should have investigated that place on my own. I did get some crucial information, but I know this all could have gone differently. In that case, I wouldn't be lying here right now in this lovely gown." She tugged at the starched white material.

John burst through the doorjamb. "My God, woman! What were you thinking?"

Jason intervened. "You just missed the apology."

"Oh, did I?"

Vivien covered her face with her hands.

Neal quickly blocked John's path. "She needs to heal, and she won't be pulling a stunt like that again."

Vivien let her hands slip down the sides of her face and dared to look John in the eyes.

With the wind taken out of his sails, John moved closer and gave her a kiss on the cheek. "Well, I'm just glad you're still with us."

"Maybe we should all go now and let Vivien sleep," Shawn coaxed, sensing her exhaustion.

"Wait! I need to talk to all of you. Shut the door."

John closed the door, peeking out the small square window into the hall. "You'll have to be quick. The nurses won't stand for this."

Everyone gathered around Vivien's bed.

"I climbed those stairs because they talked about Dagda's intention, and I couldn't get the whole conversation with just my mind. He plans on entering our world in human form on the morning of the winter solstice. I already got a vision of them conducting a ceremony on the grounds of the lighthouse. That's when Dagda will possess a body, and then all hell will break loose…so to speak."

"But hasn't it already?" Shawn grimaced. "I mean, look at the creatures you've banished."

"Those were just a warm-up."

An eerie hush fell over the group. Neal crossed his arms and stared at the floor.

Jason put his arm around Shawn, and she leaned into him.

"Hey, this is good news. I'll fight them that morning with all my warriors from Ireland, and together we'll stop this thing from happening."

John stepped forward. "So, does this mean we're not going to have any more entities show up until they do this ritual?"

"Exactly! They will lie low until he enters our world. Correction—until he attempts to enter our world. We are not going to let that happen."

Shawn sat on the edge of her bed. "What about that Nicholas guy? Isn't he involved with Dagda?"

Vivien saw Neal's face harden at the mention of Nicholas. He instinctively moved closer to her.

"Actually, I believe Dagda has chosen his host. The group I encountered last night broke off from the Foundation, and their leader Dean will sacrifice himself."

"You mean he's going to be possessed willingly?" Jason erupted with wide eyes.

Everyone turned on him. "Shhhh!"

"Sorry." Running to the small window, Jason nodded; the coast was still clear.

"Yes. Dagda will take over his body."

Shawn scrunched her face. "That's gross."

"I agree." Neal placed hands on hips and shook his head.

Someone knocked on the door. Everyone looked up to see the face of Sheriff Andy Harris pop into view.

"Oh, no." Vivien gestured for him to enter.

"Good morning." Glancing at the group before turning to Vivien with troubled eyes, Andy came to the bedside. "How do you feel?"

Shawn got up from the bed to join Jason.

"My body is tired, but I'm going to be all right. How did you know I was here?"

Andy's brows arched with a glint in his eyes. "Really, Vivien? News travels and you should have called me yourself, but at least I'm here now. Also, I'm not buying that ham hock story. So, before I ask what happened, I should tell you that your neighbor Mrs. Anderson called my office just a few hours ago."

A nurse strode in. "Why was this door closed?" She turned. "Oh, I'm sorry, Andy. I didn't see you. How long do you need? She must rest."

"Just a few minutes, Rose. Do you mind if we close the door again?"

Rose nodded, stepped back, and took the doorknob. "You've got five minutes, then everyone has to leave." With a swing of her arm, the door slammed shut.

Vivien already felt the answer with dread in her heart, but she still had to know. "What did Mrs. Anderson say?"

Pulling his small black writing pad out of a pocket, Andy began reading. "At exactly five o'clock this morning, we received a call from Mrs. Anderson, who saw two suspicious men crouched outside your library windows. We sent a car over, but the perpetrators had vanished. Two sheriffs on the scene found a compound used in many arson cases." He flipped his pad closed.

Shawn inhaled abruptly. "Oh, my God!"

"I'm just glad you and Simba weren't there," Vivien declared, on a long release of breath.

Neal, Jason, and John exchanged looks of shock, mixed with relief.

Andy put his arms behind his back. "Now…do you have any idea who the attempted arsonists might be?"

"I know precisely who they are. They're responsible for my current condition," Vivien told him without missing a beat.

Voices blasted as the remainder of those in the room screamed questions at Andy.

Andy held up his hands. "Everyone calm down. I need Vivien's answers."

All eyes turned to her. Vivien smacked her hand down onto hard white sheets. "Those imbeciles!"

Andy cocked his head. "Who are the imbeciles you're referring to?"

Vivien gave him what she knew of their names, along with their physical descriptions. She even told him they meet in the lighthouse tower, but he'd never find them there.

Andy took a pause in his note taking. "Why won't I find them there?"

"Because…"

"Because?"

"They have a strong paranormal force on their side, and he's hiding them. Why do you think the grounds men haven't heard or seen them yet?"

Andy wrote on his pad. "I'll still check out the lighthouse and grounds. Your descriptions do match two of the men your neighbor saw, thanks to your motion-sensor outdoor light. Good idea. Anyway, I advise you not to go home for at least a week. I'll have a car swing by regularly. Is there a place you can stay?"

"Yes." Neal's voice came out a bit louder than intended.

Andy smiled.

Vivien glanced at him. "But Simba has to stay too."

"Of course."

Andy put the pad back in his front pocket. "I'm going to talk to these guys and see what they have to say for themselves." He caught her eyes. "I suggest you file a restraining order."

"Damn straight!" John seconded.

The door flung open. Rose glared at Andy.

"I'm done." He glanced at her compassionately as he touched Vivien's shoulder. "I'll talk to you soon. Get some sleep."

"Thanks, Andy."

Rose continued to glare at everyone else in the room.

Shawn came to her side. "I'll come back tomorrow morning. Feel better."

Jason angled his head toward Neal. "Since you're picking up Simba, you can follow us to my place."

"Okay."

Jason gave Vivien a sympathetic smile. "Bye."

"Bye."

Shawn and Jason left her room hand in hand.

John looked her square in the eyes. "For one day, just try and forget about all this crap and take care of yourself, all right?"

"I will."

"See ya, Neal." His voice trailed off as he cleared the doorway.

Neal waved as John exited.

Alone again, Neal sat on the bed. "I apologize."

"For what?"

He considered her tenderly. "I never should have demanded you stay at my place without asking first."

Vivien grinned. "I would love to stay, as long as you know I'm not moving in."

"Understood."

Noticing the nurse had gone, she gazed at the door. "Hey, why isn't she bellowing at you to leave like the others?"

Neal flashed his brilliant smile. "She likes me."

"What's not to like?"

His smile faded as Vivien felt his energy change. "Seriously, aren't you concerned about what happened at your house? You seem almost unaffected."

"I discovered their secret lair. It made them furious. I think Mrs. Anderson went to her kitchen sink, turned the faucet, and looked out her window at the perfect time. Thank goodness she's an early riser. Also, Shawn and Simba had already gone, safely settled in Jason's house. The sheriffs arrived before they could start the fire, and it's all because I'm being protected. It's a miracle it didn't happen. A perfectly timed miracle."

"I believe you, but it doesn't keep me from worrying."

"Me too, but we have to stay strong."

"You stay strong for all of us." He kissed her, then eased back.

Gazing into his beautiful sea-green eyes, Vivien realized why those three precious little words refused to issue from her lips. Her deep-rooted fear of losing the man she loved still lived inside her like a virus. She longed to heal and needed to take a step toward that healing.

"My parents died in a plane crash on their way to Ireland when I was twenty-seven."

She sensed Neal's surprise at her sudden revealing of her past, and happiness that she shared it with him. Caressing her cheek with one hand, he came closer. "I'm sorry. I wish I could have met them."

Vivien smiled widely. "They would have loved you."

"Likewise." Neal gave her one last peck on the lips. Then, he picked up his book and placed her purse next to the bed. "If you need me, just call and I'll be over in a shot. Your phone is in there, completely charged."

"Thanks. I will."

"Sleep well." Stretching his arms, Neal yawned as he grabbed his jacket hanging on the back of the chair and headed for the door.

"You were here all night, weren't you?"

He turned with one hand on the door frame. "Yeah."

"Now listen to me." Vivien wagged her index finger at him. "I want you to pick up Simba, go home, get into bed, and fall asleep with Simba curled up beside you."

Neal chuckled. "Okay, I will. But I'll be back as soon as I can."

"What about visiting hours?"

There was that smile again. "They don't apply to me." With that, he walked out the door.

Vivien gently laughed to herself, slipping deeper under the sheets.

Footsteps of sensible shoes echoed off the linoleum floor. She moved her head to see the nurse. Vivien got her first good look at her. She appeared to be in her mid-forties, stern, and wise beyond her years, with a kind heart.

"Finally, you can rest." The nurse puttered around the room.

"Rose, isn't it?"

"Yes, that's my name."

"Thank you for your help."

Rose tucked the blankets in around the mattress. "That's my job. You know, your fiancé is a lovely man."

Feeling her eyebrows knit, Vivien began to correct her. "He's not—"

"Oh, now don't be modest." Beaming, she stopped next to her bedside. "I know a good man when I see one, and he loves you very much."

"But—"

Abruptly, Rose grabbed the empty carafe. "I'll be back with more water."

Rose's white nurse's uniform walking away was the last thing Vivien remembered, along with Neal's charming deviousness. He obviously borrowed that fiancé line from the film *While You Were Sleeping*. That warmed Vivien's heart as she fell into a peaceful slumber.

Chapter Twenty-Three

Horselaughs blasted through Java Hut as Matt's surf buddies cracked another joke at his expense. That morning Matt had missed the biggest and most beautiful wave of all. A couple of the other guys caught it and enjoyed an awesome ride. Matt had a reputation of being the best surfer in the group. So, each time they praised the cherished wave, they enjoyed his embarrassment to the fullest.

Matt pounded his fist on the table with a twinkle in his eye. "That's it! No more coffee until you all shut up!"

"Just because you prefer little baby waves, we get cut off?" Mark stuttered, in between chuckles.

A new outburst of laughter ricocheted off the walls.

Ron stood, holding his sides. "Okay, I've got to get out of here, or I'll bust a gut. It's getting late."

Matt, Mark, and Tom rose in agreement as the laughter finally died down.

"Tomorrow I'll make you all eat your words! You'll see!" Matt predicted, wagging a finger.

Filing out, they thanked Matt with a few smacks on his back.

After shouting goodbyes down the street, Matt ducked inside and locked the door. The only one left, he'd already tended to the details for the morning opening. He shut off the lights and made his way to the rear of the coffee house.

From the corner of his eye, Matt caught weaving tendrils of black smoke over his left shoulder.

"Damn it!"

Running back to the front, he went over every electrical item until he felt satisfied nothing had sparked. Lastly, Matt checked the fuse box and snapped it shut. Everything appeared normal. With a tired groan, he pulled on a denim jacket and turned to leave.

Searing hot pain propelled up his arms and quickly spread to Matt's chest.

He involuntarily grabbed at whatever lay close, a small framed photograph of a glorious aqua and white Hawaiian North Beach wave, which he clung tightly in his hand.

A hollow thud echoed through the back room as Matt's body fell to the ground.

****

Angelo made his way up a grassy knoll and noticed Dean pretending to read a newspaper on a bench hidden by trees. Sitting in Golden Gate Park amongst family picnics and dogs chasing Frisbees was not his idea of fun, given the dreadful conversation looming before him.

Wooden slats dipped down once Angelo sat. "Hi, Dean."

"Shhhh! We have to lie low."

Angelo looked up and down the jogging path. "I don't see any cops. Just chill, dude."

"Why couldn't we meet at my apartment? Why did it have to be in a public place?" Dean asked.

Angelo caught Dean's eyes, which at the moment became hard as steel. "Just in case."

"Just in case what?"

Drawing in a gulp of air, Angelo held his breath for a second. "I want out."

"What?" Dean moved in with eyes like dark wet stones. "There is no getting out. There's only getting dead. Vivien's neighbor couldn't identify our guys in the lineup. Dagda made sure of that. This is how you repay him?"

"I wasn't involved in that, so I'm not a suspect. I don't want to be tangled up in his dirty work anymore." Pushing back against the bench, Angelo persisted in a tight murmur. "I didn't know we'd be starting fires and committing murder. I thought the New World was going to be a simple transition. You never mentioned killing."

Dean's brows came together. "I'd hate to lose you. You're a great addition to the team, not to mention the smartest one besides me."

Angelo suppressed a hearty chuckle.

Lifting his chin, Dean actually smiled. "Tell you what. I'll give you twenty-four hours to come back with your decision to stay or go. But when I tell Dagda, I can't be responsible for his reaction."

"I thought we weren't supposed to say his name."

"I can say his name, but no one else can." Looking down, Dean folded up his newspaper.

Glancing up at playful clouds hovering amongst a powder blue sky, a smile came to Angelo's lips. One tight ball of puffed white blended with another, creating a balloon with a ribbon attached. How could he let this beautiful world be covered in darkness? No—he'd made his decision. For his own survival he'd have to join the competition—the Kelly Society.

Angelo pushed off the bench. "Can we get some lunch. I'm starved."

Dean smashed his paper down. "Fine!"

****

Grateful the fogginess had cleared from her head, Vivien sat cross-legged with hands in a mudra. She brought her thumb and second fingertip together in a circle like Katherine taught her. In Buddhist culture, the thumb is identified with natural elements of sky, wind, fire, water, and earth. Breathing deeply, her body felt each element while basking in the orange glow of dawn seeping through window blinds.

Vivien's favorite spot became sitting in Neal's living room in front of the hearth—the heart of the house. Reflecting on her journey of recovery, it had been tough relinquishing her body to a caretaker—namely, Neal. However, by day three she'd relaxed into his home as if she'd been wrapped in a warm blanket after a deep chill.

On a long slow exhale, Vivien closed her eyes.

Bare feet racing down the hall interrupted her meditative state.

"Honey." Neal caressed her cheek. "Are you all right? What happened?"

Kneeling bare-chested in boxer shorts on the chocolate brown throw rug in front of the fireplace, those troubled sea-green eyes peered into hers. Vivien grasped Neal's hand upon her cheek. He obviously felt she wasn't well enough to be out of bed. The farthest she'd gotten was sitting in a patio rocking chair swaddled in a wool blanket. Would that she could go back and redo that fateful evening at the lighthouse. Of course, that was impossible, so instead Vivien would convince him of her recovery.

Silently, she pulled down the capped sleeves of her favorite lilac silk nightgown.

"What are you doing?"

With a finger to her lips, Vivien pushed Neal's shoulders back until his body lay flat, quickly pulling his boxers off and capturing his mouth in a french kiss.

In a cracked voice, Neal pulled away from her advances. "Wait a minute." With composure hanging by a thread, he took Vivien's face in his hands. "Seriously. How do you feel?"

"Wonderful." She slithered out of material and magically molded her body onto his.

"Oh, God."

As she shifted on top of him, her long moan didn't even seem her own as all muscles in her body tingled with heat. Pushing her hips down, Neal grew even harder. Lifting herself up, she felt him slide inside of her. His firm hands grabbed Vivien's waist as their passion made up for the past week's celibacy.

Curling her head onto his chest, Vivien clasped his shoulder blades and surrendered to unbelievable bliss, breathing in his musk scent and loving energy.

A long time later, she lay beside him and sighed. "Now that's what I call good medicine."

Neal's deep laughter blended with her own.

****

"Wow! What's with all the peanut butter?" Vivien shouted toward the hallway after opening a cupboard revealing three jars lined up in perfect order.

With a sheepish face, Neal ducked into the kitchen. "What can I say? I love peanut butter."

Holding the cupboard doors with each hand, she

leaned back and grinned. "Well, now I know what to get you for Christmas."

Neal laughed with gusto. "I'm jumping in the shower."

As he padded down the hall, Vivien called after him. "Wait! Where's your cooking pot?"

"On the bottom shelf to the right of the sink."

"Okay. Homemade oatmeal coming up!"

"Great! I've got chicken thawing out for later, so just leave it on the counter."

"You better hurry!"

Guffaws continued until the bathroom door closed.

Crouching down into the cupboard, Vivien grabbed a thick silver handle and stood.

Air suddenly caught in her throat. The metal pot catapulted from her clutch and bounced off the floor. Her hands instinctively cradled her face as her mouth hung open. Standing immobile, Vivien looked like the frozen figure from Edvard Munch's painting *The Scream*.

Matt stood before her in the middle of the kitchen sink.

"Seriously, Vivien?" He chortled. "I thought you were used to seeing ghosts?"

As she looked him up and down, speech failed her.

Matt followed her gaze and let out a belly laugh. "Holy crap, I'm in the sink!" Moving to the center of the kitchen, he shook his head. "I'm new at this, you know."

Vivien's hands dropped from her cheeks and instantly snatched her waist. "Matt..." She couldn't finish her sentence. Tears burst forth as she huddled into the nearby window seat.

"Vivien, please listen to me. I don't have much time." Matt sat opposite her.

Nodding, she wiped her eyes. "I understand. I'm sorry."

"First of all, don't be sad. I'm surfing every day, and every wave I ride is the best ever!"

Vivien smiled for him, in spite of her chest constricting in despair.

"Be careful! The people who killed me want to control you. They made it look like an accident. You know who these people are, right?"

"Yes, it was Dean and his gang. They killed you because I found their hiding place. I never gave you a crystal for protection. I promised I would, and I forgot. Your death is on my hands."

"Oh, stop the dramatics!" Matt boomed with a big dumb smile.

Vivien's tears halted midstream.

"I didn't tell anyone, but I got diagnosed with cancer a month ago. You know how I hated doctors and tolerated pain. I waited too long. I had no treatment options. So, if I'd stayed on earth I would have gone through a hell of a lot of pain. Don't worry about me. But you—I want you to pull yourself up by your bootstraps and nail these bastards! Okay?"

While her mind processed everything he said, Vivien managed a whisper. "Okay."

Matt's hands smacked onto hers. They felt like vibrating energy. Beaming, he spoke with conviction. "I don't know the outcome of your winter battle. But I do know that I believe in you. You have the power to beat them."

His essence flowed over her—love, confidence,

and strength to get the job done.

"Thank you, Matt."

As soon as Vivien uttered those words, Matt dissolved like a light bulb slowly flickering out.

Upon gazing out the window, Vivien wondered how much more she could take. After she tightened a white terrycloth bathrobe over her nightgown, Vivien buried her head. Tears began anew. Her anguish had been exactly what they aimed for in killing Matt. That sent Vivien fuming. The past week with Neal gave her a taste of what life would be like with him, making her feel cherished and safe. This felt like home. Neal felt like home. That's all she wanted, but Vivien's past life still haunted. All the pain of the present came back to Boudicca's relations centuries ago. If she were just a normal woman, Dagda would have no interest in her. But it had become Vivien's responsibility to stop him from changing the world. Just thinking about it drove her mad.

Neal smoothed back wet hair. He wore shorts and a T-shirt. Picking up the cooking pot, he placed it on the counter. "What happened?"

Standing, Vivien peered out the window but didn't answer.

After seeing her face, Neal pulled her close. "What is it?"

She gazed upon him with a deadpan expression. "Matt is dead."

"What?" Neal wheezed out, on a gasp.

"He appeared to me a few moments ago. We'll get a call from John soon. The same people who attacked me made it look like an accident. Ironically, Matt had been diagnosed with stage four cancer a month ago and never told anyone."

Pushing out of his embrace, Vivien pulled a large knife from the counter block. She stood above the still frozen chicken sitting on a large wooden cutting board and spoke in a strange monotone. "I'll cut this up for you. I know you want to barbecue later."

A vision of Dean and his gang within the Drombeg circle of stones struck her mind. Boudicca slashed them one by one. Blood flew across rocks, soaking into dirt below. Boudicca showed no mercy and did not rest until they all lay dead beneath her crimson-stained blade.

"Vivien! Stop!"

One more remained. She attacked with full force.

Heavy breathing filled Vivien's ears. She opened her eyes, only to find herself on the kitchen floor. Neal straddled her with his hands holding her wrists in lock down mode. The knife lay a couple feet away.

"What the hell happened?"

Neal didn't look frightened, only concerned. "Vivien?"

She laughed in dismay. "Yes?"

After examining her eyes, Neal rose and helped her up. He didn't speak but plucked the knife from the floor and dropped it into the sink. The previously whole chicken, now annihilated into small pieces, covered the kitchen counter.

Vivien's legs gave way, and Neal ran back to her.

A vision of her turning on Neal and the butcher knife flying from her hand with pure intent to kill, surged into her brain. Neal darted from the knife's path, rotated her arm, and forced her down by holding her body with his. It took Neal's entire strength to control

Vivien's shrieking, powerful form. After speaking her name several times, Vivien finally came back to awareness.

They held each other tightly. Pulling back, she cradled Neal's face in her hands. "Oh, my God! I could have killed you! I'm sorry!" Kissing him softly, Vivien wept. "You've been trained in martial arts, haven't you?"

Neal nodded.

"I guess you'd have to, being with me." Suddenly panicked, her body twisted away. "I have to go. I can't be around you. I'm not safe!"

Neal slammed Vivien to the ground again, his face in hers. "If you don't know anything else, know this—I'm not leaving you. I'm not going anywhere, and I'm not afraid of you, even if you can move objects with your mind."

Muffled words emerged from a mask of fingers. "I knew you'd find out. I saw an image of myself killing all those men with a sword, but that's all I remember. I can't seem to control myself."

Pulling Vivien's hands down, Neal spoke with command. "Now—listen to me."

Sniffling, her eyes returned his powerful gaze.

"This warrior energy you channel from that other life—you can come to peace with it. I promise you, if you can balance that power with your own, you'll whip this evil thing completely out of the universe."

Absorbing his words, Vivien let out a long, exhausted breath. "I believe you."

"Matt's murder threw you over the edge."

Leaning her head against his arm, Vivien gazed into his eyes. "How did I ever come to deserve you?"

Neal wrapped her body into a tight hold. "We're more alike than you think."

A half sob, half snicker escaped her. "So—fireman, and now martial artist?"

"Yeah. I'm a black belt."

Pulling her face back to peruse him, Vivien's brows arched. "Any other skills I should know about?"

Rolling his eyes upward as if in consideration, Neal shrugged. "No. That's it."

Soothing herself, she curled into his chest. Then, Matt's friendly face came into mind. "I loved Matt."

"I loved him too."

When she gazed up, Neal's eyes brimmed with tears. He turned away, but Vivien pulled him back.

They clung to each other for what seemed like eternity.

Then the phone rang.

It was John.

Chapter Twenty-Four

The Beach Boys played full blast on the back patio of Java Hut. Dressed in their finery, people danced to the music while others sang along loudly. Mai tais and margaritas flowed, and for those who didn't drink, coffee brewed.

Matt's memorial party fell on the most gorgeous August summer day she'd ever seen. He'd requested cremation—he didn't want to take up space on planet earth. In lieu of a funeral, Matt asked for everyone to gather at Java Hut and party—complete with a DJ, caterer, and bartender. He'd set it up months before. The weatherman predicted clouds, but Matt would have none of that. Instead, rays of ginger sunshine bathed in crystal light flooded the crowd, carrying with it a mystical buzz of harmony.

Vivien knew planning a joyous farewell for his friends kept Matt going after his diagnosis. Matt was a widower with no other family, His friends were his family. All who knew him attended, swarming the white round tables and matching chairs laid out upon the small planked deck. The Java Hut was unable to house everyone, so tables, chairs, and people overflowed down a short wooden stairway into a grassy area surrounded by trees.

Leaning against one of those trees stood Matt, smiling like a blissful idiot. He waved at Vivien, laughing to himself.

Inclining her head in response, Vivien bit into a pineapple slice impaled by a green plastic sword, which she'd removed from a sweating, ice-packed glass of red-orange swirls. After toasting Matt and swallowing the fruity alcohol drink, she edged closer to Neal. "He wants us to dance."

"Who?"

Her glass found its way to the tabletop. "Matt."

Examining the patio, Neal's eyes became giant.

Vivien pointed. "He's by that tree. It's his last request."

"All right." Neal took her hand with a sad smile as they glided to the middle of the patio.

As if in slow motion, Vivien savored wrapping her arms around the back of his neck. Moving to the music while gazing into Neal's tender eyes, troubles fell away—if just for a few moments.

Tom, Mark, and Ron took places in front of the makeshift bar. All in their mid-fifties, they still sported sandy-blond hair mixed with grays, except for Ron, who'd surrendered to complete gray.

The music stopped when Tom stepped forward.

Neal led Vivien back to their table.

"Okay…people, settle down!" Tom shouted with a giant grin. "I know some of you are in your cups, as my grandma would say, but try to listen up." Looking to one table, he pointed. "Hey, Joey! Wake up and drink some coffee, will ya?"

Joey lifted his head. "What? Huh?"

The whole patio burst into laughter as his friends shook him out of his drunken stupor and another brought him a fresh espresso.

"That's better. All right then, since Matt didn't have any family still living, he has bequeathed the Java Hut to Ron. Ron shall continue the tradition!"

As Ron raised his hand in acknowledgment, loud applause, hoots, hollers, and appreciative comments sprang from the crowd.

Vivien rotated her body to face the table where John, Shawn, and Jason also sat. "I'm so glad. I didn't know what was going to happen to this place."

Donna and Roger, who sat at the table just across from them, cheered as well.

"We also have another announcement." Tom eyeballed the crowd. "Abby and Josh! Front and center!"

Ascending from their table, Josh held it together as best he could, awkwardly moving in a three-piece suit his mother had bought for him. Abby, in a yellow summer dress, dabbed away tears with a tissue.

"Matt put something else in his will." Ron held up two white envelopes. "Here are two checks for twenty thousand each to help you both with college expenses." Amidst a roar of applause, he gave each of them an envelope.

Abby wept openly, in contrast to Josh's stunned face.

"Come here." Ron pulled them into a group hug and then faced the crowd. "Oh, and by the way, you've still got your jobs if you want them."

Neal leaned close. "That's wonderful. Matt was such a good man."

"I know." Vivien nodded while a tear descended her cheek.

Passing her a white cocktail napkin, Neal eased his

arm over her shoulders.

She dabbed at her eyes and then reached for her drink. "I thought I was done with tears."

"It's okay." He soothed, in that deep calming tone Vivien loved.

This time Mark moved out from the line. "We have one more thing to do. I'm paraphrasing here, but in his will, Matt said this gift will probably embarrass and piss off the two recipients, but he didn't care. That sentence also had an exclamation mark at the end." He smiled at Vivien and Neal, and then disappeared behind the bar.

Vivien choked on her mai tai.

Neal straightened, pulling his arm off her shoulders. "Why did he look at us?"

"I think we're about to find out."

Mark appeared holding a large white box tied with a thick, silver satin ribbon. Instead of having them come up, he placed the box on their table.

A deafening gasp of joy rocketed from Donna's throat one table over. Vivien darted eyes at her, and Donna covered her mouth.

Mark addressed the crowd once more. "Neal...Vivien—behold your wedding gift from Matt!"

They sat in stunned inertia.

"Also, he didn't want this opened after the wedding. Matt wanted you two to open it here at this party."

The crowd laughed themselves silly to see them in dazed shock. Then, the laughter turned into applause, which escalated into loud chanting of "Open the box!"

Helpless, Vivien glanced at Neal, not sure what to do. Satisfying the restless mob with a lift of his hands, he stood. "Okay, okay, we'll open it." After falling back into his chair, Neal nudged the box over to her. "Open it."

Letting out a sigh, Vivien pulled the ribbon and raised the box top.

Peeking inside, Neal turned to the group. "It's an Italian espresso maker!"

A round of hollers and clapping followed.

"So, when is the wedding?" Tom brazenly probed in a booming voice.

Neal stood again with arms akimbo and cocked his head. "Well, I have to propose first."

To their horror, a round of chanting began. "Do it now!"

Vivien buried her face in her palms, praying Neal would get them out of the situation.

"I'm sorry to disappoint you all, but I won't be asking her today."

Groans of frustration rippled across the patio.

Neal raised his index finger. "However, when I do, you will all be the first to know!"

"But only if she says yes, right?" Mark bellowed with a wide grin.

Another round of guffaws cracked the air.

"That's right!" Neal got out through his own laughter and immediately sat back down.

Ron jumped in to finally relieve them of the limelight. "A toast to Matt!" He raised his margarita. Everyone lifted their drinks as a tranquil hush waved over them. "To a beautiful man!"

Several people mumbled, "Hear, hear." A few guests stood and made their own unique toasts or shared an anecdote. They shed tears, but also laughed.

When Ron made sure everyone had spoken, he switched gears. "Okay—more dancing!" He glanced at the DJ, who got people up and moving instantly. Bringing over two fresh mai tais, Ron draped his arms around Vivien and Neal. "You two earned these. Thanks for going along with his wishes."

"I'd expect nothing less from Matt," Neal proclaimed with a crooked smile.

Ron turned to leave, but Vivien snatched his hand. "Ron, I'm so happy you'll be the new proprietor here."

"Me too." Ron grinned, squeezing her hand before dashing off.

Donna leaned over them, even as Roger tugged on her hand. "Next time, the real thing, right you two?"

"Would you please just dance with your husband!" Vivien rolled her eyes while attempting to hold back laughter.

"Okay, but I can't wait! After all, I'm throwing your bridal shower!"

Roger finally twirled his wife away.

John and Shawn observed from across the table with expressions of sympathy, while Jason tried to hide continuous chuckles.

John's eyebrows lifted. "You two okay?"

"Yes, and I must say you handled that very well," Vivien stated quickly, looking at Neal.

Neal shook his head, but before he could answer, Vivien moved on. "Okay, now I have an announcement. Some of the men I trained with in Ireland will be here in October. By November, the entire clan will be here, so we'll have help by the time the winter solstice is upon us."

"Good, because I have some news for you." John

propped himself up on his elbows.

Vivien pulled her waist to the edge of the table. "Yes?"

"I attended a Foundation meeting last night."

"What?" Her voice came out as a shrieked whisper. "I told you to surf the internet, not go to one of their meetings!"

Jason's eyes nearly popped out of his skull. "Are you insane?"

Tossing up his hands, John stood his ground. "Now, hear me out. First of all, there's zip on the internet. They're keeping it clean. No one knew who I was, and it was a good thing I went. Guess what their mantra is for their opening meditation?" After waiting just enough time to spin their minds, he uttered in a chilling murmur. "Dagda."

Slowly, Vivien's body straightened. "That's why his energy is spreading so fast. With every chapter and every meeting chanting his name, it's like a signal going out into the world."

Vivien eased a bit when she felt Neal's hand along the center of her back. "That's one thing I don't think you can stop, honey. I'm sorry."

Not caring her entire team watched, Vivien softly stroked her fingers along Neal's cheek.

"What is it, Jason?" He had a burning question for her, so she turned to face him and placed her hands on the table.

"On the subject of this demon and his minions...I have the feeling Matt's death wasn't an accident."

Neal locked eyes with him. "I don't think we can discuss this here."

"He's right." Shawn gently touched Jason's

shoulder.

Jason had a right to know. They all did. She pulled her torso over the table, careful not to damage her black knit sheath dress. "Your instinct is correct, but Andy found no evidence. He told me the investigation remains cut and dry. No signs of foul play. On their paperwork Matt's death occurred from accidental electrocution. That's also why Mrs. Anderson couldn't identify the jerks who tried to light up my house in the police lineup. He's protecting them."

"Fucking bastards!" Jason growled with eyes blazing.

John stared him down. "Stop it. Remember where you are."

Neal checked to see no one lurked nearby. "I know this won't help much, but when Matt appeared to Vivien, he told her he'd been diagnosed with late-stage cancer. That's why he had this party planned out."

Desolate faces surrounded the table.

"Gee...anything else you want to tell us?" John asked, after a long, deep sigh.

With a feeling of hopelessness attacking them all, Vivien opted for a pep talk. "Look, the only way we'll get through this is to stay confident and positive. The creature we'll be fighting loves dark, depressed, angry energy. If you dwell in those emotions, you'll play right into him. I'm not saying you can't express grief—of course you can. Neal watched me slash a whole frozen chicken into molecules inside of a minute the day I heard of Matt's murder." Vivien shoved away the memory of trying to kill Neal as well, with a flying butcher knife. "But when we go into this battle—own your personal power. They want us to be frightened, so let's disappoint them."

Jason slammed a flat palm onto the table. "Hell, yes!"

"I'm in." Shawn slapped her hand on top of Jason's.

"I'll be there in spirit." John winked, placing his palm on the stack.

Neal laid his hand on John's. "I'm moral support."

Vivien smacked her hand on top of the heap. "*Dibir!*"

"What is this? A drinking game?" Mark laughed, leaning over their table.

They chuckled as their hands disbanded.

John rose. "Nope, just a pep talk from Vivien on how to chase away spooks."

Mark grabbed his sides with even deeper laughter. "I could use that information."

"I could use some coffee." John followed Mark to the bar.

"Me too." Neal got up. "Let's go home and try out our new espresso maker."

"Sounds good to me." Vivien stood, and then froze. Neal said the word "home." It sounded so natural. After being settled back into her house for a week, she enjoyed inhabiting her own sacred space. But part of her missed living with Neal. As he picked up their box, she searched his eyes. "Which home? Yours or mine?"

Neal's eyebrows furrowed. "I don't know."

"Let's go to mine. I have some cheesecake in the fridge that would go great with espresso."

"Done."

After saying goodbyes, Vivien wondered if Matt had tapped into his own psychic abilities as Neal carried their first wedding gift to the car, even though no wedding had taken place.

Only time would tell.

Chapter Twenty-Five

Neal repaired cobwebs by tucking strands of white cotton fiber back into place around his mantel, then frowned at the perpetrator. "Next time you sweep your arms out to hug a pretty woman, can you not take half the Halloween decorations with you?"

"Sorry, Neal. I didn't even feel them," Tom slurred. He quickly removed a pair of Jules Verne-inspired glass goggles—the perfect complement to his flowing steampunk coat, thigh boots, and nineteenth-century layered suit. "Also, I can't see through these things!"

Laughing heartily, Neal's hand fell on Tom's arm. "Is someone driving you home?"

"Yeah. No worries."

"Good to hear. You know, it's great that you and Mark helped Ron get Java Hut up and running again."

Nodding thoughtfully, a small sigh left Tom's lips. "Ron's gonna do a fine job. We just pitched in during the transition."

Walking away and glancing over the living room, Neal never would have guessed five months ago he'd be hosting a Halloween party in his own home. His life back then consisted solely of work and a few close friends. Neal also wondered how he and Vivien had lived in the same city for two years and never met. But he'd come to realize timing and fate kept their paths apart—perhaps only by inches at times. Feeling a tap on his shoulder, Neal turned.

"So...Ares...have you started a war?" Vivien slapped her hand onto one hip while balancing a full pewter and glass dragon goblet of wine with the other.

Resting a shoulder against the mantel, Neal leisurely looked her up and down. "Not yet, Warrior Princess. I'm too distracted by your beautiful leather-clad body."

Vivien let out a zesty laugh, almost spilling her vampire wine. "Mine's vinyl, silly! So is your costume."

After giving Neal a passionate kiss, she tested his composure by tracing one finger down the center of his chest. Vivien could barely keep her hands off him. Neal knew it wasn't just the wine, but the Ares, God of War, costume. When he first tried it on, she nearly attacked him. The tight-fitting black pants, wide silver-studded belt, coupled with thick silver armbands, and an open-breasted tunic would never invade his closet of normal attire. McGregor's Hollywood friend made their costumes and shipped them out weeks in advance. Even with vegan leather, they looked as if they jumped right out of a Warrior Princess episode. They'd been showered with compliments all night.

With Julie and her friends still present, Neal reminded himself to maintain a PG-rated party for another half hour. He'd recruited his niece and her gang to design all the decorations and had to admit they were the best he'd ever seen. Choosing the theme of a haunted mansion, the living room held a zombie butler offering a bowl of candy corn on a tray, a knight in shining armor, and four framed pictures whose eyes followed guests around the room—all amongst a sea of cobwebs. With light dimmers turned halfway down, eerie darkness and billowing fog from dry ice machines brought forth the Gothic element.

Every time a scream came from the hallway, the girls giggled. "The lady in white strikes again!" they chanted. Thanks to Neal's poker buddy George, whose IT skills surpassed many, the murky hall displayed a projection of a small woman in a flowing white dress. The tiny specter stood in front of a funeral parlor's horse and buggy from the turn of the century. Her beckoning sent a chill through each guest as she pronounced, "Room for one more!"

The little lady in white became a source of hysterical laughter every time someone made their way to and from the bathroom. No one could enter or exit without hearing her sinister message.

Suddenly the iconic song "Thriller" blasted from the patio.

Smacking her goblet onto spider webs, Vivien yanked Neal across the living room. "You have to dance with me!"

"Okay, but that's a long song."

"I don't care!" She ran, while her golden chakram bounced off her hip.

As they grooved to the beat, Vivien cast an eye over the scene. The white wizard—also known as John—tried to execute the song's classic choreography, which sent her reeling with laughter.

Neal shook his head and chuckled hard, following her gaze.

At the end of the song, it happened. Exclamations filled the living room as Brendan, Finn, and Aidan, dressed as warriors from ancient times, entered the party marching through dark fog. They'd brought costumes back with them after assisting McGregor in L.A. with combat training for a new sci-fi trilogy. They swaggered in with leather loincloths, flowing red capes, leather sandals, shin guards, and barbaric-looking spears as the atmosphere electrified instantly.

They thrust their spears forward in unison. "Happy Halloween!"

Booming applause followed. After bowing to their captive audience, Finn plopped a case of Irish stout onto the kitchen counter.

With arms crossed, Vivien glared them down. "Subtle."

Aidan glanced at his fellow warriors. "Aye but look at herself!"

Unfortunately, they had her there.

"Those spears better be blunt," Neal warned. "I've got kids here."

Jason slapped his hand on the counter. "Hey, what about us adults? They can harpoon us too, you know! You guys look so cool!"

"Arrrgh!" Finn formed his best pirate face. Jason and Shawn matched as pirate queen and pirate king.

"I want one of you to train me," Jason announced out of the blue.

Shawn caught his arm. "What?"

"I want to fight with them."

Brendan planted a mighty grip on Jason's shoulder but gazed at Shawn. "No worries, lass. He'll be fine with us."

"Aye." Finn and Aidan agreed.

Shawn managed a weak smile.

Vivien felt her stress. Neal possessed the same worry for her but hid it well. He didn't buy the idea that a demon could control the world, so part of him rested in denial. But in his gut, Neal knew it could be true.

A stillness fell over the kitchen as Shawn's fear became palpable.

Vivien quickly pointed to the banquet spread in the next room. "Okay, guys, there's food on the table in the living room, and we've got pilsner glasses for that stout."

"No need." Finn grinned. Popping cans open, her warriors turned away with brews in hand, leaving three spears lining the wall next to the refrigerator.

Placing the remaining cans on a different counter with the rest of the liquor, Vivien shook her head with a smile. They felt like the younger brothers she never had. In fact, four weeks earlier she had rented the house next door for the warrior clan. The universe conspired in Vivien's favor with the neighboring house being put up for rental just before the first Celts became due to arrive. Between her home and the house next door, they would just fit everyone.

"C'mon!" Jason pulled Shawn out to the patio to distract her with a dance.

"I've hardly talked to you. I'm sorry." Vivien grabbed the arm of Cleopatra as she whisked past.

"That's all part of being the co-host of a party. You miss talking to your friends." Donna hugged her tightly.

"Oh, your reading! Let me do it now before I drink too much wine."

"Good idea!"

"Cleopatra and I are going to your bedroom for privacy."

Neal nodded. "I'll take care of things out here."

Vivien and Donna maneuvered in between the revelry of party guests and disappeared into the hall. Once a year, she gave Donna a psychic reading for her birthday. Since it had already passed, she wanted to make good.

"I didn't realize Mark Anthony wore designer glasses."

Roger gave Neal a sideways grin. "Yeah, little known fact."

"Well, we're off!" Pam whirled into sight with Julie and her friends. It seems she waited too long to stop their candy feast, and now they all needed a tall glass of ginger ale.

Giving his only niece a hug, Neal bent down. "Take care of your tummy. Thanks again for all your hard work."

"I already have ideas for next year!"

"Can't wait!" Neal smiled from ear to ear. Julie truly possessed artistic talent and probably would her whole life, just like her mother. He waved to her friends as they walked out. "I wouldn't have had a Halloween party without all of you!" Fetching his wine glass, Neal and Roger soon got into their favorite subjects of architecture and engineering as the party rocked around them.

A half hour later, Donna reappeared, clinging to her husband's leather armor. "I have so much to tell you when we get home."

"Why don't you tell me now?"

"Okay!" She pulled him away to a quiet corner.

Vivien skimmed the kitchen counters. "Where's my wine glass?"

Neal pulled a new glass from the cupboard, filled it, and placed it in her hand. "There's your glass."

Words hummed seductively from her mouth. "Thank you, Ares."

Wrapping his arms around her waist, Neal yanked her close. "Do you know what happens when you drink too much vampire wine?"

"No. What?"

He nuzzled her ear. "You become a sexual animal, and so does your mate."

Instantly raising the glass to her lips, Vivien took a big slug.

Throwing his head back with a sly smile, Neal kissed her like a man hungry for his last meal.

"Get a room, you two! Or at least go down the hall." John snatched a stout from the kitchen counter.

"Hey, don't talk to me that way! I'm a god!" Neal declared with a dramatic sweep of his arm.

John shook his head. "I knew it wouldn't take long for you to believe your own hype." Marching away, he searched for his lost wizard hat. One of the girls had hid it hours ago, and it was still missing.

Busting up in guffaws, Vivien relished her own ability to enjoy life again. It had been years since she allowed herself to enjoy her favorite season—autumn.

In Half Moon Bay, orange pumpkins dotted along lush green hillsides brought elated anticipation of Halloween to kids and adults alike. The area become known for its pumpkin patches, and people drove from all around just to see them. Highway 92 backed up with cars, descending into an enchanted valley of nurseries, pottery studios, glass blowers, organic produce stands, wineries, and even rust-colored metal dinosaurs, rhinos, and giraffes on artisan display.

Vivien and Neal had already taken Julie to the annual Art and Pumpkin Festival. After having their photo taken with a giant pumpkin weighing in at 1,969 pounds, they entered the haunted barn. Julie insisted on standing between them giggling and screaming the whole way through. Neal drove them back to his house for pumpkin carving as he shared a trick or treat story from school days past. She and Neal's relationship had blossomed over the last few months. It just kept getting better and better.

"What are you thinking about?"

With confidence, Vivien looked him square in the eyes. "Happy stuff."

"I'm very glad to hear it."

Neal's kisses traveled down her neck. That area being highly ticklish, Vivien squealed. Neal loved hearing her laugh, so she knew he'd done it on purpose. After smacking his arm, Vivien took him by the hand. "C'mon. Let's rejoin our party!"

As the evening wore on, they replenished zombie finger sandwiches, frozen grapes masquerading as eyeballs, filled a black cauldron with frozen blood red sangria, and still found time to dance and schmooze. Ultimately, Vivien realized she'd drunk way too much and needed to sit. They were almost down to the core Kelly Society group, and she figured they would go home in another hour.

Just then, Angie, Tom's girlfriend, approached her. "Vivien, Donna said she has one more question. She's waiting in the library."

As Vivien rose from an overstuffed chair, her eyes grew in astonishment. "There's a library in this house?"

"I guess so." Angie shrugged, her grass skirt swishing as she walked away.

Following a sliver of moonlight down the hallway, Vivien found a door ajar at the far end of the house. When she pushed it open, a round-shaped room with built in bookshelves and a fireplace welcomed her. Neal had kept the curtains closed so she couldn't look in. He told her he had a surprise near completion, so she'd forced herself not to get psychic and find out.

"It's a library."

Vivien's lone whisper floated up to the ceiling. No furniture graced the space yet, but Neal had created this room just for her. She could feel his love within its walls. Now Vivien regretted Angie accidentally revealing his gift. In fact, before Neal realized her discovery, she figured she'd better leave.

"Wait a minute. Where's Donna?"

Three bodies slammed into her from behind. A piece of duct tape smacked over Vivien's lips, a large sheet wrapped around her, and someone tied her arms back with a rope. It felt like more than three men—about six.

In slow motion, Vivien fought back, impaired by the wine. Her intoxicated state also slackened her ability to move things, but only for a few seconds. Managing to shove back two of her assailants, she heard muttered curses. Her legs now freed, Vivien landed on her feet. Before her fingers could rip off the duct tape, all six men jumped on her, wrapping more rope around her thighs and calves. She thought she must look like a mummy. Why wasn't she scared? Their intent was not to kill. They wanted to take her somewhere. Vivien couldn't get a hit on exactly where or why, but still fought back. Grunting with effort, they barely held onto her.

Rhiannon's calm voice pulsed into Vivien's mind. *Let them take you.*

What? Are you mad?

Her spirit guide sent solace. *Trust me.*

Vivien eased off, and her body promptly became airborne, thrown into the back of an SUV.

Whatever Rhiannon needed her to experience, it had better be worth abduction.

****

Roger and Donna said their good nights, but Donna wanted to thank Vivien again for her birthday reading.

"Angie, have you seen Vivien?"

"What are you talking about? Didn't you just meet with her in the library?"

"What?" Donna's wispy voice eked out as she rubbed her suddenly clammy arms.

"Come with me."

Walking down the hall, they came up against a closed door.

Angie turned the knob, but it didn't budge. "That's weird."

"Tell me what happened!"

"Ten minutes ago, I saw you in front of this door. You asked me to tell Vivien you had one more question about your reading. Then you walked right into this room with the door left ajar."

"I never knew this room existed, and for the past half hour ,I've been talking to Roger and Neal."

Angie went pale. "Then who did I see at the end of the hall?"

"C'mon."

A Hawaiian hula dancer and Cleopatra burst into the living room, almost breathless.

Before they could speak, Neal came forward. "What's wrong?"

"Where's Vivien?" blurted Angie, like a frightened child.

"What do you mean?" Neal shot back.

They relayed what happened, and Neal ran to his den to retrieve the key. Sprinting down the hall, he unlocked the library door and swung it open. "Vivien?"

Ivory curtains blew gently against open French doors. Neal stood immobilized. Everyone else stacked up behind him within seconds.

"Oh, God!" Shawn screamed.

All eyes turned to the pirate queen. The Irish clan already knew her to be Vivien's protégé, so they counted on Shawn's psychic instincts.

Neal took her by the shoulders. "What is it, Shawn?"

"They've taken her."

"Who? Where?" he shouted at the top of his lungs.

Jason gripped his arm. "Take it easy, Neal."

"We have to know!"

Aidan turned to Neal with a hard gaze. "We'll find her."

"Yeah." Releasing Shawn, Neal raked back strands of hair with controlled wrath.

Jason took Shawn's palm. "Are you feeling anything?"

Lowering her head, she went silent. Suddenly throwing Jason's hand off, Shawn darted to the open windows. "I can't get anything with all of you here. Get out!"

The group slipped away quietly.

Shawn's heart pounded a mile a minute. Fear for Vivien enveloped her, not because someone intended her harm, but because Vivien's soul would be tested. Clearing her mind, she took a deep relaxing breath. That's what Vivien always taught, because panic would block psychic visions. Hoping to help, Shawn projected white light for strength—wherever Vivien now dwelled.

Now more centered, the images came. She could not see the faces of her abductors, but she saw enough.

"I've got it!" Shawn ran back to the others.

****

A jolt of power flashed through Vivien's body. Smiling, she knew it came from Shawn. One more wiggle and her ropes fell away. Her captors' stupidity knew no bounds. They didn't even tie the knots firmly. Now free, she ripped duct tape from her mouth. A big surprise awaited her kidnappers when they opened the back door.

The car stopped. Closing her eyes, Vivien tapped into their location. Redwood trees. Actually, they weren't far from Neal's house. All they'd done is drive up the highway into the mountains. It was a popular spot for hikers in the summer.

Doors opened and shut. They discussed getting her out fast.

Pulling up her legs, Vivien held position. On the verge of executing a Warrior Princess move in her Warrior Princess costume, she curved her lips into an ironic grin.

The door lifted, and her legs shot out. Two guys fell instantly to the ground.

"Shit!" one shouted.

She leapt out of the back, her boots falling firmly onto a large stack of pine needles. They'd pulled off the pavement into an opening in the forest. Staring down a group of mid-twenty-year-old men with strong bodies, Vivien stood tall and tried to focus her swirling mind.

Just then, she remembered a sword rested against her back. Even blunt, the blade of steel intimidated. Vivien reached to pull it out, but it wouldn't budge. The sight of her tugging at the sword stopped the men in their tracks. She couldn't understand why it wouldn't come out. Exploring further, her fingertips felt the safety lock at the top. If she could just get it undone, she'd have a sword in hand. When Vivien's boot suddenly slipped, she swayed, scrambling to keep vertical.

Her captors howled with laughter.

"She's drunk!"

Swinging back the opposite way, their accusation made her mad, mostly because they spoke the truth. Vivien steadied herself. "Hang on a second!"

The men sniggered while she yanked at her sword again. Then they whispered to each other, making bets on whether Vivien would get the blade from its sheath. Finally, as she fell over a large branch, her face made contact with a patch of green moss, which went right up her nose. "Ick!"

Roaring laughs infiltrated the redwoods. Some of the men held their abdomens, while others tried not to pee their pants.

"Stop!" a powerful voice boomed.

A chill ran through Vivien's body.

Nicholas.

His men halted their merrymaking.

Suddenly sober as a judge, Vivien jumped to her feet and willed every fiber of her being to alertness.

"Wait in the car." Nicholas didn't even glance at the others. His gaze stayed fixed on her.

Obeying, they jumped in the SUV, drove about fifty feet down the road, and parked. Obviously, they'd been instructed to give them privacy.

Nicholas's sweeping gaze dissected every inch of Vivien's body. "I love the costume. It's very apropos."

The past few months had changed him. Nicholas's energy used to hold some goodness, but the purity of his soul had diminished from joining forces with Dagda. Maybe Dagda would bring Dean and Nicholas together in the end, but Vivien wasn't sure. Nothing came through clearly anymore.

"What happened to you?" Her voice held genuine compassion. "The Nicholas I used to know—"

"Is gone!"

All of a sudden Vivien noticed he'd donned jeans, a blue T-shirt, and leather jacket. "I've never seen you casually dressed."

Nicholas laughed, eyes glistening at her random observation.

She pointed. "See, right there! That's the real Nicholas!"

Any spark left in those eyes quickly transformed into smoldering blackness. "You don't know the real Nicholas, but you're about to." He took her wrist in a steel grasp.

Every cell inside cried out in danger. Vivien attempted to coax him. "Please, just tell me what this is about. Why don't we go to a coffee shop and talk?"

Without warning, he body-slammed her. Draped over him, Vivien fought back with full strength. Amazingly, Nicholas held onto her while taking long strides through the forest. How did he get so strong? She should have crushed him by now. Then a horrible thought entered Vivien's mind. Nicholas had already attained a portion of Dagda's power. The transition had begun. That's why his strength matched hers. Intuitively he'd been Vivien's equal, but never physically.

Nicholas threw her down ten yards from where she jumped out of the SUV. The second he let her go, Vivien charged, catching him unaware. Abruptly, Nicholas's body crashed against a tree trunk as her arm closed off his windpipe. "You're an imbecile, Nicholas! You could have chosen another path, but no—you had to go with an evil demon!"

Not seeming to care that she began choking him to death, Nicholas glared back with delight.

Vivien released him in disgust.

After a few coughs, he spoke. "I have a gift for you." Extending his arm, Nicholas gestured to something behind her.

Skin prickled at his words. Knowing escape would be futile, Vivien turned, cold dread vibrating through every muscle.

Life shifted into slow motion. Strands of her hair, air in and out of her lungs, the movement of her costume—all elements of reality slowed down. There, duct taped to a tree, stood Philip's murderer and the man who almost killed her five years ago.

"Vivien, I believe you know Joseph Delano," Nicholas announced, as smoothly as if they spoke over

349

martinis.

The skinny, dark-haired man stood just as Vivien remembered. Now he would be about thirty years old. He smiled blissfully at her. Nicholas had drugged him. He didn't want Joseph begging for mercy, so instead Joseph looked happy. Vivien's logical mind wanted to run away and call the cops, but her body wouldn't obey.

Run, Viv!

Philip's last words echoed in her heart. His voice reverberated just as clearly as if he stood before her. Images flashed in Vivien's mind, each one brilliant and real. Shutting her eyes tightly only made them clearer. Splattered crimson blood on his white tuxedo shirt, blood on her hands where she leaned against his chest, and her own heart beating slower and slower until darkness took her.

Rage reawakened, even though Vivien knew the scene before her to be a calculated test of strength. If she could just rely on what Katherine taught her about forgiveness, she could get through this.

Then, Vivien looked into his dead black eyes. The eyes she saw after Philip hit the floor, choking out his last words. Words to save her life. Even after being shot twice in the chest, Philip tried to save her. If it never happened, they would have started a family and been living happily in upstate New York. They'd already looked at houses and envisioned Christmas decorations and sledding with the kids.

Can sorrow kill a person? That question tumbled in Vivien's mind as she fell to her knees in gripping sobs. Tears gushed down her face, but she barely noticed. Not even realizing, Vivien wrapped her arms around her body and began rocking. No thought, no logic, no strategy—only grief.

Someone pulled her hand open and placed cold metal against her skin. Instinctively she clutched it.

Maniacal laughter rebounded off the trees. Who laughed? Slowly Vivien's head rose. Joseph, with his dark homicidal eyes, laughed at her.

A long, desperate scream sliced through the forest.

Lunging, Vivien pressed metal against Joseph's neck. The dagger trembled as her hand shook, drawing a drop of blood. Her other hand viciously clutched Joseph's dark curls, arching his head back. She didn't even remember getting up from the ground or grabbing a knife.

Joseph smugly tittered in her face.

"Shut up! You son of a bitch! Murderer! Shut the fuck up!" Vivien searched his eyes trying to find some shred of remorse, even humanity in his drugged body—she found nothing. The man who robbed her of pure happiness could be gone in an instant. One quick slice of his throat, and justice would be served, and the scales balanced.

In that moment, Vivien knew how easy it had been for Boudicca to kill her enemy as power captivated her body. She felt invincible. The blade instantly became steady as a rock.

"Kill him, Vivien!" Nicholas screamed behind her, losing patience.

Whirling on him, Vivien thrust the dagger in his face. "Keep it up and you're next!"

Nicholas backed away, the blade almost slicing his nose.

Turning to Joseph, Vivien pulled her arm back, ready to strike. Then, her eyes caught blood trickling down his neck. Blood she spilled.

Now images playing in Vivien's mind consisted of Neal and their growing love—tickling each other on the beach at sunset, stargazing from rocking chairs on Neal's back patio. Portraits of Katherine, the clan, her team, and her friends also panned across her personal memory movie. She had a chance for a beautiful life. If she killed this man, that life would be over. Another thought struck—she'd lectured Jason about taking revenge on Dean after Matt's murder, and here she stood inches from slitting a man's throat.

Abruptly dropping the dagger, Vivien stepped back. A crisp thud from the blade hitting the forest floor shook her. She couldn't believe how close she came to destroying everything she loved. "Call the police." Vivien turned to Nicholas, knowing he had his cell phone. "I can identify him, and he'll finally be behind bars for good."

"Are you crazy?" His voice thundered, rattling the leaves around them.

"No, but you are."

Roughly, Nicholas grabbed her. "I brought him so you could have closure!"

"This is closure? You want me to kill a man in cold blood? Well, I'm not the person you think I am. Just because I killed centuries ago doesn't mean I'll do it now!"

"What are you talking about? You had me cringing a minute ago." Nicholas's eyes glazed over. "You possess that darkness, Vivien. Just surrender to it and we can move forward."

"No!" She threw his arms off and shoved hard.

With a face like stone, Nicholas steadied himself.

Yanking out his cell phone, he speed-dialed. "Come get him." After a pause, he continued. "Yes, he's still alive."

"I take it that wasn't the police?" Vivien uttered with a sinking feeling. "Give me the phone!"

Hurling his cell far into the woods, Nicholas pushed Vivien away. "His fate is no longer your decision!" His chin came down as he analyzed her. "I gave him to you as a gesture of hope for our future and you tossed it aside. You've ruined everything."

Vivien needed to know his true motivation. Grabbing his arms, she commanded an answer. "Why did you really do this? I know there's a deeper reason." When Nicholas refused to speak, she shook him violently. "Why did you do this?"

He avoided her gaze.

Vivien could run away, but an uncontrollable urge to hold him overtook her, so that's what she did. The moment she embraced him, he gave in to her. She felt the authentic Nicholas deep down inside and realized he truly loved her. Now, Vivien understood why he'd offered up Joseph. Nicholas believed the only way she would love him back was if she crossed over into the darkest part of herself.

As Vivien inhaled to speak, a powerful vision threw them to the ground.

Chapter Twenty-Six

A weary battlefield ached for peace. Pain, blood, and open flesh poisoned the air. Earth suffered alongside her warriors.

As sunlight slipped away, Boudicca pulled red-stained steel from the torso of a young Roman. By the age of him, he could have been her son. She watched as life left his soft eyes.

Boudicca knew her last day of life had arrived.

A swift gust sent her thick hair in all directions. When she pulled it back, there stood Gaius Marcus Antonius at the edge of the field. Her eyes said goodbye and as Gaius ran to her, she turned. Screaming toward more soldiers, Boudicca would not perish without a final stand. If she died in combat, so be it. If she didn't die in battle, her vial of lethal fluid hung ready under her tunic.

Fury thrust full force when Amergin caught Boudicca's gaze. He'd witnessed the exchange between her and Gaius.

"Amergin!" She tried to reach him.

Boudicca's youngest daughter had been killed weeks earlier in a particularly bloody battle. Now, her older daughter fought proudly with her mother. A large soldier sprinted with his sword ready to pierce. Luckily, Amergin stood between her daughter and the attacking Roman.

Amergin glared at Boudicca, then ducked out of the attacker's path.

Shouting a warning, Boudicca sprang forward, even while watching her daughter die. Blood and fire took over as she charged the Roman who just made her childless. Slicing off his head brought little satisfaction. A dark veil descended upon her spirit. Falling at her daughter's lifeless body, Boudicca clawed at the earth in living horror.

Amergin turned her around. His jealousy, always his fault, jolted him into deadly rage. "Traitor! Making us believe you lead us to glory, when you lie in our enemy's bed!" Like daggers, Amergin's eyes shifted to Gaius fighting against her clan members.

"You killed my daughter! You could have saved her!" After she broke his nose, Amergin fell hard. Swiftly straddling him, Boudicca hoisted her sword above his chest. "I never invited Gaius to my bed! He tried to help us. Gaius hates Nero and wants to leave us in peace, but he must obey his emperor!"

In that moment, devastation contorted Amergin's expression. Holding her by the wrists, tears threatened to shed. "There are no words to forgive me."

"It is too late for forgiveness!"

Amergin's face suddenly changed, glowing with a peaceful light. "If I could take us backward in time, I would love you in a world without war."

To Boudicca's amazement, Amergin released her wrists, sacrificing himself for his heinous act. His courage took her by surprise.

"I love you." Seizing Boudicca's hands, Amergin plunged her sword through his heart.

****

Two bodies lay together on an All Hallows Eve, trying to catch their breath.

Leaping up, Nicholas brushed off annoying tree needles from his leather jacket, sneering with venom. "Why didn't you tell me the truth about your meetings with Gaius? I might have behaved differently!"

Prepping for a fight, Vivien faced him head on. "Right! And you would have believed me?" She shed new tears for a child centuries lost. "How could you let my daughter die?"

"You never gave me a chance!"

Vivien wondered if he'd flee the scene. Then she noticed the tree. Duct tape hung in strips. Joseph had been removed.

An abnormal smile possessed Nicholas's lips. "Since we are now officially enemies, you need some enlightenment. Joseph Delano, a pure junkie, works for me. In fact, I gave him a job to do in Manhattan, oh…let me see…about five years ago." His smile turned poisonous. "I ordered him to kill Philip Bedford."

Pure shock infected Vivien's body.

"Joseph is under my psychic control, but when he almost took your life, I beat him to a pulp."

"It was you who made that noise down the hall in Philip's apartment building. That stopped him from shooting me in the head." Vivien's voice rasped, as she clutched quivering arms.

He pointed at her. "Right!"

"You were the black figure that ran through the wall."

"Right again."

"You also appeared when I arrived at Katherine's

in Clonakilty—but why?"

"I knew you were about to get excellent training from her, and I wanted to do that for you."

Signs of Nicholas's sabotage bypassed her at every turn. Emotions from her former life had clouded her vision, but no longer. Thoughts slashed into Vivien's mind in quick spurts. Nicholas had no knowledge of Dagda's smoky presence covering Philip's face that night in the limousine, or of the chasm she saw as she lay on Philip's living room floor bleeding out. Dagda kept it from him, creating a connection solely with her.

She needed answers.

Maintaining outward calm became vital even as fury tightened, ready to burst. "The blackness I saw in my vision that day we met for lunch was Philip's murder. It took all your energy to keep me from seeing it."

Nicholas's eyes flashed playfully. "Not that much. You didn't want to see it. I suppose, because it would be too painful."

All symptoms of shock ceased. Vivien's heart went from red to black. "How did you find me in New York five years ago?"

Nicholas shrugged. "I lied to you. Dagda and I have been connected for a very long time." With raised brows, he folded his arms. "He saved me from a life of litigation and paperwork. With his help, I found you, and you couldn't marry someone else. I had plans for us."

"You lured those four teenagers to the sea cave that night in Clonakilty. Then, Dagda killed them so they wouldn't talk about what they saw."

"You're catching on quickly." As if giving a

lecture, Nicholas paced. "At that time, I wasn't strong enough to pull Dagda into our dimension myself. But the eager innocent ones are the perfect medium for dark energy. They brought him forth, and he became my partner."

Vivien's body moved closer, akin to a tiger moving in on its prey.

"If you truly love me like I know you do, because I can feel it down in that cold black fucking grit you call a heart, you never would have taken the one person who brought me happiness."

Shifting, Nicholas held his ground.

Boudicca's magnificent cranberry hair rose high on the mighty wind. Romans charged with death in their hearts—death for her. With a cry of combat, she welcomed them—as Vivien welcomed the Celtic warrior queen's spirit. "I know more than you think I do. Are you so sure Dagda is your partner? Think about it, Nicholas. He's playing you. You know what I'm saying is true if you really are psychic like me!"

A piece of brown vinyl took flight as her safety latch erupted. Hard thick steel came into vision as Vivien swung to slice Nicholas open. Her left hand seized the bottom of his jaw in a clutch so tight, one would have thought it could only be removed by surgery.

Never before had she seen fear in Nicholas's eyes. Knowing his chance to live was now in her hands, apologies spouted from pitiful lips. How dare Nicholas beg for life now that he'd unleashed her full spectrum of vengeance. He knew revealing his murder of Philip to be a mistake. The young man with the gun had nothing to do with it. The shooter stood before her.

Dagda's energy departed Nicholas's body the moment Vivien grabbed him, but she would battle Dagda on the winter solstice. That actually made things easier. By letting Nicholas's blood flow here and now, she would be doing her clan a favor.

Bubbling panic replaced his pupils.

Vivien's arm swung hard, but a gentle thought prevented her from finishing the act.

Patience, Vivien.

At first, she believed Katherine entered her mind, but this came from within. Vivien spoke to herself, shoving impulses from Boudicca into a corner of her brain. Boudicca's desire to kill seduced her like a long-lost love, but her modern, rational mind halted all action.

You will do battle with Nicholas soon. Wait for the lighthouse. He must be there to achieve his goal. That is when you will strike him down.

Vivien's fingers let go and like the tail of a comet, Nicholas fled—right into Neal's fist.

Nicholas bounded up the moment his body flattened out onto the ground.

"The next time you even entertain the thought of hurting a hair on her head, I'll be there, and I'll kill you," Neal whispered with chilling calm.

After an expression of bottled-up rage, Nicholas ran off into the night.

Vivien felt her body sweep up into Neal's arms. His loving energy released all tension instantly. Her blade dropped.

"We'll have our chance at him," Finn assured through gritted teeth when Aidan swiveled to give chase to the fleeing Nicholas.

Brendan couldn't resist. "You're a right bastard! Keep running!"

Vivien's pained eyes met Neal's. "He killed Philip."

"What?"

"He killed Philip."

Falling against Neal's chest, her body and mind could take no more.

Chapter Twenty-Seven

On Thanksgiving Day, Vivien's house bustled with excitement. Vivien sought to help with dinner prep but instead sat in bed propped up by pillows. Hanna, Brendan's wife Maggie, and Shawn insisted she lie down and let them do everything. When she objected, McGregor almost hauled Vivien up the stairs.

McGregor, his family, and most of the clan were comfortably situated in the large house next door. Aidan and Finn moved into her extra bedrooms, while Brendan and Maggie took her guest house. Shawn opted to stay with Jason until January.

The only problem lay with Simba, who began turning into a fat Cheshire cat from all the extra treats his precious face demanded. Posting a chart of his feeding times became the only way of monitoring his new admirers. Simba was none too happy with Vivien for limiting his treats, but he still got neck rubs, chin rubs, pets, and his favorite couch cushion to curl up on.

After the incident on Halloween night, Vivien fell ill. The doctors couldn't figure out what strain of flu ransacked her body for over three weeks. On this second day of feeling symptom free, everyone still treated Vivien with kid gloves. They weren't taking any chances. Neal, her team, and the clan cared for her through the entire sickness. In fact, Donna and Roger made sure a stick of sandalwood incense burned in the corner of Vivien's bedroom at all times. The aroma aided her healing process.

Vivien relayed every one of Nicholas's heinous acts—from Philip's murder to the past-life tragedy of Boudicca and Amergin. Her inner circle needed to know the depth of what he'd become, for it would help them in combat. Everyone in thought or deed wanted to kill Nicholas—especially Neal—but they knew it must fall on her.

A week into Vivien's illness, as she lay in bed sipping her third bowl of vegetable broth, a news report came on. A man found lying in a ditch near a local mountain road by day hikers had apparently died of a drug overdose. The face filling the TV screen was none other than Joseph Delano. Nicholas wanted him out of the picture after Vivien refused to kill him. She also knew Joseph's life ended by the time they emerged from their final past-life vision on that Halloween night.

Resting her head back, Vivien heard noises of moving chairs and clinking pots echoing from downstairs. It felt so good to be part of a family again. The fact they weren't actually blood related made no difference. Checking her vintage rose red velvet dress for Simba hairs, a joyous smile embraced her face. Vivien's trusty feline had been by her side nonstop during the sick spell, and his warm purrs comforted her many a night.

Someone knocked on her bedroom door.

"Come in."

A very handsome Neal entered. He wore her favorite hunter green sweater with black pants. Gazing upon his radiant face made Vivien's heart glow.

Sitting on the edge of her bed, Neal enveloped her.

"You're early," she whispered sweetly, lingering in his essence.

"Pam and Julie are coming in their own car. I was sent to bring you downstairs."

With a playful smile, Vivien huffed. "Well, it's about time."

Neal kissed her gently. "Happy Thanksgiving."

Brushing his lips with her own, she lengthened the kiss. "Happy Thanksgiving."

Laughing, Neal pulled her up. "Okay, none of that. Maybe later." He winked. "C'mon."

As she descended the staircase, Vivien's breath caught. Small white lights dangled from curtain rods while her lungs took in cloves, lemon, cinnamon, and allspice berries from hot mulled wine simmering on the stove. A gorgeous autumn cornucopia of acorns, sunflowers, and mini pumpkins flowed onto her cherry wood dining table adorned by a white lace runner. They'd gone to great lengths to make sure she experienced a beautiful Thanksgiving.

Vivien blinked back tears. "The house looks gorgeous, and it smells so good."

Stepping out from the group, Hanna gave her a glass mug filled with crimson liquid. "Here you are, love. Careful. It's hot."

Bringing the spiced wine to her lips, warm bliss streamed into Vivien's body. "Mmmmmm."

Everyone stared back in silence until she could take it no longer. "Okay, please go back to what you all were doing. I feel silly with everyone looking at me."

"Let's go, guys!" Jason commanded, as all her warriors followed him out of the room. He peeked back into the doorway. "I'm teaching them the nuances of

American football."

Vivien glanced at Neal. "I didn't know football had nuances."

He laughed. "Evidently it does."

Maggie held out her hand. Hazel eyes, accentuated by short black hair and creamy skin, beckoned. "Come."

"Okay." Clasping Maggie's palm, Vivien suspiciously eyed Hanna. Whatever they cooked up, she was behind it.

Maggie gestured for Vivien to sit on her own living room couch as Neal leisurely sat next to her.

"Seriously, you don't all have to wait on me."

A matching steaming glass mug of warm wine passed from Shawn's hands into Neal's.

"Thank you."

Maggie, Hanna, and Shawn formed a line. Donna would have been part of that line, had she and Roger not been at her mother's house in Sonoma for the holiday. Hanna wagged a finger at her. "Now, you listen to me, Vivien Kelly! You just became well again from a flu that even your doctors didn't know of. So you are going to relax and be a guest in your own house this day!"

Maggie chimed in. "Agreed?"

"Yes, I agree!" Vivien raised her right hand, as if taking an oath.

"Good!" Shawn turned with a sparkle in her eyes.

The ladies paraded back into the kitchen on a mission. Vivien instantly knew Shawn adored Maggie and Hanna. Speaking of Hanna—Vivien knew her to be strong but never assumed she could take charge. Though, being married to McGregor, Hanna would have to be bold or be run over.

Neal lazily draped his arm around her.

"You don't want to watch football?"

"No, I'm fine right here."

Snuggling into the crook of his arm, Vivien felt as if she'd found a cloud in heaven.

Unexpectedly, powerful emotions of gratitude mixed with past sorrow made Vivien's body tingle. The feelings came from Neal, but he didn't want to tell her what caused his emotional state. He cherished this moment with the woman he loved, but after that, Vivien hit a blank wall. Neal's resolve became even stronger as she got to know him, stronger than she ever imagined. For just a second, Vivien caught a glimpse. A man fell to his knees and wept, knowing the pain of someone's death would never leave his heart. After that image, the white wall came back up. Vivien did know Neal's memory came from a previous life. He must have lost someone he loved very much, many centuries ago.

Vivien's hand caressed his cheek. "What is it? What are you thinking about? For some reason, I'm not getting it, but I know it's killing you inside."

Kissing her palm, Neal glanced thoughtfully. "I worry about you."

"No more worries, okay?"

"Okay."

They clinked mugs and drank.

"Oh, and by the way I never thanked you for my library. Does this mean you expect me to live in your house permanently one day, or that I just pop by and visit it?" Vivien faced him boldly with a crinkled grin.

Neal's eyes locked with hers, hovering above a delighted smirk. "You're welcome, and as for your question—only time will tell."

Nestling closer, Vivien let out an extended, peaceful sigh.

The afternoon blended into evening, and somehow everyone fit among four rather large tables. They ate themselves silly and after partaking of pumpkin and cream cheese pies, Shawn suggested a game of charades.

The diversion of pantomime enthralled them. But later on Ronan had to be disqualified for picking names of Irish ballads the American group didn't know. With very little coaxing Aidan performed those ballads, and after learning the words, everyone sang along.

Upon the final note of their tenth ballad, Vivien became fixated on the front door. Slowly, she rose. Someone approached. Danger and longing hovered. A quick sigh of relief escaped her knowing Pam and Julie had gone home.

"What is it?" Neal got off the couch.

Vivien walked into the hall. "Someone's at the door."

The doorbell rang three times in succession.

"I'll get it." Neal stepped forward. "Stay back."

McGregor anchored himself at Vivien's side with the clan close behind.

A dark form appeared on the other side of the beveled glass.

"Who is it?"

"I need to talk to Vivien. Please let me in!" A muffled voice pleaded.

Vivien nodded. "It's all right."

"You're sure?" Neal's eyes narrowed.

She nodded again vigorously.

Reluctantly, Neal turned the knob.

A dark-haired man crossed the doorstep and then fell to the floor.

Neal quickly shut and locked the front door behind him.

Her warriors instantly circled the scene when Vivien darted forward. Turning the stranger over, she kneeled down and pulled off his padded sports jacket. "What happened, Angelo?"

"How can you trust him?" Neal demanded.

Angelo's suffering face spoke. "I left Dean's group. I mean you no harm." He clutched his waist with a grimace. "Dean tried to stab me to death."

Three surface cuts displayed on his torso. Angelo's white T-shirt appeared red around the marks.

"It's a trap!" McGregor shouted.

"No. Angelo is with us now. He wants to fight Dagda."

"She's right!" Angelo declared.

McGregor set his arms akimbo but kept a scowl. "Aye, if you say so."

Pulling off Angelo's T-shirt, Neal got to work. "I need to dress his wounds. Where's your first aid kit?"

"Sean, it's in the hall closet on the left. Can you get it?"

"Aye." Sean ran.

"We'll only help you if you tell us everything you know!" Finn bellowed with arms crossed and a smoldering glare.

Standing, Vivien threw Finn a weary gaze. "He doesn't know anything. Can you guys get him to the library please?"

Liam and Michael lifted Angelo, but before they

could go, he turned to Vivien. "I was their IT guy. Instead of putting stuff on the internet, I made sure you guys couldn't find anything about us. But I didn't know they wanted to set your house on fire or that the demon was going to kill your friend. They told me we were gonna trash the place as a warning." Angelo caught his breath. "I'm sorry."

"Thank you."

"Dean is planning something new. He was about to tell me, but I screwed up. Is the demon really going to take over his body?" Angelo gasped, waiting for the answer even before his wounds were tended to.

"No. Now my bet is on Nicholas. Dean and his group will be killed. You just saved your own life by leaving. Beyond that, everything is murky. Dagda will only reveal so much, but like I've told my clan, this vision may change. We must be prepared for anything."

"Can you wield a sword?" Liam interjected, in a thundering voice.

Angelo shook his head. "No."

"You'll learn, lad!" Michael chortled as they helped him down the hall.

Neal threw Vivien one last look of concern and trailed behind them.

McGregor tossed up his arm in exasperation. "Are ye sure you're not after getting us killed?"

"I know you think I'm daft, but he's telling the truth. Angelo will have to stay here until battle day or he's dead. But it behooves us to have another warrior. Don't you agree?"

"Aye, but I never thought it would be one of them." McGregor grunted, shaking his head.

Chapter Twenty-Eight

Admiring her beautiful feet, Vivien knew the gold wave pumps showered with diamonds would make her the envy of all ladies at the gala. But then—she usually was. A gold-leafed designer gown already fitted for her complemented the shoes perfectly.

Stifled screams interrupted Vivien's pleasant thoughts. Curious, she approached the window of the exclusive shoe salon. Nicholas didn't want her to go out, insisting the store send their top sales rep to the castle, but after she pitched a fit, he relented. Now, two bodyguards stood at the front and rear doors for Vivien's protection. Upon exiting, they would surround her. Even though Nicholas and his legions had things well in hand, a group of humans incessantly confronted the New World order causing revolts. Beginning in Paris, their movement grew slowly, but steadily. Nicholas worried they might harm Vivien—hence, the guards.

Swirls of blackness covered the outside of the window until Vivien noticed a cape. A businessman standing on the sidewalk yelled, but a banshee covered his mouth with its gray, claw-like hands. Shrieking above the man, the creature scooped him up as he struggled. They disappeared in an instant as streaks of darkness fizzled away.

Vivien wondered what trespass the man had

committed. They called it a "trespass" if a citizen deviated from the established societal rules. They were never heard from again, and no one tried to discover their whereabouts, or they would be taken as well. It became easy to keep obedience that way. Banshees replaced all police and military to keep order in the New World.

Two black-eyed children on patrol stopped in front of the window and bowed to Vivien in honor. There stood a boy and a girl about ten years old. They looked completely normal, except for the black emptiness of their eyes. True evil lived within, and Nicholas only used them for very special jobs. Vivien acknowledged their protocol by inclining her head in return, grateful to be their leader. They gave her the creeps. The other creatures Vivien could deal with.

"Your Majesty?" The clerk approached. "Would you like to see another pair?"

Looking down, Vivien cocked her head. "No, I'll take these."

"Very good." The counter clerk gave her a slight bow and went back to the counter to ring up her purchase.

Unconcerned by the incident outside the window, Vivien moved away. Turning her attention to more enjoyable thoughts, she imagined which piece of jewelry would complement her beautiful gold ensemble.

****

After eyelids fluttered open and Vivien recognized her own bedroom ceiling reflecting a slight orange glow from the fireplace, she clung to Neal's body dry-mouthed and panting. Her dream had been so real,

Vivien felt her toes sliding into those expensive gold wave pumps.

"Hang on," Neal whispered, so as not to wake the household. Nudging her up, he placed a water bottle into her palm. "Take a drink."

Vivien drank voraciously, wiping her mouth with the back of a quivering hand and fell back amongst the pillows.

"Now…what did you see?"

Holding nothing back, Vivien relayed the horrifying visions in his arms, amidst the glow of her bedroom hearth.

Stroking her rich brown hair as golden light pulsed off the strands, Neal remained silent for a moment. Then, he spoke. "It was just a dream."

Embers slowly died.

Vivien edged away from him. Switching on the small lamp beside her, she turned her frozen gaze to his. "You do understand this is real. Everything I saw in my dream will be reality if we don't succeed in two days."

Exhaling, Neal massaged his forehead. "Look, I realize you need to do this, but I can't even fathom it being the end of the world. Can you understand that?"

His words felt like a slap in the face. "You think we're all making this up? I don't understand…When were you going to tell me this?"

"Tell you what?"

"That you don't believe a word I've been saying for months."

"It's not that I don't believe you. I saw a banshee in my own home."

"Damn straight!"

Neal took her by the hands. "Please listen to me. I

know there is something evil out there you have to destroy. I worry about it every day. I wish you didn't have to do this. But I know there's no way I can stop you. I just can't believe it could be the end of our world. I mean, that's crazy."

Vivien's heart sagged into cold dread.

"Are you telling me I'm crazy?"

Neal shook his head emphatically. "No, no. I didn't mean that."

As she sat up in utter disbelief, her eyes expanded. "Not only are you saying I'm crazy, but my whole team, all the clan members, and their families?"

"Vivien…please."

White linen ascended as Vivien flung out of bed, pacing in a strange circle on the hard wood floor. They were never going to see eye to eye on this issue. Intuitively, she knew Neal believed everything else, but his survival instinct kept him from accepting the possibility of an impending dystopian world.

Neal had to leave at that moment. Vivien couldn't have his doubtful energy near her. Every inch of her body, mind, and soul had to center on victory.

She stopped midcircle, Vivien's cream silk nightgown reflecting the dim amber glow of fading cinders. "I think it's best if you leave now."

"I love you. You know that."

Looking down, she could not bear the pain in his eyes. "I just need to focus, and it's very difficult with you here. It's about me and the preparation I need to do these next two days."

Neal leapt from the bed and took her face in his hands. "I wish this was all over and we could begin our lives together."

Wrapping her arms around his waist, Vivien buried her head against his chest. Neal held her tightly. It lasted only a few seconds but felt timeless.

She knew Neal had to force himself to walk away. He dressed and moved to the door. His emotions came at Vivien as a wave of love and rage—love for her and rage for the monster that forced her to fight. Neal stared intensely, as if he needed to remember her face.

"As soon as you've won your battle, we will celebrate. Right?"

"Right." Vivien's voice came out soft, accompanied by a wispy smile.

Giving her the lightest of kisses, he stepped into the hall. Beginning to say something, Neal paused. With warm, loving eyes, he continued. "I'm not saying goodbye. I'll see you in two days."

Vivien clung to the door frame for strength. "I'll see you in two days."

Why wouldn't those three little words come out? I love you.

Starting down the hall, Neal stopped. With a countenance of power, he gazed back. "Honor and courage."

Vivien's lips moved on their own. "Honor and courage."

Moving down the stairway, Neal left her sight.

Shutting her bedroom door felt like closing a coffin lid.

Neal had remembered the words Vivien uttered from Boudicca's memories. How sweet. Instead of reaching the bed, her body slid to the hard floor as tears gushed from Vivien's very soul.

****

The war goddess, Morrigan, in full battle gear washed a bloodstained shirt in a creek of clear water—now running red. Sympathetic gray eyes connected with Vivien's. Slowly, Morrigan lifted the garment to reveal black lettering against its beige backdrop.

Mick Finns Presents
Sons of Blarney

Beneath the heading, she gazed upon the signatures of each band member written with a black sharpie.

The shirt belonged to Brendan.

Images clicked off as swiftly as they'd taken up space upon Vivien's bedroom wall.

After adjusting her eyes, a scene unfolded before Vivien. Rhiannon and Macha assembled at the foot of her bed, while Morrigan and Badb observed her from the french windows—all were outlined against brilliant, almost blinding amethyst light.

Vivien's bedside lamp careened toward Morrigan's head in the blink of an eye. With a lift of the goddess's hand, the lamp stopped in midmotion and slowly lowered to the floor.

Pointing a vicious index finger at Morrigan, Vivien demanded an answer. "What the hell was that? Why did you show me that vision just now?"

"I only show what I see. Warn him, Vivien. That may help."

Vivien screamed inside a hollow whisper, so as not to alert the others. "May help? What do you mean, it may help?"

Rhiannon spoke next. "Battle is battle, Vivien. We must face all possible outcomes."

Nodding fast, Vivien wept openly. "Okay, that may be true, but I'm not going to let Brendan die!"

The goddesses remained silent, yet compassionate.

Closing her eyes, Vivien took in a deep cleansing breath. "Today is the day."

Morrigan and Badb approached the bed, speaking in a synchronized echo. "We may be in the form of a horse, crow, falcon, or wolf, but we shall assist you in time of need."

"Thank you."

Rhiannon zoned in, cobalt eyes twinkling. "What are you feeling?"

Vivien pondered her excitement and pre-nausea. "Fear and courage. Is that possible?"

The goddesses laughed, but they were not laughing at her.

"That is how most warriors enter battle," Macha answered, tightly clutching the leather strap attached to her pouch of many arrows.

Vivien searched their faces. "Any advice?"

"Clear your mind," Badb stressed, her fingers trailing down a shining gold sword. "Be connected to your intuition at all times, for things are not as they seem."

Silently, they glared at Vivien.

"You all know something, don't you?"

Silence again.

Vivien's arms crossed in annoyance. "Anything you'd like to share?"

Morrigan touched her arm as a slice of moonlight sparked off her long silver dagger. "All will be revealed."

A pulse of power warmed Vivien where Morrigan's fingers had lingered. She knew the goddesses could not disclose everything, but that was not the answer she'd hoped for. "Are you sure about this? Are you sure about me?"

Instead of answering, they linked hands and invited Vivien in. She joined their circle and the goddesses proclaimed in one voice: "*Go maire sibh bhur saol nua!*"

May you enjoy your new life!

Their purpose had been to project energy that Vivien won the battle and moved on. As they shimmered away one by one, their supportive power remained behind.

Vivien would need it now more than ever.

Chapter Twenty-Nine

Vivien dressed in black bamboo carbon-wicking fabric from head to toe, matching the blackness outside. She needed full flexibility, and they had to reach the lighthouse before sunrise. Snatching her Celtic blade from where it rested against the wall, Vivien took one last look at herself in the mirror. "My enemies die today, this I vow." Boudicca's timbre joined her voice as the proclamation issued from her lips.

Descending the stairs at a clipped rate, Vivien did not hear the expected sounds of battle prep from the clan. In fact, she faced an empty foyer. Finally, reaching the family room she found them glued to her flat screen television.

"So, you guys thought you'd take in a movie before we left?"

Faces of grim stone met Vivien's astonishment.

"What now?"

Rather than answer her question, the clan moved back. McGregor increased the TV's volume.

"We're getting reports that the same dark clouds above the Sahara Desert are covering several other areas. Antarctica, the South Pacific, and many other locations have been affected. The clouds are expanding at each spot, and at the current rate of growth, the planet will be concealed in twenty-four hours. Top meteorologists are frantically trying to identify the cause. They're asking the public not to panic, as it is most likely a temporary climate-change side effect. One theory is—"

Grabbing the remote, Vivien clicked the pictures off. Tension pervaded the room. This had to be what the goddesses warned her about—things not being as they seemed. Dagda had got an early start on his dark New World. Vivien had to set the tone for the coming fight, even though she flinched upon seeing Bora Bora Island covered in charcoal clouds. They waited for her reaction.

She flung the remote onto an overstuffed chair. Vivien's smile actually brightened the room. "I don't know about you all, but I'm forecasting a hot, sunny day!"

"Aye!" The men roared in unison.

"I seem to remember a wise man telling me never to assume the outcome of a battle before the last drop of blood has spilled."

Slapping hands on hips, McGregor's face turned into one massive grin.

Michael began a round of cheers which quickly escalated in volume, pumping them up.

Vivien held up her arms, and they quieted as Vivien's focus turned to Brendan. Rubbing the hilt of her sword, her voice took on a commanding life of its own. "I received a warning early this morning. A warning for Brendan." Sweeping the group with an intense glance, she continued. "No, I don't know the future in this instance, but we all need to look out for him today. Do not fear for him. Envision him well."

Instinctively the men surrounded their brother in arms. Brendan remained courageous, but his muscles coiled for an instant. Vivien sensed his concern—for Maggie more than himself.

McGregor spoke softly. "You heard her, lads."

A faint glow of candlelight caught Vivien's eye from down the hall. The clan followed her gaze. "It's time to say goodbye." Not waiting for a reply, she approached the library as they all trooped behind her.

Shawn, Maggie, Hanna, Gregory, John, Donna, and Roger sat in a circle. Shannon slept under a blanket on the couch. They explained to young Gregory that a special ceremony needed to take place, but not the details. Hanna and McGregor preferred their children be with them, in case the worst came to pass.

Candles flickered, casting a glow on their faces. The group would remain in meditation the entire length of the battle, sending powerful white light energy. That would be their contribution to the fight. Neal and Julie also participated from Pam's house, as well as Katherine, Bridget, the gang at Mick Finns, John's dream group, Donna's meditation team, and the Quilting Club of Clonakilty.

In the peaceful stillness they'd created, a portion of Vivien's mind cherished a quiet moment just before the biggest fight of her life.

Brendan went to Maggie, Jason approached Shawn, and McGregor moved to Hanna and his children. He didn't awaken Shannon but simply stroked her hair.

Vivien moved to gaze out a far window, not able to bear the sight of them saying farewell to their loved ones. Such a feeling of sorrow swelled inside. Her thoughts turned to Neal, and her sorrow found a new depth. Vivien said goodbye to all the people sitting in her library the night before. They'd agreed it would be too emotional just before her confrontation with Dagda and Nicholas.

Taking a deep breath and finding her center, Vivien turned. "It's time."

****

McGregor drove Vivien's car. She needed to concentrate solely on the battle, but her leg kept fidgeting. Sitting still seemed an impossible task. After trying three different positions, her body moved again.

"What ails you, lass?"

Vivien shrugged. "Oh, I don't know. I'm about to fight a demon to save the planet, as well as the man who killed the love of my life. That's all."

McGregor remained still.

"I need a distraction. We still have a ten-minute drive, and I feel like I'm coming out of my skin." Considering McGregor closely, Vivien's voice took on a curious tone. "You know, you never told me what got you into the combat business. I already picked up that it's very painful to talk about. But since you are my coach, I'd really like to know."

McGregor's eyes stayed focused on the dark road ahead.

She didn't budge.

He sighed deeply.

Vivien crossed her arms. "It will take my mind off—"

"I was fourteen," McGregor began, as his shoulders slightly tensed up. "There was a neighbor girl about twelve, named Samantha. I saw her sitting by a small creek not far from our houses. I realized Samantha had wandered from her own backyard, and I walked over to take her home. Shamus, a boy I knew who was a couple years older than me, ran past and grabbed Samantha. He came out of nowhere, but Shamus must have been behind me. I jumped on his back, but he threw me off. Shamus swore he would kill me. I screamed at Samantha to run back home, but her fear kept her rooted to the spot. Shamus attacked me, and I didn't know how to protect myself. I hit him a few times, but it had the impact of feathers falling on stone. So, it didn't take Shamus long to knock me out. My parents found me a few hours later."

Sad, dead silence stretched between them for the next half mile.

Finally, Vivien blew out a long, sorrowful breath. "I'm so sorry. That must have been horrifying. What happened to the girl?"

After a few hushed seconds, McGregor's dreadful answer rose to the surface. "Shamus raped her. Then, Samantha became agoraphobic and wouldn't leave the house."

Vivien shuddered, and her palms covered her face. Agonizing grief rushed through her from the girl and her parents. After it dissipated, Vivien lowered her hands and inhaled deeply. "I understand why you took up self-defense."

"Later on, after years of therapy, Samantha came around. She even enrolled in one of my female self-defense courses."

Vivien straightened in her seat. "That was smart of her to take your class and actually empowered both of you." Then, her brows knitted. "I'm almost afraid to ask, but whatever happened to the boy who raped that sweet innocent girl?"

"He did a short sentence in juvenile prison and then his family moved away. But I came across Shamus when I turned seventeen. After three years of training and growing ten inches, I beat the living crap out of him!" McGregor paused, staring at the open road. When he spoke again his voice sounded far away. "There is inter-dimensional evil, and then there is human evil."

Vivien could have asked him more but knew McGregor wouldn't answer. He vowed no woman or child would ever suffer in his presence again. That's why he opened a special session of defense classes just for women.

"I knew it was something like that." Staring at the rugged profile of a man who cared so much for people and yet wielded such physical power, Vivien addressed him as a Celt. "I honor you for sharing your story."

McGregor looked out the driver's window. "I never want to speak of it again." Then, he made direct eye contact. "Understood?"

"Understood."

Smiling, McGregor grunted. "Now, let's go kick some demon ass!"

Chapter Thirty

Six enormous flaming torches lined the edge of the lighthouse cliff. Each glowed in orange-ruby splashes against predawn darkness so deep it seemed the entire world waited.

Gravel crackled under tires as McGregor and Vivien inspected the scene.

Her brows lifted. "A bit dramatic, don't you think?"

"Aye, they're making a show of it." McGregor cut the engine. "This is it, lass."

"Aye," Vivien echoed, breathing in confidence like an elixir. "This is it."

Suddenly, a rush of icy grief attacked Vivien's lungs as she opened the door. Falling back, she fought to catch her breath.

"What happened?" McGregor's face turned stern.

Vivien's voice came out like a wee bird. "Something's wrong. Something's gone horribly wrong."

"Where's the Trestle?"

Fumbling, she clutched the Celtic talisman, and within seconds emotions came back into balance. Grabbing her sword, Vivien stepped out.

McGregor came around the car, pushing the ignition key fob into his black leather pants pocket. "Better?"

"For now."

The rest of the clan, which now included Jason and Angelo, emerged from two SUVs with swords in hand. Vivien watched as they approached.

"Come, lads. Let's help Vivien kill a demon," McGregor told them with a sideways grin.

Vivien gave her warriors one last look so strong, they looked back, entranced. "Something doesn't feel right. Let's stay sharp."

After acknowledging Vivien's warning, they rounded the caretaker's house. Hovering above the earth's soil swirled a maelstrom of pitch-black smoke, accompanied by the stench of sulfur, almost choking them. Blood-red torchlight reflected off the unnatural vapor as the disturbing scene sank into each and every warrior. They had no choice but to step into it once the battle began.

Clothed in a black robe and grasping a silver skull atop a giant pewter blade, Nicholas proclaimed himself. Next to him twenty handpicked brawny men lined up, all clad in black leather with swords at their sides. Being outnumbered, Vivien silently gave thanks for the goddesses' help. Lifting her gaze upward, she noticed a primitive-looking wooden post protruding behind the Foundation men.

Gloating in triumph, Nicholas caught Vivien's eyes. She found that odd. Yes, Nicholas reeked of arrogance, but to celebrate victory so early was strange even for him. With a nod of his head, Nicholas and the other men stepped away from the wooden post.

As soon as they moved, Vivien's breathing stopped. Nothing could have prepared her for the image she now beheld. There, tied to the post with thick ropes, stood Neal. He was not gagged or drugged, but blood clung to Neal's mouth and nose.

It took a moment for reality to smack into awareness. A clinking sound lingered as Vivien's sword slid from her hand, hitting small stones below. Numbing despair filled every cell in her body. There had been plenty of time to stop this event—plenty of time. Neal would not be seconds from death if it weren't for her. Vivien could have halted all romance until this horrible morning had ended. Who was she to think she could protect him?

The clan quickly surrounded her. Vivien's body shook. Neal's mouth screamed the words "I'm sorry!" It was all her mind took in, against the pounding of her own heart—the words occupied Vivien's mind like a horror movie soundtrack.

Suddenly, her head flew violently to the left. Fixing her gaze on something right in front of her, McGregor's shouting face came into focus.

"Vivien, wake up! Wake up! Listen to me! You have to concentrate. Nicholas is trying to control you!"

It was McGregor who had been shaking her body, finally slapping Vivien hard. She still felt no pain.

Katherine's voice echoed in Vivien's head, all the way from Clonakilty. *Clear your mind, love. Clear your mind.*

Looking past McGregor to Neal, she finally heard his cries.

"Vivien, I'm sorry! I didn't believe you! It sounded like Julie got hit by a car, and when I ran out, they grabbed me. I'm sorry!" Neal didn't sound scared. He sounded angry—angry he hadn't believed Vivien, the woman he loved.

Donal snatched her sword from the ground and thrust it back into Vivien's hand. "Hang on to that."

McGregor came face to face with her like a controlled storm. "Just like the black clouds, they're using Neal as a scare tactic. We can save him, all of us, and the world, if we just do what we came here to do."

Absorbing McGregor's words, Vivien closed her eyes, inhaled, and rejected all feelings of guilt and shame—they would only weaken her quest. Paralyzing fear still breathed through her body like a living thing, but channeling terror into the rage she felt toward Nicholas would be disastrous for all of them. Then, something Donna said clicked into Vivien's brain—*the only reason Nicholas hasn't killed Neal is because he knows if he did, you'd never truly be his. Your love belongs with Neal.* Suddenly everything became clear. Vivien's eyes snapped open.

"I'm ready."

Nicholas's piercing scream cut through the atmosphere. "Vivien!"

Vivien nodded to McGregor, and he moved aside. Her warriors spread out around her as she met Nicholas's glare.

With a diabolical smile, Nicholas raised his sword dramatically. "I have the perfect human sacrifice for Dagda!" Wrenching Neal's head back, Nicholas held the blade under his chin. One quick swipe and Neal was dead.

As Vivien stepped into churning blackness, none of Nicholas's men stopped her. She had to be unwavering, risking something she'd never done before.

Lifting her Celtic sword with eyes closed, Vivien rested the blade against her forehead. While her energy intensified, glowing white light projected from the Celtic Trestle hanging from her neck. She mentally called out to Neal.

I love you, Neal. I always have. I loved you from the first moment I saw you. I dreamt about you for years before we even met. I was just too afraid to tell you. Our love is stronger than anything that happens here today—no matter the outcome.

Vivien knew Neal heard her. She dared not open her eyes, lest she lose her concentration, but even with eyes shut Vivien saw him—and felt him. Vivien's proclamation of her love covered Neal like a shower of serenity. Neal professed his love back to her, echoing that no matter what befell them, they shared this moment of peaceful bliss.

Warriors, anticipating a resounding ring of that first blade striking another, stood stupefied. A tunnel of golden light spread between Vivien and Neal, pushing away anything in its path, including Dagda's black vapor. Peering at brilliant light—some in awe, some in fear—the men stepped back.

Nicholas, enraged at her unconventional tactic, attacked.

Because it took a few seconds to snap out of her loving meditative state, Nicholas's blade sliced Vivien's forearm open.

Battle screams commenced the moment Vivien's blood flowed. Clanging metal rang out from all directions as Dagda's toxic haze churned beneath their boots.

Vivien noticed something while fighting for her own life. Whenever one of her clan got ganged up on, a black crow or falcon suddenly attacked the eyes of a

Foundation member. A gray wolf jumped on a man about to charge Jason from behind. Then, a white horse appeared, rearing up and holding off two men from swarming Sean. Albeit rattled by the animal attacks, their enemy kept up combat.

As Vivien fought, she sent an intense message to the goddesses. *Free Neal! Please free Neal!*

A stunning gray wolf ran to Neal, instantly chewing through ropes holding him hostage. Vivien kept peripheral vision on him, even while she battled. At the sight of a wild wolf charging, Neal squirmed like a man about to be devoured. Then, after the ropes came loose, Vivien could have sworn the wolf winked at Neal before speeding off.

Knowing Neal had been freed, Vivien focused on Nicholas. Lunging on him, she brought their swords into a tight clinch. Face to face, Vivien held him in her power, her voice dripping with venom. "How's Olivia?"

Nicholas's blue eyes turned black as he pushed against Vivien, but she held fast.

"You're nothing but a common murderer, Nicholas. That's all you'll ever be." Vivien pulled her sword back, ready to finally slice his neck open. Nicholas was hers for the taking. Time to kill. "I do this not only to save our world, but also for Philip!"

An enormous rumbling boomed from behind them, shaking the ground beneath their feet and abruptly jerking them apart. Warriors and Foundation members fell to the ground.

A tall blond-haired man appeared, descending the hill, followed by Dean and his gang. The leader wore black leather pants, black boots, and a white satin shirt unbuttoned to the waist. He looked as if he leapt off the cover of a romance novel with a flawlessly chiseled face and a muscular, toned body.

Vivien whispered in terrorized shock. "It's Dagda."

"It can't be." Nicholas narrowed his eyes.

"It is." Vivien thrust the tip of her sword into the ground and stood in combat stance. "Dagda betrayed you, Nicholas. He already inhabits a body."

Abruptly, Neal grasped Vivien's arm. Now shirtless, and only in jeans, Neal began wrapping her up with tattered pieces of fabric. He'd obviously torn his shirt off to create primitive bandages. "Sit down!"

"But I can't!"

"Sit!"

Vivien plopped down without argument.

With the battle temporarily paused, Neal called out to Liam. "Hey! Put pressure right here."

Liam obeyed immediately as Neal finished dressing Vivien's arm.

Nicholas had bounded off to confront Dagda. His Foundation men lurked behind.

As Vivien touched Neal's beaten face, tears welled up. "I'm so sorry. I know they tricked you."

"All I care about right now is getting you to a hospital. You'll need stitches," Neal growled, avoiding her gaze.

She swam in confusion. "Are you mad at me?"

Neal kissed her, and in that kiss, his fear of losing her spread through Vivien's body in waves.

All at once, a blasting image of Nicholas being struck down and Dagda taking power overran Vivien's psyche. Now that Dagda had become an enemy to them, Nicholas would finally fight the demon alongside her, and all his men would follow. Afterward, she and Nicholas would have their own private showdown. Only one person would walk away—and Vivien intended it to be her.

Bolting up, Vivien snatched her sword and screamed back to her clan. "Get Neal out of here!" Neal was next on Dagda's list.

"He wants to kill you, Nicholas." Vivien's blade rested on her shoulder, with her other hand on her hip.

The blond-haired man glared back. Except for simmering red eyes, he looked human. Smiling, Dagda's arms widened. "Here we are together again after all these centuries!"

"So…Dagda. Where did you get that body?" Vivien questioned with a quick wave of her arm. Showing a casual demeanor had to be the only way to approach him. The demon sniffed out fear like a bobcat.

"I jumped into the body of a man they call a model about to meet his demise. I burned his assailant to a crisp. Now, I can enjoy my New World in my new superior body!"

Vivien went for broke, smiling sarcastically. "How nice for you. Okay, what's the plan, guys? I don't have all day."

Dagda pointed at Nicholas while dissecting Vivien's body with crimson eyes. "He dies, and you become my queen."

Nicholas's face reflected, once and for all, the cold truth. Dagda strung him along from the beginning. Nicholas gazed upon her. After a flash of pain for his own stupidity, his face softened with compassion and grief for all the acts he'd executed. Nicholas suddenly looked like the young man whose true dream was to be a professional surfer. A caring smile crossed his lips. *I believe in you, Vivien. I always did. It's up to you now.*

Dagda—not one for sentimentality—lashed out. He formed a fireball aimed at Neal, who'd moved closer to help Vivien, but Nicholas threw himself in its path.

Electricity sizzled, and a scream shot out. After rising up from where her body ricocheted from the impact, Vivien barely made out a human form under dense black fog.

Nicholas lay dead.

Panic suddenly seized her heart. "Where's Neal?" Vivien shouted, swinging around to the clan.

"I'm not leaving!" Neal shot back, looking very at ease with a sword in his hand. They'd brought extra steel, but until now she didn't know why.

"He's a stubborn lad!" Ronan yelled with a huge smile.

Neal's bravery didn't surprise Vivien, and dissuading him would be futile. If she were to die, he wanted to go with her.

The Foundation men backed up and joined Vivien's clan, unsure how the demon would react to them. With Nicholas dead, all the rules had changed.

Dagda moved fluidly, as if he already owned the planet, and extended his arm in Vivien's direction.

Three sets of hands thumped against Neal's bare chest, stopping him from running to Vivien.

Dagda chuckled.

Spotting her sword on the ground, Vivien grabbed it and pivoted, thrusting thick metal into the demon's face.

"Take my hand and join me in the New World—or else," he commanded in a subterranean voice.

Forgetting her fear, or perhaps going mad, Vivien's eyes rolled. "Oh, for fuck's sake! Are we in high school? Or else—what?"

Thick black vapor under their feet split, opening a wide chasm in the earth. Banshees instantly shot out— hundreds of them. Mixed in with banshees appeared *dullahan*s, *bodach*s, and dark figures she knew as shadow people. Growls, screams, and hissing sounds emitted from the entities, creating a unique chamber of horrors.

Then, reality came to a chilling standstill. In front of a row of banshees stood the black-eyed children— the exact boy and girl from Vivien's nightmare. With frightening smiles and dead eyes, they bowed to her.

Vivien never knew what it felt like to have her flesh crawl, but now she did. Displaying fear was not an option. She raised her head and cocked it slightly to one side, her etiquette in Boudicca's time. The move showed courage and respect to Dagda.

The little boy turned to a Foundation member about to run away. "Will you help me?"

"Don't answer!" Vivien reached her arm out, but the man succumbed to the child's spell.

"What?" The man seemed confused yet drawn to the boy.

"Will you help me?"

Vivien yelled out another warning.

"Yes, I'll help you," he whispered, as if in a trance.

Smiling victoriously, the child touched his wrist.

The man fell to the ground like a rag doll.

After the children backed away to join the banshees, another Foundation member kneeled at the side of his fallen comrade. He placed his fingers upon his neck, and then stood. "He's dead!"

Rushing the hill, the other members sprinted in panic.

"Don't run! They'll kill you!" Vivien shouted.

Obeying her command, they stopped.

Ironically, the distraction of the black-eyed children's first homicide gave Vivien time to aggressively probe Dadga's new brain. He only needed her. All other humans standing on the hill were expendable, including Dean and his group. Dagda planned to take Vivien and gather his energy into a lethal electric explosion that would kill everybody present. Then, he could begin his New World with no witnesses to the morning's event.

Alarm took command as Vivien ran out of ideas. She could only buy time, so she pitched her sword. A blade was no match against Dagda and his lethal beings. Turning, Vivien winked at McGregor and Neal, making them believe she had a smooth plan composed. They nodded back. The rest of the men held their own, even against the monsters surrounding them.

I'm asking for guidance, please!

Rhiannon and the war goddesses shimmered into view.

Roaring, Dagda jolted back once they appeared. He would have charged, but until the demon attained Vivien's full consent and power, the goddesses could still injure him. He would wait, but she only had seconds.

The goddesses transmitted information quickly within a boundary Dagda could not penetrate. Since the demon now occupied a human body, Vivien could kill him. That was Dagda's error. He didn't believe her capable of overcoming him. With protection from his army of dark creatures, the demon believed himself untouchable—an illusion created by his ego. Once Dagda died, the entities would be forever banished into their own dimension beneath the earth's core.

Clarity changed Vivien's thinking and brought confidence. But with confidence came a challenge she'd put off her entire adult life. If Vivien invited Boudicca's primitive power to enter her body, this time it would be permanent. Her final test in Clonakilty had been a momentary blending of her inner spirit and the Celtic queen's potency. What if Boudicca possessed Vivien and changed her modern life to one of barbaric existence in a faraway land? It's a risk she'd have to take. With only seconds left, Vivien arched her back, sucked in a long breath, and called out to Boudicca. Fully embracing her power—past and present—would give Vivien the edge she needed.

Boudicca blazed into vision. She smiled with a cock of her head, glad to be welcomed. *Dagda expects me to possess you, but we can fight him together. You must make a choice, Vivien. You must receive me with all my light and darkness or not at all. There is no in between anymore. Know that my passion was always to protect my family and my people. I had to fight. We were being slaughtered, our girls made into whores, and the rest of us into slaves. I had to act or turn my back on my very soul.*

Vivien nodded. "Honor and courage."

Boudicca instantly lunged into Vivien's solid body.

Golden power flowed through her molecules, creating a luminous glow upon Vivien's skin.

Taking in Boudicca's life experiences as her own,

Vivien cried out as the memory of hot pain ripped skin from her bones. Falling down, her body relived her whipping commanded by a Roman general. Then, unbearable agony transmuted into modern life images—Vivien stood in a basement glaring at pure evil. After the homeowner acquired an authentic Nazi officer's uniform, wickedness had entered her client's house. Not able to take her eyes away from silver skull buttons on the black German officer's jacket, she saw a Jewish family beaten and the father shot. The officer who wore that uniform, albeit dead, tried to strangle Vivien by the throat.

As two lives collided, cathartic scenes continued to purify Vivien's energy until all pain ceased. Having accepted every aspect of herself—the dark, and the light—Vivien became Dagda's equal.

Tapping into Dagda's mind once more, Vivien found anxiety. The corners of her mouth rose up in a grateful smile. The demon hid it well, but the only thing he feared was not being able to control her. He needed Vivien and feared her at the same time.

"I'm losing patience, woman!" Dagda knocked down the six gigantic flaming torches with a wave of his hand. People and dark creatures alike ducked the falling flames.

The hilt of Vivien's Celtic blade rose out of dark smoke covering the ground and hovered before her. Watching Dagda's surprise, she clutched her floating weapon with a death grip and faced him, eyes brilliant with purpose. "Change of plan! You're going to die, and we shall continue living in our world just as it is—thank you very much!"

Resounding cheers burst forth from her warriors

and she actually allowed herself to laugh.

Rhiannon sent Vivien a message. *He must be decapitated to die.*

Seriously? I've never decapitated anyone!

As Boudicca's energy calmed Vivien, she echoed from the back of her mind. *I'll help you, Vivien. I've done it many times.*

Exhaling slowly, Vivien connected to her core and accepted a brand-new fact—she must separate this man's head from his body.

Arms akimbo, Dagda guffawed, appearing amused by Vivien's magic trick. The demon snapped his fingers, and Dean threw him a large sword. "Very well! I will allow you to fight me human to human. Later, when you're lying in my arms in spent bliss, I can say I gave you a chance."

"Wait a minute." Vivien bent over at the waist. "I think I'm gonna throw up."

Dagda angrily came at her with unnatural speed. Popping up just in time, Vivien met his blade full force. They fought aggressively, and as clan and Foundation members moved in, the monsters pushed them back.

Catching a glimpse of a *Baobhan Sith* taunting McGregor, Vivien knew it to be the same one she banished from Julie's bedroom. Horrified that snapshot would be their new existence, she attacked harder. She was too fast for the demon, and a long bloody scar appeared across his chest. "That's for that sweet little boy, Daniel, and my friend Matt! Both killed in cold blood because of you!" Vivien spat.

In utter shock, Dagda examined his wound. Quickly shock turned to rage. Hoisting Vivien up by the throat, he dangled her legs in midair. She was barely able to breathe as choking sounds squeezed from her mouth.

"Let her go!" Vivien heard Neal scream from far away. Again, her men held him back.

Face to face, Dagda gritted his beautiful white-capped teeth. "You hurt me, Vivien. Now I'm going to hurt you!"

Unceremoniously, her body fell back to earth. Recovering quickly after a tuck and roll, Vivien snatched up her blade. But a banshee's shriek halted her next charge on Dagda.

Pulling back a bloody sword, the banshee flashed a lecherous grin.

Brendan dropped to the ground with a thud as the clan gawked in frozen terror. He'd been impaled with his own sword, and no one even saw it move, much less get into the hands of the *Baobhan Sith*.

Blinding heartache rushed over Vivien's mind. "No!"

Neal, McGregor, and the others surrounded Brendan, but the attacks had just begun. To torture Vivien into submission, Dagda telepathically commanded the banshees to kill her clan one at a time.

"Stop! I'll come with you, but you have to promise to let everyone go." Flicking her hair back like Donna taught her, Vivien ventured further. "What do you care? You're going to rule them all anyway, and if someone annoys you—you simply kill them."

Dagda smiled like a real human being. "Agreed. Come then, my queen."

Boudicca's power burned to fight the demon on the spot, but Vivien didn't want more men to die. Her new plan became to murder him as soon as they got out of sight.

Confident Vivien belonged to him, Dagda's fingers wrapped around her elbow tightly as his dreadful command followed. "Kill them all!"

"What? Wait!"

Roughly yanking her against him, the demon's essence entered Vivien. Dagda's dark supremacy stimulated all her senses at once. It certainly wasn't heaven, but the ocean below sounded loud and beautiful. Plants rustling in the path of a breeze magnified to incredible intensity. Her human frame stood omnipotent. Noises from humans on the hill faded as Vivien's lungs filled with the demon's black, passionate mist. She and Dagda levitated in a swirling funnel cloud of seductive, rich darkness. The old world seemed far away...so far away.

No one could destroy Vivien Kelly, surpassing even the goddesses she used to take advice from. Men on the hillside shouted at her. Mouths moved fast, eyes expanded in alarm—none of it seemed to matter. Vivien tried to remember why she opposed Dagda. He only wanted to give her a glorious life.

Incredible energy amped up through her body, but the purity of Vivien's soul could not submit. Turning her head back to Dagda, Vivien suddenly saw his true form—green, slimy, and evil. Did she truly desire to surrender her heart and soul to this monster?

All at once, Vivien twisted from his titanium grip, her feet touching ground again. Knuckles sharply clasped the hilt of her blade.

Dagda floated down to the ground and held up his arm. The creatures suspended their murderous intent. "Put the sword down."

She didn't answer.

"Put the sword down, Vivien. You will obey me!" The demon's voice created an earthquake where they stood. Reaching out to grab her Celtic steel, Dagda's arm hit a brick wall.

Vivien stood within her unleashed energy, but something new came into sight. Golden light flowed into her body from the groups meditating in America and Ireland. The illumination then expanded as she tapped into masses of people on earth. Anyone who wanted a better life encompassed Vivien's being without them even realizing.

Dagda's face betrayed him, reflecting panic.

Peering into the demon's soulless eyes, Vivien's voice bewitched. "Pain of your darkness we shall no longer abide. From this day forth, you shall no longer thrive."

"Your chanting won't stop me, woman!"

Vivien knew Dagda finally had enough. As he calculated how fast he could find another modern-day sorceress, a swarm of electric fire came hurling at her face.

"Earth's light you can no longer hide!"

Envisioning Dagda's head leaving his body with only seconds to spare, Vivien raised her sword and cleanly sliced through his neck at supernatural speed.

Blood dripped from her blade in strands. Vivien watched his head roll to the cliff, flying off the edge into the ocean with amazing speed.

Monsters roared, the sound like ten thousand train whistles blowing at once. Every human covered their ears. Entities flew about, attempting to outrun a black hole opening upon the hillside. But they had no power once Dagda ceased to exist. Dark edges sucked them in and closed for good.

Rays of warm yellow light struck her face. Pulling back flying hair, Vivien lifted her head, as if it were the very first time, she embraced sunlight. In her mind's eye, she saw all the other black clouds disappear from earth instantly. Raising her sword to the sky, Vivien cheered through tears of ecstasy.

Her warriors magnified Vivien's joy—some jumping, some shouting.

Neal snatched her up.

Resting her head in the soft crook of his neck, Vivien's body relaxed. Then, she remembered Brendan, on the edge of tears. "Is he dead?"

"No!" Brendan choked out.

Stunned, Vivien looked up the hill. She received a vision of Brendan's body turning just in time, preventing the blade from penetrating his heart.

Neal and Vivien ran to him, and Brendan actually attempted a smile.

Gasping tears issued forth as Vivien's hand covered her mouth.

"You heard the man. He's not dead!" Michael exclaimed with a scowl.

"I heard. These are tears of joy!"

"Aye, but we have to get him to hospital, and you too!" McGregor commanded as he finished wrapping Brendan's waist with pieces of a tattered shirt.

"I know, I know. Soon they'll give me my own wing. But please take Brendan first."

Sean and Carroll eased Brendan to a standing position and then helped him up the hill. Scanning the scene, Vivien found her clan with small cuts here and there, but nothing critical.

The remaining Foundation men had already run off, but Dean and his group lurked just yards away. They spoke in a circle until Dean marched with intent toward Vivien.

"That's far enough!" Neal moved in front of her with his sword upheld.

McGregor stood next to him, his blade drawn.

"This isn't over! You'll hear from us as these people again!" Dean proclaimed, waving an arm at his small crew of men.

Stepping out, Vivien faced him with hands on hips. "Have you ever taken English as a second language?"

The clan broke up in raucous laughter behind her, Angelo almost choking on his guffaws.

Dean charged at her. "Fuck you!"

Tossing his sword away, Neal punched him hard in the face, grabbed his arm, threw him over his shoulder, and onto the ground, all in a matter of seconds.

Dean was out cold even before landing on gravel.

Neal stepped back with a steely glare at the rest of Dean's group, challenging each of them.

Slowly, Hutch and Joe approached, pulling Dean's unconscious body up the hill without a sound.

Neal pulled Vivien against him.

After throwing her arms around Neal's waist, Vivien eyeballed Dean's gang skulking toward the parking lot. "Dagda intended to kill them, too. Dean doesn't even know. Should I tell them?"

"Ah! They wouldn't believe you. Morons that they are," McGregor grumbled.

Out of breath, Jason joined them. "So, what are we going to tell the authorities this time about three dead bodies on the lighthouse grounds? I don't think a ham hock is gonna do the trick."

Sean, collecting swords, nodded to her. Vivien gave him her steel. Observing the scene at her feet, she burst out in a radiant smile. "Let's tell the truth! Call Sheriff Harris and tell him to bring everyone. Nicholas Williams, founder and head of the Foundation made a human sacrifice in a demon-worship ritual but ironically got murdered in the process. Who knew the founder of such a growing self-help group worshiped a demon? Social media will kill them! The Foundation is done for!"

Jason laughed. "I'm on it!" Marching up the hill, he yanked out his cell.

She caressed Neal's bloody, yet beautiful face. "It's finally over. We're free."

"Yes!"

"I love you." The words issued from Vivien's lips effortlessly.

Neal's smile radiated. "I love you, too. Now, let's get out of here."

Her arms flew up. "Breakfast and first aid at my house!"

"After I take Vivien to the hospital—again!" Neal quickly added.

Yells of triumph pervaded the clan as they broke out in an Irish victory song led by Aidan. Neither she nor Neal knew the lyrics, but they sang along anyway.

All of a sudden, life lost all motion and the song silenced. Vivien turned her head toward the open ocean.

Something lurked out there. Something that wasn't supposed to live.

In the next moment, Vivien's environment came

alive again.

Neal noticed the look on her face, stopped moving, and grabbed her tightly. "What's wrong?"

Vivien's head moved back and forth, scanning the hillside. "I felt a sliver of vile, raw energy." After laser-focusing with all her intuitive strength, she picked up absolutely nothing.

"Honey, you've lost a lot of blood. I'm surprised you're not seeing blue elephants. Now, let's get you to the hospital."

"You're right."

Wavering, Vivien rested against Neal as he walked her up to the cars.

Chapter Thirty-One

Styled in a classic black and white tuxedo, Neal peered out the rental car window taking in a charming Clonakilty tavern named Mick Finns.

Vivien wanted Neal to meet Katherine and her Clonakilty friends in the flesh, and Bridget was only too happy to host a victory party for Vivien and her clan, combined with the annual New Year's Eve bash. In fact, Bridget's e-vite stated the party required black tie attire, and anyone not dressed accordingly would be tossed out into the street.

"Well…this is it." Neal's shoulders raised in nervous anticipation.

Gently, Vivien clutched his hand. "Katherine will love you."

As Neal opened her passenger door, Vivien folded herself into a thick wool coat, covering a gold beaded-sleeve foil pebble evening gown. Usually West Cork's January hovered in the low 40's, but tonight the temperature fell to the mid-30's. Taking Neal's offered hand, she sprang from the car and snuggled against him on the sidewalk. "You look like the new James Bond in that suit." Vivien's lips brushed against his, ever so softly.

Neal chuckled deeply. "There will be time for that next year."

Laughter swirled from a joyful place inside. Vivien

loved his humor, and she loved him.

As they crossed the threshold arm in arm, Vivien hardly recognized Mick Finns. White linen on round tables, adorned by gold glitter "Happy New Year" pop-up signs, caught her eye first. Nestled on each tablecloth sat frosted golden candles, matching china, and wine glasses. From the ceiling hung white curly ribbons and strands of little white lights as far as the eye could see. To the left of the bar extended a beautiful buffet with oysters on the half shell, salads, whiskey-baked ham, meat cobbler, shepherd's pie, Irish potatoes and cabbage, Irish potato soup, and finally, ending with delectable desserts, including her favorite—chocolate potato cake. Bridget had outdone herself.

McGregor, Hanna, Gregory, and Shannon pulled them into a group hug after someone whisked off their coats. Then, the clan pounced on them with cheers, greetings, and slaps on the back.

Black and metallic-gold-paper top hats adorned many heads, and horn blowers deafened all ears. It felt like a new year and a new era.

Pulling her head out of a tangle of arms, Vivien's gaze caught a banner above the bar which read "Congratulations!"

A beautiful red-haired woman came forward. "I'm Bridget! Come here, Neal!" She wrapped him up in her arms.

Vivien laughed. "Your reputation precedes you."

"I guess so!" Neal grinned widely.

Slowly, bodies parted—and there stood Katherine.

After greeting her with a kiss on the cheek, Vivien turned. "Katherine, this is Neal."

Eyes lit up with delight as Katherine's arms spread

out for a hug. "Welcome to Clonakilty, Neal."

"It's an honor to meet you, Katherine." Neal smiled softly and took Katherine into an embrace.

Winking at Vivien, Katherine unabashedly proclaimed, "This is a good one."

"Yes, I know." She nodded with a chuckle.

"Come, lad!" Ronan pulled Neal to the bar, smacking an Irish stout down so hard white foam flew.

Shaking her head, Vivien left Neal to experience the clan's ritual of that first stout, even though she knew it wouldn't be his first. "You guys sure clean up nicely!" She smirked, admiring their formal attire and clean-shaven looks.

Michael jerked his head toward the bar. "Danny didn't think so."

Danny, the barkeep, shook up a martini and ignored him. He was a friend of the clan but should have known better than to tease them in their finery.

Liam brushed a stray crumb off his shoulder, no doubt from the paté on toast precariously placed on a white napkin. "He called us the penguin brigade."

McGregor came up behind Vivien. "Brendan punched him in the nose."

"No!"

"Aye, but not hard. That's why there's no blood." Brendan smiled.

Vivien tossed a quick apology to Danny. He shrugged, as if it were a daily occurrence to be socked in the nose.

Perusing the room, Vivien admired all those in attendance. If she didn't know better, she would have thought she'd walked into the Vanity Fair party after the Oscars. Touching the sleeve of Katherine's royal blue chiffon gown, Vivien shouted over party blowers. "Your dress is gorgeous!"

"Thank you. I got it just for tonight."

"Out of our way!" McGregor's blasting voice shook the walls. Everyone looked up to see him clearing a path for Neal. "Quiet! Be quiet now!"

Neal stood before Vivien in the middle of the pub.

Katherine stepped aside and linked arms with Hanna, Bridget, and Maggie. All four women beamed with excitement. The quilting club ladies began weeping behind them.

"What's going on?" Vivien looked around in confusion. Then, her world got even brighter.

A man kneeled in front of her. It was Neal.

Her heart raced.

Reaching out, Neal grasped her left hand. "Vivien, I've loved you from the moment you came to my house to banish a banshee."

Muffled laughter came from the men. Katherine shushed them instantly.

"There was a time I thought I'd never love again, but that ended the day I saw you." Neal reached inside his jacket pocket and pulled out a small, black velvet box. As his fingers tugged the box open, the most gorgeous ring Vivien ever saw revealed itself—a princess cut in a diamond square frame.

"Will you marry me?"

"Yes!" She gasped through tears.

Neal slipped the ring on Vivien's finger and gathered her up in his arms.

Whooping screams and champagne corks exploded around them, but she focused only on passionate kissing. When their heads parted, they were quickly surrounded. Shannon eagerly tugged on Vivien's dress.

"Look!"

Bridget pulled the banner further out. Now it read "Congratulations, Vivien and Neal!"

Vivien's head whipped around to Katherine and Hanna. "Did everyone know about this but me?"

Laughing uncontrollably, they answered in unison. "Aye! This is your engagement party!"

Neal pulled her close. "I hope you'll forgive me. I wanted to surprise you. I can't believe I actually did! You must not be that psychic." He teased with a charming smile.

Vivien kissed him fully on the lips.

The crowd went wild.

Someone threw white confetti all around them. It reminded Vivien of the season's first snowfall she'd watched with her parents from their brownstone window. It became a tradition—to stop everything and watch snowflakes descend to earth. At that moment, Vivien thought about her parents and Philip, feeling their delight for her. She'd finally found her happy ending, as her father would say.

Vivien's handsome fiancé whispered against her ear. "Would you like to dance?"

Sons of Blarney played "Here Comes the Bride," and as they flew onto the dance floor amongst accolades, the band quickly blended their impending song into the Irish favorite, "Molly Malone."

Love and celebration encompassed Mick Finns that night, and for the first time in a long time, Vivien relished her present and looked forward to her future.

A word about the author...

When Starra Andrews wasn't swimming the Pacific Ocean in her hometown of Laguna Beach, California, she busied herself by writing fantasy stories and acting on stage. Having grown up watching Rod Serling's *Twilight Zone* and *Night Gallery* shows on TV, Starra quickly fell in love with paranormal tales with a message of wisdom and love. Also, being a fan of romance novels and non-fiction ghost stories, she decided to marry the two and write paranormal novels of suspense, adventure, and intrigue with a strong romantic foundation. The sense of adventure inside her came from summers of camping with her family in Mexico (Baja California) and walking along beaches with no other footprints but hers, as her family members unpacked the camper and got ready to collect clams right off the shoreline for dinner. Starra attained a B.A. degree in Theatre from University of California, Irvine, and a Professional Acting Certificate from LACC Acting Academy. She is also a member of the International Thriller Writers, which hosts the Thrillerfest writers' conference every year in NYC.

The beautiful Hudson Valley in upstate New York is where Starra now calls home. She loves being a quick train ride from New York City, but also enjoys country life. Her two tabby cats Audrey Hepburn and Vivien Leigh are her constant writing companions, and love to curl up on the table next to her laptop.

Bay of Darkness is the first book of her trilogy The Kelly Society.

You can visit Starra at:
https://www.skandrews.com/

Thank you for purchasing
this publication of The Wild Rose Press, Inc.

For questions or more information
contact us at
info@thewildrosepress.com.

The Wild Rose Press, Inc.
www.thewildrosepress.com

To visit with authors of
The Wild Rose Press, Inc.
join our yahoo loop at
http://groups.yahoo.com/group/thewildrosepress/

CPSIA information can be obtained
at www.ICGtesting.com
Printed in the USA
BVHW041343131019
560767BV00013B/150/P

9 781509 227792